IXth

The Story of the Lost Legion

© James Perry, 2000

This book is sold subject to the condition that it shall not, by way of trade or otherwise, be lent, resold, hired out, or otherwise circulated without the publishers prior consent in any form of binding or cover other than that in which it is published and without a similar condition including this condition being imposed on the subsequent purchaser

All rights reserved.

James Perry asserts his moral right to be identified as the author of this work in accordance with the Copyright, Designs and Patents Act, 1988.

This book may not be reproduced, in whole or in part, in any form (except by reviewers for the public press) without prior permission in writing from the publisher.

Published in the United Kingdom in 2000 by James Perry, 84 High St, Tonbridge, Kent, TN9 1AP.

ISBN 0-9539219-0-5

Printed and bound in Great Britain by Wordperfect Ltd, Tonbridge, Kent.

Thanks

When I had finished the first draft of this book, it was very different to how it is now.
I have been extremely fortunate to benefit from the consistent input of Katie Kotting. She has in effect edited the book, reading through draft after draft suggesting changes and improvements throughout. Her insight and belief, more than anything else, have got me to a stage where I have been ready to publish it.

I would also like to thank a few other people. Jules Acconci designed the cover as a favour at very short notice despite having never met me (!) Sophie Walker drew the beautiful map of the empire. Special thanks to my Mum & Dad, my sister Rosie and Wangair for reading earlier drafts, suggesting improvements and most of all for encouraging me to continue with the book.

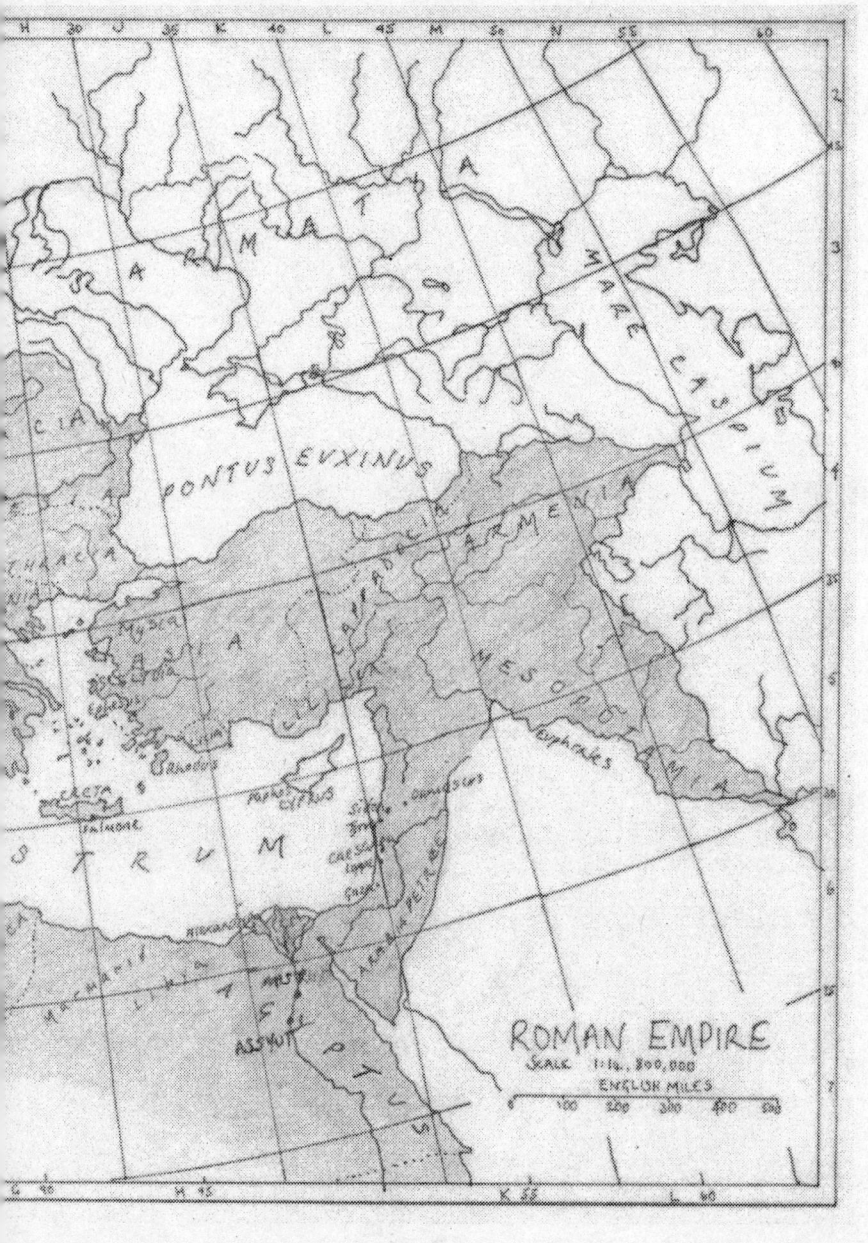

"Men who suppress the truth by their wickedness are without excuse. They have become filled with every kind of wickedness, evil, greed and depravity. They are full of envy, murder, strife, deceit and malice; They invent ways of doing evil;
They are senseless, faithless, heartless, ruthless.

They have exchanged the truth of God for a lie".

The Holy Bible, St Paul's letter to the Romans, Ch1 verses 18; 20; 29-31.

Prologue

Mare Nostrum, 59AD

The water streamed down his long, flattened nose and dripped on to the thick grey hairs that covered his upper lip. He held the wooden rail at the prow of the skiff so hard that his knuckles showed white in the fading light. All the sails were stowed, for to set sail in this gale would be suicide. Without warning he leaned forward and retched over the rail. His long white beard dug into his chest as he revealed his few remaining teeth and a pink tongue. Nothing came out of his mouth but a long sticky trail of saliva. The contents of his guts had long ago been spewed into the sea.

He turned and lurched back to the bridge using the rail as support. The captain, an experienced seafarer, fought the storm as best he could with the tiller.
"Where are we?" shouted the old man.
The captain replied with a shrug. As the old man made to return to the prow the captain grabbed his sleeve. His brow showed his concern.
"Pray, Mark. We can't take much more of this".

*****

The huge stone walls around the docks seethed with life. The harbour was dominated by the most extraordinary structure that Mark had ever seen. The Pharos tapered upwards above the swell of the Mare Nostrum. It looked like a giant elongated pyramid that touched the sky. Every night a great fire was lit, the fire that had given them hope in the midst of that storm.
As soon as the captain had shown his catch to the landing authorities and been issued with his permit to land, Mark walked across the tiny deck to him. He grabbed him by the shoulders and looked into his face.

"Thank you again for everything, brother. God will remember you for what you have done for me."

The captain smiled. "Just to be able to tell my children and grandchildren that I conveyed you to Aegyptus under the noses of the bastard Romans is reward enough."

Mark laughed and kissed the captain on the forehead. He grabbed his small bundle of possessions, laboured into the neighbouring boat and disappeared towards the shore.

*****

Nearly four centuries previously, Ptolemy I had built the great library of Alexandria. Following in the footsteps of the great Alexander he continued to sponsor academic learning. Academics flocked to Alexandria to enjoy his protection and in return they were forced to surrender their texts. The result was the greatest collection of Greek writing, and now of Roman writing, ever assembled. Mark reasoned that there was no better place to keep a document that he wanted no one to read.

The street itself was oppressively hot despite the shady gloom. The sun blazed in the sky but muslin screens blocked direct sunlight from the seething marketplace. A severed camels head hung from a hook outside a stall, tongue hanging lopsidedly out of its closed mouth. It had been hewn from the rest of its body high on the neck and flies buzzed around the bloody sinews coming from the wound. Beneath the hanging head the counter opened onto the street, a dizzying array of spices and delicacies displayed in front of a small boy. His owner yelled his patter at point blank range into the throng, showing blackened teeth and projecting stinking breath. Mark walked past oblivious, barging his way through the crush of buyers and sellers. He hated carrying anything precious into such a place, but he had no choice. The bazaar had grown up around the library.

Mark himself looked as he had since leaving his home in Caesarea – just one more piece of displaced flotsam riding the tide of humanity who roam the empire in search of peace. But underneath his grizzled beard and weather beaten face his brown eyes shone.

Mark believed in his life's work. He believed that the book he had written of his time with Jesu, the prophet he knew as the Christus, was a document that could help to save countless masses.
He also believed that the manuscript strapped to his torso was more important than anything that he himself had ever written.

Introduction

Assyut, Aegyptus, 153

The heat oppresses here in the land of the ancients, but Snofru takes good care of me. She even brings me dampened muslin to put on my forehead and orders her grandchildren to fan me as I write. I am an old man now, unable to earn my keep. I write in a small cell in the corner of the house of Snofru's son. They are really very kind to keep me when they have so little themselves. Assyut on the Nile is an ugly village, really just a stop-over point for traders and their camel trains on the desert road to the eastern ports. Along with the Nile traders they continue to make the place a hive of debauchery and violence. The Roman overlords give us a wide berth here in Assyut, partly I think because it has become something of a stronghold for the Copts. The Romans like to encourage them for the damage that they do to us with their heresy. I flatter myself that if they knew who I was, they would not be giving us such a wide berth. But to them, as to everyone else in the empire, it is as though I had never existed.

So I was happy here, enjoying the hospitality of the daughter of Horemheb and the departed Smenkhkare, God rest his soul. I was happy living by the irrigated grain fields in their narrow strip by the Nile, looking out over the desert in the distance and playing with the children. And I loved my wife. I was happy until I finally gave in to Snofru and agreed to tell my story. It is not really my story, though. It was the marriage of an orphan who wonders who she is that finally persuaded me that I must tell her father's story. If I must tell it at all I must tell it for her.

This is my fifth attempt to start. On each previous occasion I burned the manuscripts in the desolate hours before dawn. I think that if I burn the manuscripts then the nightmares that they induce will leave me. But they don't. I have awakened the demons and it looks like they will not leave. I only hope that Snofru's son is right when he says that by telling this story I will exorcise them.

I was present for many of the events I am to describe. I have heard first hand accounts of what transpired for many of those at which I was not present. I have deduced the rest from what I know. This is my story, but more importantly it is the story of another, and it is true.

My name is Tolus. I was a commander of men in the legions of the glorious empire of Rome. God help me, but I know the fate of the great IXth Legion, the proud ranks that marched out of Eburacum on 23rd November in the year of our Lord 119 and vanished. I know what happened because I was one of the 6,000 men who marched with it. But more than that I know why it happened. I know why it happened because I was in Aegyptus and Rome in 118AD and on the edge of the empire in Britannia in 119AD. I was in all of these places because it was my honour to serve the greatest Roman general who ever lived, the soldier who would change the course of history. I was the servant of a man whose name until now has been scrupulously erased from history. A vague myth still survives amongst a small group of fighting men, but they do not talk of events that no one wants to hear about. This is my story, but more importantly it is his story. This is the story of Marius Sextus.

PART I

AEGYPTUS

1

Assyut, Aegyptus, 118AD

Smenkhkare looked weary as he ambled slowly up the mud path between the fields. He was troubled, but he gave away no hint to his companion. The sun's strength was spent and the long cool of the evening would soon come. The lines in his face deepened as he squinted across orderly fields scarred by irrigation ditches stretching out to the river. Far in the distance, beyond the fields and trenches of the opposite bank, the craggy shelf that marked the edge of his world was silhouetted against the darkening sky. Beyond the fertility of the river plain there was nothing but burning desert and a few camel trains.

Smenkhkare had a large scythe slung over his shoulder. His back ached, the familiar pain that made him consider himself too old for hard labour in the fields. He only had one more year before he would allow himself to stop and rely on his sons to provide for Horemheb and himself. Although she was just forty two, he was fifty three years old already and he looked older. A shock of white hair tufted up above his wrinkled skin and sun scorched face. As usual, he was wearing a white linen shift and loose trousers that reached his knees. They were heavy with the dust that had flicked from the heads of corn as his scythe cut through their stems. Beneath his knees the patchy hairs were coated in mud where the dust had mingled with his sweat. Harvest was here, and the whole village spent time in the fields.

As the path reached the river and joined the road that followed the bank he bade farewell to his companion. Smenkhkare walked the last few minutes to his house alone, along a dusty and rutted mud track. His house was set back from the main track, away from the river on the edge of the fields that he worked. Sitting outside on wooden boxes three men too old to work were playing a game of mandoneb, a complex and endless distraction for the old involving the conveyance of rice grains about a series of wooden bowls on a vast board. He yearned for the days when he could play with them and leave the fields for good.

Smenkhare's heart lightened at the sight of the neat patterns of mud bricks and layered straw roof that had been the home of his parents before him. He didn't notice the squalor of the street outside or the open sewers running into the Nile. Their stench, and the rubbish left to rot and dry in the sun by the sides of the track were as much a part of his life as the river. As he approached the door, he could hear the lively voices of his wife Horemheb and of Rani, his eldest daughter. As so often, they were in the middle of what to a stranger might sound like a fierce argument.

"It's theft. They have no right to take them. Those buildings make us what we are. You cannot say that anyone who wants some of the masonry can just dismantle them". Twenty four summers passed, and Rani was an idealist despite already being a widow.

"Rubbish, Rani. You must live in the real world. The buildings have no purpose at all other than as a haven for thieves and vagabonds. They were built on the bodies of thousands of people who died beneath the whips of cruel men. They were built to glorify ridiculous gods. Why should we keep monuments to a time of such suffering?"
As she spoke of the ancients, Horemheb instinctively reached for the beautiful soapstone carving hanging by a thin leather cord around her neck. The shape was simple but unmistakable - the shape of a fish. She continued, still touching her talisman.
"We might as well make use of the stones. Why should people build from mud when there is such an abundant source of hewn stone on our doorstep?" Horemheb was ever practical.

"I don't care about the rights and wrongs of the ancients. What I do know is that their buildings are the most beautiful in the empire. I have heard that even the circus of Maximus and the great Pantheon in Rome cannot compare to our pyramids and temples. We should be proud of them, not destroying them by stealing their stones".

Neither Rani nor Horemheb had noticed that Smenkhkare appear at the doorway. He smiled to himself as he listened to the passion in his daughters voice and watched the fire flicker in her eyes as she spoke. Rani was tall, with her dark hair cut short. She was lithe and her body supple. Her face was not gentle or classically beautiful, but had a luminescence that caught ones attention. Her dark eyes sparkled, often with fire but more often with laughter. But it was her manner that gave her a presence and attractiveness that was striking to everyone. It amused her father to think what a bundle of trouble and joy she would be to anyone brave enough to marry her. She certainly had been to her first husband, before he had died of the fever.

As Smenkhare advanced into the room, Horemheb left her vegetables on the wooden table and walked over to kiss her husband. She sat him down and filled a wooden mug from a large ceramic pot of water on the floor.
"Your daughter, Smenkhkare, is a dreamer. It's time she found another husband and had some children. That should make her a bit more practical."

Rani glowered at her mother but remained silent.
"When is your official period of mourning over, Rani?"
"In two months, father", she replied.
Smenkhkare looked thoughtful. "Well Akhattes has certainly been making his intentions clear, hasn't he? I think we will take him".
"What? What about my say? I am twenty four years old and a widow. I have a right to make up my own mind".
Smenkhkare cursed himself. He had things of his own to discuss with them, and he knew that this conversation would end in the usual row.
"You will do as you are told! I am in no mood to have an argument about a husband. We will discuss it some other time."

Rani was furious, but she recognised the disquiet in her father. She turned to light the fire whilst Horemheb silently chopped vegetables at the table. Her husband would speak eventually.
Yet even as he dismissed the subject of Rani's future, Smenkhkare's mind was already elsewhere.
He was a mellow man and he rarely snapped, particularly at his beloved daughter.

Rani was the eldest child. Traditionally their secret had been handed down to the eldest son, but when the time had come Smenkhkare believed his eldest son to be too irresponsible. He had decided that Rani would be a better guardian. How he had fought against that decision! Although her brother would never know, he knew that to Rani it would seem such a confirmation of his favouritism.

As Rani stoked the fire and Horemheb worked at the table, Smenkhkare's voice broke the uneasy silence. He spoke very quietly and very deliberately. "I have had a message. Someone is coming for that of which we do not speak."

******

Horemheb stopped dead, her crude metal knife embedded in a ripe aubergine. Rani still squatted by the fire, but her face was turned to Smenkhkare and her eyes were wide and bright. Neither spoke as they looked at the old man. No one had come for their secret in all the generations that they had been its guardians.
"Who brought the message? What did it say?" asked Horemheb.
"I do not know who brought it. I found it in my shift this morning". He felt beneath his clothing, brought out a small roll of papyrus and handed it to Rani. She read it out loud.
"Greetings brother. David the smith will arrive in the summer. He has been sent by me, and you will tell him where he can find that which you have. Give it to him, for the time is at hand when we

must rise. Our time is coming. Peace in the name of the emperor of all. Origen".

"What are you going to do?" asked Horemheb. Her voice was unsteady and she did not notice that her hand had begun to shake.

Smenkhkare looked her full in the face. "I do not know. I do not know why it has been left for so long, nor do I know why it is being sought now"
He paused and lifted his head to the ceiling, eyes closed in concentration. He opened his eyes and continued in a weary voice. "It must have seemed so simple when our family were first made its guardians. We were just a stop off point on the way to the manuscripts retrieval. But after all this time, I feel that we have a responsibility. We can't just release it to anyone who demands it. We will be judged."

Horemheb and Rani were horrified.
"We will be judged if we do not do as we were bid. It is not for us to meddle in these things"
Horemheb could think of nothing but her desire to be rid of the responsibility for this legacy, and it showed in her strident tone.

On Rani's fourteenth birthday, the day that she celebrated her coming of age, she had been taken aside by Smenkhkare to be told what she could repeat to no one. Her whole adult life had been lived under the shadow cast by its responsibility. She did not believe in deferring to her elders and now she let her frustration show.
"I hate this. You're so bound by your feelings of 'duty' and 'obligations' and 'honour'. How honourable was the person who passed on this responsibility all those years ago? It is us who have been left with it, no one else. We never asked for it. Those who conferred it on us no longer have any right to make demands on us. We have been the guardians of the manuscript for generations, so it is ours to do with as we wish. We should do what is right for us, regardless of what anyone else says."

Smenkhkare was getting frustrated. "We're all frightened. We will meet this smith and we will discover from him why Origen wants the document now. But I am not prepared to . . . ."

Suddenly the door was flung open and the rest of the children bundled into the kitchen. Snofru was fourteen, Huni nineteen and Mycerinus twelve. Conversation quickly turned to Akhattes. Snorfu had met him on her way home and said that he had been hanging around waiting to talk to her. Knowing her, it was more likely to be the other way around. Snorfu was always stirring people up. According to Snorfu, Akhattes had been angling for an invitation to dinner. At twenty five and unmarried, their neighbour's son was showing serious interest in the widowed Rani. As the handsome son of Smenkhkare's best friend, his chances were perceived to be good. The problem was Rani, who seemed oblivious to his advances. With a mischievous grin Snorfu announced that she had invited him for dinner. Rani rolled her eyes and braced herself for an awkward evening.

2

Lucius made his way through the early morning fog that engulfed the Via Flaminian. The high facades loomed threateningly in the gloom and Lucius cursed the hour. Old men like him should be tucked up in bed at this time, not wandering the streets like vagrants. The only sound of the daybreak routine in this usually busy thoroughfare was the slapping of sandals against stone paving, punctuated by soft chanting emanating from cavernous doorways. The streets had been swept during the night, and he passed some Numidian slaves loading their tools onto a donkey cart. Lucius looked with approval at the small pouch set over the donkey's hindquarters under its anus. A great innovation, stopping the beasts of burden turning the streets back into the sewer that the administration had spent so much to move underground. Outside the Mausoleum of Augustus, beneath a great columned monolith that stood facing the barren hump of the Pincian hill the slaves were packing up. Past the mausoleum and glancing to the sides of the street, Lucius could just make out faces softly lit by wax candles in the houses to the left and right. The early morning devotions could take half and hour, and should be nearing completion by now. The working day would shortly commence. Lucius lowered his grizzled head and concentrated on speeding his step. He felt too old to be walking this sort of distance through the streets. He would have preferred to be sitting on a litter. The order to appear at the trade entrance of the Emperor's private residence without ceremony had prevented this, and it irritated Lucius. Hadrian was a rude little fool. This was just his style, to get into a lather about some irrelevance and seek to turn it into a crisis. Retirement had become an increasingly attractive option since Hadrian's accession.

The Via Flaminian forked. Out of the gloom rose a v-shaped wall that was so high that the top was lost in the mist. The left fork would take him to the forum, where on the south side was the main gate to the emperor's villa. The other fork would take him down a narrow lane where he would find the service entrance.

Just before sunrise Lucius entered the lane and passed the fruit sellers setting out their wares on their large wooden trays. In pride of place in the front of the trays was now the curious yellow curved fruit that had been such an instant hit with Hadrian. Called "annannasium" these fruits had just begun to be imported in volume from the colony of Aegyptus and they were proving exceptionally popular.

Lucius walked straight up to the door and knocked loudly. A peephole opened, and upon seeing him the doorman instantly opened the door and bowed low. Lucius ambled past, through the storerooms and outhouses and through a gate into the walled garden. It was enormous, with its elaborate statues, series of ponds and bathing pools, arched walkways and pavements warmed in the winter by heating under the ground. It led to the rear terrace of the house. Through an enormous archway and across a brilliantly coloured mosaic of semi precious stones covering the floor, Lucius could see the others who had been summoned. As he saw the three men who reclined in that room, Lucius felt a shock of concern. With him as the fourth, the group essentially ruled the empire. All the major power blocks and decision-making processes could be manipulated and controlled by these men. This was no formal body. This was the essential quartet who could deliver the support that the Emperor might need to do almost anything.

Emperor Hadrian reclined on a couch absentmindedly feeding himself grapes. Lucius noticed that his nonchalance was a little forced. He was tense. A small man approaching his autumn years he wore his long hair, black as jet, slicked straight back. His face was dominated by large, carefully tended eyebrows which made his small intelligent eyes look almost as black as his hair. His eyes were constantly on the move as if they were looking for what you were not telling him, or what might be more interesting to him than you. He was small, and his soft pale skin and lack of stubble made him appear younger than his fifty years. This, combined with his fondness for painting the rims of his eyes and lips, gave him an effeminate air. Across from Hadrian sat Decimus. In contrast to Hadrian, Decimus was young, just thirty two years old. His father had been granted an unprecedented three triumphs for his glorious campaigns in all corners of the empire. He was still acknowledged as Rome's greatest general and had been determined to establish a political career for his only son before he died. Like his father, Decimus was a strong, intensely masculine man and like his father he was unusually quick witted. But the fierce eyes often gave a hint of irritation and of violence barely suppressed. Lucius feared Decimus for his ambition and impetuosity, but most of all he feared Decimus for his influence over Hadrian. Their affair was an open secret and had been going on for almost a year and a half, since six months before the death of Emperor Trajan. Lucius had little doubt that Decimus had entered into the relationship for his own advancement rather than out of a genuine love for Hadrian. His reward had been the military. Decimus was the supreme commander of the vast might that was the combined armies of the empire of Rome. He was answerable only to the Senate and to Hadrian.

The third and final person in the room was Alexander. He had beached rather than sat, a massive flabby presence extending over the fringes of the soft velvet and onto the short carved legs of the couch. Affable and over privileged, Alexander had been born to the greatest family in Rome. From birth he had never been allowed to forget his calling to greatness. Having been mightily indulged by everyone, and adored for his straightforward goodwill, Alexander found one true greatness: His social life was legendary, his invitations the most sought after in Rome. His popularity and pedigree made him a useful ally, but it was his enormous, endless wealth that made him one of the most powerful men in the empire. It was said that Alexander controlled so much wealth that he could underwrite the mortgaging of Rome itself. Despite his easygoing manner and socialite reputation, Alexander had repeatedly shown himself to be no fool. On the contrary, he managed his fortune with a guile and ruthlessness that belied his clumsy appearance.

With Lucius present, whose forty years of uninterrupted service in the Senate made him the most senior and highly respected senator alive, the square was completed. Lucius had proved over the years that he could deliver more votes in the senate than anyone, including the emperor.

With the servants dismissed and Lucius settled with a gold goblet in his hands, Hadrian began to speak. He was impatient and agitated.

"Thank you all for coming, and please be sure that I do not gather you here lightly. I understand the potential repercussions if it were to get out that we have met like this without the knowledge of the Senate and the Plebs".

Hadrian shifted uneasily in on his couch, his beady eyes flitting around the room, looking at nothing in particular. Abruptly he cleared his throat, emitting a shrill rasping sound. He made a visible effort to summon some dignitas as he continued.

"I think that you will agree when you hear the reason for the meeting that I had little choice. Last night one of our spies returned from Sidon in Ituraea. I thought that it would be simpler if he was to report to you direct".

Hadrian turned and pulled a cord that dangled from the ceiling behind him. A few seconds later, the heavy door to the room swung open, and a swarthy middle-aged easterner strode in. He wore the brightly embroidered cotton garments of the Ituraeans. He was clearly tired and afraid, and he wasted no time in starting his story. His voice was slightly tremulous as he began.

"My name does not matter. For several years I have been on an assignment to infiltrate the followers of the man they call Jesu in Sidon. Three weeks ago, a meeting was called which was attended not only by the leader of the movement, Origen, and his predecessor, Tertullian, but also by other leaders who had come from Gallis, Italia, Hispania, Asia Minor, Mauritania, Aegyptus and many other parts of the empire".

The spy looked nervously around the room and saw that he had the complete attention of everyone present. Even Alexander had levered himself up and was leaning forward with his belly resting on his knees and his large brown eyes peering intently from his jowly face.

He continued. "Towards the end of this meeting, Origen summed up. In a quiet voice, so quiet that all in the room had to lean forward to hear he said that he had news of the gravest importance that he must share with the assembled leaders. He spoke of a message that had been brought to him that claimed that they had the means to break Rome and thus allow their new religion to grow unchecked."

At this point the spy broke off. He retrieved a small piece of papyrus from inside his colourful tunic. His hands were shaking slightly and his voice was taut. The atmosphere of fierce concentration amongst those in the room was beginning to unnerve him.

"Please forgive me, I want to be as accurate as possible with regards to what was said next. I have notes which will help. I am going to repeat as best I can the exact words of Origen:
He said that he had received word about a document that "would finally prove the Roman conspiracy of lies about Jesu. It reveals what we know to be their ancient and successful plot to create a false history of "fact" about Christ".

Through this document Origen claimed that he could reveal to Rome's client rulers the contempt with which she regards them, and the lies with which Rome has endangered their souls. He claimed that he could do this directly to every client king and chieftain, as well as to countless Roman citizens all across the empire. He ended by saying that he would soon have in his possession the means to make these clients rise up and expel their overlords".

"In the meeting there was uproar. People demanded to know what this proof could be, and where it was. All Origen would say was that it had been left by the great writer Mark before his death and that it was somewhere safe. He finished by urging all present to return to their respective lands and prepare their people for the proof. To prepare for the proof so that when it arrived the uprising would be swift".

The spy folded his paper, his hands shaking more noticeably now.

"This is as it happened. As soon as the meeting closed, I returned to my unit commander to make my report. He in turn reported it to the general, who put my commander himself on stand-by to leave at short notice. He was to follow any of Origen's men seen leaving Sidon in the hope that they might lead to this document. I was dispatched here to make my report. The day before I sailed I received notification that one of Origen's inner circle had left Sidon equipped for a long journey and was being followed. That is all".

Finished, he stood silent. Hadrian looked at his quivering form with distaste and dismissed him.

When the doors had closed behind him, Alexander was the first to speak. Deep concern showed on the faces of Decimus, Lucius and Hadrian. Alexander's usually jolly expression had given way to a frown of anxiety.

"Origen is just a paranoid delusional like the rest of them. No one will take any notice", he muttered. But there was no conviction in his voice for he knew better. The manuscript left by the "prophet" Mark was known to all of them, although none had seen it. The emperor Trajan had been careful to ensure that his very closest advisors, Lucius and Alexander amongst them, knew about the confession of the emperor Nero. Knew that it was at large, and that it had the power to ignite fires in the hearts of all men who heard of it.

A brooding silence descended on the room. It was Lucius who took it upon himself to speak. His experience as a chairman told him that there was nothing to be done except to sum up the situation and the options that faced them. As he did so he watched as concern turned to horror on the faces of the most powerful men in the empire. He fought to keep his voice level as he outlined the options. They were so limited that Lucius felt embarrassed to offer them, despite the fact that he bore no responsibility for their insufficiencies. Yet as he spoke it became increasingly clear that their only feasible option was to keep close watch on Sidon and allow events to play themselves out. And they had to hope that the man sent to follow Origen's courier knew what he was doing.

The lethargy that creeps in when powerful men face an intractable problem had settled itself over his audience, and when Lucius finished there was no reaction at all. Decimus was peeling grapes with his teeth, an implacable, dangerous expression in his eyes. Alexander looked towards Hadrian whilst Lucius closed his eyes as if in deep thought. Hadrian spoke more out of a sense of duty than out of conviction and when he did so his voice was dull.
"I don't like any of these options but I don't see that we have any choice. Assuming that the man currently following Origen's courier is competent we will leave him on the trail. He must remain in regular contact".
With that he turned and wearily pulled on the cord behind him. The head housekeeper was abruptly ordered to summon the messenger back to the meeting.

*****

When the spy was shown back into the room he did not notice the subtle nod that Hadrian gave to his housekeeper. Lucius did, and although he knew what it would mean for him he wasn't surprised.
If anything, the messenger looked even more nervous when he returned. Hadrian was not wasting any time. "What is the name of the man sent to follow the Origen's courier?"
"His name is Marius Sextus, sir"
"Do you know him?"
"Yes, sir."
"Tell me of him"
"He began his service with the XXXIIIth legion over eight years ago. Before that he served in the XIIth in Cyrenaica and Epirus, rising to the rank of centurian. There he quickly rose to prominence for outstanding bravery on the field. His men were devoted to him. In the XXXIIIth he was quickly promoted to the staff of the commander, where his council was highly valued. He was made the praefectus castrorum of the legion two years ago. He has a reputation for fairness and integrity in peace, brutality and audacity in war".
"How do you know so much about him?" Hadrian asked.

"He was my commander. But it is more than that. Tales of his exploits are frequently told by the men of the XXXIIIth. It is their belief that he is the greatest Roman soldier alive. Sir, Marius Sextus is something of a legend in the legion".

3

The crossing had been quick and uneventful. It got steadily hotter as our boat had neared Aegyptus, and as we docked in Alexandria the heat was almost unbearable. My eyes were aching. The light reflecting off the sea, glaring off the sandstone harbour and shining down from the sun itself made even squinting painful. I watched the huge stone walls around the docks seething with life, but the others attention was focused on the most extraordinary structure that they had ever seen. The great Pharos dominated the harbour.

The briefing in Rome had been simple. We were to travel to a caravanserai, a traders rest house, at Tanta twenty miles south of Alexandria in Aegyptus. We were given papers that identified us as civilians. We also carried permits and licences to recover the treasures of the ancients from the tombs at Luxor and the Pyramids at Misr. When the papers were issued to us in Rome, the official had looked sheepish.
"It was the only thing that we could think of that would explain the presence of so many young Romans wandering about Aegyptus. Sorry".
I could not understand why we could not be given papers that simply told the authorities that we were soldiers on Rome's business and to leave us be, but apparently Rome did not want anyone in the government of Aegyptus to know of our mission. Even we did not know what our mission was to be. We had simply been told to get ourselves to this caravanserai, where we would be approached by a man who would know us.

I was travelling with eight men, and I was their leader. Bless us, for that day we believed that we were invincible. We all belonged to the Praetorian Guard and had been serving a tour in Rome. I had been approached to lead a mission abroad. In truth I didn't really have an option, but I was pleased. Back then I thought that I wanted glory and that it would make me happy. When I recruited my men I wanted people like me. So many people in the guards are afraid, are trying to escape something. I wouldn't have them. I wanted the glory seekers, the men who had nothing to lose and everything to gain, and I found them. I found Greto, too. I had served my first tour with him in Achaia. He had led me well, and I had asked for him by name as soon as I was appointed. He was my second-in-command. His skin was like tanned leather and looked about an inch thick. His short legs and wide shoulders made him seem indestructible. He looked dependable and he was dependable. He rarely smiled and that was because he rarely saw anything to smile about. Neither did he often see anything to get angry about. When he did, he was terrible. I knew because I had seen it. With us were Numba, Cassius, Artorius, Silus, Alaric, Petrus and Tobias. They ranged in age from eighteen to thirty one. They had two things in common. They had all earned commendations for bravery on the field, and none valued their life highly.

*****

On the voyage we had all been boisterous. All except Greto. He had seen too much to be like us. There had been rumblings amongst the men about him. Just after we rounded Sicilia we were all sitting out on deck, enjoying the morning sun and a good following wind. Greto stood at the prow of the boat, watching the sea. Silus spoke in a low voice. "What's up with the miserable old mule? He's so old he'll barely be able to lift his sword. Who does he expect to carry him when he gets tired?" The others laughed. Numba stood up and waddled about the deck with his backside sticking out and his back bent. He used a pike as a walking stick and complained of backache and irregular bowel movements. I laughed with them. I laughed with them but thought that I had better put them straight.
"I wouldn't let him see you doing that, Numba, or haven't you heard?" I had their attention. Numba came and sat down with the rest. "I've heard that Greto is strong, but that's it. I'm not so bad myself," he said defiantly.
I turned round and called out "Greto. Come over here a minute."
Numba looked apprehensive as he approached.

"These boys want to hear a story, Greto, and I can think of none better than one which will introduce the man who we are on our way to meet". I turned to the men.
"I have never met this man, but Greto has. And when I served my first tour in Achaia one of our men persuaded him to tell the story of one of his battles". I turned to Greto. I knew that he hated to tell stories, particularly stories in which he featured, but he knew me well enough to know that I would not ask him to do it unless I had good reason.
"You know the one I'm talking about. Tell them of Marius".
Greto looked reluctant, but the enthusiasm of the men for a good story to pass a couple of hours on that long voyage was too much for him to refuse. He sat down and settled back. He paused to look round before he started. His audience looked back eagerly.

*****

"Marius Sextus was just a young decurian, and I served on one of his early tours in Moesia. It's a wild place and it must have been like cutting your teeth on granite. Marius led me then despite still being in his early twenties".

"Pintreich, the chief of Moesia had refused to pay his taxes, so the legion was sent there to help him change his mind. It's a dark mountainous territory south of the Danuvius river. I thought that I was hardened, but a few days on the march with Marius made me realise that I wasn't. He just scowled at us all the time and only spoke when he had something to say. We arrived in the autumn, and as we marched the leaves were turning on the trees. There is only one metalled road running from Dalmatia through Moesia, and we were on it. We were a full strength legion and Pintreich just a barbarian upstart who could quickly be bullied into handing over some gold. We were over two hundred miles from his headquarters. It should have felt safe but it didn't. There was something about that land that unsettled us. The hills were hard, and covered in woods. The trees were a blaze of gold and red and every colour in between. Conditions were rough. The road sought out the valleys and passes, but it was still gruelling. The weather was bad, more often than not rain and low cloud whipping across the hilltops. We saw more boars and wolves than people. The only good thing was the food, the best that I have ever had. I do not know who was the tribune in charge of the food, but it was fantastic".

"Our scouts said that there were many people too, hiding in the woods. Those that we did see were filthy, little more than animals with wide black eyes looking out from under hair matted with pig fat. They were all dressed in black rags and were invariably scampering like rabbits in search of cover. We passed few villages and even they were difficult to spot. All had been abandoned in advance of our arrival. To untravelled eyes they would have been shocking. The evidence of pigs, horses, chickens and donkeys was all over. The villages virtually swam in excrement, although like the inhabitants there was no sign of the animals themselves. Their huts sat in a morass of mud, filth and years of accumulated rubbish that formed a quagmire, marking the village territory from the green grass and woods around. The villages were always located in a narrow cleft between hills, and the huts were built right into the hillside. For each hut they had dug out a section of the hill and set the hut right into it. They had used mud bricks for the walls, and then used turf on their roofs, making their huts look like an extension of the hills".

Greto paused and looked around. I was pleased to see that all of the men were leaning forward so as not to miss a word. This was the sort of story that they loved to hear, the sort of story that they longed to better through their own exploits. He continued.
"Marius could not understand why they would build like this, and why they would go to so much effort to set their dwellings in such pokey little clefts when there were pleasant wide valleys all around. I was marching behind him, and he turned to ask me. To be honest, at the time I was feeling a little put out by being commanded by this wide eyed novice in such a place. I faced him squarely.
"You really do have a lot to learn, don't you Marius? Look at these people. Look at their huts. You are looking at raw terror. Not the instant terror of battle, but constant terror as a way of life. This is a land that reeks of death. Where do you think all the livestock is?

Where are all the people? They are in the woods, hiding from us. These people know all about fighting men, Marius. They know all about armies passing through. And you can be sure that the fighting men that pass through here are not governed by the discipline that forces us to remain on the road when many of us would rather be seeking them out. These people have been meeting fighting men for generations. They have built their villages in places that cannot be seen from any distance. They have sought to build their homes into the hillside, so as far as possible they become one with the hills. Scouts on high ground will never see them. When the legate sends out reconnaissance, he will not be asking them to find us a pretty little spot with a lovely view and a big sign on it saying "come and get us, we're here"".
Greto chuckled as he recalled his insolence. "I don't suppose my reply did anything for my young Decurian's confidence".

"We had been marching through that dark country for four days. That night we set full defensive camp in a large flat valley to the south side of the road. The valley extended one mile from the road before coming to a dead end. There were high hills to the east, south and west of us. Scouts were posted on the hills around, and a century was put at either end of the entrance to the valley as the rest of the legion settled down to sleep".

"The sound that woke me chilled me to the bone. Hundreds upon hundreds of voices were emitting a high pitched howl. There were tremors in the howl, and as my head cleared of sleep I realised that it was because the howlers were running. I pulled my jerkin over my head, grabbed my sword and shield and ran outside the tent into the gloom of the receding night. I looked up to where the sound was coming from. It was the eastern hill, and at that moment I felt true terror. I know that anyone caught in a surprise attack feels it, but it shook me then. As my eyes followed the sound I saw several hundred men charging down the hill, silhouetted by the dawn breaking behind them. They were dressed in great animal skins covered in thick pelts. They had used some kind of fat to stiffen their hair into long spikes, and they had drying blood all over their faces. Their priests or druids stood behind them on the hills. They stood with chickens and knives, and as the tribe charged they were disembowelling the chickens and smearing the innards over their heads. I stood taking this in for a few seconds, and when I got a grip on myself I frantically looked about me and saw Marius with his other men. He looked in complete control as he systematically barked out orders. I didn't realise it at the time, but he was already forming up the basis of a defensive wall by the rampart. Men were rushing to join him, so I followed them and easily found a gap to fill. Marius looked at me and winked. That tiny gesture of frivolity seemed so inappropriate yet somehow it steeled me".

Greto was excited about the memory, and as he continued his voice quickened.
"The howl was petering out as the attackers bounded down the hill. It took them another few seconds to reach us. When they were about ten yards away the howl became a great animal scream. An enormous hairy warrior ran straight for me. His face was sticky with the blood of the sacrificed chickens and he wore a great bear skin with the bear's head over his own, forming a sort of helmet. His maddened eyes looked out from under the bear's teeth. It was at about this point that I realised I had forgotten my pike. It was too late to do anything. The man swung a great axe, and it smashed into my shield. I thought my arm would break with the force. The blow knocked my shield to the left, exposing my right side and my sword arm. He was off balance, his body still twisted to his right exposing his side. I lunged out at him wildly, and experienced the great joy of battle as I felt my sword enter his lung. I kept pushing it in, and felt a sinewy resistance before it sank like a knife into water. He turned his head and looked at me like he was going to ask a question. Blood retched its way up his throat and began to flow out of his mouth in great waves. It swamped the congealing chicken blood already on his chin. He fell, and I lifted my shield again".

"Just as I was bracing myself for the next barbarian I felt a tug on my shoulder and ignored it. Hands on each of my shoulders dragged me backwards out of the line. My place was instantly taken. I looked round, furious. It was Marius, and he had his other nine men with him.

I saw the chaos and carnage around me. Our defensive shield wall was holding, with slain attackers lying at our feet. Marius had remembered his training when he had ordered the wall to step back three paces. It prevented the corpses from getting under our feet, and formed a stumbling block for our attackers in their last few paces before reaching the wall. They were now forced to break step and look down to secure their footing. Hundreds of attackers were still hurling themselves at the wall and the noise was almost unbearable. The screams of the attackers and the injured, the scraping of metal on metal, the shouts of orders all mingled into an insensible cacophony.
"I saw that, Greto" shouted Marius with a nod of approval. Then he ordered us to follow him. I realised that Marius was a great commander then. He had that extraordinary ability to remain detached in the chaos, to see the bigger picture and yet make each of his men feel his personal approval"

"By now the sky was lightening with the day break, and we ran the from the line to the edge of our camp. Some of the legion had been slower to get out of bed than us and were only now moving out of the camp. Some were moving to reinforce the line and some were forming up a wedge to drive into the flank of the oncoming attackers. Unlike those who had formed the first desperate line, these had managed to arm and dress themselves properly. Marius stood in front of us.
"It looks like we've got them held for the time being, but we haven't seen their commander. We would usually expect him to attack with the main body, but we think that he's holding back".
How Marius had been able to think about anything other than our desperate defence I had no idea. I began to learn that Marius would always surprise you on the battlefield.
"I've been authorised to lead a search for him, and I've volunteered you for the job. We're going to climb up that hill there" he pointed at the southern hill, upon which there were several druids hopping about holding dismembered chickens above their heads.
"When we reach the top, we're going to shut those druids up and see if we can find where their chief is hiding. Then we're going to kill

him. Stick close to me and keep your ears open. And before we go, get dressed, would you?"

We climbed the southern hill. When the druids saw us coming they ran east, towards where the attack had come from. It took us half an hour, through bracken and thick shrubs. By the time we got to the top, the battle going on below looked to be almost over. Our wall held firm to the west and the attackers were becoming squeezed. Even from the heights of the hill I could see a vast pile of bodies at the foot of the shield wall. Limbs stuck out at unnatural angles, and the whole scene was covered in red blotches as blood ran into the earth. There were about three hundred dead, and four hundred or so still fighting. They did not stand a chance against the four thousand that they faced. But we wanted the battle to last as long as possible as it would give us more time to find their chief.

At the top of the hill we found the bloody corpses of three of our scouts. Their heads were lying back at an unnatural angle, and their necks gaped open like a vast second mouth. Their throats had been cut so deeply that their heads had been half severed. Their uniforms had been removed, and their bare chests revealed that their nipples had been cut off. Their genitals had been removed and stuffed in their mouths. They had been scalped, and their hair was nowhere to be seen.
I had never seen anything like this before, and I'm pretty sure that Marius hadn't either. I vomited where I stood, but Marius just looked grim. "That explains our surprise this morning. We're moving round to the east".

I followed Marius' glance, and looked down the other side of the hill. There was nothing there, just a narrow steep valley with a stream running down the centre. Following the druids, we worked our way around towards the east. As we passed a shoulder to our right and saw over it, the scene became clear. Another valley ran parallel to the one in which we had camped. I could see the road in the distance, just beyond the mouth of this second valley. On the floor of this valley, about five hundred metres from the bottom of the hill began a seething mass of bodies. There must have been about seven thousand barbarians. Their number began close to the mouth of the valley and spilled out into the main valley, over the road and round to the right out of view. They were just milling around, and I couldn't work out why they hadn't joined their comrades.

The clouds darkened and it began to rain. We could hear the distant sound of the battle going on way below to the left.
"Welcome to Moesia" said Marius in a dry voice.
He was looking north. We all turned to follow his glance, the direction in which the druids had fled. Across the hill that divided the two valleys were about five druids. They were facing us in a semi circle, dancing on the spot. They had their elbows dug into their sides, and their hands and forearms were making strange jerky movements in our direction. They were waving the scalps of our scouts. Below them, above the thick woods of the eastern slope stood perhaps fifteen men facing the main barbarian army. They were split into two groups and each held a standard aloft. One was a long pole topped by the skull of an animal, a dog or a wolf. The other was a pole with a huge bear skin spreadeagled across the top. Two of the men stood slightly ahead of their respective groups of henchmen, and even from where we stood their shouting could be heard above the sound of the far away battle. They were having a furious argument.

There was urgency in Marius' voice. "We haven't got long. We'll take those men down there in the woods as they return to their army. They will have to go down the eastern side of the hill, as their force to the west is just about routed already. We have to approach the woods from here or we'll be seen. That means taking out those mad priests. Is anyone squeamish about killing druids?" Legionaries always were superstitious and two of our company were no exception. Marius understood, and ordered them to the back. "Stick together and move fast."

We ran at the druids. I was expecting them to turn and flee, but instead they simply remained jigging about in their semi circle, continuing their strange jerky movements. When we got close we slowed to a walk. I could smell the stench coming from them. They were dark red from the congealed blood that covered them. Each had chickens entrails smeared over his face. They howled and spat at us as we approached. I don't think that they expected us to touch them. In their own wars, barbarians never touch a priest or druid. Marius casually walked up to the one nearest to him and thrust his sword deep into his belly. The druid doubled up and slumped to the ground. The others all looked at Marius with astonishment for a second, before turning and attempting to run away. It was futile, we were too close. I hacked at one from behind and caught him on the neck. My sword only sank in about an inch, but blood sprayed out of the wound, forming a great arc before sprinkling the grass. I looked round. All five druids lay dead. Marius was already running on, turning to hasten us. I ran with the rest. We reached a depression in the hill and ran down it to the right. We carried on running until we reached the woods. In the woods we blundered through the undergrowth bearing right to loop behind the place that we had seen the barbarian leaders arguing. Marius stopped suddenly and raised his hand. I was right behind him, and nearly went careering into his back. The first thing I noticed as I stopped was voices. They were still raised in anger, and they were very near. I looked over Marius' shoulder and saw why he had stopped. Several metres ahead of him was a clear path leading down the hill. Marius crouched and motioned to the rest of us to follow. We hid behind the bracken and watched the two groups of seven barbarians pass us.

"Damn". Marius' face was set. "We really needed to ambush them as they descended. We're going to have to take them from behind. Greto, you come with me. We'll try to loop round them through the forest and then join the path ahead of them to cut them off. The rest of you, wait until they have got out of sight, then attack from behind. Julian, you're in charge."

With that, Marius charged off through the wood. I followed him. He could move incredibly fast and I struggled to keep up. When we had gone three hundred metres he veered off to the right and we saw the path. We couldn't see the barbarians so we crouched and waited. As we did so, Marius looked at me out of the corner of his eye.

"You've done this before" he whispered, more as a statement than a question. I nodded, afraid that I had been showing myself up.
"You've been wasting your years, old man. You will use them better in my command".
My initial terror when I had realised that we were being attacked had shaken me and damaged my confidence. Somehow I thought that everyone could see it, smell it. Yet Marius had chosen me to come with him. Maybe it was because he wanted to protect the rest from my fear, or maybe he really did think that I was good. Either way, at that moment he made me feel strong and he earned my respect. To this day he has never done anything that would shake it".

As he remembered the moment a rueful look came into Greto's eye, but he quickly turned his attention back to his story.

"Very soon after came shouts and screams that told us that Julian and the others had attacked. Almost immediately we saw four men running straight towards us. When they were ten metres away, Marius gave me the nod and we jumped out in front of the group. They stopped dead, shocked. The biggest one let out a great howl, and charged at me. I sidestepped to get out of his direct line and before I knew it I was falling headlong towards the path. My foot had got caught in the bracken. Both of the barbarian's arms were above his head, gripping a huge sword. Helplessly I looked up as he began to bring it down. I would have died had Marius not stepped in front of me, and quick as a snake thrust his sword into the belly of the giant. The howl died on his lips as he fell next to me. The three remaining men attacked together. I just had time to get up before I had to desperately parry a sweeping blow aimed at my legs by a small wiry man. I thrust forward at his sword arm as it recovered, but he was too quick for me. As I regained my balance and freed my foot I saw his face. He had a grey beard and several large warts on his forehead. His nose was bulbous and made me want to cut his head off. I recognised him as one of the men who had been arguing with the other. He was quick. After the stab of fear when I fell, I again felt the great joy of battle. I advanced towards him. He thrust at my sternum. I sidestepped, grabbed his arm with my left hand, and thrust my own sword towards his throat. I do not know why, but I stopped the thrust as I reached his windpipe. He looked into my eyes. I rammed the point home, and his legs buckled. When I turned round, I saw Marius regarding me intently. He had two corpses at his feet. I recognised one as the other of those who had been arguing. We ran back to help the others. When we got there, we saw eight corpses. Julian and two more of ours lay dead. On the ground lay the two standards.

When we got to the top of the hill and looked down on our encampment we saw a scene of carnage. It was clear that the legion was on the move. Formed up into centuries, they were marching out of the valley and back onto the road. The legion was going to attack the main barbarian army, which was still milling about aimlessly in the neighbouring valley waiting for orders that would never come.

It turned out that Marius had killed Pintreich himself. I had killed Rheistoln, a lesser chieftain. The bear standard was that of Pintreich. Without their leader, Pintreich's army fled as soon as they saw our legion approach. The legion gave pursuit, and some were killed. Most got away. Rome lost seventy four men that day. We counted six hundred and sixty nine dead on the field. All of them were Rheistoln's men. His tribe was virtually wiped out. Marius was decorated for his bravery and offered promotion. He refused it because at that time he wanted to remain with his men."

"From what I have heard, that day in Moesia was Marius' first taste of the ecstasy and abandon of battle. And from that day he was hooked. He found that he was good at something. He was good at killing. Marius Sextus is among the best soldiers that any of you will ever meet. If you find yourself in a fight, there is no one who you would rather have alongside you".

Greto had finished, and after a brief silence everyone began to ask questions at once. It was obvious that the story had been a great success with the men, and as I'd expected it was clear that they had a new respect for Greto. That night, as the sun went down over the calm swell of the Mare Nostrum I was amused to watch Numba go out of his way to ensure that Greto was the first to get his food.

*****

After disembarking at Alexandria, the onward journey to Tanta was uneventful. It would have been marginally quicker to take a boat, but we opted to walk despite the heat. We had been idle for too long on the crossing from Rome and needed to stretch our legs. The road was dusty and busy. It ran along the palm-lined Nile and was fringed with small shacks selling figs and coconuts, bananas and oranges. Numba was in his element, joking with the stallholders and making us all laugh. Silus and Tobias had never been outside of Italia before, and were shocked by what littered the road. People with withered arms and deformed legs, lepers and madmen squatted and lay on the ground wherever there was any shade. Many were so badly crippled that they could not move themselves and as a result they urinated and defecated where they sat. Most of my men had witnessed the brutality of battle. We were hardened to it. But seeing these pathetic, helpless creatures sitting in their own excrement got to Silus and Tobias. Scorching heat, an overpowering smell of their own rancidity and total isolation were all they would ever have. They insisted we give them coins and food, and felt guilty as we moved on for not stopping to wash them.

The walk was long, dusty and hot, so we were relieved when we got to Tanta in the late evening.
The caravanserai was like every other caravanserai. A mud wall built more to mark the limits of the compound within than to keep anyone out, and an open gate leading into the compound where horses and camels can be tethered. On three sides of the compound straw covers were erected beside the walls to provide shelter from the sun and occasional rain, and great kilims set on the dust and sand on which to sit and sleep. Fires were only permitted in the open of the compound away from the kilims and the shelter of the straw covers, and usually one could purchase produce from the proprietor for cooking.

The caravanserai at Tanta was busy, full of traders coming up from the fertile Nile plains to the south, and the hardy camel trains travelling from oasis to oasis through the desert. Despite the crowds, it was not difficult to find a section of kilim that was unoccupied, and large enough to sleep us all. We settled down to enjoy the gossip and entertainments of the caravanserai. The compound was already a dotted with small cooking fires when we arrived, and as darkness fell more and more were lit, including ours.

Numba immediately took charge of the cooking. He was from a village in the unforgiving plains around Carthage. When he was not yet a man his tribe had been hit by drought. His parents had been farmers and forced him to leave home, to preserve the food for those too old to travel. Numba spent several years wandering the roads of the empire, labouring for his bread and fighting in the streets to stay alive. Eventually he returned home to find that his family had starved, along with most of his tribe. He joined the legions straight afterwards, when he was sixteen years old. That was two years ago. He had a mouth, Numba, and he wasn't afraid to use it. When he had been mocking Greto on the voyage from Rome, he did so without concern for his safety. Although not a big man, Numba was sharp as an arrow and quick as a snake. He knew how to look after himself because he had been forced to learn on the streets. He would have been long dead had he not.

*****

For three long hot days we waited at the caravanserai. We played gambled, sang, told each other stories and met our fellow travellers. The dice and cards were spoiled somewhat by Alaric. Alaric was a small, sinewy man from a tribe near to Dalmatia, and he had joined the legions in order to escape the boredom of life in the mountains. His latin was not good, and no one really felt they knew him. He kept his own council but he pulled his weight and clearly knew how to handle a sword. But his great talent was for dice and gambling. His quiet demeanour hid an amazing memory and a ruthless instinct, and he had won everything of value amongst all the men within the first day.

On a couple of occasions we had travellers try to pick fights with us, and I was impressed by the discipline of the men as they refused to be goaded. On both occasions Artorius used his massive frame to dissuade the protagonists from pursuing the matter, ably backed up by the solid looking Silus and Tobius.
On the third day, we were all beginning to get frustrated, but knew that there was nothing we could to but wait.

After we had breakfasted on the fourth day, a man approached me. I had noticed him arrive the previous night. He was olive skinned, and his face deeply lined. His eyes were a piercing blue, and as he approached they had me fixed in their gaze.

"My name is Marius Sextus and I seek Tolus the Corsican" he said simply as he arrived.
"You have found him, Marius Sextus. We are at your service."
Marius smiled at me, and took me warmly by the hand.
"I am glad to have found you" was all that he said.
I was slightly awed, but I was also annoyed.
"Why did you not introduce yourself to us right away?" I asked.
He smiled, and his reply revealed that he had noted my irritation.
"One night was not going to make any difference, and I used the opportunity to observe you".
Something dawned on me, and I turned round. All my men were standing behind me, regarding Marius with fascination. All except Greto. I was furious with him, but not for long. As soon as I saw the expression on his face I burst out laughing. Greto had the most extraordinary look that I have ever seen. It was a mixture between squirming embarrassment for colluding with Marius in not identifying him to me, pleasure at seeing his old commander and nervousness as to what my reaction was going to be. Marius put Greto out of his misery by walking over to him and embracing him.
"Thank you for keeping your mouth shut, old friend. You are lucky that your leader has a sense of humour". He turned and winked at me.

"Did you like what you saw?" I asked mildly.
Suddenly Marius became serious.
"Yes and no. You are young and strong and no doubt beautifully trained. I was very impressed by the way that you handled those thugs last night who wanted a brawl. If we get into a fight then I'll be happy to have you. But look at yourselves. You stick out like group of old Jewish women at a pig market. Anyone with half a brain will spot you from a mile away as Roman soldiers. What, precisely, are you planning to say to the authorities when they ask you who you are and what you are doing?"
I dug in my pocket and found the permits given to us by the official in Rome. I handed them to Marius and he read them quickly.
"Recovery of artefacts? What idiot gave you these? Tomorrow, Tolus, we're going shopping and by the time we've finished you are going to look like good Aegyptusis".
He then turned to my men.
"You are all ordered not to shave from now. You are going to look inconspicuous, and there is nothing more conspicuous than a clean shaven Roman!"
The men were surly. They had liked the sound of Marius, and they liked what they saw. But we all knew that they would not be instantly his. It would take time, and it would take some killing before he could truly rely on them. I knew it, the men knew it and Marius knew it too.

We left almost immediately, and by the middle of the morning we had chartered a boat to take us to Misr, eighty miles down the river. Marius told us that he would brief us on the boat. As we made our way down the track outside the caravanserai, we passed a group of peasants listening to a man who spoke beneath an olive tree. He was speaking of the "prophet" Jesu. Had we been in uniform we might have arrested him. Instead we just picked up a few rocks and threw them in his direction. One struck him on the forehead, which immediately began to bleed. As the men laughed I noticed that Marius was not joining in, but rather standing to one side looking uncomfortable, almost as if he was ashamed of us. I did not think much of it at the time.

*****

The felucca was comfortably big enough for all of us, and Marius had found one whose skipper did not speak any Latin. We glided easily down the Nile, the sail filled with the soft hot breeze that came from the north. Oxen dragged heavy wooden ploughs in the green fields on either side, and donkeys passed down the road pulling mountainous carts of hay. Women were at the river edge beating clothes with flattened wooden bats. Frequently, hippopotami would break the surface of the water and snort loudly. In quiet stretches of the river we saw crocodiles basking in the sun. They would suddenly come to life and bristle into the river if the boat approached too close. Occasionally we would pass a magnificent and ancient villa, flanked by palm trees with beautifully kept gardens running down to the river bank. It was with this as his backdrop that Marius told us why we had come to Aegyptus.

"Friends, I am the reason that you are here. I was supposed to be operating alone, and it is my error that has brought you here".

"This strange mission began back in Tyrus, the main base of the XIIth, for whom I was acting as praefectus castrorum. My general summoned me to his headquarters in the old royal palace and what he asked me to do staggered me. He asked me to follow a courier wherever he went. I am not a man who believes himself too good for anything, and I hope that as you get to know me you come to see the truth of it. But to send someone in my position to follow a messenger personally is, I think you'll agree, a bit odd.
The general was specific in his instructions. I was to keep in regular contact with him and most importantly I was not to allow the man to realise that he was being followed. He added that he had sent a messenger to Rome to request further instructions.
I thought that he must have gone a bit mad, overreacting like that, but what I have learned since has caused me to wonder".
As Marius spoke he was looking right at us, ensuring that he had our attention. He need not have bothered, for we all wanted to know why we had been sent to this place.

He continued. "There had been a meeting of the Christian leadership at the house of Origen, their leader, where they had discussed the retrieval of an important document. At dawn the following day a traveller had been seen leaving Origen's house. He headed down the inland road towards Capernaum on the Sea of Galilee. He left on horseback, heavily laden as if for a long journey. The traveller was one of Origen's inner circle, a man known as David the smith".

"I procured a horse and set off with my pack roped across the horse's haunches. I followed the road southeast towards Capernaum, and soon saw a lone horseman ahead. He was going at a fast walk. At that rate he would cover over thirty miles in a day, more if he rode from dawn to dusk.
I left the road to pass him unseen. The land round there is barren and rocky. There is barely any water, so it is necessary to carry at least two day's supply for yourself and your horse. For this reason, the road is fairly empty. There is nothing between Sidon and Capernaum on that road, no villages, people, vegetation or beast. There are many hills and it is easy to avoid being seen, but it is difficult terrain, slow going even with a horse. I had to move as fast as I dared to skirt round him. I wanted to get ahead so that I could have a good look at him".

"I ended up following him through Ituraea into Galilee. He then followed the Jordan river through Decapolis and Peraea until we approached the great salt sea. David talked to no one on the way and he moved fast. For the first part of the journey, he set off at dawn and did not stop until dusk. After Galilee where it began to get much hotter and the roads became busier he began to start an hour before dusk and stop an hour after dawn. I was relieved, as it is much easier to ride through the night on those roads than to ride through the day in the relentless heat. It was good for the horses too, as they were able to keep going for longer and did not require so much water. David was a tough man. He was also a careful man. On several occasions he checked his tracks to ensure that he wasn't being followed. On each occasion, I thought that my precautions had proved sufficient".

Water lapped at the sides of the boat as it fought against the current and made it's way slowly south. The sun was at its height, and usually we would have slept through the heat of the day, enjoying the soothing sounds and motion of the boat. But sleep was far off as we listened to Marius' story.

"One night we were approaching the great salt sea. I was to the west of David so that he was in between the river and me. By doing so I could be sure that I was not going to lose him unless he swam the river. It also meant that I could hang back a bit more and reduce any possibility of being seen. Everything was as is would normally be. The road was empty, since most of the traffic uses the boats of the Jordan rather than slog along the road. The sky was cloudless, the stars crystal clear and a cold wind was blowing up little spirals of sand and grit. David made his tidy little camp under a rocky overhang slightly earlier than usual. There was still over an hour until dawn. I ensured that he was settled in and then settled down myself. I don't know how long I was asleep for, but it felt like I had only just closed my eyes when I was woken by a sharp blade digging into my neck. A rough voice asked in broken Latin when I had started following him. I tried to bluff him by saying that I was a thief who worked this stretch of the road and had begun trailing him two days before. He applied some pressure to the knife and ran it down my throat so that it lightly sliced my flesh and drew a few droplets of blood.
"You lie! You have follow me before Peraea before Pella. Why?"
There was nothing I could do, as he would have his knife in the back of my throat before I'd got my hand to my sword.
 "Like you, I am a soldier", I replied.
I knew that I had to do better than that or this man would just kill me and continue on his way.

I gambled.
"I was sent by Origen to follow you. He wanted to be sure that you would do as he bid you".
David instinctively believed this story, and as a result he did not see me as a threat to his safety. Subconsciously he let his hand loosen its grip and his knife slipped a few inches from my throat.

I began to say something, and in mid sentence I struck at his hand. The knife flew from it, and he instantly jumped at me. I had no choice but to kill him".

The men nodded with appreciation. I was impressed by the casual way that Marius spoke as though there had never been any doubt that he would prevail in a hand-to-hand fight.

"I was very afraid. David was an expert. He was deadly serious in whatever this mission was, and he didn't seem mad to me. As a result, I began to believe that my general had not been being paranoid when he assigned me to this mission. I began to think that he had not told me everything when he sent me to follow this man. Preying on my mind was the fact that my mission was briefed to Rome direct without going through any of the regional authorities. I was very afraid because I was given two clear instructions. Follow this man come what may and do not reveal yourself. I had failed on both counts. I was furious with myself.

I searched his body but found nothing of interest so I walked down to his camp and searched his pack. Again I found nothing. In my desperation I began to check the linings of his clothes. I ripped open his sleeping roll with my knife. As I threw the padding aside, I noticed a large bundle of papyrus. I grabbed at them and started to read. They were writings of the new religion. On the first papyrus were written the words "To Joshua of Hebron, with love in the Lord, Origen".

I gathered all of David's possessions, loaded them back on to his horse, and returned to my own camp. I tried to bury the body, but the rocky ground made it hard work. Eventually I had him adequately covered, but by then it was nearly noon. I slept in the shade of a rocky outcrop until sun down".

"When I woke, it seemed obvious what I should do. Rather than return a failure, I would take on David's identity and try to find this Joshua myself in Hebron. My three years in Ituraea had given me a good command of their language, and my eight years in the region had given me a fairly comprehensive understanding of their customs and habits. I felt that I could pass for an Ituraean".

"Hebron is a large village at the top of the escarpment above the great valley of the Salt Sea. People come from all around on market days to sell their crude produce, but for most of the rest of the time the village is quiet. The innkeeper pointed Joshua out to me. He is a water seller, so I just followed the ringing of his bell. He was a kindly old man, childishly trusting. He had never met David but knew much of the christian movement and of Origen. He was expecting David, and the "gospel" that I carried with me. I thought that the more I knew about the Christians the better, so I had taken the opportunity to read it on the journey. I had not been with him long when Joshua told me that he had received a message for me from a Mishac in El Arish in Sinai. The message said simply that David was to lodge with him at his earliest convenience. I spent two days in Hebron. Joshua was a lonely man, and like all lonely people he talked too much. He chattered constantly for two days. I listened and I remembered. He told me of the christian movement. He told me myths from nearly one hundred years ago concerning the Christus. He told me of Origen and of the modern movement. He told me of heroism and cowardice, but most of all he spoke of Roman brutality. He was a kind man and seemed sincere in his beliefs. He had an interesting view of the Romans. He hated what we do but claimed to love us. I think that he had probably spent too much time wandering around in the sun listening to his bell. Unfortunately when I tried to move the conversation to the document for which we search it was clear that he knew nothing".

Marius paused and shifted on the deck of the felucca. There was a wide bend in the river ahead, and the palms leaned right out over the banks, shading us for a few seconds from the sun as we passed underneath. When he was comfortable, Marius resumed his story.
"Before leaving Joshua I sent a despatch to the general explaining what had happened. I also explained that I had successfully passed myself off as David the smith at the first contact point and was moving on to the second. I thought that when I got to Aegyptus it was

possible that I might need some help. I suggested that he sent me ten trusted and clever men".
Marius looked up with one eyebrow cocked in mock reproach.
"I requested these men to meet me at that caravanserai. Instead it appears that they sent you lot".

Marius' face broke into a wide smile. "After Hebron I continued on into the desert for several weeks to El Arish. There I found Mishac and stayed with him just long enough to eat a meal. He was impatient and jumpy, and told me that I was late and that I must continue on my way. Before I left I sent a report to Rome. Mishac gave me the next contact, and it is to there that we are travelling. Now, if you don't mind I'm weary and the sun is hot and I'm going to have a bit of a sleep."
With that, Marius leaned back, closed his eyes and fell asleep.

There was silence on the deck of the felucca after Marius had finished. I looked around and all of the men looked pensive. The story that Marius told was, indeed, odd. Odd that this small group of religious zealots should be so paranoid about a document. Odd that such a senior soldier had been assigned to retrieve it. Odd that we had been sent to support him, but were unable to do so as Roman soldiers. But most of all, odd that all of the regional authorities were being bypassed and the mission seemed to be being run directly from Rome. As Marius began to snore lightly, I asked the men what they thought. They were as unsettled as I was. No one liked the idea of engaging with an enemy that we did not know in search of something we did not understand. What written words could be so important as to justify all of this effort and secrecy? No one had any idea, and as we continued upstream, we all, I think, did so with an uncomfortable feeling of foreboding.

4

Mycernius came charging around the side of the house, screaming. His thin little legs were grazed and covered in dust, his impish face filled with excitement. Behind him, breathing heavily, came a young man a few years short of his prime. Akhattes was good looking, and he knew it. Mycernius turned and taunted him, enjoying the fact that he was now of an age that some grown men could no longer catch him. Breezily the boy turned and skipped off, leaving Akhattes with a rueful smile. With the shadows lengthening about him in the evening light Akhattes listened to his breath slow. He wiped the perspiration from his elegant forehead and entered the house.

Snofru was putting dinner onto the table, and Rani sat in the corner silently. There was a tension in the room that Akhattes put down to Rani's shyness in his presence. He knew that he had raised her hopes, and relished the thought that he had the power to dispel the tension that gripped her with the simple proposition that he was planning to put to her. He would have done it sooner, but he was enjoying the thrill of the chase too much. Rani pretended to be indifferent to him, but he was sure that she would yield the moment that flirtation turned into anything more serious.

Rani could have killed Snofru. Having Akhattes mooning at her all evening was just what she did not need. She felt as though her whole world had been rocked that day. She knew the danger that the manuscript represented because she understood the lengths that certain forces, forces that she had no desire to ever understand, would go to in order to claim what her family had in its possession. Because of this she did not have the energy to lock wills with Akhattes. She chose instead to ignore him.

Smenkhare and Horemheb entered the house, and all of the children rose to their feet.

Smenkhare half raised his hand to indicate that they should sit down, but he was not really concentrating. Both he and his wife looked distracted, tense. Silently Huni dished up the rice into wooden bowls.

Akhattes was mildly surprised. He had been careful to hint at his intentions towards Rani over these last few months, but he could not remember what he had done to give away the fact that it was this night that he planned to propose marriage to the beautiful girl who had grown to be such a lively widow. Nevertheless, he was encouraged by the nervousness in the household. Like the excitement of being on the brink of agreeing an important deal, he thought happily. The match would be good for their family. They could not wish for better for Rani, and Rani would be grateful for him. What luck for her! To be tainted by the touch of another, and to still have the opportunity to marry one so young, handsome and with such prospects as himself!

Dinner was a noisy affair. Snofru spent more time flirting with Akhattes than eating. Huni had picked up the tension in her elder sister and parents, but was soon distracted by the banter. Mycernius watched with glee at the proceedings and roared with laughter at the repartee between Akhattes and Snofru.

Eventually Akhattes turned his attention to Rani.
"You are quiet, Rani. Something troubles you?"
It was said with a conspiratorial, slightly arrogant smile. Akhattes knew what was troubling her, and enjoyed the fact that she could not voice the thought.

Rani's eyes flashed with irritation. Akhattes was being even more unbearably smug than usual, and his outrageous flirting with Snofru was obviously designed to rile her. What is more, she had a terrible feeling that his smugness was caused by an impending proposal of marriage. The unpleasantness of rejecting him was more than she could face today. She knew that she should ignore his baiting, but she could not help herself.

"What is troubling me is you. You are slimier than the weeds in the Nile, and talking to you I feel a residue collecting on my skin. Leave me alone."

Akhattes was delighted. She had obviously been very annoyed by his flirting, and that revealed how much she cared for him. Nevertheless he lowered his eyes in feigned hurt.

Rani felt guilty. Akhattes did not deserve such brutal treatment. He was only trying to be endearing. It was not his fault that his vanity repulsed her. In her regret she looked up for the first time and her eyes met the beautiful long lashed eyes of her suitor. She held his gaze and smiled.
"Forgive me, Akhattes. I have had a long day and I'm tired. If you'll excuse me I need some fresh air".

Rani stood with her eyes to the floor and walked out into the cool evening air. The moon had risen over the river, reflecting in silver shards off the water in front of the bulrushes. The snorts of hippopotami disturbed the silence, and their movements in the water sent ripples across the stillness. She wandered down to the riverbank, subconsciously checking for hippo prints. Everyone brought up by the river was careful to avoid letting themselves get between the water and the fleshy river beasts that grazed the banks at night. She sat on a tuft of grass close to the waters edge allowing the breeze to cool her and her thoughts to clear.

Someone was coming. Someone was coming to their small village to disrupt their peaceful family. None of them had asked for the danger, the threat that hung over them all. Rani felt herself go taut with anger at the injustice of it. She thought of Huni, of Snofru and most of all of Mycernius, so full of the joys of life. They were totally ignorant of the impending darkness, of the powers that could at any day intrude into their lives and tear their close family apart. She remembered being twelve years old. She remembered the simple joys of discovering the secrets of farming, of religion, of the ancients. She recalled the slow realisation that the world was a great rich tapestry as complex and beautiful as one wanted it to be. And she remembered the dark day that she had turned fourteen, how she had felt when her father had told her that which she could tell no one. She remembered how the world had suddenly seemed ominous, threatening. The unknown had been transformed from something exciting and fun to something she feared. Ever since that day she had seen the world through different eyes, and her love for life had been tinged with fear. She knew that she could never tell Akhattes their secret. He could not be trusted, and he was not a man who would grasp the implications. He was too apathetic, too vain, too sure of himself, too ignorant. He would not fear it as he should, but persuade himself that he was too clever and too strong for the forces that threatened them. And then, one day, he would learn how wrong he was and all of her family would die because of it. For this reason she could never love Akhattes, and she could never marry him. The man was a fool.

Rani felt lonely and trapped. She could not allow a man to come into her life, for it would mean sharing her secret and putting his life in danger. How could she do that to someone she was supposed to love? Rani knew she was too young to be a widow. She longed for children. She longed for peace and for normality. But most of all she longed for freedom from the yoke of her secret.

Rani jumped as she felt a hand on her shoulder. She half rose as she turned, and saw Akhattes standing straight behind her. He put out a hand to calm her fright. He spoke softly, his eyes lit by the moon.
"You are like a thoroughbred, Rani. So delicate, so highly strung, so intelligent. Yet you have such strength and such extraordinary beauty".

Rani felt her heart sink. She had hoped that he would have got the message from her premature disappearance from dinner. He had never complimented or tried to seduce her like this before. His approach had always been to flirt with playful banter. This was an ominous sign, and she did not know how to proceed.

"Akhattes . . . I think . . . ." she made to turn away from him.

Akhattes grabbed both of her hands, interrupting. Suddenly he was urgent, ardent.
"Rani, you know why I am here. I love you. I am young, my prospects are good and we will make a fine match. I can look after you, and the union of our families will strengthen them both. You need to make a match, and you cannot hope to make a better one. I am going to ask your father for your hand, but I want to do so with your blessing".

Rani felt herself flushing with anger. The arrogance of the man! To tell her that she could not do better, that he was what her family needed! He had no idea of what her family needed. Even worse, he managed to make the whole thing sound like a transaction at the market. She forced herself to be calm. She raised her eyes to the sky and allowed the spectacular sight of the millions of stars burning brightly above the palms to bring some degree of peace. As she lowered her eyes, she looked at Akhattes. Handsome, young, stupid, arrogant Akhattes, and for the first time in all of her life she saw him in a new light. He was vulnerable, expectant and nervous. Suddenly he looked like a young child to her. She could hardly bear to say what she must to this man, her friend who for the first time had laid himself bare. But she forced herself to harden her heart, and when she spoke it was as if the harsh words came from somewhere else.
"I am sorry if I have led you to misunderstand my feelings, but I will never agree to marry you. I do not love you, and you could never make me happy. Through my unhappiness I would bring you only grief, and I am not prepared to enter into something so destructive. You must forget about me now and never allow yourself to think of me again".

Akhattes could not believe his ears. Rani must have taken leave of her senses! How could she reject such a generous, advantageous offer?

It was not long before it became clear to Akhattes that this wilful girl did not know what was best for her. She seemed oblivious to reason, and to his charm. He had to fight to prevent from showing her his anger as he left her alone by the river.

As soon as he was gone, Rani wept.

5

The sun was low in the sky as the boat approached Misr. As soon it came into view I woke Marius. I couldn't have allowed him to miss such a sight.

We were passing through a large settlement surrounded by fields. Unusually it was on both banks of the river. The spectacular palaces on the edges of the settlement would probably have been enough to cause me to wake Marius. However, what had really caught the attention of us all was the distant sight, far from the banks of the river, of the great pyramids rising out of the desert. Surrounded just by sand were these enormous monuments to the ancients. Other than the owner of the felucca, none of us had ever seen such a sight.

"What are they for?" asked Cassius. Cassius was a tall, thin man with receding hair on an outsized head. He was quiet and thoughtful, unusual amongst us as a man who liked to think before he acted.
"I don't know. I have heard that they might either be monuments to their Gods, or they might be tombs of great kings. I do not believe either explanation", I replied. As I did so Cassius looked thoughtful, and as so often I got the impression that it was I who should be asking Cassius for an explanation.
"What do you think, anyway?" I asked him.
Cassius was slow to answer, but when he did it his ponderous tones were characteristically measured.
"Many men must have suffered to build something so great. The only thing that men care about enough to cause such suffering is themselves. Whatever reason they gave for building these things, the only real reason can have been to prove their own greatness. They are magnificent, but they are terrible". His voice was a strange mixture of awe and disgust.
Instinctively I liked Cassius, but I was reserving judgement until I had seen what he was like in a fight.

"Dock, captain if you please" shouted Marius from behind us. The captain looked back at him blankly.
"Excellent! He absolutely doesn't speak Latin".
Marius was in good spirits as he wandered back to the captain and gestured to him that he wanted him to dock for a short period. When he came back, I handed Marius the two things that I had been given for him in Rome. The first was an official stamp. It bore the crest of Rome and the mark of the Governor of the Imperial Roman Province of Aegyptus. "I was told to tell you that you cannot under any circumstances reveal your identity and enlist the help of the local authorities. Therefore you have been given this. Use it, only if you have to". I thought that I saw a flicker of shock in Marius' eyes. If I did, it was gone in an instant.

As well as the stamp there was a sealed papyrus. Marius broke the seal and read it, and as he did so the shock returned to his eyes. Only this time, it did not vanish. He looked as though he had seen the dead rise. He handed it back and gestured for me to read it. As my eyes followed the text an icy chill ran down my spine. The papyrus was an order from none other than the leader of all of the armies of the empire of Rome, Decimus Marcellus, and it was simple. From now on, Marius Sextus was to report on the progress of his mission every third day, and the messages were to be sent directly to no one other than Decimus himself.
"Ye Gods" I whispered.

*****

Marius led us off the boat into the crowded marketplace of Misr. Like the market at Alexandria, it was a seething chaos of shouting traders, a bewildering kaleidoscope of colours and images coming from high set stalls. The stench was worse than in Alexandria, the stench of rotting fish, excrement and filthy human bodies. Muslin screens covered the market to keep the sun out. As the sun went down it became almost black under the screens, and oil lanterns lit up the market. It had a close and threatening feeling. The narrow streets were labyrinthine, so narrow as to prevent even a donkey and cart from passing. We squeezed and pushed our way through the bazaar, which seemed to take over most of the village. Occasionally we would pass a few streets with no stalls, no traders and very few people. But these small side streets would always lead back to a heaving thoroughfare. Soon we found a stall selling simple peasant clothing. Marius ordered us all to purchase two sets. He told us not to forget a yashmak to guard against the sun and cover our faces, and a long robe of at least knee length.

"You'll soon all have beards and then everyone will know you by sight as locals. Let's get back to the boat." Silus, Numba, Tobias, Alaric and Greto were sent to buy food for the evening and morning meals and were behind the rest of us. Marius, Artorius, Cassius, Petrus and myself all continued back to the boat.

Marius led us back the way that we had come. I was relieved to get out of the chaos of the market and into the back streets for a brief respite. After a few minutes I became aware of a large man dressed in a long brown robe approaching me. It was gloomy but not completely dark, as the back streets were not covered by the screens that kept off the heat of the day in the bazaar. I was only half watching the man when suddenly there was the sound of scuffing feet and I noticed movement out of the corner of my eye. Just as I turned to face where it came from I was violently spun round and felt the sudden bite of a knife blade above my hip. I felt breath on the back of my neck that carried a strong smell of fermented drink. I froze, and my assailant turned me round to face the others. Cassius and Petrus were already held by strong grips, and had curved knives pressed against their sides. Marius had jumped to his right. A knife was already in his hand and he stood cat-like facing four attackers. Artorius, a tall, wide shouldered man with an impressive reputation as a fighter, was at the rear, and had not yet been reached. I saw Marius gesture backwards to Artorius with a subtle move of his eyes. A weasely looking man emerged from the shadows and grabbed Artorius from behind as he edged back. Artorius was quick to see what was going on, and intelligent enough not to resist. Marius stood facing us. A man stepped from the shadows and spoke in rough Latin in Marius' direction.

"There are eight of us and five of you. Drop your knife or your friends die".

Marius dropped his knife and was grabbed, a knife to his side. There were a further three men looking on. They were all street scum wearing similar brown robes held with rope, and from the look of their eyes they had all been drinking. I was looking at Marius. His eyes were on fire and seemed to be appealing for attention. I kept my gaze on him, while he looked round to ensure that he had the attention of Cassius and Artorius. The leader of the attackers walked towards Marius. I had a horrible feeling that they might be Christians who had learned of the murder of David the smith. As their leader spoke he revealed a few brown, dakkar stained teeth and a twisted grin.

"So you are the leader of these pilgrims".

"Pilgrims have no need of a leader", replied Marius.

The man ignored his defiant tone. "Drop your bags and empty your pockets" he ordered.

As their leader finished, Marius gave a vicious elbow to the ribs of the man who held him. Instantly he turned, drawing his stabbing sword and turning the man to face his leader. He held his sword to the man's throat.

"You do not want us to empty our pockets or our packs because they will bring you only death. Release my men and you can go with your lives".

On the final word he gestured with his free hand. All three of us instantly took the signal, and elbowed our attackers sharply. They were slow, probably because they were fuddled by drink. I felt the knife drop from my side as I grabbed the man by the hair and twisted him round. With my other hand I reached to my calf to draw the dagger that I keep there and had it at his throat. I looked up, and saw Artorius bury his knee with awesome power in the face of his attacker, who fell unconscious to the floor with blood spurting from where his nose had been. The cerebral Cassius had a knife to his assailant's face. I looked to Petrus. He had been too slow. Blood already soaked his side, and was forming a puddle on the floor. He was crumpled but still upright as his attacker tried to recover his sword. Immediately I slit the throat of the man in my grasp. Cassius did the same. Both men fell to the ground.

The remaining bandits began advancing towards us. "Enough" shouted Marius. Then he spoke more slowly to their leader, who still had Marius' knife at his throat.
"No more. Call them off or you will all die here". With this, Marius released the man. He looked wide-eyed at the carnage around him and fled into the darkness. His remaining men followed.

Petrus was dead. We wrapped his body in one of the white robes that we had just brought, picked him up and carried the body north out of the village. We left the corpses of our attackers where they lay. We found a quiet place between the fields two miles north of the village and dug a deep grave. The dark rich soil was soft, irrigated by the long drainage channels that flowed from the Nile to feed the fields. When the hole was about the height of a man, water began to seep in. We put Petrus into the puddle at the bottom. Cassius spoke some words of poetry about summer and autumn and the sun and the moon that he had memorised from somewhere. It did not take long, and when he finished we filled the hole in and returned to the boat.

At dawn the following morning our felucca pulled into the small village of Assyut. We disembarked onto a small wooden jetty, and made our way through filthy black streets to the rear of the village. There, at the fringes of the fields with the hills of the desert rising beyond we found the caravanserai. Marius had been planning to spend some more time with Christians. He wanted to become more proficient at passing unnoticed among them, but he was nervous about spending too much time in Assyut with all of us at the caravanserai. We could only spend a few nights there without attracting any attention. So Marius decided to seek the man whose name he had been given by Mishac in El Arish straight away.

We waited. We sat around the caravanserai and did not talk of Petrus. We had lost friends before, and this was no different. He had been too slow. We could not afford people who could not look after themselves and this was the unspoken verdict. It was harsh but it was also the truth. Instead we settled back into the routine that had started to develop.

As usual, Numba took charge of the cooking. He could make food go further than anyone we knew, and had a talent for making it taste delicious no matter what it was. He would bark out orders, insults and jokes in equal measure, and the rest of the boys loved it. Artorius was his assistant, good humouredly fetching water, stoking the fire and absorbing Numba's ribbing.

Cassius took up his customary position by the fire. He looked into the flames and sat reflectively, chuckling at some of Numba's more outrageous comments with Alaric beside him.

Silus and Tobias, the last of my men were from the same village in northern Italia. Both were professional soldiers, the sons of legionaries who had been discharged and given plots to farm. They were good Romans – clever, educated, solid, witty and strong. I sat with them that evening, talking of the wonders of Aegyptus and of the men who had built it. We speculated as to their methods, and we guessed at their motives.

*****

Marius found the house by asking at the riverside. He arrived there well before dusk and sat watching. An elderly woman was in the house going about her chores. Marius waited. Eventually, an elderly man who matched the description he had been given by Mishac approached the house. He had obviously come straight from the harvest and looked weary. When he entered Marius approached and knocked on the door, and when it was opened he drew his breath. A girl with fresh, striking features peered out. Her full mouth was formed in a hesitant smile, and despite a deep tan her skin was almost luminescent. Her smile gave Marius a glimpse of flawlessly white teeth. Although her features denied Rani a classical beauty they were perfectly formed. She stood there with her eyebrows slightly raised in mild enquiry and an instinctive look of welcome on her face. Marius was surprised to feel his heart pounding in his chest and hear his breath shallow on his lips. For reasons that he did not understand he felt clumsy and ungainly. Unaccustomed to being so flustered, Marius just stood there and stared at this girl in the doorway.

Rani looked straight at Marius and saw a man reaching the end of his prime who had seen too much sun. She saw a handsome face creased by grief and weighed by responsibility. She saw eyes that had seen too much death and become hard. She saw Marius for what he was. She saw a soldier, and she had no need for soldiers. Yet she sensed a depth to him. She recognised some of his pain and sadness and her instinct was to soothe it. Despite herself she found herself wanting to know him.

For some moments Marius and Rani just stood looking at each other. There was no awkwardness about them, just a spontaneous fascination. Marius' first thought was that this girl was the most beautiful thing that he had ever seen. It took some time for reality to intrude back into his thoughts. He fought it, for he just wanted to be here with this woman, alone. But he had come to deceive her and her family, and he could not ignore it. Marius was used to doing this. It had always been part of his duties as praefectus castrorum. But somehow, here, it felt wrong.

Slowly Marius gathered himself and gruffly announced that he was seeking a man named Smenkhkare. Rani went white, and quickly turned to summon her father. Smenkhkare appeared on the doorstep and politely asked who had travelled so far to see him.
"My name is David and I am a smith" replied Marius simply.
Immediately Rani was sent in to despatch Horemheb to the house of Akhattes parents with the rest of the children. When the house was empty of them, Smenkhkare invited Marius in and sat him down in the family room. Rani fetched water and then came to join the two men. Marius could not take his eyes off her. When Smenkhkare spoke Marius reluctantly dragged his eyes back to her father.

"I believe that you have met Rani, my daughter. She knows everything, so we may speak freely in front of her."

Marius looked back at Rani and felt his heart leap as he nodded to her. She looked squarely and slightly quizzically back at him. Smenkhkare continued.

"Why have you come, David the smith?"

"I have come to recover that which you guard", replied Marius

"What is it that I guard, David?"

"In truth, I do not know. I was told little by Origen. All I know is that you are in possession of a document that can be of great benefit to our cause. Origen believes that it can be used to alter Rome's attitude to us".

Smenkhkare was silent, lost in thought. Rani glanced at Marius and caught him as he took in her features. He quickly looked away, and as he began to blush he sensed her wry smile.

Suddenly Smenkhkare started. "I received a letter from Origen that virtually ordered me to hand the confession to you. Tell me, David. Why does Origen believe that he should be given the confession? I will not part with it unless I know his intentions".

Marius had no idea of the answer. Nor did he know why Smenkhkare was referring to a "confession". He certainly did not feel that he knew enough to guess.

"I do not know, sir. I do know that Origen is a good man, and I also know that he will use it according to God's will. As I understand it, you are under obligation to surrender it when it is requested."

Smenkhkare's face hardened.

"I do not need reminding of that. I also have a responsibility to do what is right in the eyes of God. But I need not concern you with that if you do not know the use to which the confession would be put".

Rani was looking restless. She did not think that Marius looked like a smith.

"How do we know you are who you say you are?" she burst out. "Tell me of Origen and of how you know him".

Marius blessed the openness of Joshua in Hebron. He had practiced his answer to this question time and again in his mind over the past few weeks. Yet as he came to say it Marius felt an unfamiliar emotion. He felt guilt.

"Origen is forty eight years old and is the leader of our movement. I was born to christian parents and they brought me up in the church in Sidon. My father was a smith, and I too became a smith. I grew up with Origen. He was older than me and I feared him. Origen is a big man. He has a hunched back and looks like a bear. As a child I was terrified of him. He was a bully. When he grew he became a big drinker and a street fighter. He was a notorious thug. When he was converted he changed. He studied the texts of the apostles. He became a learned man. He became a good and compassionate man. But he has seen too many people who he loves die at the hands of the Romans. He has heard too many stories of their brutality to our people. He hates the Romans almost as much as he loves God. He is a great scholar of the writings, and a great leader of our people. He wishes only for peace for our people, and for the salvation of the empire".

"You know Origen. Now tell me how Tertullian is" demanded Rani.

Marius knew all about Tertullian. "He is well"

Suddenly the atmosphere changed. Smenkhkare sat up. Rani looked shocked.

"Well?" asked Smenkhkare. "How can he be well with that wasting disease? I am told he will be dead within the year"

Marius knew that Tertullian was old, but he had not been told that Tertullian was dying. Probably the news had not reached Joshua. Unaccountably Marius was beginning to feel sick, but he recovered quickly.

"Tertullian is well compared to how he has been. When I left Sidon his wasting disease appeared to be in some kind of remission. He was stronger than he had been for some months."

Their suspicion remained. Both sat with furrowed brows and regarded him intently.

"Tell me of Tertullian" said Smenkhkare softly.

"No one knows how old Tertullian is. We believe that he is over seventy years old. He is small and shrivelled and frail. He is also the greatest christian alive. He knows more about the ancient writings than anyone, and his knowledge has deepened since he handed over his responsibilities to Origen. He is gentle and wise. His eyes are full of light, and he forgives what Origen will not. Some say he is too soft, that he is bullied by Origen. I do not agree. I believe that he recognises what Origen is trying to do and agrees that it is necessary. I also believe that he realises that he was not capable of it himself. Otherwise he would not support Origen and act as his advisor".

Smenkhkare relaxed visibly. Marius could not read Rani's expression.

"Thank you, David. You know Tertullian and you know Origen. Now, you will have some food with us and stay?"
Part of him wanted to remain. For some reason, Marius could not bear the thought of leaving the presence of this girl. But another part of him could not wait to get out. Caution took over and he spoke with genuine regret.
"I have already eaten, sir. Thank you for your offer, but I have left my pack at my lodgings and I would prefer not to intrude."
"Very well but you are welcome. Rani, please show our visitor out. You must return in the morning, David, and we will tell you what we are going to do. I do not yet know myself, but we will discuss it and have an answer by morning."

Marius rose. Smenkhkare kissed him on both cheeks, and Rani accompanied him through the kitchen.
"You do not look or act like a smith. You're more like a soldier" Rani said as she led him through the kitchen. She did not even try to hide her suspicion.
"I was brought up watching Roman crimes against our people. It makes soldiers of us all"
Rani stopped. Her voice softened "Is it that bad up there?"
"They know that we have a headquarters there. It is sport to the local legion to harass us, to rape our wives and to murder our children."
Marius said this with such bitterness that he took Rani aback. Marius surprised himself with his tone, but he recognised it as guilt for the behaviour of his comrades and disgust at himself for things he had done as a young soldier and for what he was doing now.
"You have lost loved ones?" she asked quietly.
Marius did not understand what was happening to him. He had an urge to tell this stranger of himself. He answered truthfully.

"Apart from my parents I have never had any loved ones. I have seen too much death, Rani. I have seen too many people broken by grief. I never wanted to put myself in that situation. I thought that I was protecting myself. I thought that it would spare me from being hurt."
Marius stopped himself. He couldn't explain the feeling that had overwhelmed him earlier when Rani opened the door. That first sight of her made his whole life seem empty, nothing but immense loneliness. As a servant of the empire, he had never had the opportunity to marry and until now he had never been sorry. What he said about protecting himself from grief was true. But now he felt different, and was startled to find himself wanting to tell Rani. He had a terrible urge to tell her everything, tell her who he really was and who had sent him.
Rani understood the implication. She could see that she was having an effect on this hardened man who stood before her. She took his arm and their eyes met.
"You must not be afraid to love, David. You must allow yourself some happiness".
He felt that if he did not flee he would blurt out the truth. He quickly turned from her. For the first time in years he felt the hot flush of tears in his eyes, and he did not want her to see.
"Be here tomorrow" was all he could say as he fled into the night.

6

The coliseum was packed. Fifty three thousand Romans were crammed onto the stone benches baying for blood. The sun shone overhead as the gladiators went for each other with fatal brutality.
In the Imperial gallery, Hadrian reclined on his couch with half an eye on the proceedings. Behind him a young girl played a harp that was largely drowned out by the shouts of the crowd. Decimus and Alexander sat in a corner, paying little attention to the entertainment. Lucius stood on the edge of the balcony lost in thought. One of the gladiators fell. His helmet was roughly removed by the other, who raised his sword high and decapitated his opponent. He lifted the severed, dripping head high above his own and showed it to every part of the giant coliseum. The crowd roared their approval as the stewards ran on, removed the body and helped the surviving gladiator off the compound. A band marched out from a tunnel in the amphitheatre and began to play.

Lucius turned to look at Decimus and Alexander and wondered what they were talking about. Ever since their clandestine meeting a few weeks ago the atmosphere between the four men had been strange. Although no one spoke of what had been said Lucius was sure that the subject had been weighing on all of their minds. He was an experienced enough politician to know that such news could be seen as an opportunity to the ambitious. There had been a slightly fractious atmosphere between them, a sort of jostling jealousy that Lucius did not fully understand. He knew that all who were at the meeting would be aware that it could bring about the downfall of the empire itself. It would not be particularly surprising if certain people put their own ambitions ahead of what was best for the empire, and it was natural that the thought had unsettled him. But what concerned him more was the powerful sense of foreboding that had accompanied it. The fragility of the foundations upon which Rome was built was always something that had seemed vague and unreal to him. Just to look at the great power of the city and the might of her grip across her provinces was to banish any fears over her solidity. But that Ituraean spy had been real. A loud fanfare of trumpets interrupted Lucius' thoughts.

Hadrian sat up. Even Alexander and Decimus broke off their conversation and walked to the front of the balcony. The main event was about to begin. It had been personally ordered by Hadrian, and he was determined to enjoy it. Three huge lions were released into the paddock. They sprinted into the arena, looking all around them. They stopped, and walked round uncertainly in circles. At the opposite end of the arena large double doors were opened. About fifteen men and women and about ten children reluctantly stumbled out. All were naked. Behind them were men with whips, forcing them to enter the arena. When all were in front of the doors, they shut behind them. The lions had stopped, and were regarding the reluctant people intently.
"Excellent. The Christians have arrived to show us the power of their god" said Hadrian loudly. Lucius turned away and went in search of a refill for his goblet.

The lions had not eaten for a week. As the Christians huddled together against the closed doors, they began to slowly walk towards them, crouching down as if they were stalking them. The crowd had gone silent in anticipation. When they were a short distance from their quarry the lions sprang forward. The Christians scattered, running in every direction in blind panic. The first lion, a young male, jumped at a young woman. Whilst in mid air it swung a paw at her body and knocked her off her feet, the force of the blow spinning her around. In a flash both of its forelegs were pinning her to the ground and it had her neck in its huge jaws. Her legs and lower body flung themselves around, trying to get free. Her chest and upper body lay still, totally pinned by the lion. After just a few seconds her lower body became still and began to twitch. Without releasing its grip on her throat, the lion sat down. After perhaps a minute, it looked up. The fur around its mouth was stained red, its white teeth covered by a thin red film. The lion briefly surveyed the arena, and then lowered it's head to begin tearing at the flesh of the woman's belly. Within a minute it had opened up her stomach and had it's head deep inside, eating out her warm organs.

Meanwhile the other lions had each found a victim, one a young man and the other a girl of about twelve years. The crowd were cheering wildly. The other Christians had returned to the front of the door, and were huddled there again. The doors opened and they ran through the gap as soon as it was wide enough for them to get through.
The doors closed while the lions continued to eat.

"First blood to the animals" shouted Hadrian. He was grinning widely and had a nasty look in his eye. "Next on are the wolves. We have far more of them!"

Lucius was sickened. He was about to make his excuses when a senior centurion of the Praetorian Guard approached him.
"Sir, I have an urgent message for the emperor".
With that he handed Lucius a rolled and sealed papyrus. Lucius took the papyrus to Hadrian who immediately read it. His face betrayed no emotion. Silently he handed it to Lucius without even looking at him.

"SIR
THE MAN WHOM I WAS SENT TO FOLLOW, DAVID THE SMITH, WAS A PROFESSIONAL. I FOLLOWED HIM THROUGH GALILEE AND DECAPOLIS TO THE JORDAN RIVER. IN PERAEA HE ACCOSTED ME. I WAS FORCED TO KILL HIM. I DISCOVERED IN HIS POSSESSIONS A CONTACT NAME. I ASSUMED HIS IDENTITY AND PROCEEDED TO THE CONTACT. THIS MAN GAVE ME FURTHER INSTRUCTIONS AND A FURTHER NAME TO CONTACT IN EL ARISH. I AM PROCEEDING THERE NOW AND INTEND TO CONTINUE UNDER THE IDENTITY OF DAVID THE SMITH. I WILL REPORT FROM EL ARISH PRIOR TO DEPARTING. I AM CONFIDENT THAT I CAN PASS FOR ORIGEN'S COURIER AND RETRIEVE THAT FOR WHICH YOU SENT ME.
MARIUS SEXTUS
HEBRON"

Lucius finished and looked at Hadrian. Hadrian was on his feet. He walked round his couch and out towards the private chambers at the rear of the balcony. He casually beckoned Decimus and Alexander as he passed. In his chamber, he was silent as he gave the message to Decimus and Alexander. As soon as they looked up Hadrian began to rant. "Who is this fool? If he can't even follow a man, what chance does he have of passing himself off as an Ituraean? It's a complete catastrophe. What shall we do?"

Lucius couldn't believe his ears. As far as he was concerned this was good news. This Marius Sextus had already passed as the courier, so it was clear that he could. They found themselves in the position of having a senior Roman soldier successfully infiltrated as the man who had been sent to retrieve the Neronian confession. It was the perfect scenario. They could never have ordered it, as it would have been too risky. If they had they would have wanted it to turn out like this. The faces of Decimus and Alexander were unreadable, and no one was willing to break the silence. Hadrian was getting impatient. His voice was threatening as he once more insisted upon advice.
"The exposure of the confession of Nero is the most potent threat that the empire faces to its stability. Do not underestimate how close the empire was to falling apart when the Christians were allowed to peddle their stories to them to the client rulers. I am party to information that no other man alive is and it will stay that way, but if you had seen some of the supplementary information that Nero put in the bequest about events at the time you might be taking this a little more seriously than you appear to be now. Whilst this manuscript and the persuasive zealots from Judea pose real danger to our power, recent events represent greatest opportunity since Nero's original foul up to eliminate the threat forever. I shall shortly ask each of you for your council on how we should proceed, and when I do I expect you to have thought about it properly, and to have a good answer."
With that, Hadrian rose from his couch pulled the cord that dangled behind it and strode out of the room. The head housekeeper walked in. Decimus took control ordering him to fetch refreshments and light snacks. Usually small talk was easy. There was plenty to gossip about

in Rome, from the latest scandals of which senator's wife was sleeping with which of their colleagues to who was making a name for themselves in the administration. Today there was no small talk, but rather deep silence as the company sat lost in thought.

Hadrian was gone for some time, and from the cheering we could hear that the entertainments had resumed. When he returned he was a little calmer.
"This had better be good," he said as he sat down.

Alexander was the first to be asked for his views, and he measured his words carefully.
"I want to start by making it clear that I fully understand the implications of what might happen if this Origen were to use this confession as effectively as we fear he might. From my perspective the scenario is every bit as grim as it is from anyone else's. The whole financial system of Rome could collapse. Most people do not understand money and the abstract of our financial system. The system is based on confidence, since the collateral used to underwrite our activities is often not liquid. In plain Latin, if we were threatened with the loss of a number of territories simultaneously, investors would want to convert their assets into something flexible and portable – cash. In other words they would seek to convert the collateral. However it cannot be converted into cash readily, if at all. Inflation would escalate and the denarii would collapse. To all intents and purposes, money would become worthless. Anarchy would ensue and the empire could collapse. So as I see it the question is not "what to do?" but "how to do it?" I cannot speak as a military man. But as a man who understands more than most about protecting things of value I would say that Origen will keep the details of the search and the exact location of the document known to as few people as possible, perhaps as few as two. I was always taught that to catch a rat you send a cat, because the cat can track the rat and kill it at its pleasure. A big clumsy bear would never find the rat. So one option would be to use the cat already sent. But in Origen we have a more obvious place to start. He knows more than anyone else and most importantly he knows how to get his hands on the confession. I suggest we bring him

in and force him to tell us. I understand we have ways to extract this sort of information?"

Listening to this fat, over privileged patrician describing his beloved legions as a "big clumsy bear" had visibly annoyed Decimus. When he spoke there was an edge to his voice.
"It's not always as simple as that, Alexander. People who do things out of conviction rather than fear or ambition or greed have an awkward tendency to die before they talk. Origen could be just such a man."
He paused to flick away a fly that had landed on his toga before continuing in more measured tones.
"No, we must find another way. I have two legions stationed in the region. The XIIth is based in Tyrus and the XXXIIIrd is in Alexandria. I can deploy both legions to search every single home in Aegyptus. I can put soldiers out undercover posing as Christians on the roads. I can have every bed in every caravanserai on the way searched every night. With two legions we can find this manuscript. The area is small. To use your analogy, Alexander, if you put a rat in a cage with a bear, there will only be one winner. I can turn that region into a cage".

With that he picked a bunch of grapes and began peeling the skin of them with his teeth. Lucius could hardly believe his ears. It beggared belief that a man that stupid could command the might of the entire military machine of the Roman empire. But he realised that he must watch his tone with Decimus. There were two senators who were unable to speak in the senate, for they had given Decimus a verbal mauling in the presence of Hadrian. Hadrian had taken it personally and now they no longer had tongues in their heads. With this in mind he quickly modified what he was about to say.

"I agree with Decimus that his method is the most likely to succeed in finding the document. Let us speak plainly. The whole point of this discussion is to seek to understand how we can keep a deception covered up. If two legions were to ransack a whole corner of the empire on our orders to create Decimus' cage, the news would get out.

Questions would be asked in the Senate. This would either lead us to allow the secret out - tantamount to doing Origen's job for him - or it would force us to refuse to tell them. The Senate will not agree to trust us, without explanation, if we use two full strength legions to ransack a peaceful part of the empire."

Lucius looked around. He sensed that thus far he retained their attention. "I also agree with Decimus that Alexander's suggestion of bringing Origen in for torture is too risky. Yet Alexander has a point when he says that cats are extremely effective at catching rats. They are also discreet. Impersonating the man sent by Origen to retrieve the document will by definition lead us to it. It is simple, discreet, and has as much chance of being effective as anything else. What is more this is a plan that is already being enacted. Thank goodness for the presence of mind of that general in Tyrus who sent this Marius Sextus to follow Origen's courier. If he fails we still have the option to fall back on to either Alexander's or Decimus' plan. So I think we should do nothing and await Marius' next report".

Nero stood up. "Nothing? Do nothing? I do not like your council, Lucius. Decimus?"
Decimus had a calculating look in his eye, but he did not hesitate for long.
"I agree with Lucius, sir"
"Alexander?"
"I also, sir"
"I don't like this. I want more regular reports, Decimus, and I want them quicker."

When Lucius returned to the balcony, the sweet music wafting above the men clearing corpses from the arena went unheard as the instinctive feeling of dread once more overtook his thoughts.

7

The men and I spent the evening looking out over the rolling dunes of the great desert and telling stories. Shortly before sunset we were distracted by a group of traders. We saw the cloud of dust that they threw up on the desert road long before we saw them. As they came over the brow of last of the desert hills we counted the camels. There were twenty one, all roped together in a long line, with heavy loads under blankets on their backs. There were eight men of all ages accompanying the beasts and they were a cheerful bunch. When they arrived they acknowledged us with curt nods before unloading their camels and tethering them in the compound for the night. Before long they were all slumped on their packs in the courtyard of the caravanserai. One of them had a strange wooden stringed instrument shaped like the head of a cobra, another a pipe made from a large stick. It was pleasant there, listening to the haunting tunes that they sang before they settled down for the night.

Marius returned to the caravanserai soon after the traders had settled. He told us that everything had gone smoothly, but was virtually silent as we ate a late evening meal. As soon as he finished eating he withdrew quietly. After some moments I followed and found him looking out over the desert outside the caravanserai. I was still in awe of Marius. I was in awe of his calm handling of events, his way of dealing with people, his reputation. I sat down under the brilliant stars in that vast silence on the edge of the emptiness and said nothing. Presently he began to speak. He was reflective and spoke softly.
"For the first time in my life, Tolus, I do not know what is right any more. When I was young all I ever wanted was to be a legionary. When I first joined up I was sure that I was the happiest man alive. I threw myself into every part of life in the army. If there were orders to be followed I followed them enthusiastically. I thought that I was married to the legion and that it would give me all the fulfilment I

needed. Of course I went out with the boys to find women. But it was never more than physical relief."

I was perplexed by his words, but I stayed silent as he continued.
"The last few weeks have made me start to think. We blindly do what we are told. We never question the wisdom or integrity of those who order us. I'm starting to feel as though we are getting involved in something that too big for us to properly understand. And I am beginning to wonder whether we are on the right side. Tonight in that Aegyptusis house it was I who felt like the vindictive madman. I have learned much of these people, Tolus. I have learned that they are not mad. They are not simply after our money. Their writings teach peace and love and charity. They are good people, I can see it. And yet here we are, unquestioning as we do the bidding of some of the most powerful people in the empire. But what of them? Are they good people, Tolus? I do not know. I believe in Rome, and I believe in the rule of law. I will not see anyone harm that. I will do what I have been sent to do but I'm beginning to find that I do not like myself for doing it".

It sounded as though Marius was beginning to crack up. A soldier is often ordered to do things that may be distasteful to him. It is part of the job.
"Marius, I don't understand. You're not soft or fickle. You've served Rome all your life. What has suddenly changed?"

He thought for a few moments about his reply. "It's impossible to explain. Our leaders in Rome must be badly shaken by these people and by this document they have. But I cannot understand why. We were all educated. We were taught that these Christians are con men. We know that their great prophet was a hoaxer. We know that their beliefs were fabricated by this man Jesu to extract money from the foolish. And we know that they seek to bring about the end of the empire so that they can prey on people more easily". Marius paused. He looked out towards the dunes and the fire flickered as it was reflected in his eyes. As he continued it was as though he was thinking aloud.

"And yet . . . . and yet these people have a quality. The writings that I read on the road from the great salt sea to Hebron have a quality. They challenge what we know to be true, and they have a beauty about them that is difficult to explain."

I was staggered. "Come on, Marius. Next you will be telling me that you are thinking of converting".

My tone annoyed Marius. Something in him snapped and he was suddenly furious. "Don't be ridiculous, Tolus. If you want to be sarcastic, go and do it in the guardroom with the recruits." There was something in his answer that suggested that his anger was directed more at himself than at me. I was offended by his attitude.

"Marius. You are obviously troubled. You can choose to tell me what it is and you can choose not to. Either way, don't take it out on me."

Marius was silent for a while. "You're right, I'm sorry. Part of it is that I don't like this mission. I feel that we are interfering with forces that we'd be advised to leave well alone. I don't know whether what we are doing is right, but I know we have to do it. But more than that . . . ." Marius' voice petered out. I sat silently. There was something he was not telling me.

I wanted to push the point but something about his distracted look stopped me. He would tell me if he could, I reasoned. Instead I broke his reverie with a simple question. "So what are you suggesting we do, Marius?"

"I am suggesting that we have no choice, Tolus. We will complete the mission, and we will complete it well. We will return to Rome, accept the congratulations, and move on to our next posting with a nice promotion. All I am saying is that doing it will cause me to hate myself."

We eventually returned to the caravanserai in the early hours. Everyone was asleep and the fires burned low.

*****

Marius departed soon after dawn. He found his step quickening as he approached the centre of the village. He was striding briskly, paying no attention to the morning rituals that were going on around him. His mind was elsewhere, buried deep in the soft image of Rani. He thought of nothing but the ideal of comfort and security with the exhilarating girl from this scorching land.
He reached the house of Smenkhkare without really noticing, and as he approached he was mentally unprepared.

Marius felt a curious relief when he saw that Rani was there. She smiled at him from the doorway and greeted him with a playful kiss on the cheek. Marius began to waver again. He went inside.
When he was sat down, Smenkhkare began to speak.
"We have decided what to do. I have to confess that I was not ready to trust you and Origen, but Rani has convinced me that you are a good man. She is more circumspect than I, so I trust her. However, she also argued that it would be unfair to allow you to continue with your mission without knowing the danger into which it puts you. In not knowing you have less chance of succeeding, so by telling you we will not only be protecting you but more importantly we will be protecting the document".

Smenkhkare paused. His rheumy eyes narrowed as they looked straight into Marius'. He seemed to be making his mind up about something. Before long he sighed, and when he began to speak his voice was low. He started by explaining the problem that Nero had been confronted with. He spoke of a man known as 'the rock', and of how the actions of this man had precipitated a crisis.

"What you will take to Origen is a document that was dictated by the emperor Nero in 59AD. It is known as the Neronian Confession and it bears his seal and his signature. It is utterly and unambiguously authentic. In it, he sets out how Rome decided to deal with the "threat" of the Christians. He outlines an invented history, which the document explicitly declares to be invented. This history is the one that is familiar to all of us. It is the pack of lies that deliberately sets out to discredit Jesu and us, his followers. Nero portrays Jesu as a con man, a scholar of the Jewish Torah who deliberately set out to "fulfil" the prophesies of the ancient prophets. He is portrayed as a conjurer who played clever tricks on gullible peasants, a confidence trickster who planted stooges as "cripples". He is characterised as a liar who married Mary Magdalene and sired five children by her. Nero even produced these "children" as proof at one point. The claims that he rose from the dead are ridiculed. After all there is precisely no evidence for this phenomena. The motivation that they invented for Jesu is the most believable possible. Doctrines such as "it is easier for a camel to pass through the eye of a needle than for a rich man to enter the kingdom of heaven" and his insistence that his followers "tithe" their income are cited as proof that the man's true motivation was money. So his followers are characterised as credulous fools who had fallen for the trick. The "disciples" who had known him in life and had gone out from Judea to all parts of the empire to "spread the word" are said to be in on the trick. They are portrayed as opportunists who sought to profit from the ignorant, so keen to give up earthly possessions. So were the leaders of the new religion. The whole thing is made out to be an example of the clever preying on the stupid, and relieving them of their money. A very clever, successful and elaborate con trick. And Nero made this version sound very convincing."

Smenkhare paused to take a sip of water from the clay pot that sat on the table in front of him. Marius had a sick feeling in the pit of his stomach as he listened to Smenkhare's words. What he was being told was impossible, yet it rang true to him. He had been brought up with this knowledge. He had never questioned the truth of it. Yet somehow he felt that he what he was being told now was the truth. He was being told of a great conspiracy perpetrated by the very institutions that he was here to serve and he found himself beginning to believe it. Before his thoughts could run away with him, Smenkhare's voice continued:

"Yet the manuscript is more than this. A good part of its power lies in the strategy of disinformation that it outlines. It clearly shows the disdain that Rome has for all her clients. It directs regional governors to use the disinformation with all local client kings and chieftains. It directs them to use it to ensure that none of them convert. It also outlines the reasons for this strategy – the protection of Rome as the sole sovereign authority in the empire. The emperor is divine. Any rival claimant to divinity could bring the whole edifice crashing down. It would inevitably cause the clients to question the basis of their loyalty to Rome".

"In other words the motivation for this disinformation campaign is rendered transparently obvious by the manuscript. Generations across the empire have been misled for one reason and one reason alone. To preserve the power of the empire."

Marius had gone white. His right leg began to shake. He felt that at any moment he might start to shake all over. Suddenly everything became clear to him. The interest of such senior men and the importance that they attached to his mission. His misgivings about the righteousness of what he was doing. He also saw that his imminent betrayal of Rani and her family would lead to her death. He fought to maintain his composure.

Marius shook his head involuntarily, trying to rid it of these chaotic thoughts. When he had dispelled them sufficiently to be able to listen once more to what was being said Smenkhkare was not talking. He was looking at Marius with concern. Rani leaned over and touched his arm. "I know that this must be a shock, David. Origen should have told you the danger into which he was putting you before he sent you. It was unfair of him to let you go without such knowledge. It was also careless, for now you will be more cautious. You must realise the value of this document to the Romans. And believe me, they know of its existence. It has been used before. Of some comfort is that we have no reason to suggest that they know that it may soon be used again. It has been in our possession for nearly sixty years and they have never

come anywhere near us. They know nothing of us or of its whereabouts. You will be safe, I am sure".
Marius just wanted to get out of there. "I wish you had never told me this. I must leave as soon as possible. Can you give me the confession so that I can be on my way?"

"We do not have the confession, David" replied Smenkhkare. Marius looked up at him with incomprehension. Smenkhkare gave a wry smile. "But we can tell you how to find it".

8

Ruth was sweeping the floor with a bunch olive twigs. She was going at her task with the controlled vigour of the elderly. She was furious. Tertullian had just received word that a large delegation from the churches of Mysia, Asia, Lydia, Phrygia, Pisidia, Pamphylia, and Lycia had arrived on a ship from Ephesus. He was already exhausted. Ever since Origen had disappeared "on church business that cannot wait" Tertullian had been having to bear the strain of leadership. He was too old and frail. His wasting disease had returned with a vengeance. He was fading before her eyes and the work he was being forced to do was accelerating his decline. She wanted to strangle Origen for abandoning his place. But most of all she wanted to take Tertullian far away to somewhere where his sense of duty to the cause could be forgotten. Yet she knew that he would never stop working for the cause, or at least not until he was dead. She was also wise enough to recognise that someone had to lead in Origen's absence and that Tertullian was the best man available. Whatever it was that had called Origen away it had better be serious.

By mid morning it was getting hot. Tertullian sat outside. Their house sat at the end of a dusty track some way from the centre of Sidon and the sea, over two miles from the Roman road. Behind the single storey mud bricked house was a large fenced dust bowl. There were troughs for the goats and several olive trees. Other than that there was nothing but dust. One of the olive trees had branches that extended far enough to provide a significant area of shade. A colourful kilim was spread out under the tree and was faded in patches where the sun broke through its branches. On the kilim cushions were strewn around a long low table. Tertullian's eyes were closed and he appeared to be asleep. He did not watch the occasional gaggle of women who strode along the path that ran along the fence. They carried pots on their heads as they trod the path to the spring that lay beyond Tertullian's home. Ruth was inside. She no longer collected her own water. One of her only concessions to her age was allowing her niece to do it for her.

The visitors arrived and Ruth showed them to Tertullian. He rose to greet them. Perridac looked at Tertullian's wasted body and shrivelled features and could not hide his shock. The last time Perridac had seen the old scholar he had been a lively bundle of energy. Despite his shock he embraced Tertillian warmly. They all sat under the olive tree and watched in silence as Ruth brought figs and olives, and water for them to drink. All of the group were dressed in long robes and had long beards. Most were in their forties and fifties and their hair was grey. Perridac was their leader. In response to a question of how things fared in the lands of the Mare Nostrum around Ephesus, Perridac spoke of an incident in which two thousand Christians living in Lycia had been massacred by the Romans and the local community. The reason was given as their refusal to pay taxes to the governor, although everyone knew that they did. There had been three Christians who had been caught evading taxes. The Romans had used their example to denounce all Christians as thieves. The slaughter had not been officially sanctioned but Roman soldiers had started it and had encouraged the participation of the local community.

"The streets ran red with blood that day, Tertullian. I wish that I could say that our people, secure in the knowledge they were going to meet their Father, behaved with dignity and honour. But they did not. They panicked and they tried anything to save themselves. Many even tried to renounce their faith, but by then the frenzy was upon the mob and they were cut down as they pleaded. It was ugly and it has done our credibility no good. Of course the Romans loved it and couldn't wait to tell everyone what we were really like when our piety was stripped away and they got to look at the decay beneath. It was a bad day."

He paused, and seemed to be making a conscious effort to brighten up. "But we did not come to mourn the failings of the past. We came to talk of the future, and particularly your idea for the book of God's word. Let us pray for guidance in our discussions."

*****

When they had prayed for the souls of all those martyred for the cause, Perridac got straight to the point. "Tertullian, we are concerned that you and Origen are going to disregard the decision of the congregation of Rhosus. The Gospel of Peter must be included in your "New Testament"".

For most of the latter part of his life Tertullian had been working on a project that he saw as his calling. He had been trying to consolidate the writings about the Christus into a single, universally accepted work. It was Tertullian who had first called Jesu by this new name. No one had argued when he had started to refer to him as the "Christus", meaning 'the One sent from God'. Much more contentious had been what was to be included in the story of the man's life. He called this story the New Testament, meaning "new promise", a name he regarded as appropriate. His vision was for it to be combined with the books of the Jewish Torah, which Tertullian described as the "Old Testament" to create a complete "Word of God". The debate over which writings should be included had raged ever since Tertullian had first muted the idea in the years before he stepped down in favour of Origen. The younger man had been supportive from the start.

At the mention of the writings of Peter, Tertullian had to work to hide his exasperation.
"Perridac, you know the history. The congregation at Rhosus did indeed adopt the Gospel of Peter. But you also know that the main reason for this was that Serapion had not properly read it. As soon as he did he said, and I quote, "we accept Peter and the other apostles as Christ, but as men of experience we test writings falsely ascribed to them, knowing that such things were not handed down to us". Rhosus was an aberration. Both Justin and then Tatian were clear that there were the four true accounts: those of Matthew, John, Mark and Luke. The gospel of the Egyptians, of the Hebrews and of Thomas were disregarded by Tatian and by Rhosus. The only reason that we are having this conversation about Peter is the error made by Serapion. Do not cause disagreement on this point Perridac. The four are God's true word".

Perridac was persistent. He and his companions had travelled all the way from Ephesus, and part of the reason was to ensure that the gospel of Peter was included.

"I am concerned about what is being done, Tertullian. I am concerned that you people sit in Ituraea and massage the words of God to suit yourselves. I am concerned that you sacrifice the truth in order that you might create consistency. I understand that Peter's writings have inconsistencies with those of the four. Yet to refuse to include them for this reason makes us no better than the Romans. The only thing that we have going for us is the truth. If we sacrifice that, we have nothing. You cannot ignore parts of the truth because they are inconvenient. You will destroy our credibility, Tertullian, and I cannot sit back and watch you do it".

Tertullian was furious. "Listen to me, Perridac. Matthew, Mark, Luke and John are unique. Either they were apostles themselves, or were closely associated with the apostles. Origen puts it well when he talks of "the four Gospels, which alone are undisputed in the Church of God beneath the whole of heaven". You do not dispute the four. No one does. You do not advocate the inclusion of Thomas or the others. Yet you argue for the inclusion of Peter despite his denial of the manhood of Christ. By excluding Peter's writings, we are not massaging God's word. We are simply restricting it to those sources that have real credibility. We are not forbidding the works of Peter to be read or used for devotional purposes. We are simply continuing the policy of the great scholars. Yes, Peter was included by the congregation of Rhosus. But as I have said, that was a mistake that Serapion himself acknowledged."

A younger man whispered to Perridac. He then turned back to Tertullian. "We must discuss this, Tertullian. I agree with Origen. I agree with the importance for unanimity. I agree that the Word of God of which you speak must be definitive and uncontested. You are tired. We will leave you and return tomorrow. Thank you for your hospitality, and thank you for the work that you do for us".

They prayed together, and then said their farewells. While the delegation walked across the dusty bowl to the house Tertullian lay back on his cushions and closed his eyes. Ruth showed the visitors out and looked out at Tertullian. She was worried. She left him there for some time before going out and quietly removing the empty glasses of water and the plates of olives and figs. Flies buzzed around and Tertullian opened his eyes a fraction.
"Are you alright, my love?" she asked.
Tertullian had to make a conscious effort to sit up and open his eyes.
"I feel tired. I'm going to rest out here for a while" he replied.
"You must stop working, Tertullian. You are too old and too ill".
The sunlight was dappled on her grey gown.
"What is Origen doing? It is so unlike him to just disappear. He knows how ill you are. What work could be so important that he can just abandon the co-ordination of the message and organisation of God's church? What can be so important that you just give me vague answers when I ask? I've had enough of watching you kill yourself with work whilst you refuse to tell me why Origen has gone away. You won't tell me how long he'll be gone or when he'll be back. I need to know, Tertullian. I deserve to know".
Ruth began to weep. She did not want to. She did not want to do anything that might increase the wear on her husband but she could not help herself.

Tertullian beckoned her and she came and sat beside him, resting her head on his shoulder. He stroked her white hair and started to speak.
"I will tell you. I will tell you what it is that cannot wait. You will know why we have told no one when you hear".
Tertullian told Ruth of the Neronian confession. She had heard rumours of such a document, but had never been sure that such a thing existed. After he had told of the circumstances that led to its formulation, Tertullian continued.

"Over the next few years, this "official history" was spread throughout the empire. It would probably never have worked as well with the client kings had it not been for the fact that we did desperately need money. The early brothers were travelling extensively to spread their word. They needed money to pay for their subsistence, their manuscripts and their travel. They accepted donations from anyone willing to give to them, and there probably was some degree of abuse of these funds by the unscrupulous. All the Romans needed to ask the client kings was whether the Christians solicited donations or took them when they were offered. The answer was always "yes", and in the minds of the clients this confirmed the empire's version of events. Thus the clients were controlled and their loyalty assured. A close watch was kept on them, and anyone being seen to waver was discreetly removed and replaced by someone more pliable".

"This strategy could have been successful for all time had it not been for one crucial necessity. Nero remained convinced of the power that our new religion could have over the uneducated, the non-citizens. He also realised that to prevent the threat from re-emerging his strategy of misinformation needed to be maintained forever, or at least until we had given up and disappeared. Otherwise a similar crisis could arise at any time. Therefore he ordered a history to be written of the events surrounding Agrippa - the climate that precipitated the crisis, and the steps that he had taken to avert it. The document was full and frank, explaining in detail the thinking behind the strategy and the rationale for the false "history" that had been its product. This document bore his signature and the seal of the emperor. It was to join the few documents that are passed from one emperor to his successor, documents known as the Imperial Bequest. No one alive other than emperor Hadrian knows what the imperial bequest consists of. But not even Hadrian has seen the original Neronian Confession."

Ruth was fascinated. She had been surprised that her husband had felt unable to confide in her, but now she understood that he had been trying to protect her. But what was puzzling her was how the confession came to be within the reach of Origen. Tertullian nodded as she asked.

"One of the scribes who worked for the Imperial Secretariat was secretly a Christian. Because he worked in the palace he knew of the arrest, torture and execution of Peter and was incensed. Since he was one of the men trusted to put Nero's words to papyrus, he also knew of Nero's conspiracy of lies. Like all who worked at Nero's court the scribe was judged completely trustworthy. As with all of his officials and private staff, Nero had also taken out the insurance of making it clear to the scribe that his family were under the threat of execution should Nero become displeased with him. This had proved to be an effective sanction in the past, but Nero had not banked on the bravery that God inspires. The scribe stole the confession. The ink of Nero's signature on the completed document was barely dry when he just walked out of the palace with the document hidden under his tunic. He had been entrusted to return it to the bequest room. The guards simply assumed he was leaving for the day, an assumption that they paid for with their lives and those of their families. It appears that the man left the palace knowing that by doing so he was a dead man and that the lives of his family too would be horribly ended. Nevertheless he passed the document on to an individual who was never traced. He died in agony shortly afterwards. Nero rewrote the confession and included in it the tale of what had happened to the first confession as a warning. We believe that the second confession is still part of the imperial bequest. Nothing was heard of the first confession for a generation. It was assumed that it had either been lost or its "owners" had not worked out what to do with it. Then, just over thirty years ago Emperor Domitian received an anonymous letter claiming that proof existed which could prove that emperor Nero had invented the "facts" about Jesu the Christus to preserve his empire. Domitian was originally an enthusiastic persecutor of Christians. His viciousness rivalled that of Nero himself and his appetite for their capture was insatiable. The letter he received simply threatened him with the disclosure of a document. But Domitian knew the document and he knew the consequences of it being used against him. Fires could have been set raging across the empire. Domitian was shaken and his brutality towards our brothers changed to apparent disinterest. Until now, nothing more had been heard of the document".

As he spoke, Tertullian's voice was getting thinner. Ruth was having to lean forward to hear. Usually she would have stopped him and insisted that he rest. But she wanted to know when Tertullian would be spared all of this work and be allowed to rest. She silently reproached herself for doing it, but she asked him when Origen might return.

El Arish, Sinai

Origen was in a bad mood as he walked up to Mishac's house from the port. He had been continually sick on the sailing from Sidon, and he had become increasingly convinced that he was wasting his time. No doubt the message David sent from Hebron had simply got lost. But a nagging doubt remained. He should have received word from here by now too. He quickened his step as he approached Mishac's house.

Mishac was at home, sitting in the large cool living room of his stone house. He was a prosperous merchant and not afraid to show it. Origen knocked on the door. A servant answered, and as soon as Origen disclosed his name he scampered off to announce the arrival to his master. Before long Mishac himself came to the door.
"Origen!" he exclaimed. "to what do I owe this honour?".
"You owe it to my disquiet, and quite possibly no more than my paranoia. I have come in search of David the Smith".
"You have missed him, I'm afraid. Come inside and have a drink. You must be thirsty".
Origen entered and sat in the cool dark room. He was glad to be out of the sun. "So he has been here then?"
"Yes, he passed through about ten days ago. I had been expecting him before and knew that his mission was an urgent one. He left almost straight after I told him how he could find Smenkhkare."
"Was he alright? Did he ask you to send word to me?" asked Origen.
"He looked fine if a little weary. He did not make mention of sending a message to you and I am sure that he did not send any message whilst he was here. Once I had told him of Smenkhkare he seemed keen to be on his way and I was not going to hold him up. To be honest I wanted him gone as soon as possible myself. He is a dangerous man to know right now".

Origen was troubled. David was reliable, and would have been sure to send word. Origen thought for a while. It would have been normal for David to ask Mishac to send word, or at least to ask him how it could be done in El Arish. There were no big towns for miles around, so he would have had to do it here.

"You had not met David before, had you Mishac?".

"No, never."

"Tell me of him"

"Why?"

"Just describe him to me" he snapped. Origen was fighting to keep calm.

"Six foot tall, medium build, dark skin, burning blue eyes"

Origen felt the bottom fall out of his stomach.

"Stop". He said it louder than he had meant too, almost shouting it.

"Blue eyes, you say. Are you sure?"

Mishac regarded Origen strangely, as if he feared that Origen might be demented.

"Absolutely. I was quite struck by them. Unusual in an Ituraean."

Origen gritted his teeth. "David the smith has brown eyes" he stated deliberately.

"I'm afraid that he very definitely has blue eyes".

Origen's eyes narrowed. "Oh my God" he muttered.

9

Smenkhkare leaned back on his wooden chair. His eyes looked to the ceiling and he began to chant in a monotone. The chant had a hypnotic effect and despite his fascination with the words Marius found it difficult to concentrate on them. He had to make a conscious effort not to just stare with horror at Rani as he thought of what he had to do. Smenkhkare's chant described the exact location of the document in the great library of Alexandria.

Rani made Marius repeat the details twice to ensure that he had them. He then stood hastily and kissed Smenkhkare on both cheeks. Smenkhkare grasped both his hands. In one he was holding a small piece of folded papyrus. As they separated Smenkhkare left the papyrus in Marius' hand.
"Go in peace" was all that he said.
Rani accompanied Marius through the kitchen to the door. On the doorstep he turned. She looked at him with bright eyes. She had a shy smile on her lips but Marius could not meet her gaze.
"I must leave now" he said.
Rani could see that he was stricken. "You must. Will you return?"
"You do not know how dearly I would like to"
"Does that mean you will not?"
"It would be impossible"
Rani looked hurt. As she spoke, frustration rose in her voice. "You confuse me, David. You are lonely. You say you do not know love. You look at me with so much longing it's pitiful. And then you say that you will not return. I am a widow, David. I must make a match. You are a fine man and you can see how much you need me. You look at me and I can see how I touch you. Yet now you pull away. . . . ." Marius looked into her eyes. Again he felt his own fill with tears. He looked away.
"Look at me David".

She grabbed his chin in her hands and pulled it up. She looked straight into his shining eyes and there were tears falling down his cheeks. He moved forward to kiss her, but suddenly pulled away.
"My God, what a pain you bear" said Rani gently.
At that moment he came within an instant of telling her what he was. Abruptly he turned around and fled once more. If he had turned round he would have seen Rani flee into the house with tears of her own.

*****

Marius was away for most of the day. The men and I were getting increasingly bored, just sitting around in the caravanserai. I said nothing to them of Marius' state of mind. We began to worry shortly after noon and when he turned up a short time before sunset we were all relieved. Marius was quiet again as we ate in the evening. He did tell us that he had successfully obtained the location of the document. At dawn we would depart Alexandria, its resting place. This success seemed to give him no pleasure and the men were perplexed. Yet they soon forgot, and their high spirits were infectious. They were excited at the way things were progressing. But I was worried about Marius.

After dinner Marius withdrew. Again I followed him back to the edge of the desert. When we were sure that we were out of earshot, Marius immediately told me everything he had learned from Smenkhkare. He started at the beginning.

"By the latter days of his reign the great Emperor Nero had a problem. In the twenty five years since the death of the prophet Jesu, his followers had dispersed themselves to all the corners of the empire in their zeal to spread their "good news". They found a willing audience among the peasants and paupers, mainly those who did not hold citizenship. The message they brought promised "divine citizenship", citizenship of an empire far greater than Rome's. More disturbingly some of the regional leaders and chieftains were becoming influenced by the conversion of their people. There were rumblings that leaders throughout the empire were being seduced by these zealots. We all know that the emperor commands absolute and unequivocal loyalty from everyone because he is divine. The Christians began to deny the divinity of the emperor by claiming that there is only one God, their own. Had this message been allowed to gain currency, the basis of Roman authority could be destroyed. Allegiance to the emperor would not just be unnecessary and superfluous to them. It would not be legal".

"Nero did not know how to react. The zealots who were spreading the message would not raise arms against him. They would not directly challenge Rome in any way. They simply sought to persuade people that they were governed by a power higher than Rome. This new message was spreading like a virulent plague, and Nero needed a cure. He would dearly loved to have crushed them but they were too widespread, too numerous and too indirect in their challenges to Rome's authority. Nero's sadistic treatment of captured Christians is well documented but was simply the way that he chose to vent his frustration with them".

"The fourteenth year of Nero's reign proved to be the year of reckoning and something of a turning point in Rome's policy toward the Christians. Peter, who they called "the rock" was passing through Dalmatia on his way to Rome. King Agrippa of Dalmatia, ruler of the Illyrians, had received him in his court and had become influenced by him. In the early summer and completely without warning Agrippa sent a messenger to Nero. The messenger not only confirmed all of Nero's most outlandish paranoia about the Christians but also acted as a harbinger of what might become the fate of Rome itself. The ambassador politely thanked Rome for its protection in the past and announced that henceforth Dalmatia would no longer be requiring it. He requested Nero to remove all Roman forces from his kingdom. He added that Agrippa understood that this may take time and gave Nero until the end of the year to complete the withdrawal. Agrippa even offered to compensate him for some of the Roman money that had been invested in Dalmatia's infrastructure".

I was aghast. It was not possible that a client ruler could say such a thing to the emperor of Rome. Marius noted my look of disbelief, and he gave a rueful smile. He also anticipated my response.

"This is not the worst of it, Tolus. It wasn't as simple for Nero as just crushing an arrogant upstart. The strength and ethnic cohesiveness of Agrippa's kingdom, it's proximity to Italia and Rome across the Mare Adriaticum and the huge numbers of Illyrians serving in legions raised in Dalmatia made it a serious threat. But what shook Nero more was that, rightly, he saw this as the first in what could become a flood of client leaders opting out of Rome's control. Whilst he knew that he could forcibly suppress Agrippa, he also knew that he could not suppress client leaders all across the empire. His intelligence suggested that Agrippa was not the only leader to be under the influence of the zealots from Judea. He feared that by crushing Agrippa he would provoke a reaction from many of the other wavering kings and chieftains. Then, as now, Rome's power was based on the rapid deployment of overwhelming force in concentrated areas, and her great vulnerability was her inability to fight significant campaigns on more than two or three fronts at any one time. Nero's fear, reasonable in the context of the time, was that in suppressing Agrippa he could ignite rebellions in a multitude of client territories simultaneously. It could have torn Rome apart."

Marius eyed me carefully to make sure that I was following him. What he was saying could not be possible. That Rome could be "torn apart" was unimaginable. Surely it was.

"Nero gathered his closest advisors together to devise a response. What they decided upon was typical of Nero. It was ingenious and insane. They examined their enemy and realised that it was their choice of tactics that had made them such an awkward threat. Rather than choosing to fight with armies they fought with words. Rather than fight on contested land they fought in people's hearts. Nero decided that they must fight the Christians using their own tactics. They would use words to reclaim people's minds. And they would start with Agrippa."

"Scholars and spies were brought in to concoct a story that would convincingly discredit the Christians. They decided that the best way to do this would be to base the story on the very beliefs of the Christians. They took many of the stories vital to the new religion and twisted them. The result was the "facts" that have been taught to everyone educated under Roman rule since Nero".

I was horrified. I wanted to close my ears. I wanted to not know what I had just been told. But Marius was relentless.

"So the official history of Jesu the Christus came about. Nero sent his most trusted advisor and one of the inventors of this 'history' to Agrippa. By the time he arrived Peter had departed for Rome where, incidentally, he was picked up on arrival and secretly executed. Agrippa might not have believed Nero's envoy had it not been for a crucial stroke of luck. Agrippa had given Peter a significant amount of gold to support him in establishing a church in Rome itself. The envoy spent many days convincing Agrippa, and it was this donation to Peter that was used to convince Agrippa of Nero's version of events. It was reinforced by the subsequent return of the gold found on Peter along with fictional accounts of Peter's debauchery in Rome. Agrippa's loyalty to Rome was thus secured"

Marius paused, still shaken himself by what he had been told. I think at the time I was barely capable of understanding the magnitude of his words.

Marius continued, telling me how Rome had endangered the souls of countless masses over the generations in order to protect her own power. He was bitter as he recalled the ignorance with which he had casually arrested and mistreated the Christians. Up until the last few days we had all thought of them as nothing more than dangerous lunatics who posed a threat to decency and law.

*****

If what Smenkhkare had said was true, our mission would lead to the deaths of many innocent people. I had killed many people in the name of Rome, but all of them had been soldiers. Soldiers expect to die on the battlefield. But the empire had been persecuting these people for centuries for her own reasons, and they had never been soldiers.

But I was weak. At that time, as far as I was concerned we were Roman legionaries. Soldiers do not question orders. They obey them.

Marius on the other hand was furious. He saw himself as a man of honour. He had served Rome faithfully for so long because he believed in the empire and what it stood for. All of a sudden he felt as though he had been betrayed. He had begun to question all he had ever done in the name of Rome. He began to see his whole life as corrupt. "What is truth, Tolus? What are we to believe? We are told all these things by Rome and we believe them. Our lives are led according to what we believe to be right. And what we believe is dictated by what we are told by Rome. But Rome lies to us. Rome manipulates and exploits us." There was a note of despair in his voice.

There was silence. After a few minutes I spoke. "What are we going to do?" I asked him.

Marius sat for a long time under the stars. It got cooler and I pulled my cloak about my shoulders. A wind had got up, and blew sand and dust about the vast emptiness ahead of us. Eventually Marius spoke. As he did so he was reasoning with himself more than he was talking to me.
"We have our orders. All my life up to now I have never questioned my orders. But orders are no longer valid if they instruct us to commit or help others to commit crimes. If this confession contains what Smenkhkare says it does, by returning it to Decimus we will be helping him to commit murder. Therefore surely our orders are no longer binding. But unless we see the manuscript we will not know. Therefore we are going to retrieve the document, and we are going to read it".

As he said the last sentence his voice grew louder. It was as if this idea had dawned on him as he was speaking and God help us but I think that that is exactly what happened.

I didn't like it. Marius' words were a capital offence. We would be executed for if we were to do what he suggested.
"What if it is as Smenkhkare says? What shall we do then?" I asked.
"I do not know". Marius replied. He turned to me, and looked me full in the face. I felt his eyes burrowing into my soul. "Are you with me, Tolus?"
I was very clear about what I wanted to do. I wanted to retrieve the document, deliver it to Rome and forget the whole business. I wanted to ignore the questions that Marius was raising. They were too big for me, too complicated, out of my control. I was a soldier. I did what I was told and asked no questions. But despite his strange behaviour, Marius was my commander and he needed me.

"Yes Marius. I am with you." I replied.

10

It took us two nights and one day to reach Alexandria on the felucca, and we should have enjoyed the voyage through the beauty and calm of the Nile. The sun shone, it was close and hot throughout and we had nothing to do but lounge on the deck of the boat watching the business of the river and the slow pace of village life on its banks. Yet the atmosphere on the boat was tense. Throughout the journey Marius had been withdrawn, his jaw set and his eyes closed for most of the time. He was unsettling the men, and although I did my best to keep their spirits up, in truth I too was out of sorts. During the early part of the voyage Marius had told us the exact location of the document by recounting Smenkhkare's words verbatim. We debated how we would retrieve the manuscript. According to Smenkhkare's legend, it was in a chamber deep inside the library at Alexandria. The ancient piece of papyrus that Smenkhkare had slipped into Marius' hand as he left had on it a floor plan, and it made the library look labyrinthine. Marius ordered us to memorise it.

Greto, Silus and Artorius argued that we should seek permission to enter the library. Marius refused to even discuss it. To do as Greto suggested would be in contravention of the direct order to remain under cover at all times. What is more, he argued, we could not afford to waste any time. At any moment Origen could learn of the death of David the smith and discover that an impostor had stepped into his shoes.

I knew there were other reasons for Marius' refusal. He was not sure what he was going to do with the manuscript once he had read it. Greto's plan made it inevitable that it would go to Rome. He and the rest had compelling reasons why we should go through the authorities. It would guarantee success and it would prevent us having to kill fellow Roman soldiers, a real possibility if we broke into the library. They would not let their plan go easily, but still Marius would not agree. He insisted that we must follow orders and had no time to send a request to Rome. Eventually the men accepted this but they were unhappy at the prospect of breaking into a building guarded by their colleagues - colleagues who may have to be killed if we were to succeed.

We were unlucky with the moon. It would have been better had it been new, but instead it was nearly full. The pale blue light was so bright that it left shadows.

*****

The library was an incredible structure. It was approached by a flagstone road that was so wide that it was almost a forum. At the edge of the boulevard was a long colonnade. Columns taller than a house rose vertically to an arch that connected them to their neighbour. When the library was originally built the wide boulevard that led up to it had been kept clear. Over the years peddlers had moved in to sell their wares on its wide open space. They had not been moved on so they set up stalls. More and more peddlers moved in so that the whole place had become a thriving marketplace.

At the end of the wide approach was the imposing bulk of the library itself, with vast square towers at each end. There were hundreds of tiny windows which seemed to be randomly dotted about the mighty façade of this great monolith at irregular heights. A long tapering staircase led up to the front entrance, and standing high up those stairs there was a panoramic view of Alexandria. The seething marketplace was immediately ahead. Beyond lay the harbour with its diverse array of ships nestling side by side. The great Pharos that dominated the harbour also dominated the view from here, reaching towards the gods. To the left and right an unruly chaos of buildings made up the central area of Alexandria while the fertile lands of the delta stretched out beyond. It truly was a great city, and this library was a great cavernous hulk squatting over it.

*****

We spent three days in Alexandria watching the library. After that time we knew the exact movements of the guards over the cycle of a full day. We knew every exit and entrance and what time they opened and closed. We knew what sort of people went in each entrance and where each one led. Marius and Greto had tried to find out if there were any covered drains that led into the library but found none.

*****

On the third night Marius summoned us all together. He wanted to discuss what we had learned and decide whether we had enough information to formulate a plan.

The following day was spent making final preparations. Silus was sent out to get some chalk. Artorius tested the oil lamps that we would take with us. He was big and he was strong, but he was also most skilled with his hands. The lamps in the library were wall lamps and could not be easily carried without burning one's hands. Alaric procured some black robes for each of us, and some clothes that would enable one of us to pass as a household slave.
Numba was the best liar among us. He had been known to sell water to the boatmen. When Alaric came back Numba put on the slave gear. His dark Carthaginian skin and skinny frame made him look completely convincing.

In the late afternoon he left. He was bearing a message written by Marius which explained that the librarian Yuya had been summoned to the residence of the governor. There he would dine and would not be back before morning. For the first time, Marius used the stamp that I had been given in Rome. No one would argue with that, at least for a while.

When Numba returned we were ready to leave. We waited for a nervous hour, cracking jokes and telling stories of mishaps that had befallen other legions and other missions. We even managed to coax Cassius into telling a story, which he did in his dry, deliberate manner.

The respect of the boys was obvious – when Cassius spoke, he was worth listening to. Marius was the only one who was quiet and composed. This was my first time going into a possible fighting situation with Marius and I can remember being struck by his calm. His blue eyes were clear as the sky and he looked around the room with an air of indestructibility and total control. He inspired immense confidence and calm. It was a great quality and one that I was to see again in situations that were considerably more testing than this.

Half an hour before dusk we set off. We took some dice with us. When we got to the alley outside the librarian's exit we sat down and began to play. Except for Alaric, none of us paid any attention to the game. While Alaric did his usual trick of winning the game, the rest of us had our ears tuned to the door just a few metres away. Distant noises sounded close and made us jump. I was sure that I heard the door lock turn several times but when I turned, expecting to see the door open, there was nothing happening. Nothing but my mind playing tricks on me. After about fifteen minutes of mindless dice, Marius suddenly raised his head like a deer sensing a predator. He took a quick look around and then hissed at us to take position. He remained with Alaric, Silus, Tobias and Artorius playing dice. Greto, Cassius and myself moved swiftly to put our backs against the wall on either side of the door. Almost immediately the door opened inwards and I span into it. We had agreed that I would take the man who opened the door. As I spun in I drew my dagger from under my cloak. I grabbed the man who had opened the door by the throat and thrust him backwards against the wall. He was just a servant and had a similar dishevelled and poor appearance as the man who had been refilling the oil lamps in the library when we had visited a couple of days before. He was terrified and posed no danger. I looked round. Greto had the tall librarian with his face to the wall and his arm behind his back. Cassius was at the doorway giving the all clear signal to the others, sweat glistening off his balding head. They quickly joined us. When they were inside we closed and bolted the door. The light was suddenly very dim, only a wall mounted oil lamp casting a weak light in the cavernous gloom. We were in a narrow corridor with high walls. Marius spoke to the librarian. "If you do as we bid you will not be harmed. If you do not you will be killed. It really is that simple. We have no use for the servant. Show us an empty chamber where we can leave him."

The librarian was terrified. Greto kept his arm twisted behind his back as he led us twenty paces to the south and indicated a room to the left with an inclination of his head. I was following with my hand on the collar of the servant's robe and my other hand reminding him that he had a knife hovering above his kidneys. Without a word Cassius and Numba took the servant from me and led him into the small chamber to tie him up and gag him. The rest of us turned to face the librarian. Once more Marius addressed the librarian. "We have come to retrieve something that belongs to us. We have no desire to harm you or your library. We require you to guide us to the great central chamber. Will you do this in exchange for your life?" The librarian's eyes were wide. A small trail of spittle seeped out of the corner of his mouth. He began to nod frantically and a pathetic high pitched moaning came out of his mouth as he did it. He was so petrified that he couldn't even speak, and I suppose that we shouldn't have been surprised given that all of us were dressed entirely in black and armed to the teeth. "Before we do anything we are going to wait for the dead of night. You are sure that the chamber where we have put the servant will be undisturbed?" The librarian nodded. "We will wait in there then". We all entered the chamber. It was big enough for us all to sit down with our backs against the wall. We settled in for a boring and uncomfortable wait. Marius had forbidden for us to talk at all for fear of giving away some information about ourselves to the librarian. We sat lined up against the wall on either side of the doorway. Opposite sat the librarian and the tied up servant. Silus was first to do guard duty, standing in the doorway with his back to the room to monitor the passageway. We sat for what seemed like years. Time seemed to stand still in that dark gloomy silent room. After an age we heard footsteps. They were so loud that a couple of the men who were dozing instantly woke up and felt for their swords. All of us stiffened. It sounded like the footsteps were in the room with us. Artorius was on guard duty by this point and he turned round. Using his huge hands he indicated one man, twenty metres away and approaching. I couldn't believe it. I would have sworn he was less than five metres away. Artorius then withdrew into the room, amazingly quiet for one so large. Marius signalled Cassius to move the bound servant out of the line of vision of the corridor. He crept across the room, picked the bundle up and returned to press himself and the servant against the wall beside the doorway. Marius silently moved across the room and pulled the librarian to him. He put his finger to his lips and retreated across the room with him. The footsteps seemed deafeningly loud as they approached. Artorius had his dagger in his hand. He was closest to the doorway. I sensed a shadow pass the door and continue on without breaking step. At that point the gagged servant began to whimper. It began quietly and quickly grew in strength. Suddenly it stopped. Cassius was closest to him and he had cut his throat. But he hadn't cut his throat soon enough. The steps faltered, stopped and then began coming back towards us. Artorius slid back from the doorway. I saw the back of a head as it peeked into the chamber. It was looking straight at Artorius. The head suddenly lolled back sickeningly. Artorius had cut his throat without a sound. It was obvious as I watched the life ebb out of his eyes that this man had just been another servant filling the oil lanterns on the walls. I was relieved, for I had no stomach for killing legionaries. The floor of the chamber was now awash with blood. Artorius had been badly sprayed as he had cut the throat of the unfortunate intruder.

"Come on, we're moving out" said Marius.

It was impossible to tell how much time had elapsed since we had arrived in the chamber but I figured that it must have been close to five or six hours. Marius put his sword to the librarians back and followed him out into the corridor.

Marius looked at the librarian who was now shaking all over. "Right. You are going to lead us. Behind you will be my sword. If you do not lead us directly to the central chamber and keep us away from any guards you will be killed. If you make any noise you will be killed. You saw what happened to the servants. Do you understand?". The librarian nodded his head frantically and no sound other than a similar moaning to before came. This time it was lower pitched and sounded more pained. Tobius handed the librarian a lantern to hold and he led off northwards along the passage.

It was a strange procession. Artorius was covered in blood, whispering numbers. The librarian had got a bit more control over his body but was still occasionally shuddering violently in his terror. Greto at the rear making strange arrows on walls, and Tobius barely audible as he noted points of the compass. It was like a rite of the old religion. After about ten minutes of convoluted routeing and many staircases we reached a long passageway at the end of which we could see a dim light. The librarian stopped. He turned to Marius and held up his lantern. His face looked white and drawn in its weak light. He made to speak. "Er . . . . . Sir. . . . . . The . . . . the corridor leads to the central chamber. It often has guards playing games at a table". Marius looked at me. I had Smenkhkare's map with me. I took it out of my pocket and gestured towards the librarian. Marius nodded and addressed the librarian. "Yuya." At the sound of his name the librarian gave a start, and rolled his eyes with terror.
"We have a map, and you are going to lead us to the chamber that we seek".
Marius pointed at the map. "This is the chamber for which we have come".
Yuya looked at the map. "Oh . . . . Oh Gods. The only way to reach this chamber is to cross the great central court. It is in another part of the complex and can only be reached through the north gate or the great court."

Marius looked at me. His face was set. He gestured for me to advance to the end of the passageway and look into the chamber. I quickly crept past him as fast as I could. As I neared the end I slowed and pressed myself into the shadows by the side of the wall. I could hear my heart pumping so loud that I thought it would be echoing throughout passageway and into the great court. As I advanced the light improved a little and the court became visible. It was enormous. Lit by tens of wall mounted lanterns it had two galleries all around, one above the other. There were three levels of torches on the walls. The court was a huge expanse with a beautiful mosaic floor. I could

not see the ceiling as the light from the torches around the walls by the second gallery meant that anything beyond was hidden in the black. But the first thing I noticed when I had seen into the chamber was a table in the centre of the mosaic. Sitting at it, playing dice, were eight legionaries.
My heart sank and I retreated back down the narrow passage.

Marius gestured for everyone to gather around him. We formed a tight huddle. Yuya was still being held at knifepoint. Marius turned to me and told me exactly what he wanted me to do.

Marius and his men hid up a side passage as I led Greto, Cassius and Numba towards the balcony.
I thought that Marius' plan was going to involve us having to fight at some point but I could not see a better way of getting to the document and avoiding a fight. At least this way we should be able to get to the document without having to have a pitched battle with eight fully armed legionaries. The thought of fighting my own made me sick. I later found out that everyone else felt the same. If it had not been for our faith in Marius and, I later discovered, my men's faith in me we might have refused to go on. Certainly it was not their respect for orders that made them continue.

We followed Yuya's directions and quickly could see the gallery edge. I spoke loudly, and the resonance of my voice startled me.
"We'll get a fortune for these things if we can only get out of this bloody maze".
Cassius replied quickly "Why didn't you get us a sodding map, you fool? We'll never get out of this place".

There was a clattering sound in the great chamber. I looked down over the balcony to see the eight guards running towards the passageway in which Marius hid. My men and I ran through the shadows. We had one handheld lantern to see with. It projected shadows that danced about the walls crazily as we ran. We did not go far, for we were afraid of getting lost. We found a large chamber full of wooden racks containing hundreds of papyrus, hid and extinguished our lantern.

Marius and his men waited until the guards had passed them. They ran down the passageway and across the central court. When they had got across the court they dived down a passageway on the other side and slowed to a walk. Yuya led them for three or four minutes through the maze, up and down stairs. By now no one was noting the direction or counting the steps. He stopped outside a chamber and told them that this was the one that they sought. Marius walked in alone with a lantern and the plan of the room. It showed individual flagstones on the floor. To see anything in detail Marius had to draw the light across the part of the flagstones he was looking at. The atmosphere was close and the light gloomy. On one of the flagstones there was supposed to be a tiny mark in the shape of a fish. Marius drew the light over a flagstone. He looked puzzled and drew it back over the same stone. Suddenly his face lightened. He had found the mark. It was so small and shallow that it was barely discernible. Marius said he would have missed it if he hadn't known to look for it. He drew his sword and put the tip in the narrow cleft between the flagstones. He shoved it in as far as he could and heaved backwards trying to lever it up. Nothing happened. He summoned Silus and Alaric. They too drew their swords and shoved them in the cleft. They all heaved, and again nothing happened.

"Artorius, get over here". Artorius left Yuya and joined the others.

Yuya was unguarded but he was so fascinated that he just stood there, watching. He loved his library, that man, and knew that it was about to surrender one of its many secrets. He could not allow himself to miss it.

"Once more, on three" said Marius.

On three they all gave a mighty heave and the flagstone lifted. They removed their swords from the now large cleft and threw them away. At that moment Yuya not only had the opportunity to run but also to grab all the swords of his captors. He did not take it. Instead he watched the men intently. Without their swords they were able to get both hands beneath the flagstone and pull it back. It took the combined strength of four strong men. The stone yielded and scraped along the floor to reveal the foundation of perfectly level mud. It was rock hard and must have been brought up from the banks of the Nile when the library was built all those hundreds of years ago. On the mud sat a wooden framed housing for the flagstone. In the gap sat a modest looking dark brown leather pouch. It had a flap that was folded over and sealed with a greasy substance that had been smeared on and was now hardened like rock. It looked like some sort of fat or wax. Marius leaned forward and removed the pouch.

*****

Upstairs on the first balcony level we sat huddled in the black chamber. The sound of the guards came and went as they searched for us. They were restricting their search to the area around the balcony and they could have come into our chamber at any time. At the time I thought that it was nothing more than luck that they didn't. Presently the sound of their search moved away and was lost completely.

*****

Marius turned round to see Yuya looking at him open mouthed. His eyes were alive and it was obvious that he wanted to see what the pouch contained. Marius instantly realised that Yuya was not being guarded. He swore afterwards that at that moment Yuya had completely forgotten he was a hostage. He was just an excited academic who had witnessed an important discovery. Marius stood, retrieved his sword and walked over to guard Yuya whilst the others replaced the flagstone. It was a huge effort for the three of them but they did it. They never would have managed without Artorius' immense strength. When it was back in position they retrieved their swords, joined Marius and moved off towards the great court. They hurried up and down the stairs with Yuya, who was closely followed by the point of Marius' sword. Yuya appeared to have shed most of his earlier terror. Our discovery had relaxed him. Marius reached the great court and ran across it. As he reached the end of it he let out a great shriek.

The signal echoed through the dark and sounded mystical, almost other worldly when it reached us. We stood and began to hurry out of the room. It was black as pitch in there and I walked straight into a papyrus rack and knocked it over. There was a massive crash as it fell over and I could hear scrolls of papyrus rolling across the floor. We found our way out and returned to the base level. Marius and the men were waiting for us. As soon as we arrived, Marius turned to Yuya "Get us to the nearest unmanned exit right now and you will live".

Yuya set off to the east. The guards who were looking for us had, we believed, headed off to the south. We were all tense. We dreaded having to fight them. The corridors were endless, up stairs and down stairs, constant right angled turns. We barely noticed chambers on either side as we hurried on. Finally we got to a long straight corridor. "This is the outside wall" said Yuya. "The door is a little further on".
We quickened our step. There was a shout of alarm from behind. Artorius was bringing up the rear and had heard a noise behind him. It was the guards. I don't think that they were following us. We had just been unlucky. Marius grabbed Yuya and passed him backwards towards me.
"Get him to the back" he said.
He ran on and Yuya went to the rear of the column. As soon as Marius reached the door he frantically began to unbolt it. I knew the guards behind were close when I heard the sickening sound that a man screams in violent death.

11

It had been one of those northern days so grey that it had never quite got light. Dark angry clouds raced across the sky above the huge hills of the highlands. It was late afternoon as Gwdloych marched back into his camp, a place known as Dunn Sccyrebb. He had been marching all day with his three hundred men and he was well satisfied with his work. Gwdloych was not a tall man. He had a squat, muscular torso and long, filthy, matted black hair. His beard was long and bushy. Two things were striking about him. The first was his flattened nose. The bone had been broken so many times that it was crooked and jutted out straight ahead in two places that were not aligned. It gave him a rutted, pugilistic air. The second were the trinkets that adorned his body. Both of his ear lobes were pierced, as were his eyebrows and his lower lip. In his eyebrows he wore a variety of metal rings. In his lower lip was a horseshoe shaped piece of bone, carved so that it had two sharp ends protruding down and to one side. It somehow gave him an evil quality. But it was what he wore in his ears that marked Gwdloych out. Hanging by a string from each ear was a tiny dried human head. They were the wrinkled heads of foetuses, and they had been retrieved from pregnant women that Gwdloych had raped before he killed them. In a brutal place among brutal people Gwdloych had always stood out for his viciousness. He wore a huge bearskin over trews made from hides. His feet were bare. Behind him his three hundred men trailed down from the pass into the wide valley. They were all as filthy as he and carried large bundles. Most of the bundles were food. The rest were trinkets that had caught the men's eyes as they passed through villages on the journey home. To the rear of the group were several hundred sheep, being directed by twenty or so young boys who had been taken on the raid to herd the booty back home. Many of the barbarians had bloodstains on their furs. Some was their own blood and some was the blood of others. Roman blood. They were a wild and dangerous crowd, a motley army of killers who were governed by no law save that of Gwdloych's whim. And they loved Gwdloych. They loved him and they feared him. His brutality and success as a leader were greater than any could remember. There was always enough to eat and their women were safe. These frequent raiding parties ensured that.

It began to rain as Gwdloych reached the floor of the valley. He was just outside the village, within earshot of the women and children who had come out of their homes to watch their men return. He let out a monstrous roar.
"Tonight we feast" he shouted.
The women and children cheered. His own two children had run out of the village to greet him. He bent down to scoop them up and smothered them with kisses. With his children in his arms he looked at the several hundred wattle huts of the village. They were set in a quagmire of refuse and excrement, surrounded by grazing animals. He felt a surge of pride. Gwdloych was the chieftain of this village, and soon he planned to be the chief of the great tribe of the Brigantes.

*****

One hundred and twelve miles to the south east of the village, Flavius Ignatus reclined on his couch in the private chambers of his official villa within the city walls of Eburacum. The villa was low set and had a beautiful promenade outside, an arched walkway that was used as a loggia in the summer. Flavius was in the main reception room. It had thick glass in the windows, strong walls and extensive under floor heating to keep out the northern cold. There was no hint of a chill in the room which was just as well, for Flavius was naked. As he turned onto his side his penis flopped over and the rolls of his belly wobbled as he settled himself. The room was enormous and the floor covered by a deep soft carpet. He was being fed grapes by a naked Numidian slave. One at a time, she held them between her teeth and brought her mouth to his. He touched his lips to hers to make sure the grape did not fall to the floor and extended his tongue to scoop the grape out of her mouth.

In the room were seven other men, all senior legion officials. Most were completely naked, or naked under loose fitting togas. There were about twenty female slaves in the room with them. They were young, between the ages of thirteen and twenty, and all were nubile. They came from various parts of the empire but the majority were from Britannia. Three of the men were having nonchalant sex on the floor with slaves whilst one was watching two of the slaves perform sex acts on each other. Two of the men were giving each other the pleasure of the Greeks, and the last man was standing with is back against the wall recovering his strength. "This is more like it", thought Flavius.

Flavius had looked forward to his posting as the commander of the IXth to Eburacum. He was not especially ambitious and this backwater had seemed perfect. He could relax with plenty of time to indulge in the worship of his favourite god. But it had not worked out like that. It would have done had it not been for an aggressive barbarian chieftain, the upstart named Gwdloych. How he cursed that man. His constant sniping across the borders, his vicious raids and impudent attacks on the fortresses that guarded the roads were having a terrible effect on morale. But more irritating still was the fact that these raids forced Flavius into frequent sorties to try to quieten him down. Today's revels were the first opportunity that they had enjoyed for several days.

Two of the men who had been having sex with slave finished. Flavius was just about to order his Numidian to begin placing the grapes in places other than her mouth when the door opened and his assistant walked in. He looked concerned. He walked right up to Flavius, completely ignoring all the others in the room including the girl on Flavius' knee. He spoke in a low voice "Flavius. You must come. We've just had word of another raid. A bad one this time. They got one of the forts on the road."

Cursing, Flavius stood up sending the Numidian crashing to the floor. He grabbed his toga and wrapped it round himself briskly. As he stormed out he threw the loose end of the toga across his shoulder imperiously.

12

We all got out of the library. The legionary at the head of the guards had seen Yuya in the half light at the rear of our column and had not hesitated. He had just brought his sword down on the unarmed librarian's head. I was sorry for him, for he had deserved to survive. But despite Yuya's death scream none of us hesitated for an instant. Marius had the door open and the men at the front were hurrying out. Artorius was backing down the last few metres of the corridor towards the door, holding his sword out to defend himself. I got out into the night air. I heard the clash of steel on steel and quickly turned to see Artorius leap out of the door. We were already running.

*****

It was mid morning and the place was silent. We had all split up after breaking out of the library. We would be more difficult to find in pairs than in a large group, so Marius had ordered everyone to meet in two days at the caravanserai near Misr. He had been insistent that I accompany him. The two of us had ridden hard through the boiling expanse to get here and had made it in just half a day. Our horses skulked around the water trough, completely spent.

Marius and I sat beneath the palm trees, the only travellers at the oasis. We did not disturb the silence as we sat, each lost in our own thoughts. Marius had folded the document and returned it to its wax sealed pouch under his clothing. To be honest I was finding the whole experience overwhelming. I could not believe what I had just read, and yet there it was with Nero's own seal and signature. Both Marius and I well knew that imperial seals could be forged. But this hadn't been. Just to look at the document, to read its words and discover it in that place we knew it was genuine. At that time both Marius and I were looking into the horror. Horror was all that this thing could bring. But Marius was a step ahead of me. Not only was he looking at the horror, he was also looking at his salvation.

The implications and consequences were too much for me. Had Marius asked me what I would do, and had I answered him truthfully I would have told him that I wanted to run far away. Run from the responsibility, run from the lies, run from the murder and the evil. I wanted to be where they couldn't find me. I wanted to dig a hole in the ground and hide. I felt like those Moesians that Greto had told us about. I was terrified and I wanted to be invisible. But more importantly I wanted to be where I couldn't find myself. I was slower than Marius, and more cowardly. This cursed document was tugging at my conscience. I could not just forget about it and hide, but I did not face it.

Marius did, and I nearly killed him for it.
"My God, Tolus", he said.

My God? I thought. Not "ye Gods" as we Roman's say, but "my God" like the Christians say.

My memory of our conversation is odd. I was in a sort of suspended reality and I think that Marius was too. I felt numb. It was like my head was full of wool and I could not understand what was happening very clearly. At the time I thought that Marius was seeing things clearly, but looking back I suppose that he felt much as I did. The one thing that I did understand was the significance of Marius words.

God forgive me, but I so nearly murdered him then. I so nearly murdered him to give myself the easy way out. I would have returned to Rome with the manuscript, taken my promotion and sold my soul. But I didn't.
Maybe it was simply cowardice, although it would have been more cowardly to kill him than not to kill him. Maybe it was my respect for Marius. Maybe it was that I did have a conscience. In the end I think that I just didn't have the will. I knew what was coming because it was the truth. Marius was strong, and he had conviction. He would

work this out as only he could. He would do what he thought was the right thing regardless of how difficult it might prove. I did not have long to wait.

"Tolus. You realise what this means, don't you? The Christus could have been who he said he was. All that we thought we knew of him is false. I have read their "gospels", the good news that they wish to proclaim. They risk their lives to spread this news. They believe that it is more important than their own lives. Their writings are beautiful and tell of the son of their God. In Hebron Joshua told me that he loved Romans, despite everything that we do to his people. They ring true, Tolus. Rani and Horemheb and Smenkhkare, they ring true. They are not mad and they are not stupid. It is the Romans who are mad and stupid. We might be jeopardising our souls, our eternal souls for our ambition and greed. Nero and Decimus and no doubt Hadrian have suppressed this new religion. They have deliberately suppressed it to satisfy their craving for power and wealth. Yet by doing so they could be endangering the souls of everyone. We could all be condemned for eternity due to the greed of a few powerful men. And if we give them this document we give them the only means of stopping it. I do not know whether there is any truth in the works of the Christus, but from everything that I have seen and read and heard I can no longer say for sure that he was just a liar. And while I harbour this doubt I cannot hand over the manuscript to Rome. I will not do it."

Marius had got up. He was pacing about like a caged lion. He was angry, and as I remember it now probably a little frightened. I myself was petrified. Marius was my commanding officer and the words he spoke were treason. It was my duty to kill him, but I agreed with most of what he said.

I had to decide what to do but my head had gone numb. I barely understood any of it, and I felt that which ever decision I took was going to lead to horror. Horror from within if I did my duty, and horror from without if I agreed with Marius. I could not separate out all of the issues clearly. But my heart knew what I must do. It was telling me to back Marius, to fight the crimes that were being perpetrated by our leaders in Rome. Yet I was revolted by the prospect of rebelling against the power that I had devoted my life to serve. I felt like I might explode. The torment must have shown on my face, for Marius looked at me kindly.

"I know Tolus. I speak treason. Yet I cannot allow myself to forget what I have seen. I cannot allow the murder of these innocent people to continue at the hands of liars. I cannot continue to see the souls of the whole empire being risked by the jealousies of a few powerful men. You must kill me now or you will be with me."

He stood and spread his arms wide. I could have rammed my sword into his chest and he would not have resisted. I think that in some ways he would have welcomed it as relief from the awesome responsibility that he was taking upon himself. I stood up and walked towards him. I did not know what to do so I embraced him. He looked like he was inviting it, standing there with his arms apart. An embrace or a sword. That was my alternative. No half measures, no walking away. It was too late for that. As I embraced him I felt hot tears on my cheeks. I had not cried since I was a child and I do not know why I cried then.
Perhaps it was for the end of my life as I had known it, or for the years of service devoted to something that I was now turning my back on.
Perhaps it was for the horror to come.

When we separated I tried to hide my face. Marius lifted my head and looked into my eyes. He too had tears in his eyes. At that moment he knew and I knew that I would follow him anywhere.

"We have chosen the difficult road. We must be clear about why we are doing it. I am not a Christian. Nor, I believe, are you. We have turned our back on Rome for its lies and for its injustice. People must have the right to choose, to learn about the Christus and to make up their own minds. What Rome has done is wrong and I will not be a party to it".

Marius paused. He looked into the distance, and when he resumed he spoke slowly.

"No one can be allowed to learn of Rome's deceit. It could destroy the empire and I will not allow myself to play a part in that. I don't know about you, but I believe in Rome. I believe in law, I believe in order and most of all I believe in justice. We bring civilisation to the barbarians. We bring order to chaos. All of these things are good and I cannot play a role in their destruction".

I turned away from Marius and began to pace. I felt a great relief at his words. We would not be turning our backs on the power that we had served for our whole lives. As I walked across the sandy shade under the palms of the oasis, I felt the burden lifting. We were not to be part of a plot against Rome.

*****

We were both restless and jumpy. There was so much that was not resolved. The oasis was made up of a well in the centre of some palms and a patch of coarse grass. I pulled on the crude twine and drew a wooden pail up the shaft. The water was clear and cool, and I drank deeply. Marius had sat down in the sand under the shade of a large palm, so I took the pail and joined him.

We sat there and we discussed the options that faced us. I argued that since we had agreed that we could not give the confession to Hadrian and Decimus we must give it to Origen. Marius did not reply immediately. He just gazed out from under the palms into the desert. The land baked under the burning sun, the dusty ground a tawny colour. In the evening as the sun set it would gain a reddish tinge but now, in the heat of the day, it had a bleached and very dead feeling. A few ugly rocks punctuated the landscape but otherwise there was nothing to see other than a vast parched flatness. As he leaned forward he began to tell a story.

"Joshua told me of Origen. The man was a hellraiser. In his late teenage years he was constantly in trouble with the authorities in

Sidon. It was rumoured that his parents hated each other and argued constantly. He worked as a labourer on the docks and it was said that he supplemented his income by pilfering some of the cargo that he unloaded. One of the things that his parents argued about was Origen. It gave him a fury to think that he was a cause of his parents unhappiness, as their unhappiness was the cause of his own. He took it out on himself and those around him. His drinking feats were legendary, second only to the tales of what he did when he was drunk. On one notorious occasion, after a heavy drinking session, he walked down to a jetty where the cripples and beggars pleaded for food and money. He picked them up, one by one, and methodically hurled them into the deep water of the port. Many did not have limbs to swim and others were too weak. Eight drowned. A few did get out to tell of his exploit. Apparently he had not taken any pleasure in doing it. He was very drunk and he was full of pain and desperation.

The Roman administration heard of his actions but did nothing. It was thought that they secretly approved of his actions. Origen was unrepentant. If anything it made him more offensive and obnoxious. The community thought that he had a sickness in his head, and shunned him. For several months he was ignored by all but the most unpleasant thugs and vagrants.

Then one day he walked into a tavern in the docks. Some taverns would not have him because he was such a troublemaker but most valued his custom too highly and were prepared to put up with him. That night there was a new serving girl in the tavern he chose. She was named Nemwab and had recently arrived on a ship from Tyre, just down the coast. By all accounts she was beautiful and gentle, from a reputable family. Her parents had both been killed in a raid by pirates and their wealth taken over by relatives who had thrown her out and forced her to leave the city. She took a boat up the coast and arrived in Sidon with nothing. The tavern in the docks offered her lodging and food in return for labour. By all accounts Origen was love struck from the start. He managed to keep his drinking under control and visited the tavern every day after his work. Nemwab saw his anger and could identify with the suffering. Over several weeks they became friends, and then lovers. Origen's behaviour improved. He virtually stopped drinking all together and people stopped being afraid of him. In time Nemwab began to attend meetings held by followers of the Christus in the taverns by the docks. She and Origen moved into a small house of their own and when she became pregnant they were married. She continued to work in the tavern. She had learned of his pain and of the things that he had done. Origen spent much time seeking to make up to the community for his actions. The couple apparently even provided food and shelter for cripples and beggars from their miserly income. Origen was reinstated into the community and forgiven. Nemwab was given much of the credit".

Marius' voice softened. "About ten years ago a galley full of soldiers came from Rome to relieve some of the garrison. When they arrived, like all Roman soldiers after a long voyage the first thing that they did was head for the taverns. They were mostly a group of boys who had never been outside Italia. There was trouble in many of the inns around the docks. Some of the newcomers tried to buy Nemwab for the night, and wouldn't take no for an answer. When they began to cause trouble the tavern keeper asked them to leave. A fight ensued and soldiers were called. The boys were removed and disciplined. Three nights later they returned to the tavern late and waited outside for it to close. They were drunk. When Nemwab left to return home they followed her. Origen was at home asleep when she came in, and she went straight to bed. Half an hour later the legionaries broke into the house and pinned Origen down. They took turns raping his wife in front of him. Origen could not bear the sight, and he is a strong man. He bucked out from under the men who pinned him down and broke the neck of the man who lay on top of his wife. The legionaries went berserk. They pinned Origen down once more. One of them buried his dagger deep in Nemwab's chest. Their son had been woken by the noise and tottered in as his mother was murdered. The soldiers were drunk and their lust for blood was aroused. They grabbed the boy and slashed him repeatedly before they fled. Apparently Origen's son survived for several days before he died. Origen burst into the garrison commander's quarters and demanded justice.

He was publicly flogged for killing a Roman soldier. It would have been worse but for the mitigation of the death of his wife and son. The men who had broken into his house were sent back to Rome".

"Origen was broken. He could not even reap his revenge on the men who had destroyed his family, as they were lost untraceable somewhere in the empire. Most thought that he would descend back into his previous drunken behaviour and were fearful. Instead he went to the christian group that his wife had attended. He had always refused to go whilst she was alive, but now he threw himself into it, searching for some kind of solace from this new religion. I suppose that it was something of his wife's that he could hold on to. He learned about it obsessively. He became the most learned of scholars. He was driven and passionate. He was also totally devoted to the cause. It was like he had transferred his immense love for his wife and child to the new church. Under the circumstances it is hardly surprising that he did well. Yet the only cause for complaint about Origen from his new community was his attitude to Rome. He despises Rome with a consuming passion."

Marius paused and looked thoughtful. He wiped a few beads of sweat from his brow with the edge of his robe. When he resumed his voice was hard.

"We cannot give the confession to Origen. I will not see all that is good about the empire destroyed by a bitter man with revenge in his heart. There must be another way".

I understood Marius' concerns. I had a vague impression of the inevitable conclusion that we were coming to. But my head had gone woolly again. I had the numb feeling that it getting too much for me again. My spirits were sinking, and as they sank my head cleared.

Marius was silent. I thought that he was thinking about what we were to do. He wasn't. He remained deep in thought for several minutes. I was impatient. I felt that my whole life hung in the balance. A small camel train came into view across the expanse. All I could see of it was several small black silhouettes, but the shape and gait of the camels was unmistakable. They were still at least five miles off. This image of life continuing with its day to day routine contrasted sharply with my uncertainty. Anxiety rose uncontrollably from my chest towards my head. I sensed vultures circling over my head. Marius just stared at the camel train approaching. It would be more than an hour before they reached the oasis.

Suddenly Marius jerked forward and seemed to brighten.
"I don't think that we can make this decision alone. You have not met Smenkhkare and his family. They are good people. They know all about the document and they are reluctant to give it to Origen. I had a clear impression that they share our concerns about him. They do not want to see him use it to create anarchy and for that reason they very nearly refused to tell me where to find it. I think we should return to them and ask for their advice. I think that they will see things as we do".

I am afraid that I lost my temper then. I thought that Marius had lost his mind.
"You're mad! You're suggesting that we go back to the people that we have just robbed and ask them what they think we should do with the thing that we have stolen from them? You're out of your mind, Marius. It is the one place that both the Christians and the Romans know as the key to the manuscript. It is the place where both will start their search for us. I'm not going back to Assyut. I want to get out of Aegyptus and I want to get out right now. We must go somewhere safe and we can decide what to do when we get there. I'm not walking into the lion's den". By the time I finished speaking I was shouting, red in the face, almost hysterical.

Marius stood up. He walked over to where I was sitting and before I knew it he had punched me hard on the face. My lip split open and blood started to trickle into my mouth, onto my teeth and down my chin, dripping onto my robe. I looked at him, stunned, as I used my tongue to stem the flow. The blood tasted hot and salty.

"Shut up and listen to me. You are not thinking clearly, Tolus, and unless you get a grip I swear I'll kill you. Now that we've got ourselves into this we're going to have to think clearly to get ourselves out of it. Have you got that?"

I didn't reply. I was angry with him for hitting me but I was more angry with him for being right. I would have done the same in his position. Although I maintained a sulky silence, the shock of Marius' blow had cleared my head.

"I'll take that as a yes. Let's look at this clearly. The Romans are not looking for us. As far as they are concerned, everything is as it should be. The Christians, on the other hand, might be looking for us. They could have found out about what happened to David. If they have there will not be many of them. One or two would be my guess and they will not have come to fight. They will have come to retrieve a document. They know that they cannot take on the might of Rome. Stealth is the only thing that they have on their side. If we see them at Smenkhkare's house we can deal with them. There are nine of us and we are good".

I interrupted him. "Nine of us? What are you talking about, Marius. There are two of us now. The men will not just agree to abandon their mission and commit treason because you order them to. You really have lost your mind".

It was Marius' turn to lose his temper. "For pity's sake, Tolus. We need those men. We cannot just disappear. They would report our disappearance and we would become the most wanted people in the empire. Neither can we just return to them and dismiss them. They would know that something's going on and they would know that they were being deliberately excluded. In case you haven't noticed, Tolus, they are devoted to us. They believe in us. Dismissing them now would be seen as a betrayal. Their resentment could lead them to make a report. We can't risk it. Our only option is to tell them the truth and hope that they see things the way we do. Their devotion will help, as will the strange circumstances of this mission. They know that something big is going on. We've got a good chance that that they will see it as we do".

Marius paused. I was beginning to feel calmer. He had a way of doing that to people, Marius, and it was something that he used more and more.

"You did well in choosing those men, Tolus. All are fearless and good but their loyalty is primarily to themselves. They do not value their lives highly but they are proud men who crave glory and excitement. We can offer them more excitement than any of us can probably handle, and glory by the cartload. But I'm telling you, we are going to need them".

*****

We rode hard through the desert to Misr. Along the way my thoughts turned to Smenkhkare. I had not met him. I could understand the desirability of getting another view of what we should do, but it just seemed so irregular to ask for the advice of those we had just robbed. At the back of my mind I suspected there must be another reason for his desire to return, but I had no inkling as to what it could be.

It was well after dark when we saw the low-lying houses of Misr looming ahead of us in the moonlight. We dismounted from our horses and looked for a drainage channel where they could drink. We tethered them to a fence by a ditch so they could drink and graze. Taking them into town so late would be noticed so we walked the last couple of miles to the caravanserai. All of our men were already there and all were asleep. On the walk from where we left the horses Marius and I had been getting increasingly nervous about what would happen when we told them what we were going to do. We were still on edge after the day's discoveries and would not be able to sleep, so we decided to put our plan to them straight away.

As soon as we woke them they knew that something was up. No doubt Marius and I gave it away with every word and action. They were wide awake in no time. Marius told them not to bother dressing as we were just going to the stables to talk, and a chill ran through me. I wanted to be far away at that moment. I wanted to be back with the Praetorian Guard in Rome enjoying the crude banter of the guardroom. But there was no going back. I grabbed a lantern and we all walked quietly out of the main gate of the caravanserai and around the perimeter wall to the stables.

The mud floor of the stable was dry. The men sat down and looked at Marius expectantly, eyes bright in the light of the lantern. He told them what we had done and he asked the men to trust him.

*****

When he had finished there was silence. It was obvious that the men were completely stunned. Just by opening the document Marius had committed a capital offence. It was an inconceivable thing to have done. Given their shock at the news of us reading the document, I found myself fearing how they would react when they heard why we were telling them. Marius wordlessly put his hand under his cloak and withdrew the sealed pouch that contained the document. He opened it and lay the manuscript on the mud floor of the stable. I looked around the room. Despite the warm yellow glow of the lantern each of the faces sitting around it were chalk white. They looked at the manuscript with disbelief. No one had asked me what had happened to my lip, which was now swollen with a large scab of dried blood. I shuddered to think what I looked like. Everyone just sat and stared at the document.

"Will any of you read it?" asked Marius. There was silence.

Numba was first to react. "I will" he whispered. He picked up the manuscript and began to read. Artorius, Greto and Silus instantly moved behind him to read over his shoulder. After some hesitation Tobias moved forward and picked up the lantern. I thought that he was going to extinguish the light so that none of them could see the manuscript, but he didn't. He simply walked over to the others crowded round Numba, put the lantern down so that they had proper light to see, and joined the huddle. As they read it was clear from the atmosphere that they were suddenly all deeply suspicious of myself and Marius. I had not realised how used I had become to their constant attitude of respect and warmth toward me. I only really became aware of it at that moment, when it had gone and when I needed it most. They were perplexed and angry. They felt compromised and betrayed. But they believed in us enough to want to understand us and they were independent and strong enough to want to discover what was going on. They would make their own minds up. I loved them for that, but I craved their respect now that I had lost it. I was surprised at how it made me feel, because for some reason it made me feel bloodthirsty.

Alaric seemed even more hostile than the others. He looked at Marius and he had fear in his eyes.
"You bastard. By doing this you have condemned us all to death. What choice do we have now? We are all guilty by association. Well I'm not reading it. I will deny ever being here. I will say that I was asleep".
Cassius had begun to shake. His outsized head was nodding involuntarily. "I don't believe this. I've got to get out of here". He stood up.
"I'm coming with you" said Alaric as he too got to his feet.

Both Cassius and Alaric made for the door. All of the men were standing, huddled round the manuscript, watching. Greto spoke.
"Stay. Wait at least until we have all decided what to do. Don't think that you two are the only ones who are afraid. I for one think that Marius and Tolus are have lost their minds. None of us has any business getting involved in any of this. But whether we like it or not we are involved. We may as well know what we are involved in before we decide what to do".

Cassius looked at Alaric. Alaric narrowed his eyes.
"I wouldn't be surprised it those two had put you up to that, you ancient old bastard. Cassius and me, we were never even here".
With that he turned and stalked out of the stable door.

13

The camp of the Imperial Guards was the glory of the legions of Rome. A huge, semi permanent campus, it sat squat and solid within sight of the city walls as a reminder to all who came to the imperial capital of the awesome power that lay at the command of the emperor. The camp was a very deliberate show of military might.

Decimus loved coming to the camp. As the overall commander of imperial forces he enjoyed the status of a quasi god within those walls. Fighting men stopped what they were doing to stare. They nudged comrades and stood rigid, silent and respectful as he passed. This sunny morning was no different. Decimus and his entourage breezed across the ditch, through the thick oak gates in the stone walls and down the main thoroughfare with well ordered grids of accommodation blocks and stores on either side. As he did so, Decimus swelled with pride.

In the central compound he was greeted by one of his most senior generals, the Legate of the Imperial Guards. Commodius had been like an uncle to Decimus when he was growing up, and Decimus trusted him completely. He was also an experienced campaigner who was not intimidated by the able, arrogant son of his dead friend.
"Ave, Decimus Marcellus. How does this fine morning find you?"
"I am well, Commodius" replied Decimus smiling.
"To what do I owe the honour of a visit from the general of generals?" asked the older man. He did so with an ironic tone that suggested that he was not above poking fun at his powerful junior.
Decimus raised an eyebrow in mock reproach, but his humour remained good.

"Your commander comes to most humbly benefit from the unparalleled experience of his most distinguished general. He wants to discuss the deployment of his armies with one who may lend the benefit of his years to his . . . how shall we say? . . . . less aged superior". Decimus was grinning widely, and moved forward to embrace his old friend.

Commodius laughed. Decimus could be incredibly charming when he was in good humour. But the older man also knew that his mood could change like the weather in mountains. One moment he would be full of warmth, the next he could be stabbing confidants in the back – literally. Nevertheless, despite his better judgement Commodius had an affection for the brutal, spoiled son of his best friend. He had watched him grow up, seen the ambition and the greed fight against the desire to be loved. The end result was a strange mixture, a flammable combination that meant that he was always on his guard with his young commander despite their apparent ease with each other. He was not surprised or concerned by Decimus' visit. It was just like the man. He would often come to the camp when there were no pressing matters to be attended to. He enjoyed inspecting the men on parade, and he would invariably "ask for advice", really an excuse for him to indulge in a discussion of all the great strategic moves that he was making on behalf of the empire, civilising vast swathes of territory in lands far away.

Commodius was happy to indulge Decimus. He led him through to his chart room, a room dominated by a huge table which was almost completely covered by a hand-drawn map the length of three men and the width of two. In its centre was a great blue oval that represented the Mare Nostrum, and around it were marked each of the client territories of the Roman Empire. To the northwest the map showed Britannia. The southwest was dominated by Mauretania, which had been annexed by Trajan just a few years previously. In the south eastern corner was Aegyptus and to the northwest was Armenia, a great new territory stretching all the way to the vast Mare Caspium. On the map sat large discs of wood with numerals etched onto them. They represented legions, and there were twenty eight of them.

Including auxiliaries these wooden discs represented nearly four hundred thousand men.

"So what's the latest, Commodius?"
Decimus had more complete, up to date information than Commodius and both men knew it. But Commodius indulged Decimus' desire to hear about the state of the forces spread around the empire.
"The latest is that the frontiers are quiet, the clients and governors are paying their taxes almost without exception and there are no reports of any unusual dissatisfaction in any of the provinces. Rome is civilising the world at a rate unprecedented in the history of the empire. The only real question that Hadrian has to answer is whether he wants to consolidate what he has inherited from Trajan and strengthen our grip still further over our provinces, or to go back on campaign".
"Men need to fight, or they forget how" said Decimus gruffly.
"Well, there is plenty of fighting to be had if we decide to go after it. There are a good number of territories that remain unconquered, particularly in the east, and in the north of Britannia".
Decimus looked up sharply.
"Britannia?" he asked "I thought that we crushed the barbarians there long ago".
"In a way, we did. They haven't had any credible resistance since the warrior queen Boudicca and her army were massacred by Paulinus in Nero's time. But we never properly conquered the north of the province. The land is mountainous, and the tribes savage. We always had so many problems with the southern people that we did not have the energy or personnel to conquer the north."
Decimus looked thoughtful. He had heard that the Britons were a difficult people, but he had never really taken it too seriously. There had always been more pressing matters.
"What problems do we have with the people of the south?" he asked.
"It's difficult to put one's finger on" replied Commodius. "They just hate us. For some reason, their leaders are not interested in our bribes and we have failed to establish the incentive of citizenship there. They do not seem to care about status or gold or progress. They just care about hating Romans. It's a constant war of attrition, and very difficult to deal with since they never actually raise an army against

us. I think that they learned through Boudicca's experience that they could not beat us in battle".

Decimus yawned. He was getting bored, for he hated intractable problems, particularly trifling ones.

"What are we doing about it?" he asked lazily.

Commodius recognised Decimus' mood. When he was bored like this he could become dangerous.

"Caracalla, the governor of the province has been reliable in delivering his tributes. We get good income from the province, mainly from the harvesting of slaves in the northern wilderness . . ."

"What are we doing to bring the people into line?" Decimus was curt.

"Do you have a suggestion, sir?" Commodius shot back.

"Get a decent general up there, Commodius, to the north of the country. Get a decent general who will not swan about in a palace, but a general who will march around the countryside cracking skulls together".

It was not a suggestion but an order, and both men knew it. The name that immediately came into Commodius' head was that of Victrix.

*****

When Decimus rode back along the wide road to the Collina gate he was dissatisfied. He had not enjoyed his discussion with Commodius. Not only was Britannia a trifling detail that should not trouble men such as he, but his discussion had failed to dispel the unsettled feeling that had been provoked by a message that had come through that morning. The messenger had come at dawn. Hadrian had got out of bed to see the messenger in his antechamber, but had returned with the message unopened and got back into bed. Decimus and Hadrian read the message, from Marius Sextus in Aegyptus, together. He had simply reported that he had successfully made his first contact with the family who were acting as guardians of Nero's confession and was hoping to retrieve the manuscript as soon as possible. He would send a further report when he had it.

It was good news, but the reminder that Nero's confession was still in the wrong hands had left a nasty feeling with them both. Decimus thought that a visit to the camp would settle him. The great strength, the discussion of the vastness and security of the empire should have calmed the disquiet caused by events in Ituraea and Aegyptus. But somehow the feeling of dread remained. It was instinctive and irrational, and his visit to Commodius had done nothing to ease it.

*****

Lucius was having dinner with Alexander when the message arrived. As soon as he had read it, he returned to the table and passed it over to Alexander. Alexander grunted as he read it, cast it aside and immediately turned his attention back to his plate. As soon as they had finished eating, Lucius retired pleading a headache. Alexander took the hint and departed. Lucius spent much of the night lying awake, thinking about the consequences of the message from the soldier called Marius Sextus.

14

After Alaric left, Cassius looked around the stable, unsure. This quiet man, usually so dignified and composed turned to face me with pleading in his eyes. I started to walk across the mud floor towards him, meaning to reassure him. Cassius was a good man and I could understand his fear. But as I stepped forward he panicked. He turned and stumbled out of the door after Alaric. I turned to Marius for guidance, and as I did so I knew what was coming. His nod was barely perceptible and I was once more on the move almost before I saw it. We ran out after them. We could see their white shifts clearly in the moonlight as they walked fast across the sand, Cassius hurrying to catch up with Alaric. The high outside wall of the caravanserai cast a shadow. The benefit of sand is that you can move silently - I am not sure that either of them heard us but some sixth sense alerted them to our presence when they were almost within reach. But we were already running and by the time they had seen us we were on top of them. They were unarmed. I have always hated myself for that. I can understand their reaction. Much of me wanted to join them. God forgive me, but for the first and last time I helped murder two unarmed men who were under my command and in my protection. We left the corpses where they had fallen and ran back to the stable. The rest of the men were just sitting there. The horror that I was feeling showed clearly on their faces. They were staring at our clothing. I looked down and saw the fresh blood. I was holding a dagger red with the blood of one of my own men. Marius too held his bloody dagger. Greto's face was like granite.

"Dead?" he asked.

Marius nodded. I will never forget the hatred I felt as I watched their faces turn from horror to grim fastness. I perceived them tense as one.

I feared that they were going to try to rush for us. The huddle of men had become like an animal poised to strike. Marius and I were subconsciously standing on either side of the door. I had not really realised, but we were effectively guarding it. We were armed and they were not, but in the gloom of that stable I felt the intimidation that they were capable of. I thought they were about to strike, and to this day I have no idea what I would have done if they had. To my eternal relief, Greto spoke.

"Easy lads. Easy. Everybody relax". There was an unreality about his voice. I think it was the trauma of the situation but I felt as though I was not in my body as he spoke. I had a strange feeling of being completely detached. On his words some of the tension left the stable. Just the sound of a voice brought us all back to our minds. Our instincts had taken over, but the human voice brought us back to ourselves.

Very slowly Marius turned his dagger in his hand and held it by the blade. He threw it to the far corner of the room, closer to the men than to us. Very slowly he drew his sword and did the same. I followed his lead. We were now unarmed and our weapons were within easy reach of our men. I wondered for a moment if they would grab them and kill us. It was their way out. Before this thought had time to develop, Marius spoke. He spoke slowly and deliberately, and I was amazed at the authority and conviction in his voice.

"Tolus and I have just done something that we will have to live with for the rest of our lives. I have never before killed a man in my protection and I never will again. You may kill us if you will. If you do you can be free of what is in front of you. But I beg you, before you decide what you are going to do, read the manuscript. Read it and you might begin to understand why we have committed this crime".

Greto looked about him. Each of our men's faces was a grim mask. The eyes were hard and the mouths set. Artorius gave Greto a nod. "We will read it. But I would be surprised" he inclined his head towards Marius and me "if you are not dead men".

Marius and I silently withdrew. We walked out into the desert and began to dig with our hands. The sand was soft and deep. It took us a long time to displace enough sand to cover the bodies of the two men. We did not work fast. When we had we dragged Cassius and Alaric to the holes and dumped them in we brushed the clods of sand with our feet until we could no longer see the bloody marks. The graves would become exposed in a few days, but that would be long enough. When we returned to the stable the document had been cast aside on the floor. The men were deep in conversation. Silence fell as we entered. Greto looked up at Marius, his face a little softened but his expression impossible to gauge.

"Marius Sextus, you owe us an explanation. What in Jupiter's name were you thinking of? If I am not mistaken this document is our death warrant. We can understand that you are a man of honour. We know that you have a conscience. But why did you have to get involved? What made you suspect that this is what we were sent to recover?"

I was heartened by the question. It meant that the men wanted to try to understand what was going on. But I also got a clear impression that the document alone had not won them over. They wanted an explanation for what Marius had done, and I knew that the explanation was not a good one because I had heard it.

Marius told the men how his disquiet at the mission had grown as he had come to respect the Christians. He told them of his disquiet at their treatment by Rome and his reluctance to betray good people like Smenkhkare's family. He told them of our conversation outside the caravanserai in Assyut when we had withdrawn for the first time. He spoke of the outcome of that conversation – the resolution to do as we were ordered and ask no questions. But then he told them of when the contents of the document were revealed to him by Smenkhkare and Rani. He spoke of how he had agonised about carrying out his orders when it appeared that we were the agents of a great wrong being perpetrated against so many people. He spoke of the burden that his knowledge of the suffering inflicted by Rome on an innocent people was causing. And he justified his decision to read the document for himself. To be fair to Marius he did it well, and he did it better than he had to me.

Greto looked thoughtful. "That I can almost understand. Foolish, very foolish, and unprofessional. But I can understand how a good man like you might have such a crisis of loyalty in such a situation. But why involve us? Why implicate us?"

The atmosphere in the room had completely changed. From open hostility and imminent bloodshed it had transformed to interest and a degree of sympathy. "I involved you because I need you" replied Marius simply.

*****

Soon after dawn the following morning we were on a felucca pulling out of Misr. There had been a short delay whilst Marius disappeared for half an hour at dawn. When he came back he told us that he had sent word to Decimus Marcellus that we would be leaving Aegyptus shortly and would send word as soon as we arrived in Rome. He added that he had given no hint as to what we bring back with us. On the felucca that morning there were seven of us. Each of the remaining men, Greto, Artorius, Numba, Silus, and Tobius had agreed to join us. We had talked deep into the night about what to do. They saw it much as I had. We had little option. I had been surprised that fighting men used to obeying orders without asking questions had taken so readily to the idea of some sort of moral campaign. To be honest I think that they were excited by the enormity of what we were undertaking and saw the potential fame or notoriety as outweighing the risk. Nevertheless I don't think that they would have been interested if they didn't believe in Marius, and to a lesser extent myself. If they had thought that we could not succeed, they would have killed the two of us without a second thought and returned to Rome with the confession.

In deciding to join us they forgave us the killing of Cassius and Alaric. They understood that it had been necessary. I didn't forgive myself, but none of them ever mentioned it again and I honestly think that they forgot about it. They were like that. It had been an operational necessity, simple as that. I have never felt a closer sense of comradeship than I did on the felucca that morning. It's strange but I really was content as we made our stately way through the reed lined banks of the fertile Nile strip under the blinding morning sun. It really felt like we were embarking upon a glorious adventure.

*****

We got to Assyut just before sundown. Marius did not want to waste any time and as he jumped off the boat he announced that he was going to Smenkhkare's house. The men responded that they were going to join him. We were still on the landing jetty by the river at Assyut and it seemed that the whole village were moving about, coming in from the fields to return home. Carts pulled by donkeys, laden with the harvest passed. Weary, dusty men and women passed bearing their tools over their shoulders. Their faces were lined by rivulets of mud where the sweat had trickled down through the dust on their faces. On that jetty we had an argument that caused heads to turn. Neither Marius nor myself had appreciated that the dynamics of command would have changed so totally. In retrospect it seems obvious. But Marius just looked back at them in surprise. "What?" he said quietly. He said it like he had misheard them. I know now that he had other things on his mind. The last thing that Marius wanted was for anyone else to complicate the forthcoming encounter.
"We are coming with you", said Greto.
"You are not" said Marius swiftly
Greto was insistent. "We are coming with you because we are no longer soldiers. We are . . . . we are . . . . we are something else. By the gods, Marius, you've turned us into revolutionaries. You can't just treat us like subordinates any more. We're as involved in this as you are. We need to be included. We need to know what's going on. We're coming".
Marius could not believe his ears. Had anyone said this to their commanding officer in the legion they would be executed on a charge of desertion. But he knew that Greto was right. He knew that we were

now effectively a group of outlaws and by definition we operated outside established laws.

"I understand what you say, Greto, but we are going to have to establish our own modus operandi. We cannot operate as a group of individuals. We can only succeed if we follow some sort of leadership model. I suggest that we establish it later. For the time being, I must go to Smenkhkare."

Greto began to lose his temper. It was unlike Marius to acknowledge the point of another and then completely ignore it. "Marius. We are coming with you".

I could see that both sides were about to dig in. I was desperate to avoid a stand off, particularly with half of Assyut looking on. Our unit was still fragile after the upheavals of the last few hours and this was our first action together. I could not fully understand Marius' attitude at the time. It was almost as if he were ashamed of what we might find when we met Smenkhkare. I myself was intrigued and wanted to find out what it could be, so I intervened.

"Look, you've both got a point. In a way it would probably be better for Marius to go alone. But the rules of engagement have changed. We should all go together and we can decide how we will work together later".

I could see Marius about to protest. I looked at him fiercely and gave a tiny flick of my head. He got the message.

We walked through the fading light along the river track to Smenkhkare's house.

"Keep your mouths shut" said Marius as he stepped up to the door. He poked his head round the doorway and was seen by an astonished Horemheb who was preparing food in the kitchen. From outside we could hear her summon Smenkhkare. The old man came to the door.

"David!" he exclaimed. His greeting was full of affection and surprise. As he drew away from the embrace he looked over Marius' shoulder and saw the rest of us. Bewilderment quickly gave way to shock. He looked back at Marius with searching enquiry. Marius simply said "I think that we had better come in".

Smenkhkare nodded, standing aside to let us enter. The room was simple but homely. Horemheb turned from the fire and when she saw six men arrive the fear showed in her eyes. She quickly turned and ordered all her children to leave the house.

On hearing the concern in her mother's voice, Rani walked into the room. The moment she did, all of Marius' strange behaviour regarding this family became clear. As she entered and saw Marius, for just a split second I saw the look of expectant joy in her eyes. Marius' usually implacable face had softened to a look of deep tenderness. But as soon as she saw the rest of us Rani's joy was instantly overcome by suspicion. We were six strong and, except for Greto, young men. All of us had the beards and the robes of the Aegyptusis. All of us were deeply tanned from our time in the land of the ancients. Yet she immediately knew that we were not of her people. She looked at Marius with puzzlement.
"What is going on, David?" she asked.

Marius looked uncomfortable. "I have returned to tell you the truth. My name is not David and you were correct, Rani when you told me I was more like a soldier than a smith". Marius' discomfort with the situation, and with the audience made him formal. As he sought to explain who he was he sounded almost pompous.
"Until several weeks ago I was working as the praefectus castrorum for the XIIth legion, based in Tyrus. I began my service with the XIIth over eight years ago as a centurian in Cappadocia. We moved to Tyrus just over three years ago and I have been praefectus castrorum there for two years. In addition to being the camp adjunct, one of my auxiliary duties as praefectus castrorum was to oversee the legion's small intelligence section. And in Ituraea, one of the minor jobs of the intelligence section was to monitor the activities of the christian leadership who operate out of Sidon. I am a soldier and until I came to this house I had served Rome all my life."

At this point something extraordinary happened. I was watching Rani and a great fury overtook her face, a fury the like of which I have never seen. The dark skin of her cheeks reddened and her eyes glistened with hatred. She launched herself at Marius. We were so taken aback that we did not react immediately. She attacked Marius like a crazed cat, scratching at his eyes and pummelling about his ears. Marius looked stricken. He stepped back and held her by the wrists. He was so strong that despite her fury there was little she could do to escape his grip. Yet her legs were still free and she began kicking at his shins with all her might. Marius just stood there, holding her hands and repeating her name softly. Smenkhkare and Horemheb looked on in amazement, as did we. Soon her kicks lost their power and she began to sob. Marius looked around the room not really seeing us, with a terrible disconnected blank look on his face. He let go of Rani's wrists and started to talk again. His voice was lifeless.

"I said that until I came to this house I had served Rome for all my life. I no longer serve Rome. These men here now were Roman soldiers too, and they too no longer serve Rome. We were sent to recover the Neronian confession for Rome. I killed David the smith and I assumed his identity. My real name is Marius Sextus".
Horemheb was comforting Rani. Smenkhkare had sat down on a wooden stool and was slowly shaking his head. Marius paused to ensure that he still had their attention. Rani had her face buried in her mother's shoulder. Marius spoke sharply to gain her attention.
"Listen to me Rani. It is important that you understand this".
She looked up at him. Her fury had vanished and had been replaced by a look of dull hostility.
"Because of all that happened in the course of my deception I became unsettled by this mission, Rani. I became so unsettled that I read the confession. I read it and realised that I could not surrender it to Rome".

Smenkhkare's face was like the sun coming out from behind the clouds. Realisation dawned.
"So you haven't come here to kill us?"
"No, Smenkhkare. I have come here to ask for your advice".
"But I don't understand. What made you do this?"
Marius briefly recounted the events of the past few months and particularly the past few days to them. I knew the story, but as I

listened to him recount it to these people the missing part that had been puzzling me became clear. I had seen it in the look that had been exchanged between Rani and Marius. He loved her. He had partly done it for her. He had partly betrayed Rome for the love of a woman. The realisation made me angry. He had brought me with him and he could never have brought the rest of the men along without me. I felt misled. I knew that we were doing the right thing but Marius had got me into something without being honest with me. I was furious and had to make a conscious effort to concentrate on what was being said. Marius had reached the end of his tale and was outlining our options to Smenkhkare.

"So option one and two are unacceptable to us. Therefore we have to work out a third option. What we plan to do is to return to Rome and blackmail the emperor. We are going to agree not to hand over Nero's Confession to Origen in exchange for the legalisation of Christianity."

*****

I was astonished. Marius had not discussed this with any of us, and it was absurd. I looked to the rest of the men and to my surprise they seemed unaffected. Numba even had a look of amusement on his face. As I battled to understand what it meant, Marius was looking at Smenkhkare.

He was a good man, Smenkhkare. He was a good man but he was a simple man. He had led a quiet life in a farming village in Aegyptus. The concept of blackmailing the emperor of Rome was beyond him. At that moment it was beyond me.

He would not countenance Marius' plan. He was stubborn in his insistence that the right thing to do with the manuscript was to give it to Origen. Although he had doubts about Origen and his plans for the confession he had come round to the view that his wife and daughter had earlier argued. He just wanted to be rid of the thing for good. He wanted to be left to his old age in peace. Horemheb agreed. Give it to Origen and be done with it, she said. By doing so they would fulfil their ancient obligation and be free for good. What Origen did with it

was not their responsibility. Their attitude was understandable, they no longer had the zeal of youth.
Rani had begun to recover her composure. She looked washed out, but argued that there must be another way. She was firmly of the belief that the destruction of Rome could not be in anyone's interests. The conversation was going nowhere and there was a depressed feeling about it. Rani was sullen and empty. Marius had lost all of his enthusiasm and looked to be going through the motions.

We were going round in circles and the men were becoming restless. Horemheb was in the middle of repeating her lecture about their obligations as guardians of the manuscript. As head of their movement, Origen must be given it as he requested. As she spoke a deep, rich voice interrupted from the shadows by the doorway.

"Well spoken" said a voice that I did not recognise.
An enormous hulking presence stepped forward. There was stunned silence and Artorius had his sword at the man's belly.
Marius punctured the tension. "There'll be no need for that, Artorius. I recognise this man from what I have heard and if I have heard correctly he will not wish to die here tonight".
He turned slightly to face the intruder.
"You are far from home, Origen".

15

The atmosphere had been taut before, but with the entry of this huge bear of a man it became unbearable. The great man spoke in a voice like iron.
"My reputation obviously precedes me, David. But I too have heard of you and you are most certainly not the man that I sent from Sidon all those weeks ago. It is my guess that you are a servant of Rome".
"I was a servant of Rome. Nero's confession changed that. What I am now, it seems, depends on ones outlook".

Origen raised an eyebrow. He could not hide the contempt in his voice.
"A Roman spy with a conscience! I will believe it when I see it, and I don't believe that I yet have." The insult was obvious but Marius ignored it.
"Well I hope that you will recognise such a man when you do see him. Our business here was finished. We will bid you good night and a safe journey home".
With that Marius began to say his farewells to Smenkhare.
Origen interrupted. He was obviously exhausted. He was covered in dust and looked like he had been on the road all day. His voice was arresting. "Before you go, I must ask whether the manuscript has been recovered".
Marius regarded Origen. "It has".
Origen spoke deliberately. "Then I would be grateful if you were to return it to its rightful owner".
He looked straight at Marius. "Me".
Marius refused. He gave his reasons. He spoke of his refusal to see the Roman Empire brought to its knees, to allow anarchy to envelop the order of the empire. Origen was scathing.

"You say that you no longer serve Rome, but all you want to do is preserve the status quo. You are a fraud, Marius".

"I want to see what is good about the status quo preserved, that is quite true. But I want to see the wrongs that are done against your people corrected, Origen, and this document can enable that to happen".

"And how will that work?"

"We are going to blackmail the emperor. He will reverse the policy of disinformation and persecution of your people. In exchange for retaining his position and the empire he will make a few inconsequential policy changes which will give you the justice that you crave".

"There can be no justice without punishment, Marius. Had you read our scriptures you would know that. But all of this is irrelevant in comparison to the catastrophe that you are about to walk into".

As he continued, Origen made no attempt to hid the contempt in his voice.

"For a Roman, your naivety is stunning. What are you expecting Hadrian to do? Quake in his sandals and agree to do anything that you demand? Beg for your mercy? You are living in a dream world. These people are ruthless. They do not care about the empire. They care about themselves and their place in history. They will not allow you to just turn up make a fool of them. They will not start to implement changes that they cannot explain. They certainly won't convert to Christianity. The climate in Rome would make it impossible. The time is not right. I'll tell you what will happen if you proceed with your absurd plan. The emperor will kill you. He will risk the exposure of the document, but he will kill you. The likelihood is that he will also retrieve the document from you. These people are evil. They are snakes that would take great pleasure in crushing the breath out of you. You are like a small child who thinks that he can walk across burning coals unscathed. Please understand this. You have two options. You could destroy the manuscript, either by giving it to Rome or by burning it yourself – both amount to the same thing. Or you could give it to me. I will use it to achieve the ends for which you say you strive. All the things that have led you to commit your treason

I will reverse. This is who I am and what I live for. Give me the manuscript, Marius, and I will achieve the thing you have risked everything for".

Marius looked thoughtful. "But I cannot allow the destruction of the empire, Origen."

"I will not necessarily destroy the empire. If I do, it is only because the empire deserves to be destroyed. I will spread the message and the facts of the manuscript across the empire. Everyone will come to hear of them and see what Rome did. I do not know what the consequences of this will be. Yes, it will be a threat to the empire. Yes, it could lead to the whole façade coming crashing down. But if Rome is clever and if they respond fast they could save themselves. They could save themselves by doing exactly what you seek to persuade them to do with your ridiculous blackmail. Give me the document, Marius, and see it put to proper use".

Marius was beginning to become confused. Origen spoke persuasively and his rich voice inspired confidence. His scorn for Marius' plan had rocked the little amount of confidence I had in it. I could sense that it had done the same for Marius. Much of what he had said made sense. I was reminded of my own reaction to Marius' idea that he would blackmail the emperor. It was absurd. It could never work. Marius was wavering and Origen knew it. I had a sort of vague idea that I had to get us out of that place, get us out to somewhere that we could talk about it calmly. There was no objectivity in there and Origen was a man who spent his life persuading and cajoling people.

Rani was our saviour. She too sensed the atmosphere and she had her own misgivings about Origen. When she spoke the sound of a female voice seemed somehow incongruous, at odds with the mood of the room.
"You must rest, Origen. We have been remiss in not offering you refreshment after your long journey. It is late and we need to consider what you have said. These men will leave now and they will return in the morning when they have considered your words".

I was relieved and when I looked over to Marius I could see that he was too. Origen glared at Rani and began to protest. He was furious. He felt that he was on the verge of persuading Marius to hand over the manuscript. As he began to speak Marius stopped him.

"Rani is right, Origen. I have heard what you say. We must rest and will return in the morning."

With that he bade his farewells quickly and we all left the house.

We walked up the path back to the track on the road. After some moments a woman's voice called out. It was Rani. Marius hung back as we walked on. He fell into step with her a few metres behind the rest of us, and they began talking in low voices.

Marius did not know what to say to Rani. He felt nothing but desolation.

When she caught up with him he wasn't thinking particularly clearly. After she had attacked him he had been sure that she would never want to see him again. He supposed that she was following him now because she wanted to discuss what he would do with the document. He was surprised to find that he no longer cared about it. He had been so sure after he had read the manuscript at the oasis with me. He had been so sure that he would do what was right. Now he had lost his will to do anything. He felt weak and lethargic. He wanted just to be rid of it. He knew that he should not give it to Rome or to Origen. He had a vague idea that he might just burn it and return to his fate in Rome. Death would almost be welcome.

He did not want to be with Rani now, it was too painful. When he spoke he did so with empty disinterest. "Thank you for intervening. I was about to agree to anything Origen wanted."

Rani was surprised. She had been expecting Marius to beg for her forgiveness. She had at least been expecting an apology. Instead here he was, distant and apparently disinterested. How could he talk with such apparent detachment, failing to give any recognition at all to what had passed between them? She was confused, so she mirrored his coldness in her response.

"Well I could see that he was breaking you down and I thought that you might do something you would regret. What are you going to do?"

Marius was staring straight ahead. His face was an impenetrable mask. He would not look at her. Eventually he spoke. "I do not know. I just wish I had never come here. I was happy in Ituraea, I knew who I was. Now I just feel loss".

Rani was angry. She was angry at Marius for refusing to acknowledge her, for treating her like anybody else. She was angry at him for refusing to look at her. His feeling sorry for himself was the last straw. She snapped.

"For God's sake get a grip David, or Marius, or whoever you are. This is agony".

She stopped abruptly. Marius looked dolefully at his sandals.

"Look at me" she screamed. "Look at me when I'm talking to you!"

As she said the last few words her voice broke. She turned away and began to sob quietly. Marius didn't know what to do. He had never known women well and was lost when it came to understanding them. He believed that Rani would never have him because of his lies. He was the only person in the room earlier who had interpreted her attack on him as an act of hatred. Everyone else saw it for what it was - the frustration and fury that only love can provoke. But Marius was completely bemused by Rani's weeping. He did not know what to do. He walked off a few paces intending to leave her and be alone with his desolation. But he didn't. He turned, and as he turned Rani looked up at him. She looked him straight in the eye and Marius lost his composure. He felt tears spring to his eyes. All he could see was her understanding of his loneliness. He wept where he stood, on a dusty path under the stars. He stood there and wept as he hadn't wept since the death of his parents. Through his tears he chastised himself for his deception of her. He pleaded with her to forgive him. He felt he was humiliating himself and embarrassing her, but he pleaded. As she walked up to him he was expecting to feel the force of her blows once more. He did not try to protect or brace himself for what was coming. He just watched her approach. She walked right up to him, flung her arms around his neck and kissed him on the mouth. Marius was so surprised he nearly ran away. Instead he allowed his instincts to take

over and returned her kiss. After several moments he pulled himself away from her. She laughed at the puzzled look on his face.
"You really don't have any idea, do you Marius? You have no idea what is going on inside my head". Marius looked at her with incomprehension.
"I thought that you loathed me. I thought that you wanted to kill me. I would have if I was you, and you looked like you would have done if you could".
"Am I going to have to explain myself to you?" she laughed.
"I think so" he said.
"Marius, I love you. Of course I hated you for a minute. Any woman would. You came to my house to steal from us. You deceived us with the aim of betraying us to death. But you didn't! You made a decision of great bravery. You rejected everything that you have believed in all your life for us. But most of all you did it because of me. I could see it. Everyone could see it. It was obvious in that room. And then when you thought that you had lost me you lost your fire".

She grinned. "Why do you think that my parents were so keen that you should give the manuscript to Origen? They don't want him to have it. They are as reluctant as you are to give it to him. But they could see how we felt about each other and they knew the danger that we would both be in if you persisted with your plan. But if Origen got the manuscript then we would both be free of it. We would be safe. They were speaking with the well being of a daughter in mind. Nothing more."

Marius looked at her with wonder. Then he grabbed her and pulled her to him.

They broke off and Marius looked at her. A torrent of words rushed out.
"I just wanted to be out of that room. I would have agreed to anything. I came back here because I wanted to tell you the truth. I had come so close when we spoke before. I can remember your exact words. You said to me "You must not be afraid to love. You must allow yourself some happiness". In one sentence you showed that you understood me

better than I understood myself. I always thought that by controlling my feelings I was preventing myself from being open to being hurt. I thought that I was protecting myself. But almost as soon as I saw you I realised what happiness could be. For the first time, I wanted it. I wanted to allow myself to have a chance with it. But I couldn't. As long as I was lying to you, I couldn't. I was so close to telling you the truth back then, Rani. I . . . . ."

Marius was interrupted by Rani's lips hitting his. But this time there was no breaking off. He led her by the hand off the track and into a field of newly harvested corn. He sat her down on the soft banks of an irrigation channel and there he began to caress her neck and her hair. He felt her lips explore his face, and her hands explore his body. Her firm breasts burrowed against his chest and her long, smooth legs moved over his middle. Suddenly he was pulling at her shift, over her slim hips and shoulders. He felt her hands as they urgently sought to remove his robes. Naked she straddled him, the pale blue light of the moon casting soft shadows across her body. Marius had never known such pleasure. Her softness, her warmth, her tenderness were all things that he had not even dared to dream about. The stars glimmered above as Marius looked up and saw the woman he loved smiling down at him. He noticed tears rolling down her cheeks and was surprised, for the first time in his life, to feel peace.

*****

It was several hours before Marius insisted that they rise. The light of the moon still lit the field. They began to walk down the path hand in hand. Whereas he had been feeling totally drained and uninterested just a few hours before, Marius now felt a fire burning inside him. He felt he could do anything. He felt he could conquer Rome itself, which was almost what he was planning to do. As they talked of the options a plan began to harden.

I was asleep with the men under a palm tree. We had settled down in a field between Smenkhkare's house and the caravanserai and must have been asleep for several hours. The moon was still bright when Marius shook us awake.

"We are leaving Aegyptus" he said.

At these words I was wide awake. "But what about Origen and the others?" I asked.

"We are leaving now so that they will not have a chance to follow us or try to talk us out of it. I'll explain on the way".

Despite their sleepiness the men looked pleased to be getting out. All of them were ready within minutes. I was so busy getting my kit together that I didn't immediately notice Rani. When I did I was puzzled. I didn't know how to ask and I was trying to be subtle, so my question was clumsy.

"Good morning, Rani. It's a bit early for you to be up isn't it?"

She grinned at me and Marius spoke.

"Rani is coming with us. I'll explain that on the way too."

I could sense grumbling from the men and to be honest I shared their misgivings.

Although we were ready, we all looked at each other uncertainly, and no one moved.

With infectious enthusiasm, Marius shouted at us.

"To Rome"

16

As the ship approached the filthy looking port from the south, Origen felt his temper worsen again. It had been terrible for days after the skiff had weaved its way out of Alexandria's port. It all seemed so useless. He knew that he had been taken for a fool and felt ashamed. To allow the document to be within his reach, to have the man who possessed the manuscript actually in the same room and then to lose him without even following him – it all seemed too crass to be true. As the small fishing vessel approached Sidon his feeling of helpless humiliation increased once more. He knew that Tertullian would be understanding and non judgmental and that almost made it worse. He would prefer to be met with exasperation and vilification rather than instant forgiveness. That would be impossible to take right now, particularly as he knew that he would not be forgiving himself.

The ship pulled alongside the low stone jetty. Origen was first off, barely pausing to thank the skipper. He strode up the stone steps feeling none of his customary relief at being home. The stones were slimy with fish residue. From the land the stench of this port could be smelt almost before the place could be seen. The fish were unloaded here and the wooden crates passed in a human chain to the sorting room, a low wooden barn not twenty metres from the quay. It was in here that the fresh catches were sorted by type, size and weight into lots for sale. It was a place of men. Shouts echoed across the building as the fishermen announced their wares. Their calls were usually met by the approach of one or more traders. The trader would then offer a desultory price for the stock, which would be met by a stream of profanity from the fisherman. The trader would then feign offence and grudgingly offer a higher price, the fisherman's cue to bemoan his poverty and his children's hunger. So the game would go on until a price was agreed.

Origen barely noticed the stench as he stalked past the sorting room. His eyes were down and his face set. His size and reputation made Origen conspicuous and his demeanour made it clear to everyone who saw him coming that they should get out of the way. By and large they did. Those who did not were grudgingly circumvented. In a past life he would have simply ploughed through them. Origen barely looked up until he was out of the seething centre of town. With one of the three town wells behind him he turned onto the dusty track and slowed his pace for the last two miles that led to Tertullian's low slung mud house. He knew that he had to calm down and allow reason to govern his frustration. The sun was going down and the colours that lit the sky mellowed him. He reflected on the glory of God, and used the beauty of this daily show to put his carelessness into perspective. By the time he reached the chickens in the yard at the front of Tertullian's house he felt that he was sufficiently calmed to have a sensible conversation with the old man.

As he approached the door Ruth came out and embraced him. As they parted he saw the lines of worry on her face. Ruth was not the type to fuss. Origen knew that something must be wrong.
"I'm so pleased you are returned", she said.
"How is Tertullian?" replied Origen abruptly.
"I fear that he is dying". Tears had filled Ruth's eyes. Although he knew that they were not intended as such, Origen could not help feel that Ruth's tears were a reproach for his absence. He felt his frustration boil up inside him again. He felt responsible.
"Take me to him" was all that he said, and Ruth turned and immediately led him into the dust bowl behind the house where Tertullian lay in his customary place beneath the olive branches, propped up with cushions on the vast kilim. Origen stopped. Even from this distance he could see the deterioration that had come over Tertullian. He was such a tiny presence, dwarfed by the cushions that surrounded him. His bony frame looked to have shrunk even further since Origen had left him. His face had about it the mummified look of the dead ancients, with the skin drawn taught across his face, cheek bones protruding above hollow cheeks. In contrast, the legs beneath his robe were lifeless. The skin sagged heavily off them; skin and

bones. As they approached he noticed that Tertullian's eyes were closed. For a terrible moment Origen feared that he had died. Ruth gently put her hand on Origen's shoulder causing him to stop. She approached the prostrate body alone and took hold of the left hand. She knelt down and whispered in Tertullian's ear. Slowly his eyes opened and as they did so Origen was relieved to see that they still burned with the warm intensity that he remembered. When Tertullian opened his mouth Origen had to lean forward to hear his words.

"Welcome, brother. I thought that you were Perridac coming to say farewell. It is good to have you returned. Come, sit, and tell me of your journey".

Origen sat near to Tertullian on the cushions so that they could talk without Tertullian having to strain forward. Ruth got up. Before leaving she spoke in a low voice.

"Try to be as quick as you can, Origen. He tires quickly and he needs to save his strength". She then altered her voice and tried to sound cheerful "You must be hungry after your voyage. I was going to cook some eggs for Tertullian. You will have some?"

"Thank you Ruth, I would be grateful".

Origen had always looked forward to Ruth's eggs. She was one of the few people in the coastal region who insisted on feeding her chickens with grain. As a result, the eggs she served were almost unique in not having the overwhelming taste of the fish that all the other chickens were fed. Despite his hunger Origen could muster no enthusiasm for this simple pleasure.

Ruth turned to go and Origen looked at Tertullian. The waxen head turned above the withered body, giving the impression that the neck could barely support its weight. Tertullian's eyes were alight with his inner fire.

"Brother, I do not have long to live. This thing has gone too far now, and I will be departed within a few weeks." These words were said with no regret. On the contrary, there was almost an excitement about them. Tertullian's eyes shone as he finished. "Soon I will have peace. But I do not wish to go until I hear of your journey".

"Brother, I have bad tidings and I need your advice".

Origen launched into his story, speaking quickly and quietly. It was clear that although Tertullian's body was failing him his mind was still strong. He listened intently.

Origen briefly related his encounter with Mishac in El Arish, his disquiet at what he had heard, and his encounter with the curious Romans in Assyut at the house of Smenkhkare. He lowered his eyes in shame as he confessed that he had allowed the Romans to leave the house, trusting that they would return the following day. He spoke of his conviction that he could talk Marius round. The frustration was written on his face as he told of his desperate ride up the road that ran alongside the Nile, searching all the time for a boat sailing up the river containing the Roman soldiers or a group on the road that might be them. He told of his exhausting search in Alexandria, the two days that he spent watching the embarkation of passengers onto every boat that left the port. His frustration deepened as he told of these things, and Tertullian could see his self reproach. He finally told of his conversation with a dock worker who recognised the description of Marius' party and confirmed that they had boarded a boat bound for Rome two and a half days previously. As he finished his story and related to Tertullian the hopeless feeling that had engulfed him on his journey home, he looked up again and into Tertullian's eyes.

Tertullian was alert. He had been following Origen's story with keen interest. His face was full of understanding and sympathy. "There was nothing you could have done, Origen. You must not chide yourself. You did your best to persuade this Roman, and you failed. That is all".

Origen shook his head. "I've dwelt on this for too long because I haven't known what to do about it. I'm telling you, Tertullian, this Marius is obviously a brave man and he is acting out of conviction. But he will fail. I tried to persuade him of it, and I think that he listened. Something must have happened to change his mind after he left, and I'm sure that it had something to do with Smenkhkare's daughter, who disappeared with them. They were not the kidnapping kind. She would not have disappeared unless she had chosen to. I had him, Tertullian. He was so close to giving it to me. When he told me that he would return the following day, he meant it. But now he is on his way to Rome and he is going to try to blackmail Hadrian. He will be killed and Hadrian will recover the manuscript. Either that or it will be lost forever. If he knows that it's somewhere in the city Hadrian will turn Rome upside down if necessary. Marius will be dead and we will have lost our chance. It's such a waste, Tertullian, and all I've been able to do is to sit on a boat and despair. There is nothing we can do. We could send some people to Rome. If we leave right now we could be there within about a week of Marius' arrival. But what would we do when we got there? How would we find Marius? How could we persuade him? I've met the man and I'm sure that we've missed our opportunity with him. The only thing that I can think of is to try to steal the manuscript from him. But with the whole of the Roman machine also trying to find it I don't like our chances. It would be such a desperate act that I'm not sure it's even worth trying. We could have had Rome by the testicles. We could have shoved them right down their throats".

Origen's voice had a note of bitterness as he finished. His eyes had the wild quality which showed when he was angry. It was times such as these that his old suppressed life came close to surfacing. All he could see was the immense opportunity afforded by this manuscript being lost. His chance of revenge on Rome for the murder of his wife and son lost.

Tertullian regarded Origen critically. He could see the effect that this was having on Origen and knew the violent hatred that simmered beneath his magnetic charisma. He sensed that Origen was in danger of losing his salvation and embarking on a violent orgy of revenge against Rome. If this were to happen, the consequences for the movement were potentially devastating. Origen was the leader. Tertullian knew that he himself would soon be dead and once he was gone there would be no moderating influence.

There was a long silence. Tertullian appeared to have drifted off in his frailty. After some minutes Origen became concerned, and put his hand on Tertullian's shoulder. As he opened his eyes, he spoke.

"There is something that I will tell you, Origen. I have not told you before because I fear for the man of whom I am about to speak". He paused, still apparently unsure. But he did not pause for long.
"There is a debt of honour that is owed to me, owed to me and only me. It is not transferable to you. However, I am alive now so I can call in my debt. I suppose that I needn't call it in personally". Tertullian looked out across the dust bowl, past the sandy wastelands towards the sea.

"When I was a younger man, I visited Rome to learn from our patriarchate there. They were a wonderful and brave group of men. You know why we have our headquarters in this backwater – the danger to the brethren in Rome is too extreme. One of the meetings that I attended took place at the Theatre of Balbus. The keeper of the theatre, Stominius, was one of us. It was a small amphitheatre that could only seat a few hundred. Behind the stage was a large, flat roofed building. In it were several dressing rooms, a living quarter and some storage rooms for seat cushions, costumes, props and so on. It was in this building that Stominius held secret meetings of the patriarchate at night. There were about thirty present at the meeting I attended. All were citizens and most were tradesmen and men of commerce. But there was one man there who was clearly a noble. Even in the inadequate light from the torches, he was a striking figure and totally at home with the rest of us. He had been tutored by a man who was one of us and had been sufficiently interested in what he was taught of Jesu, and sufficiently rebellious to seek to find out more. His tutor had trusted him enough to bring him to a meeting. The man had converted at that meeting, and had been attending them ever since. Because of his position he was only able to attend infrequently. He had to take absurd precautions not to be seen, and often found it necessary to dress up in the clothes of a tradesman. At the time I remember thinking that it was a dangerous ploy, for you only had to look at how he stood and see how he walked to know that he was no tradesman. His posture was impeccable, the way he held his head distinctive to those of the ruling class. At that time he was twenty two years old and already a tribune. He came from a great family and I was told that he was destined for greatness. The small group that met there at the theatre were very excited to have him among them, for they had high hopes that in future years he could influence the empire to moderate their policy towards us".

Tertullian paused and gestured for Origen to give him water. Origen lifted the clay pot and held it to Tertullian's lips. The old man took a few tiny sips before settling back to continue.

"As we were praying near the end of the service, the main door to the living area crashed open. In walked two legionaries with their swords drawn. There was chaos. We were running in all directions, and one of the soldiers grabbed the coat of Stominius as he passed me. He turned wildly and saw me. He held my gaze and gestured his head towards a door and mouthed the word 'trapdoor'".

"I got the message. When I'd attended the theatre in my youth I had seen false floors being used to spirit away the players. Everyone was still running everywhere, putting out the torches and so casting the room into near blackness. In the gloom I saw this important young Roman looking desperately about him. I ran up to him and grabbed his sleeve. He gave a start, and then saw that I was trying to help. He let me bundle him to the door. I could barely see it by now. We blundered through and inside it was black as pitch. I put a chair against the door to block it and told the Roman to begin searching for a trapdoor. We both searched frantically, and before long the Roman gave a hoarse cry. He had found it. As he did, there was a great bang on the door of the storeroom. I got up and hurried to secure it, but as I did the door burst open and a little light entered the room. I knew that the Roman would not have got down into the trapdoor by then, and I also knew that I had no hope to join him. So instead I made a desperate lunge to try to get under the legionary's arm and back into the main room. I knew that I couldn't escape, but I distracted the legionary for long enough to allow the noble to escape. When the legionary turn his attention to the room to search it there was nothing in it at all."

Tertullian leaned back on the cushions and gasped a little for breath. He had become excited by his memory and had leant right forward as he spoke. Origen rearranged the cushions so that he could continue more comfortably.

"The soldiers took me away with the rest. It turned out that we never had a chance of escaping. Outside the building was a whole century. They had completely surrounded the place and each soldier carried a bright torch in one hand and a sword in the other. We were all taken to the prison outside the old rampart of Servius near to the camp of the Imperial guards. I do not know what became of the others because after three days seven of us, the youngest and fittest looking, were taken out of the jail to the forum of Julius. It was a slave market. There were people of all races for sale, but most were young like us. Some were just children, distressed. I was shoved out onto a platform early, and before the auctioneer could even start the proceedings an elderly man shouted out a very good price for me. The auctioneer looked a little put out and requested counter bids. No one wanted to compete with him, so I was led away by this elderly man. He said nothing to me as he handed me a clean robe and waited whilst I put it on, there in the forum. As we left I tried to ask him who he was but he would not say. All he said, and I remember it clear as if it were yesterday, was "I am doing the bidding of another and you will know his identity when it is time". In my state of nerves I was almost convinced that it was the archangel Gabriel who had liberated me. This strange man escorted me to the docks where he put me on a boat. The boat was bound for Sidon and my passage was paid. Once I was on the boat, my benefactor thrust a scroll into my hands and said simply "do not open this until you are out to sea. Farewell."

Origen was beginning to doubt this story. He could not see what it had to do with their predicament and began to wonder whether Tertullian had lost his mind. The old man only had so much energy, and Origen did not want to waste it with rambling reminiscences. In his impatience he had begun fiddling with his hands and looking into the branches of the olive tree above, silhouetted against the darkening sky. Because he was looking up, he did not see Ruth approach with

their food. She had made tomato omelettes and served them with unleavened bread. Tertullian saw Ruth approaching and stopped.
"Do not be impatient, Origen. My story is nearly at an end, and you will like how it ends. But before I finish it I think that we should eat". Origen looked down and saw Ruth. As he took the plate that was offered, Tertullian whispered something to Ruth. She looked sceptically at Tertullian who gave a barely perceptible nod. She turned and hurried back to the house. Tertullian picked at his omelette. By the time he resumed Origen was long finished and gazing up at the stars.

"I waited until we had lost sight of land before I opened the scroll. I was most anxious for an explanation of what had happened to me, and was sure that I had been the recipient of a miraculous intervention. I opened the scroll and read it. Rather than have me tell you the contents I will let you read them for yourself. I have asked Ruth to bring it out to us".

Ruth was returning, bearing an old scroll. The seal was broken, and as she handed it to Tertullian it gaped open at the top. Without a word Tertullian handed the scroll to Origen and he began to read.

"TERTULLIAN,
YOU WILL PROBABLY BE WONDERING ABOUT THE CIRCUMSTANCES OF YOUR FREEDOM. I OWE YOU MY LIFE. BECAUSE OF WHAT YOU DID I INSTRUCTED MY HEAD SLAVE TO PURCHASE YOU AND PUT YOU ON THE BOAT THAT IS RETURNING YOU TO YOUR HOMELAND. HOWEVER, BY RETURNING YOUR FREEDOM I STILL HAVE NOT REPAID MY DEBT. YOUR LIFE WAS NOT TO HAVE BEEN FORFEIT AS MINE SURELY WAS. ALTHOUGH I HAVE IN PART REPAID YOU, I STILL OWE YOU FOR MY LIFE SO I SWEAR THIS TO YOU. IF YOU ARE EVER IN NEED AND IF YOU ASK ME I WILL DO EVERYTHING IN MY POWER TO HELP YOU IN ANY MATTER. THIS IS MY OATH TO YOU. YOURS WITH ETERNAL GRATITUDE".

The letter was unsigned. Origen finished reading and handed the scroll back to Tertullian.

"Who is this man?" he asked
When Tertullian whispered the name, Origen immediately took his leave.

*****

The following day Origen returned to Tertullians' house several hours after dawn. He had wanted to be there earlier but he had spent most of the morning talking with Perridac.

As soon as he had left Tertullian the previous night, Origen had hurried into Sidon to begin searching for the leader of the Ephesian delegation. He had been in luck for he had soon found him in a simple guesthouse near to the docks. The next ship for Ephesus was not sailing for several days yet. He had told Perridac the story of the Neronian confession, of his search for it and it's theft by Marius. Perridac had been sceptical about the incredible story, but Tertullian's reluctance to tell him of Origen's whereabouts persuaded him that it could be true.

In the morning, Origen called back to discuss with Perridac what he hoped to do. Perridac agreed to remain in Sidon and take over the leadership for a short time. He trusted his companions to return to Ephesus and implement the decisions that they had agreed with Tertullian without him.

As Origen and Perridac walked down the dusty track to Tertullian's home they were both in good spirits. They were both excited about their respective plans. Ruth met them at the doorway and wasted no time in laying down the law.
"He was much exhausted by your discussion yesterday, Origen. I will not let it happen again. His death will be hastened by the demands that you are making on him. You must be brief."

Origen thought about arguing, but the thunderous expression on Ruth's face cautioned him against it. He realised how much it was costing her to let him see Tertullian at all.
"Very well" he replied softly.
Ruth pursed her lips and showed Origen and Perridac through the house and into the yard. Tertullian was in his customary position under the olive tree.

"Greetings Tertullian" called Origen as he approached. Tertullian opened his eyes and a rueful smile crossed his lips as he saw that Perridac was with him. Almost imperceptibly he motioned with a limp hand for them to sit.
"I see that Origen does not want to let you escape, Perridac. I feared that he would find you" he said.
Perridac was put out "Feared?" he asked with a note of hostility.
"Yes, feared. Your place is in Ephesus with your people. Your being here leads me to think that Origen has talked you into some other idea".
"Indeed" replied Perridac, "Origen and I have decided that I will stay on here whilst he goes to Rome to retrieve the manuscript of Nero."
Abruptly Tertullian sat up, with surprising vigour. "You will do no such thing" he hissed. "Origen is needed here. You are a good and wise man, Perridac. I do not doubt that. But it would be a great mistake for Origen to go to Rome. He is likely to be recognised, and he would be arrested on sight. It is too risky. We cannot afford to have Origen in a Roman jail or worse, and you cannot afford to stay here indefinitely. I will not have it".
Origen was furious. "You cannot tell us what to do, Tertullian. For God's sake, sometimes I think that you chose not to recognise the importance of the confession. You know as well as the rest of us what it could mean for our people. The end of our suffering, the end of our persecution and the salvation of countless souls across the empire. Why do you seek to obstruct us?"
Perridac shifted in his seat. He was embarrassed to witness a conflict between the two great men.
"I think that you know why, Origen. Do you want me to say it here?"

Origen was too angry to think straight. All he could think of was the prospect of getting his hands on the document, the means to his revenge.
He glared back at Tertullian. "Tell me your reason, whatever it is."
Tertullian resigned himself. "You force me to spell it out to you. You are a great man, Origen, but you bear too much pain. You are full of love for God but sometimes your hatred of Rome clouds you. You desire revenge, which is not the teaching of the lord. You know the words of the Christus that Matthew quotes: "You have heard that it was said, 'Eye for eye and tooth for tooth'. But I tell you, do not resist an evil person. If someone strikes you on the right cheek, turn to him the other also.
Yet you will not accept it. You allow your hatred to burn away at your insides. I would not be surprised if this Marius saw it. If he did it would certainly explain his reluctance to let you have the manuscript"

Tertullian leaned further forward and his eyes blazed as he continued. "You know how I feel, Origen. I too believe that the manuscript can be of great value to us. I too believe that it can be used for the deliverance of many men. But I believe that it can only be for the good if it is used with pure motives. I am not sure of your motives, and that is why you cannot go to Rome. The temptation would be too great for you in that viper's nest. You and I need to use the document together from here, from Sidon, so that we can use it judiciously. It must be used with a cool head and a good heart, not with a hot head and with an eye on revenge".

Perridac was shocked. Origen sat glaring at Tertullian. He was tensed, and looked like he might strike out at the weak old man lying in front of him. Instead he jumped to his feet and stalked across the dusty bowl away from the shade of the olive tree. He walked to the fence at the edge of Tertullian's land and stood there, his hands gripping the wooden struts.

Tertullian and Perridac looked on with concern, and after some moments Origen's body relaxed and his shoulders drooped. He

turned, and walked slowly back to them. He was standing with his head bowed when he spoke, and his voice was quiet and pained.
"You are right, Tertullian. I have constantly to wrestle with my anger. I will stay."

Perridac quickly recovered his composure and when he spoke his voice was loud and strong.
"I will go to Rome. My people can survive for a while without me. I will take a few men and the scroll that Origen told me about, and I will find this Roman who owes you so much, Tertullian".
A look of relief came over Tertullian's waxy features whilst Origen seemed listless. Ruth came out to tell them that their time was up.

The following day a mid sized trading vessel set sail for Rome. On it was Perridac, and with him were the four men that he had personally selected. He had been most grateful to Origen for giving him two of his finest young men, and the other two he knew to be tough and reliable for they were from his own delegation. As the boat cleared the harbour walls, Perridac looked out to the western horizon and felt for the scroll under his tunic. Under his breath he was repeating the name that had dominated his thoughts since he had left Origen to fight his demons.

PART II

ROME

17

Land had been spotted the previous evening. By dawn we were tacking along the coast heading for the mouth of the Tiber and by mid morning we were proceeding up river towards Rome. I cannot really describe our mood at that time. It may sound perverse but I think that we were all glad to be going home. I suppose that we should have been fearful and wary, but we were not. Instead there was almost an atmosphere of celebration among our small group on that boat. Marius and Rani were behaving as newly weds and their happiness was infectious. Marius was convinced that he could conquer the world if he were to so choose and bless us, for we believed him. We had an irrational confidence and a curious sense of family. For most of us this was a new feeling. The closest bonds that any of us had known had been with our fellow soldiers in the army, but this was different. The presence of a woman altered the dynamic, and Rani was superb at balancing our excesses with her feminine sensibilities. On that voyage I think that all of the men, even Greto, fell a little bit in love with Rani. I know that I did. Greto had even seemed cheerful at times. Numba, Tobias, Artorius and Silus had been like puppies with a new toy, and their toy was the blossoming relationship between Marius and Rani. They baited them mercilessly, led inevitably by Numba. I had been expecting sober assessment and planning to dominate our thoughts, but there was none of that. Under the sun of the Mare Nostrum we were at peace, at peace with ourselves and at peace with the world. It was the last peace that most would ever know.

As soon as we began our progress up the Tiber the mood intangibly changed. The clouds had rolled in behind us from the sea. The wide river wound its way through flat, fertile valleys. The small farms on either bank were impeccably kept in front of gentle hills rolling up from the valley floor. These hills were littered with a myriad of grand villas, many enjoying commanding views. From the river, all one could see of most were the landscaped arboriums and the elaborate peristyles so favoured by the rich. The grandeur of the view from the boat and the scale of the villas squatting over the valley served as a salutary reminder to us of the power and the interests that we had come to challenge. A sobriety came over us all as we sat on the deck. This mood did not last long, for presently the boat negotiated a sharp bend in the river and before us was Rome. Imperious, arrogant, grand, massive, intimidating Rome. It was a sight to strike awe into all who ever saw it.

The river ran straight between the rocky façade of the Janiculan Hill on one side and the rump of the Aventine Hill on the other. At the base of the Aventine Hill were the complex wharves and stores that fed Rome with food and drink and all manner of other goods from across her vast empire. The river had been artificially widened at his point to provide the space required for the tens of boats to dock at the wharves. By the stone wharves were vast warehouses, and our ship headed straight for them. As it did so I looked further up river and into the heart of Rome.

We all knew Rome well. We had all lived or been barracked here at various times in the past, but each of us still drew breath at the sight of the place. On the left bank of the river was the Transtiberine Region. This was the "wrong side" of the river and largely consisted of vast, hulking buildings that were used to house the plebs. These were the men and women who did everything from engineer plumbing systems to perform sexual acts so that Rome could be kept in the manner to which she was accustomed. There were nearly one million people living in these terribly cramped monoliths. On every one of their several storeys were clothes hung out to dry from cords suspended between the small windows. At ground level were cavernous archways cluttered by traders selling every commodity and service imaginable. Between the arches at regular intervals were small doorways that led directly up stairs, giving access to the apartments above. Marius had decided that we would find lodgings in the Transtiberine Region. Amongst all those people we could disappear instantly and stay hidden for as long as it might take.

Straight ahead the river curved around to the right and at the top of the curve was the beating heart of the city. The white marble exterior of the baths of Agrippa rose up from behind the theatre of Pompey. To the left one could see the great Pantheon, half obscured by the baths. The Capitoline Hill rose steeply to the right crowned by the centre of imperial bureaucracy, the delicately designed Record Office. The old city walls began at the base of the Aventine hill where the base of the hill met the river and rose steeply up, past the Capena Gate and curving round to the north where they were crossed by the great aqueduct of Claudio. The immense Circus of Maximus and the lavish Palace of Augustus would be visible from there.

The sight was impressive enough for all of us who had seen it before. Rani was simply speechless. As the boat docked at one of the unloading bays I turned to see her, wide eyed and open mouthed as she strained her neck to stare at the heart of the great city.

*****

Despite the familiarity of the sight we were all, I think, struck at that moment by this physical evidence of the vast power that we were about to meddle with. We disembarked quickly, bade farewell to the captain and walked the couple of hundred metres to the jetty where the riverboat men plied their trade. They had small rowing boats which paddled between the east and west banks of the Tiber by the wharves. Their main business was done at dawn and sunset as they ferried the workers from their homes in the Transtiberine Region to their work at the docks and back again. Now that it was close to noon we should have been able to get a good price. As the ferryman launched into a foul mouthed tirade of invective at the price he was offered, I smiled. "Welcome to Rome" I thought. It always was the place with the rudest and most vibrant people on earth and no doubt still is, although I have never been back there since. We were only trying to get to the west bank, but by the length and complexity of the negotiation a bystander could have been forgiven for thinking that we were trying to purchase the boatman's wife, children and livelihood all at once.

It only took us two hours to find lodgings, but it took us the best part of two days of constant walking to get to know our way around that complex, crowded little world of streets, alleys and markets. We had to know it sufficiently well that we could be confident of escaping pursuers, and even after two days we felt that our knowledge was rudimentary. Our lodgings consisted of two rooms on the fourth floor of an immense building, and the rent was astronomical. The men and I slept in the larger room. The other was no bigger than a cupboard, and once a decent sized sleeping roll had been laid out in there it left no room for anything else. I don't think that Rani and Marius were bothered.

Our two days spent finding our way around had been strange. The carefree abandon we had felt on the boat had vanished and was replaced by a quiet introspective professionalism. We barely talked to one another and when we did we spoke of nothing other than practical necessity. On the second evening Marius spoke to us of our mission for the first time since leaving Aegyptus. We were sitting in the large room playing dice while Rani prepared food for us. Marius came over to sit with us.

"We all know what is coming and we all know that there is no point in putting it off. This afternoon I sent word to Decimus Marcellus that I had arrived and would report to the camp of the Imperial Guards at dawn tomorrow morning. When I leave, you, Tolus, will go with Rani to hide the confession. I will leave the exact place up to you, but I had thought somewhere outside the old rampart of Servius behind the Esquiline hill. The area is still wild, and there are many caves and hidden glades that should suit the purpose. Make sure that you can find your hiding place when we come to retrieve the manuscript, make sure that no one sees you do it and be sure to wrap it in the skins before you hide it so that it will remain dry".

Marius looked about the room to ensure that everyone was with him. There was no hint of dissent from the men. They were all looking thoughtfully ahead of them. Marius caught my eye and I nodded my agreement. He continued.

"If I do not return, Tolus will assume command. You will have to decide whether to return the document to Origen or to continue with our original plan. My disappearance should not affect your success in that – indeed it would probably mean that I was suspected of lying to Hadrian, so you would be more likely to be believed. For my part I will be at the mercy of Decimus. I sincerely hope that he will allow me to make my report direct to Hadrian. I'll just have to take it as I find it. Once I have made my report, I will make sure that I am not being followed and will return here. I'm afraid that there is little the rest of you can do except wait here for my return. Are there any questions?"

Marius looked about the room once more. The thoughtful expressions on the men's faces remained. I don't know about anyone else, but I once again had the feeling of encroaching darkness. I didn't like the fact that we were unable to control events. As a Roman soldier I was used to manipulating events and circumstances to suit myself. We all were. Artorius was the one to speak and when he did he gave voice to exactly these concerns.

"I feel the same, Artorius, and I'm sure that we all do. We are not going to be able to exert any control over events at this stage. However, once we have made our approach to Hadrian with the truth and laid down our conditions, we will have control. But for now I will be playing the role of a legionary who is reporting on a special mission that he has performed for the emperor. Part of being a legionary, as we all know, is that our actions are governed by the whims of our overlords. This, I'm afraid, is an unavoidable part of our plan."

There was an atmosphere of disquiet and tension as we went to bed that night.

*****

Rani and I moved off fairly soon after Marius. Neither of us particularly wanted to hang about, and the distraction of our task was welcome. I had the slim leather wallet strapped to my torso under my tunic in the same way that Marius had carried it ever since that moonlit night in the great library of Plotemy I. We quickly dismounted the stone staircases and joined the throng in the streets leading to the larger of Rome's two great bridges. We were swept along in the stream of humanity that each morning pours from the Transtiberine region to the heart of Rome. We passed the Temple of Concord and continued on to the Forum of Augustus. The sound on the streets in the morning was extraordinary. The noisy chatter of literally thousands of workers, each making their way to unknown tasks in the city. Romans were not slow with their opinions, nor were they shy about sharing them with strangers. The throng engaged in witty banter with one another, conversations overheard and joined by complete strangers. At intervals on either side of the road stood great statues of the heros of Rome and Greece. Aristotle, Nero, Plato, Julius Caesar, Augustus and a myriad of other, lesser notables lined the route all the way to the Forum of Augustus. From there Rani and I joined the road to Tibur. It was not long before the great flood of people thinned to become just a trickle, and the tall grand buildings of the centre of Rome soon gave way to large residential domus with roomy gardens and columned peristyles. As we neared the Tivoli gate we entered the slums that had sprung up on the waste ground beneath the old wall. Outside the city walls there were barely any buildings at all. The hills spread out ahead of us, and far to the north we could see the vast, brooding presence of the quadrangular stockade that had served as the camp of the Imperial Guards for nearly three hundred years. Marius should be there by now.

We walked down the straight road into the valley on the other side of the Esquiline Hill. Dotted around the green hills were wild flowers; red poppies and orange honeysuckle, blue campanula and pink dog roses that gave the landscape a tranquil air. Small shrines and temples were the only buildings that could be seen scattered around the hills.

We had barely spoken to each other as we walked through the city. I was tense, and I knew that Rani would be desperately worried about Marius. I did not want to intrude into her thoughts, and it was she who broke the silence.

"I can't stand this, Tolus. I've got no idea whether any of us will see Marius again".
I nodded stupidly.
She looked at me and smiled. She was so beautiful when she smiled, her eyes lighting her whole face and the tip of her pink tongue showing between flawless teeth.
"We're going to worry ourselves to death if we're not careful. Come on, Tolus. Tell me a story or something".
My mind was blank. I was not accustomed to being alone with a beautiful young woman, and I could not think of anything to say. I felt like a halfwit as she looked at me curiously with a half smile on her face.
I stopped and looked into her eyes.
"I can't think of a story" I mumbled, reddening.
"Oh come on, Tolus. You've got to do better than that. Tell me about your childhood, your battles, anything! You've never spoken of your family".
I had never spoken of it because I did not think that anyone would be interested, but I could think of nothing better.
"I was born in Corsica, a small island in the Mare Nostrum off the coast of Gallia and Italia. We are a proud people, but have been ruled from Rome for generations. It's a beautiful island, full of waterfalls, mountains, pretty little ports, sun and sandy beaches. We fish and grow fruit and live in peace. My father and mother worked as labourers on a farm, and I was brought up working in the fields. It was a lovely place, and an idyllic childhood. I was not like Numba. We were never hungry, and the closest thing we saw to fighting was in the taverns of the ports. Really, it is not very interesting".
Rani looked wistful. "It reminds me of my own childhood. Do you have any brothers and sisters?"

"Two brothers and a sister".
I think that she saw the pain in my eyes. "You don't have to tell me" she said quickly.
"No, it's fine. My mother died in childbirth when I was fourteen years old. My second sister died with her before she was even born. My father was devastated, and never really recovered. He withdrew into

himself and rarely spoke. My brothers and I worked the fields to put food on the table, and my sister nursed him. We carried on like that for some years before he died. He just never woke up one morning. But to be honest, it was as if he had died with my mother. After he was gone I became restless. My brothers were happy there in Corsica, enjoying the peace, the good food and wine and the friendships we had. But I wanted to get away and do something with my life. I didn't want to become like my father. So I jumped on a ship to Rome and enlisted".

I looked at Rani. To my surprise she had tears in her eyes. I looked at her quizzically, wondering what I could have said to make her cry. She smiled back at me through the tears.

"Sorry, you must ignore me, Tolus. I am lucky to still have two healthy parents who love me and love each other. It's just that your story reminds me of my husband. He was a good man, a farmer like your father. He loved me more than I deserved, but I never loved him like your father must have loved your mother. I was sorry when he died, and I did love him. But it was not the end of my world. I sometimes feel guilty for that".

"But it's totally different. My father was old when my mother died. He had lived most of his life with her. You are still young, and you only had a short time with your husband. You must not reproach yourself".

Rani stopped walking and embraced me. I was embarrassed, and awkward with her. When we parted the smile had returned to her face. I lowered my eyes, blushing once more, and resumed walking.

An hour after leaving the old rampart we left the road and headed up a hill through a wild meadow. Once we were well out of sight of the road we descended into a small vale with a derelict shrine decaying by a stream. It must have been very old, for the moss and ivy grew so thick that the stones were barely discernible.

Rani slowed her pace and I looked across at her. Our eyes met and we came to a halt by the ancient shrine. It was no bigger than the room that Rani and Marius shared in our lodgings. The roof was not even the height of a man and had partially fallen in, leaving moss covered rubble on the floor. We both removed our sandals, and stooped as we entered. It immediately became clear that we could not remove any of the stones without disturbing the moss and ivy. We left the shrine and outside I asked Rani to keep watch. When we were both sure that there was no one within sight of us I fell to my knees on the soft turf. I drew my dagger, carefully cut a deep square in the grass and levered up the square of turf to remove the soil beneath. Before I lay the pouch in the hole I lifted the flap to double check that the manuscript inside was still safely wrapped in the skins that Marius had given to Rani. Once I had finished, I fluffed up the grass at the fringes. The line where the turf had been replaced could not be discerned. Before we moved off I made a mental note of the exact position of the buried pouch. As we left we were careful to keep an eye out for anyone who may have seen us. We had not seen anyone since leaving the road, not even a shepherd.

We did not hurry back for knew that it was unlikely that Marius would beat us back to our lodgings. Neither of us cherished the prospect of sitting around looking at four walls, and it was mid afternoon by the time we returned. The rest of the men were making a brave effort to concentrate on a game of dice. The dice had improved since Alaric's death, but on this occasion it was clear that none of them was interested. Rani and I were able to distract them and ourselves with a detailed description of our morning and the location of the manuscript. By the end of it we were confident that they would be able to find it without Rani or myself to help. When we finished our story there was silence. No one was much disposed to talk so we each sat and disappeared into our own thoughts. It seemed like we were there forever. As the sun went down I became apprehensive. An hour later I was seriously worried. Finally Rani broke the silence.
"I can't stand it any more. Something must have happened to him. He's been gone more than twelve hours. What can possibly keep him that long? I'm . . . ." She wanted to do something, but there was nothing to do. She stood up and went to the cooking area and began to prepare something for us to eat. None of us was hungry and I don't suppose that Rani cared. She was preparing food more for something to occupy her mind than because she felt the need to feed us.

*****

The Prefect of the Camp of the Imperial Guards had been waiting for Marius at the main gate. As soon as Marius identified himself he was treated with the greatest of deference and respect. The Prefect personally escorted him on a glistening chariot down the Via Quirinal. People dashed for cover as the huge horses cantered through the streets. To Marius' surprise they stopped some distance short of the junction with the Flaminian Way and dismounted. From there the two of them proceeded on foot through the back streets before coming to an inauspicious doorway in a high wall on an alley occupied by groups of fruit sellers. The Prefect knocked once on the door and it opened instantly from the inside. The two men walked through, past storerooms and outhouses and through an inner wall into the most exquisite gardens. Marius was led through an enormous archway and into a luxurious reception room whose floor was covered by the most arresting mosaic that he had ever seen. The Prefect disappeared and Marius was left standing in front of four men. He immediately recognised Hadrian from the busts that stood proudly throughout the empire. Abruptly he fell to his knees and was told to rise. Hadrian introduced the other three men - Alexander Grenolian Brutus, Senator Lucius Merutii Scripius and Decimus Marcellus. There were no pleasantries.

"Do you have the document, Marius Sextus?" asked Hadrian
"I do, sir"
"Let's have it, then" he snapped.
Marius pulled the pouch out from his tunic. Carefully he put it into Hadrian's outstretched hand.
He watched as the emperor examined it.
Hadrian's eyes narrowed. "There is no seal"
"No sir. That is as we found it."
Hadrian looked at Marius for a long moment, making him feel as though his legs might give way. He put his hand into the old leather pouch and withdrew the manuscript, trying to unravel it. As he did so some clumps of fell off. He stared at the rotted mulch, turning it around with wide eyes and an expression of incredulity.

Hadrian looked as though he might explode. Instead he threw back his head and roared with laughter.

He handed the dried-out mould that was all that was left of the papyrus to Lucius Merutii Scripius who looked at both sides before passing it on, grim faced, to Alexander Grenolian Brutus. He too examined it before passing it to Decimus Marcellus.

Marius just stood there. There was an uncomfortable silence as Hadrian finished guffawing and refocused his attention on the others in the room. Seeing the expressions round the room, Marius was convinced that he was a dead man. He stared straight ahead, pretending to be oblivious like any soldier would. Decimus Marcellus looked at him with something close to a sneer and said:

"I think that you ought to explain to us how you came upon this piece of excrement and why on earth you think that you should not be killed for bringing it into the presence of the emperor of Rome!" His voice had risen to a shout of indignation.

Lucius and Alexander just looked at him with raised eyebrows, as if to say that Decimus had voiced their thoughts precisely. Marius knew that his reply would determine whether he was to live or die. So he began, simply and factually, to tell them of his mission from when he left Sidon on the trail of David the Smith. He sketched over the early events until he reached the story of his encounter with Smenkhkare. He was careful to falsify the names of Rani's family, and told them that the Aegyptusis family resided in Misr. Other than that he told the truth.

Marius had always been an accomplished liar. Some of the stories of his pranks as a young soldier had become folklore. He had become well practised in explaining the inexplicable to his commanding officers, spinning yarns that were so convincingly rendered that cynical men used to the writhing of frightened subordinates were frequently fooled. Marius had been practising his story continually since leaving Alexandria, and when he finally came to tell it he was utterly convincing.

He spoke of the trip to the library in Alexandria and the retrieval of the document. He added a few crucial details. He spoke of how the wooden supports underneath the stone with the fish engraving had at some time in the past become rotten. He described a strange, dried up fungal growth that had covered the pouch that Decimus still held, a fungus that had been rubbed off during the journey to Rome. The penny dropped with them all at that point. They each came to the conclusion that Marius had been relying on. They came to the conclusion that the chamber had at some point been flooded. Marius brought the story up to the present, but his audience were not really listening. They were trying to recall whether they had ever heard news of a flood in Alexandria.

When he had finished there was an uncomfortable silence in the room. Marius retained his composure throughout the meeting. He appeared completely calm and had spoken with the conviction and consistency of the truthful. But he was struggling to maintain it. From the sceptical looks that he was getting from all of the men in the room, he felt sure that he was about to be challenged by these suspicious men accustomed to the lies and dishonesty of the influential.
Instead it was Lucius who spoke. He cursed himself for not remembering it sooner and berated himself for not realising that if the manuscript had been stored in Alexandria then there was a good chance that it would have been destroyed. He spoke of Alexandria's great flood in the thirteenth year of the reign of the Emperor Vespasian. There had been a great shuddering of the earth in the Mare Nostrum that year, a shuddering that had sent great waves crashing over the port walls and into the streets of the great city. The whole city had been submerged under a swords depth of water before the waves subsided back into the sea.

Marius had never heard of the flood. Vespasian had died before he was born. He mentally calculated that Lucius would have been a teenager when the flood occurred. But from Lucius' words he did learn that Lucius had never been to Alexandria. If he had, he would have known that the great library of Plotemy I was built on high ground with a commanding view of the harbour. Even a flood of the scale that Lucius described could never have reached the library.

Lucius' intervention was decisive. Hadrian suddenly lost interest. Decimus and Alexander too were reassured by the news of a flood. As they had nothing more to ask him, Marius was taken to a small bare cell in one of the outhouses behind the walled garden. It was part of the servants quarters, and next to a dormitory where the slaves slept. He was ordered to wait there in case the emperor had further need to talk to him. He waited for what seemed an age. Finally an orderly appeared and told him that he could leave, and that he was ordered to report to the camp of the imperial guards an hour after dawn tomorrow. When he left it was already dusk.

*****

I was beginning to lose hope when Marius walked through the door. He had been gone for the whole day and looked utterly drained. Rani ran to embrace him. He slumped into her, and she had to bear most of his weight. The rest of us looked on a little embarrassed. When they separated she looked straight at him.
"They believed you?"
"I'm not sure, but I think so" he replied.
There was an almost audible easing of tension. We all sat down to listen to Marius tell us what had happened. It was clear that he was exhausted by the strains of the day but he was also excited. He exuded a sort of staccato nervous energy. As he told us of his experience with the most powerful men of Rome his manner alternated between excitement and fatigue. One minute he was speaking so fast he began to trip over his words and the next his mind seemed so lethargic that he barely had the energy to form the words for the next sentence. It was in this strange way that we heard of Marius' first encounter with the people who would ultimately determine our fate.

Looking back now I realise how naïve we were, but at that time we did not know of the workings of Rome. We were ignorant of the duplicity that is a way of life for the powerful. We all went to bed in blissful ignorance of the danger we were in. We were far from relaxed but our belief that the first encounter of our plan had gone smoothly was of comfort to us. None of us saw any reason for alarm in the order for Marius to report to the camp of the Imperial Guards. Marius was a soldier who had just completed a mission, and it was natural that he should receive further orders now that his mission was over. We would not have slept so well had we known that as we did so we were being watched.

*****

The following morning Marius left just before dawn. The rest of us barely stirred as we heard him leave. He walked down the corridor outside our rooms and down the public staircase to street level. The street was already heaving with the tidal movement of people leaving their abodes to go to work in the city. Marius' head was still heavy with sleep as he joined the throng. He had not gone far when he felt a blow to his head. His last conscious thought was that his skull had been cleaved in two. Then everything was black.

18

Creta is a mountainous island in the Mare Nostrum that lies across the southern end of the Mare Aegius. The island had been spotted just before sunset the previous day. Perridac and his men were relieved, for they were not good sailors. The five of them disembarked in the early hours at the chaotic port of Salmone at the far eastern end of the island. It was a beautifully appointed place. The mountains rose steeply behind the port. The town was built in a natural amphitheatre facing east around the wide natural harbour. The houses of the town were dramatically situated on the steep slopes of this amphitheatre. Had the houses not been so ramshackle the place could have been imposing. As it was it just looked dirty and gave the impression that it might at any moment fall down the hills into the sea. Even the fortress on the south side of the bay was in poor repair. Salmone had certainly seen better days.

The captain of the vessel had told them that they would be in port for two days. He was taking on more cargo and had yet to purchase it. There was a large market in the forum each day where goods from all over the empire were traded in bulk. Salmone had derived its wealth from this market, but for the last fifty or more years the traders had increasingly preferred to use Rhodus as the clearing house for their high volume trade. Creta had been sidelined, but the captain still came because there were often bargains to be had from desperate traders in urgent need of cash, and rare cargoes were easier to find here since there were fewer sharp traders with their eyes out for unusually profitable goods.

Perridac was frustrated when the captain told them to report back to the ship an hour or two before sunrise in three days time to catch the tide. He knew that time was tight if they were to get to Tertullian's contact in time to stop Marius. He looked to his men and knew that they would feel the same as him about the prospect of kicking their heels on this island. Of the four men that were with him he knew two well. Beziac and Radjic had come with him from Ephesus to see Tertullian. They had come to represent the churches of the Lycus Valley in the province of Lydia. These churches had been established by Paul the apostle during his correspondence with the Corinthians. The christian community had been enthusiastic in that area, and their success was blamed by local traders for helping to destroy their lucrative trade in votive figurines and cult objects devoted to the worship of the goddess Diana. They had subjected the local Christians to the Ephesia grammata, a kind of magic formula that was supposed to lay waste to the enemies of Diana. When it had failed there had been riots. Both Beziac and Radjic had fought to defend their people and their churches. There had been much bloodshed and the losses on both sides were terrible. They had both seen death, and had inflicted more than their fair share. Neither had any family left save that of the church, so their commitment was complete and their bravery beyond question.

Perridac had never met the other two men before they had boarded the boat at Sidon. They were members of Origen's church and trusted lieutenants in his inner circle. One was Benjamin, a fisherman from Sidon. Origen had explained that Benjamin had recently lost his brother. The manner of his brother's death gave Benjamin a special interest in this mission, for his brother had been a smith named David. The other man was named Gideon, a close friend of Benjamin. Origen had assured Perridac that both could be trusted with a secret and with a sword. It was not long before these assurances were put to the test.

The five men had not disembarked when the ship docked in the silent hours before dawn. Instead they slept on deck in the same way that they had since the ship had left the coast of Ituraea. They would stay on the boat for the nights that they were in port. Soon after sunrise Perridac decided that he wanted to greet the leaders of the church in Creta, so the five men left the docks to seek them out. As they walked into town they looked for the secret symbol that Christians had began to adopt everywhere. They searched for the sign of the fish. The waterfront inns showed no sign. The men walked up the hill further into town. The road zigzagged up the hill, lined by houses made of local stone that was so ill fitted it gave the impression that the houses might fall apart at any moment. The views were stunning, with the early morning sun still low above the sea. Still they saw no fish motifs, something that Perridac found strange given the island's reputation of having a flourishing christian community. As they rounded a corner on the outskirts of the town Benjamin noticed a tiny fish engraved into the doorpost of a large wooden house. Perridac approached the door and knocked. The servant who answered summoned his master. The owner's manner was abrupt as he asked them what they wanted. Perridac explained who they were and that they wished to meet local Christians to exchange news. The man quickly gestured them inside and hurriedly closed the door behind them.

Inside was a large shady room with a kilim on the floor and cushions strewn across it. For some reason their host seemed nervous as he sat them down and called for refreshments. He was a man of about fifty years old and his belly revealed him to be a man of considerable prosperity. He introduced himself as Javan and explained that he was a merchant. Perridac introduced his companions and asked how things fared with his brothers in Salmone. Javan's look of anxiety intensified.

"We are most concerned. We have been having trouble for some months now in Creta. It always used to be the most peaceful and relaxed of places. But now we find that we are frequently threatened. Things began to go wrong two years ago when a new governor was appointed. His name is Albinus Florus. Almost as soon as he arrived he began a spiteful campaign to offend us".

Javan paused to brush a fly away from his closely trimmed beard. "Over the years, our religion has become a strong part of the life of Creta. The new governor deliberately stirred up long standing resentment towards us for the devastating effect that the good news has had on the local cults. The priests of these cults have participated in this campaign enthusiastically and just yesterday things boiled over. You will forgive me for the manner in which I greeted you. It is because I am afraid. You may have noticed that most of the Christians in Salmone have removed the sign of the fish from their homes. Things have become so bad that we fear for our safety".

In some ways, it would have been easy for Perridac and his men to commiserate with their well-groomed host and forget about it. But what he spoke of was a common problem and each of them had personal experience of the sort of ordeal that Javan was talking about. They listened intently as he continued.

"Things reached a head yesterday. I don't know if you are familiar with the story of the founding of our church here in Creta?" He looked around. Each of the men looked blank and shook their heads.

"During the time of the Christus, Creta was divided into many city states. They were constantly squabbling amongst themselves. Many of the feuds went back generations. Almost a generation after the crucifixion of Jesu the Romans arrived. They had decided that it was time to subjugate the feuding city princes of Creta. With the Romans arrived a man named Tolus. He established a brotherhood of the followers of the Christus. They flourished and made Creta a stronghold of the new religion".

Javan's face relaxed as he told them the familiar history of his town. He was clearly proud of its close association with one of the most august of Jesu's friends. He continued.

"Paul the apostle came to visit Tolus. His ship sailed straight past Salmone and put into a port in the centre of the south coast of the island called Fair Havens, near to Lasea. Paul wanted to winter there but he was overruled. So the ship set out to find a better wintering berth at Phenice in the south west of the island. A heavy wind sprang up and blew the ship out to sea. It finally landed in Malta. Paul was frustrated by his failure to visit Creta and determined that he would return. It was many years before he was able to, for Paul was arrested and imprisoned in Rome. Upon his release the first place that the old man visited was Creta. It was also the last. Legend has it that Paul died in Salmone. He is buried in the hills behind the town, not ten minutes walk from here. His grave has become a shrine that is oft visited by both the local community and by pilgrims who pass through the port".

Javan looked round to make sure that he still had the attention of his visitors. He needn't have done for they were straining forward to be sure that they heard every word. This was just the kind of story that they loved. As he continued his brow furrowed with concern.

"Yesterday the trouble that had been simmering with the leaders of the local cults boiled over. Yishdron, the most powerful of the cultic leaders gathered his followers and went up to the shrine. There were several hundred of them. When they got there they found a few Christians praying. They fell on them and literally tore them apart, limb from limb. Two or three got away and came screaming into town. I heard them pass the house but did not go out to see who they were. When they got to town and told their story a group of brethren armed themselves and climbed the hill to the shrine. By the time they got there, Yishdron's horde had disappeared. But they found the evidence of the most sickening desecration. The horde had entered the small shrine and conducted strange rituals there. Animals had been sacrificed on the stone that covered Paul's tomb. Some are even saying that they sacrificed a live child there. Worse, they removed the stone and defecated in the tomb over Paul's bones. But worst of all, Paul's skull is gone".

Whilst Javan was clearly afraid, Perridac was angry. This kind of desecration was a familiar occurrence that seemed to be happening more and more.

Presently their conversation moved to other matters. They exchanged news of their respective churches. They spoke of Origen and Tertullian, of the progress of Tertullian's "Word of God" and of their views about their prospects for the future. It was about lunchtime that Perridac and his men left Javan. They left with an invitation to dinner that night. They were to return just before sunset. As they walked off down the street Javan looked at them. The anxious look had returned to his face as he spoke his parting words. "Be on your guard".

Perridac and the others walked down the hill towards the harbour. They had a vague plan that they might go to the smaller town forum to buy some bread for lunch before returning to the boat to sleep through the hot hours of the afternoon. As they sauntered down the hill large numbers of mainly women and children hurried past them, moving up the hill. Neither Perridac nor the others paid too much attention until a man stopped to address them as he hurried past.

"Get out of town" he said. "The Christians have gone to the house of Yishdron and are demanding the return of their relic. There is going to be trouble". With that he hurried off.

Perridac moved to the side of the street to get out of the way of the increasing flow of townsfolk who were heading up the hill. He gave his men an enquiring look. He knew what they must do but did not know whether his men would agree.

"We must keep our heads down and stay out of trouble" he said "Let us follow the townsfolk up the hill".

Benjamin's blood was up. He was incensed by the story he had heard about the abuses that his Cretan brothers were suffering.

"I say that our brethren need us!" he said, a little too loudly. "I don't know about you, but I will not stand by and let my brothers be insulted in this way. I am going to help them. Who's coming?"

"You will do no such thing", replied Perridac sternly. "Origen placed you under my command. Our journey to Rome is too important to risk our lives here. I understand your feelings, Benjamin, but we must get to Rome and cannot risk anything that might prevent us from getting there. We are going up the hill".

Both Beziac and Radjic nodded and moved to stand beside Perridac. Benjamin truculently folded his arms and made it plain that he would not go. All eyes turned to Gideon. He looked uncomfortable.

"I am with Benjamin," he said softly. "I will not stand back when our brothers need us."

With that, Benjamin and Gideon strode on down the hill, leaving Perridac and the Lydians watching them. Perridac was furious but there was little he could do about it. He gestured for the other two to follow him up the hill.

As Benjamin and Gideon got closer to the centre of town the situation became more and more confused. Instead of people hurrying to get away up the hill it seemed that people were running in all directions. They passed a house that was on fire. It was a stone house but the straw roof had caught and the flames leapt high against the deep blue of the sky. The heat of the day was at its most intense and as they continued into town they noticed the crazed look in people's eyes. Benjamin looked at Gideon and they both drew their swords from underneath their tunics. They had both recognised the evil in the streets that day, from Lydia. An ancient hatred, pent up for generations was being released.

Benjamin and Gideon rounded a corner into the forum. What they saw infuriated them. A group of men, armed with clubs, stones and ancient weapons were clustered around a large house on the western side of the forum. There were about one hundred of them. On the south side of the square were about two full centuries of legionaries. They were all armed but were at ease as they casually watched the drama that was unfolding in front of them. They gave the impression that they were finding the whole thing rather amusing. On the roof of the house were several men. At the front was a man dressed in a long tattered red robe that reached his feet. He held in his hand a crooked staff and on the end of the staff sat a skull. It was Yishdron and he was taunting the Christians who had gathered outside his door. As Benjamin and Gideon watched, Yishdron bent down and picked up what looked like an old garment of some kind. It was pale, ragged and floppy, and it was clearly heavy. Two men came forward to help him as he lifted it. As they spread it out the crowd recoiled in horror. The inside of the garment was dark red, almost black. There was no doubt that it was dried blood, and the garment was in fact the skin of a human. Yishdron had skinned the small girl that he had sacrificed the previous day on the grave of Paul. Helped by his cohorts he draped the skin over his staff below the skull in a sickening reconstruction of a person. Yishdron then began to dance with the gory effigy. The skin flopped about heavily on the staff. It was too much for the watching group. With a great shout they moved forward to the door of the house. As they did so four men shuffled forward on the roof. They carried two long wooden beams, a man at each end of each beam. Between the beams was strapped a large cauldron. As the Christians surged forward to the door of the house the cauldron was tipped over them from above. The screams began as the people below watched their skin melt away when the scalding oil splashed onto it. Benjamin and Gideon stood horrified and powerless. There was a great shout from behind them. They turned to see a group of perhaps one hundred Cretans charging towards them. Benjamin and Gideon quickly got out of the way to avoid being trampled by the horde. The Cretans fell on the Christians, taking them by surprise. Few of them had heard the shouts of their attackers, as they were too busy ministering to those who had been burned by the oil. At least fifteen Christians died of wounds to their backs before they even realised what was going on. The sun was burning down and it seemed to increase people's fury. The sight of the slaughter was too much for Benjamin and Gideon. Both charged at the rear of the Cretans. At first it was easy. They were brutal as they relentlessly hacked at the exposed backs of the pagans. They had each killed two or three before they encountered any resistance at all. A few Cretans turned to see what the commotion behind them was and when they did they saw Gideon and Benjamin swinging their weapons in a grim display of lethal sword work. Gideon and Benjamin quickly became separated. Before long they were becoming surrounded. They continued to fight, but as they did so they stepped backwards. Soon it became apparent that the Christians outside the door of Yishrac's house had fled. Most pagans had followed them, but some had turned to see what was going on behind. Benjamin and Gideon realised that it was hopeless. Just as they turned to flee the Roman soldiers decided to intervene. They had thoroughly enjoyed their afternoon's entertainment but one of the centurians had decided that it was time to bring order back to the forum. No doubt his afternoon siesta could wait no longer. Benjamin and Gideon turned and ran. Gideon was grabbed by one of the soldiers. Benjamin was barely aware of it as he retreated up the hill. At first he was closely followed by a few of the pagans, so he carried on running. It did not take long before he lost his pursuers in the crushing heat of the mid afternoon and was able to slow to a walk. There was no sign of Gideon.

Once he was out of town Benjamin sat down to rest. Small groups of people sat on the rocks and scree and the small patches of coarse grass

of the hillside, and they stared at Benjamin's blood stained tunic. He had a raging thirst. Just as he was about to return to town to find a well he saw Perridac and the other two men. He approached them with head bowed and stood in front of Perridac. As he lifted his head they saw the tears running down his face.
"I owe you an apology, Perridac. You were right. We should never have intervened" he said.
"Where is Gideon?" asked Perridac.
"I don't know. I lost him in the confusion, but I think that he might have been arrested by the soldiers".
Perridac sighed. "You will obey me from now on?" he asked.
Benjamin nodded as he looked at the ground.

They remained up on the hill for the rest of the day. Beziac had a skin with plenty of water, and no one wanted to go near the town until things had returned to some semblance of normality. Just before sunset they walked back down the hill towards Javan's house. By the time they reached it a fire was burning itself out. The house was now just a smoking ruin with a few small flames lapping at the edges. There was no sign of Javan. Disconsolate the four men returned to their boat to await news of Gideon.

*****

That night Yishdron's house was broken into, and his throat was cut as he slept. No one stirred as Benjamin silently returned to his place on the deck in the silent hours before dawn.

There was no word of Gideon. Benjamin wanted to visit the jail but Perridac would not hear of it. People visiting jails were often arrested and Perridac would not risk losing a second man. In truth everyone knew that there was nothing that they could do for Gideon. His fate would be decided by the Romans and there would be no opportunity to plead on his behalf.

Although they had no word of Gideon they did hear of Javan. Rumour had it that he had been burned alive in his house. He had refused to leave when he had been told of the approaching horde. It was said that he died as he knelt on his kilim and prayed for deliverance.

The following day was surprisingly peaceful. Both communities had suffered greatly, one with disfiguring burns and twenty dead, the other with the loss of twelve people - eight of whom had been killed at the hands of Benjamin and Gideon - as well as the mysterious murder of their leader in the middle of the night. The result was a sort of dumb shock, an atmosphere of quiet emptiness.

By the afternoon that they were to catch the tide there had still been no word of Gideon. Benjamin decided to slip away and go to the jail. As he made to step onto the jetty he felt a hand on his shoulder. It was Radjic.

"You are a good man, brother. We will need you in Rome" he said gently.

"I cannot just abandon Gideon. I must try to get him out" replied Benjamin desperately

"Would Gideon want you to take that risk?" replied Radjic.

Benjamin thought. "No. He would want me to be on this boat tonight".

Radjic then looked Benjamin squarely in the eyes and smiled sympathetically. "Do not think that we do not understand the courage that it will take for you to leave Gideon here."

When the ship cast off from Salmone, Benjamin was with Perridac, Beziac and Radjic.

Gideon was left to the mercy of the Romans.

19

Marius had no idea how long he was unconscious for. His first conscious thought was the vague awareness of a faint light. He was lying on something soft and was just about to feel what it might be when he was struck by what felt like a thunderbolt between the eyes. It seemed to pierce through the top of his head and settle behind his forehead. It banished all other thoughts. Marius lay there enduring the pain until it subsided a little. The light was becoming stronger and as it did so he noticed that it was coming through a tiny slit in the wall. He tried to sit up and was struck once more by the agonising shot of pain, this time from right behind his eyes. He lay back and closed his eyes. He remained like that for several minutes in complete silence. After a while he decided to try to sit up again and as he did so he felt a sudden nausea. As he leaned across to the side of the bed he noisily retched and threw up. He noticed the spotless, beautifully fitted sandstone floor before his vomit splashed across it. Almost immediately he felt better. He sat up and looked around. There was just enough light coming in through the slit in the wall to make out that he was in a tiny cell. There was no furniture at all. He had been put on a feather bed roll that lay on the floor. The slit looked out across a gap onto a wall, so he had no way of getting his bearings and working out where he was. In the corner was a small bowl of fruit, some dry bread and a large flagon of water. His captors evidently had no intention of allowing Marius to die of thirst or hunger. He knew that this wasn't necessarily a good sign.

Marius lay back and tried to remember what had happened to him. He could clearly remember leaving the lodgings in the Transtiberine and walking down the street, but nothing after that. He had no idea who had abducted him or where he was. He began to replay the meeting at Hadrian's villa to himself. He had felt that it had gone well at the time. He thought himself to be a good judge of how people were reacting to him, and felt sure that he had been believed. As he thought

about it, a feeling developed that perhaps there had been something not quite right. He began to try to retrieve the thought but was interrupted by footsteps in the corridor. The footsteps stopped outside his door and a hard voice spoke. He could hear it clearly through the heavy wooden door.
"You are going to be blindfolded and your hands are going to be tied. You have two choices. You can turn your back and submit to this, or we can compel you. Will you submit?"
Marius replied immediately. "I will submit".
"Turn your back and put your face up against the wall. Spread your arms and your feet against the wall" said the voice.
Marius complied. He felt giddy as he got to his feet, but he managed it. He heard the cell door swing open and felt a blindfold being wrapped over his eyes and over his head. He then felt strong hands grab each of his wrists and pull them together behind his back. They were bound tightly but not brutally. The man behind him checked the blindfold and the bindings on his hands and then spoke again.
"I am going to lead you from this cell to another room. Do not resist". Marius had no intention of resisting. He believed that he would die here but resistance at this point would have been futile. He wasn't even especially curious to find out who had abducted him because he was sure that he knew. It had to be Hadrian.

*****

Marius was led down a corridor before turning sharply to the left. He was led a few more paces before he was abruptly stopped. The voice then told him that he was standing in front of a chair and that he was to sit down. He gingerly bent his knees and felt the wooden seat touch his backside. He sat back into the chair. He heard the man who had led him in leave the room and close the door behind him. Marius thought that he was alone in the room, so when a deep rich voice spoke he jumped.

There was a quality about that voice. It could have been reciting a shopping list and yet Marius felt sure that he would have been hanging on its every word. The rhythm with which it talked, the lyricism of the diction and the stature that it conferred onto its subject matter had a resonant beauty. What the voice spoke of was Marius himself. In it's unique manner the voice laid out the story of Marius' journey from Ituraea to Aegyptus.

Nothing in the story particularly surprised Marius. It contained the same detail that he had relayed in the meeting at Hadrian's villa. The man who was speaking had either been present at that meeting, had overheard or had been told second hand. Despite himself Marius was enjoying the way that this wonderful voice recited his story. However as it got to the library at Alexandria the story suddenly deviated from the version that Marius had given to Hadrian and his cronies. As it did so, the voice hardened. It revealed a granite intensity, a harsh intimidation that was completely at odds with the resonance of before. What the voice said sent a shock wave right through him.

"When you found the manuscript it was intact. There had been no flood. It was in perfect condition".

Abruptly, the voice stopped. It had spoken with a certainty that confused Marius. He was disorientated, and the waves of nausea that swept over him made him reluctant to open his mouth.

The silence was broken by the screech of chair legs on the sandstone floor. His interrogator was standing. The nausea swelled and once more Marius leaned forward and retched. Little vomit came out, but his torso convulsed uncontrollably. Marius heard steps approach him. He braced himself for the blow that would surely come. Instead, he felt the chill of cold iron as it rested against the back of his neck.

The hard voice spoke so close that he could feel the hot breath on his ear. "Why did you steal the manuscript, Marius Sextus?"

Marius had to bite his lip to remain silent. His head was throbbing and he knew that he was weak. He had failed before he had even started with his plan, and he was ashamed. But he said nothing, waiting for the sword to finish it for him.

Casually the sword ran across the back of Marius' neck. It was sharp, and Marius could feel the blade slice through his skin. Blood oozed out and warmed his back as it trickled down. It was a curious sensation - the silence, the blood, the nausea and the sound of breathing close by. Marius got the impression that he was being sized up, but still he said nothing.

Eventually the stillness was broken. When it was the voice came from the other side of the room. Marius must have lost consciousness for a few moments for he had not heard his interrogator cross the room.

"Your silence implies guilt. If you do not respond to me you will be killed".
There was a pause. Still Marius did not say anything.
The voice resumed, and when it did so it began to recount Marius' story from the moment that the confession of Nero had been found, intact, in the library of Plotemy I in Alexandria. From the description of the library it was almost as if the voice had been there with Marius. It went on to describe Marius' growing concerns about his mission as he spent time with the followers of the Christus. It talked of his disquiet when he had been told of the contents of the manuscript. It talked of his dilemma as to what he should do. And it talked of his decision to read the manuscript for himself.
As the voice concluded its story, it hardened once more.
"The confession could never have been destroyed by a flood, Marius. I know that it is intact and I know that you have it".

Marius was trying to get his brain to work. He was so shocked that it was an effort to have any rational thoughts at all. How could this man know all this? He was vaguely aware that there was something that he was missing. He fought to impress this logic onto his confusion. But he was also aware that any more silence from him would be met by violence. As the steps once more came towards him the mists began to clear in his mind.

Marius saw the only possible explanation, and it was too terrible to contemplate. After he had been abducted on the street, his assailants

must have gone to their lodgings in Transtiberine and abducted his men. And Rani. One of them must have broken down in the face of whatever pressure had been applied.
Through the fog of pain, Marius knew at that moment that it was all over for him. He saw then that his plan had been naïve and stupid. A feeling of self-disgust began to overtake him when the voice interrupted his thoughts. It was speaking very slowly and very loudly, as if repeating something to a foreigner or a child.
"I ask you again. Do . .you. . acknowledge . .what . . I . . say . .to . . be . true?"
Marius knew that he had no choice and knew that he was lost. His answer was a desperate shout of bitterness and despair.

The footsteps came towards him. Suddenly he felt a hand in the hair above his ear and the blindfold was grabbed. It was whipped off and Marius instinctively closed his eyes to protect them from the sudden glare of the room. The man was now untying his hands. Marius dully supposed that this would herald the beginning of the torture that would try to force him to reveal the whereabouts of the manuscript. He was frantic with worry for Rani. At that moment he would have told them anything that they wanted to hear in exchange for her life.
His hands were free, and he lifted them to rub his eyes. The footsteps returned towards the other end of the room. Slowly Marius opened his eyes. It took several minutes for them to adjust fully to the light. As he opened them a little, he found himself squinting down at a long wooden table. On it, directly in front of him, sat a papyrus and a stylus.
"They want a written confession" thought Marius dully.
He raised his head and looked down the table. At the other end, reclining in his seat and inspecting his finger nails sat Senator Lucius Merutii Scripius

*****

Marius was not in the least bit surprised. No doubt the unscrupulous old jackal wanted to get hold of the document himself so that he would have a hold over Hadrian. Maybe he was just Hadrian's hatchet man. Marius sullenly looked away from Lucius and fixed his gaze on the corner of the beautifully proportioned basement room.

Lucius spoke quietly.
"The first thing that I want you to do is to write a note to your men to tell them that you are safe and will return presently to them. Instruct them not to leave their rooms for any reason at all until you return."
Marius looked up lazily. "What for?" he asked dully.
And then his brain began to work. If his men were still in their lodgings and had been unharmed, then Rani might be all right. His brain began once more to race. If his men were still in their lodgings in Transtiberine, they had not been abducted and questioned. How then did Lucius know all that he had just related to Marius? The lack of a rational explanation made his thoughts spin. He became distressed and wrote the note in agitation.

Marius was a hard man. Not only did he have a remarkably quick mind, he was a man whose bravery and skill on the battlefield was truly second to none. But at that moment he came close to breaking. The confusion, the uncertainty, the surprise of Lucius' simple request disorientated him. It went against all logic. He felt completely out of his depth. Lucius had displayed knowledge that was impossible and followed it up with a request that was completely inexplicable for an enemy. A severe knock to the head and frantic worry for Rani meant that all Marius could see were the demons that he had unleashed. He passed the papyrus over to Lucius who immediately took it and strode out of the room. As Lucius walked back into the room, Marius looked at him with an expression that is the closest such a man will ever get to pleading.
Lucius' face immediately softened.
"Have you still not worked it out, Marius?"
Marius just stared at him. His brain had completely ceased to work. The throbbing in his head was clouding in, and he felt that he might at any moment lose consciousness. His head began to slump forward, and through the fog he thought he heard something that was impossible. He thought that he heard Lucius' rich voice say four words that would turn everything upside down.

*****

When Marius regained consciousness he was back in the small cell. He opened his eyes and saw the concerned face of Lucius looking down at him.
"How are you feeling?"
The throbbing had gone, and had been replaced by a deep fatigue. Marius just looked back at Lucius, his face registering nothing. Slowly his brow furrowed as he tried to remember the last few seconds of his interrogation. He had a strong feeling that something momentous had happened, but he could not remember what. As he strained, he remembered the words that he thought that he had heard. But he could not be sure whether he had been conscious or whether he had been dreaming.
Lucius gave a rueful smile at the look of confusion on Marius' face.
"No doubt you wish to know how it is that a man in my position can be a Christian?" he prompted.

Marius felt no relief at confirmation of this revelation. Instead he sat in silence for some minutes as he tried to piece together the implications. Finally he spoke, and when he did his voice was measured. He had so many questions. Lucius was enormously impressed by Marius' first question. But at the time Lucius did not know about Rani.
"What about my men?" asked Marius.
Lucius replied immediately. "I didn't believe your story. Fortunately Hadrian and Decimus hadn't even thought to have you followed as a routine precaution. I knew that if their spies were allowed to report, something that they saw might easily raise suspicions about you. It wouldn't have taken much. Instead I had you followed. When you returned to your rooms in Transtiberine, one of my spies stayed watching the building. The other returned to me to report that you were lodging with your men. I decided to bring you here. I also kept your men under surveillance and gave orders that if any of them were to go any further than the street for supplies, they were to be picked up. Fortunately none yet has. Your note should keep them where they

are. No one is looking for them, and no one will find them unless they do something stupid".

Marius was not satisfied. He was reassured by the note that he had been asked to write, but he would not believe that they were safe until he had seen them. But his brain was working again now, and he felt a new energy. He moved straight on to his burning question.

"How did you know what had happened in Aegyptus? The only way that you could possibly have known was by forcing it out of my men, and you say that you haven't".
"Think about it, Marius. I had decided that you were not telling the truth. I began to think about your motives for lying. I am not a stupid man. I put myself in your position. I know the brethren well. I have never met the individuals that you did, but we are a good people. I had you down for an intelligent man, Marius, a view that I have since come to question. I knew that you would have seen that. The spy who initially sent you on your way told us of you. He described your reputation for "fairness and integrity in peace". I suppose that should have set alarm bells ringing with us, given the nature of the mission that we were sending you on. But it didn't. We just wrote it off as part of the hero worship accorded a fine soldier in a remote outpost. Yet those words came back to me as you made your report in Hadrian's villa. They were a piece of the puzzle that led me to realise that you were lying. So given that you lied, I asked myself why you would do that. The only reason that would make a man like you do that, Marius, is if you had read the manuscript for yourself. A brave and foolish thing to do, and something that I could easily believe of you".

Lucius paused and looked into Marius' eyes. He was wanting to see if his explanation was enough. The bemusement that greeted him persuaded him that he needed to continue.
"When I told you what I 'knew' about what were doing I was speculating. I deliberately kept the story vague, but included the key things that must have happened to make you lie. That is why I asked you if what I said was the truth. I had to know from your own lips that you were in possession of the manuscript. I have to say that by the

time that you admitted it I was already sure, but the admission has served to facilitate this conversation."

Marius was furious with himself for being tricked. His gave Lucius a look of pure hatred and jumped to his feet. Lucius burst out laughing. He waited for the fury to pass, and it soon gave way to relief. Marius felt humiliated, but Lucius was beginning to inspire his confidence with his gentle and authoritative manner.

"Marius, I know that you still have the manuscript. What completely baffles me is what you were planning to do with it."
Marius looked up at Lucius. He was interested by Lucius' use of the word "were". He decided to test him.
"We are going to use it to blackmail the emperor into reversing his policy of persecution against the Christians."
Lucius regarded Marius with disbelief. He looked into Marius' eyes and said "My God. You actually were!" His expression of disbelief gave way to a shake of the head. His face had softened into a wide smile. "Well that spy was right when he described you as audacious. But he neglected to mention that you were completely insane. Thank God that I got to you before you got hold of Hadrian". Lucius continued to smile and shake his head.

Marius was indignant. "If our story was that stupid, why was it believed by three of the most powerful people in Rome?"
Lucius' smile slowly disappeared and he began to think.

"It wasn't at first. But I think that there are three reasons. The first was your skill as a liar. Although I hate to admit it, I almost believed you myself and I consider myself to be an accomplished judge of veracity".
"The second was my intervention. I said that I almost believed you, but I didn't. And I could see that the others were going to question you very closely, and then probably kill you anyway. I very much wanted the rest of those in the room to believe you, and I wanted you to live so that you could lead me to the manuscript. So I, too, lied. I am not as good at it as you, but I can hold my own".

Lucius leaned forward and poured himself some water. He offered some to Marius, who accepted. It was extremely strange to be served by the most senior senator in Rome. After he had taken a sip, Lucius continued.

"That story about the flood in Alexandria, I invented it. They would all be too young to remember. They came to that conclusion themselves and I know them well enough to know that none will bother to check. What is more, I have been to Alexandria. I know that the library is on high ground and would not be affected by any flood". Marius' look of incredulity creased into a grin. Lucius smiled back.

"What was the final reason?" he asked

"The final reason was that the news that you told us was by no means unwelcome. Hadrian was positively relieved. He is not a stupid man and he has probably recognised the power that the manuscript could have if it fell into the hands of a rival. His desire to believe you was strong enough for him not to think too critically of what you were saying. As far as Decimus is concerned, right now he is in the middle of a fight for his very position. Hadrian has recently become enamoured of a young Greek scholar who is engaged in tutoring the son of one of his friends. Over the last few weeks Decimus has become frantic. He realises that if he loses Hadrian as a lover he could well be dismissed from his job. Anything could happen to him. So he is trying to win back his status as Hadrian's sole obsession. Part of his strategy for achieving this is to avoid any disagreement with Hadrian at all costs. He has been ingratiating himself in the most nauseating manner for weeks. Hadrian is revelling in it, and it appears to be working. At present, Decimus will believe anything if it will keep him in harmony with Hadrian. As for Alexander, he simply isn't sufficiently interested to stick his neck out on this. As far as he is concerned if everyone else is satisfied with an explanation, so is he. So he saw the rotted manuscript as the end of the matter and an opportunity to return his attention to what he really cares about, the management of his vast wealth. Given that I have a reputation as a sceptic in these sorts of scenarios and had made it clear that I believed your story, it put the rest of them off their guard."

Marius realised that he had been lucky. But there was still something that he wanted explained.

"So why was I ordered to report to the camp of the Imperial Guard the following morning? What did you discuss after I had left?" he asked.

Lucius' eyes narrowed.

"If these were not such a strange set of circumstances I would regard that as outrageous impertinence and inexcusable nosiness". His face softened. "But we do find ourselves in an unusual situation. I have already told you what we said of your story. Once it had been accepted, Hadrian was concerned about what to do with you. He was concerned about what you might have gathered through your mission. No one knew how much you had found out, and no one wanted to be reminded of it. Decimus advocated having you discreetly killed. I argued that you had men who might know as much as you yourself. I argued that you had shown yourself to be a good servant of Rome. I also agreed that we needed to get you as far away from us as possible. We made no decision but agreed that for the time being we would have you report for duty with the Imperial Guard where you could be given a job that would keep you where we could keep an eye on you. That suited me as I still haven't worked out what we are going to do."

Marius suddenly stood up, wide-eyed. As he did so he felt his head spin. "I'd completely forgotten! I was supposed to report to the Imperial Guard yesterday morning."

Lucius gestured for him to calm down. "Don't worry, Marius. I sent word to the prefect to tell him that you were indisposed and would be arriving two days late. You must be there tomorrow one hour after dawn".

As he sat back down Marius wobbled a little. Lucius looked at him closely.

"You need some time to recover from the knock. I fear that they hit you rather harder than was necessary. You were unconscious all day and all night. You cannot stay here, it is not safe for either of us. Return to your men. Despite your note they will be worrying about you. I will summon you when I have decided what to do. In the meantime, for God's sake act normally!"

When Marius left, Lucius returned from the secret chambers of his basement and went to his study. He sat there for a very long time, lost in thought.

20

That time in the Transtiberine was tough for us. After Marius left we sat around in our pokey rooms getting increasingly frustrated. Rani was amazing, utterly composed and patient. I think that she was acutely aware of the need to be strong and not to become a burden to us. The men were less patient. None were good at waiting. Marius' confidence about his interview with the emperor went a long way to preventing us from worrying when he failed to return, but we became irritated by his failure to send word to us. When he had been gone for a day and a night we were worried. Shortly after that we had received the papyrus script. A strange mood came over us. His order for us not to leave the area made it clear that something was happening, yet it told us nothing. A restlessness descended, and the morning had dragged on. And then Marius walked through the door. He looked terrible. After the immediate excitement of his return Rani wanted him to rest, but he insisted on telling us of the extraordinary events since we had last seen him. When he did we all blessed our luck.

There followed a week of crushing boredom for the men. Whilst Marius went out to report every day for duty the rest of us had to just sit around staring at those four walls, waiting for Lucius to make his move. The inactivity weighed heavy on us. Marius was assigned to the staff of the deputy commander of the Imperial Guard who gave him administrative tasks that were simply meant to keep him out of the way. As it wasn't an official posting, he was expected to arrange his own lodgings in the city, which suited us all. He had his work cut out trying to bolster morale when he returned in the evenings. I had been trying my best but to be honest I was as bored as everyone else, and we all knew that my promises of an end to the waiting were baseless.

All of us were men of action. The men had agreed to embark upon this plot out of a desire for glory. They had fallen in with Marius and I on the understanding that they would have an opportunity to get blood on their swords. Just how much blood none of us yet knew. But instead we were sitting around waiting on the decision of a man that none of us had ever met. It said a lot for the men's respect for Marius that they were prepared to do it.

The boredom began to tell and the men were becoming increasingly bad tempered with one another when, on the seventh evening, we received a visitor.
Tobias and Artorius were having an argument about who was going to clean the kitchen when there was a discreet knock on the door. Immediately the atmosphere tensed and our bickering was forgotten. I got up and cautiously opened the door a fraction. Outside was a very short, powerfully built man. I raised an eyebrow and he told me that he came from Lucius. The men were on their feet, poised, as he entered and Marius stepped forward.
The man briefly looked at us all and said "I am to escort Marius Sextus to the house of Senator Lucius Merutii Scripius".
I was concerned about the effect that any further exclusion might have on the men.
"We will all come", I blurted out.
Lucius' messenger was firm. "I am afraid that will not be possible, sir. Only those who have been summoned can be admitted".
My instincts told me that the men needed to be included if we were not to lose them. I knew that Marius would disapprove of my intervention, but when he spoke he made it clear that he understood my reasons for making it.
"We are all in a delicate position. If we were all to barge into Lucius' house it would provoke interest. But if Lucius is ready to talk there is no reason why he should not do so to all of us. Each man in this room has an equal stake in what Lucius may have to say".
He turned to the messenger. "If Lucius is ready to talk to us, he must come to us here to do it".
The messenger's eyes were wide with disbelief as Marius walked to a corner of the room where he scribbled out a few sentences on an old scrap of papyrus. He sealed it and gave it to the messenger. The man looked uncertain, but Marius' purpose persuaded him to do as he was bid. He nodded to us and left the room.

*****

It was late evening and most of the lanterns in the enormous building had been extinguished when we heard a soft knock on the door. Marius opened it, and Senator Lucius Merutii Scripius strode in. We all stood up instantly. We could see from his appearance that he was a distinguished man, and we were all a little in awe of him. His thunderous expression served to increase our awe. Marius was quick to notice it and awkwardly shepherded the old man into the smaller room. He closed the door behind them. When Lucius came out he looked a little mollified.

Marius addressed the room. "In asking Lucius to come here rather than to go to him as he requested, I have done something completely irregular. No one needs reminding that our circumstances are highly unusual, and it is not surprising that Lucius is not comfortable with the way that we have resolved to run our operation. However he has agreed to tell his plan to us all, together."

Marius motioned Lucius to sit on a cushion with his back against the wall. The rest of us pulled our cushions up in a semi circle around him. Lucius looked uncomfortable as he began to speak. I was struck by the beautiful lyrical quality to his deep, rich voice. He began sympathetically.

"You have my apologies for keeping you waiting for so long. I know fighting men and I know that they do not bear uncertainty and sloth well. I have been working as fast as I can, but your aim is not one that can be easily achieved. I have spent much of the week going through options and discounting them. It was not until two days ago that I hit upon a plan that could succeed, and I have spent the time since then setting the wheels in motion".

We were indignant that Lucius would begin the preparations for his plan without first consulting with us. I looked around, and saw raised eyebrows amongst the men. Numba had reddened but fortunately no one said anything. As Lucius continued his voice hardened.

"Your plan to blackmail the emperor would never have worked. Origen showed that he knew more of the nature of Rome than her own soldiers when he told you not to be so ridiculous".

The atmosphere tightened and Lucius looked around him. He was met with hostile stares from hard men. Artorius looked impressive at the best of times, but the thunderous expression on his face as he glared back at Lucius would have been enough to put lesser men right off their stride. Silus and Tobias had flat, granite expressions. I was angry too, for none of us were going to take kindly to insults.

When he saw the coldness in our eyes he paused, deciding on an approach to take with us. Whilst he did so he met the stares of each man, including mine. His eyes were equally hard, and in them I saw an inner depth and strength that would not easily yield.

Lucius decided what he had to do. He leaned right forward, engaging us.

"I am going to tell you of Hadrian. I am going to tell you because without knowing about the man you will not understand why your plan would not have worked, and why my plan will work".

He looked round to ensure that we would all at least listen. The eyes that looked back at him were still hard, but outright hostility had been replaced by a sceptical willingness to hear him out. In his wonderful voice he began to talk to us.

*****

"To understand Hadrian it is necessary to understand the mechanisms by which emperors are appointed. To do so I will need to refresh your memories about what happened after the death of Nero. A power struggle developed between four key generals and senators; Galba, Otho, Vitellius and Vespasian. They were the commanders of the legions of Hispania, the household troops, the army of the Rhenus and a coalition of the armies of the Danubius and Euphrates respectively. By the end of the struggle only the lowborn Vespasian lived, and so he became the undisputed emperor"

The intrigues of high politics were not always interesting to soliders, but since we had left Aegyptus with the manuscript, all of our men had become anxious to know more about how our rulers established and maintained their power base. Marius had been able to tell them a certain amount, but from the way that they were concentrating it was obvious that they still wanted to know more.

"Because he had broken the precedent of exclusively high birth leading to high office, he had to institute a new system for the justification of his position. What he chose became known as "the inherent prerogatives of the principate". In plain latin, this means that power became the justification for power.
To reinforce this, Vespasian sponsored the worship of the Divi, the Caesars. It was at this time that they became "true gods". This was how Vespasian ensured that his descendants would inherit the empire".

"The plan worked for two generations until his grandson Domitian thought that he could ignore the will of the senate. He was murdered by Nerva, who succeeded him as emperor. Nerva replaced Verspasian's system with one that has survived to this day - the system of adoptive emperors. So it is that the emperor is permitted to choose his successor, and that choice has come to be accepted by the senate. So when Hadrian set out to become emperor, he did so by establishing himself as the heir apparent to the emperor Trajan. He spent years ingratiating himself, acting as though he were Trajan's own son. The old man indulged him. He enjoyed the attention and found Hadrian to be a useful ally. Hadrian was never above taking hints off the emperor and disposing of rivals and critics for him. He also used this position to intimidate and dispose of his own rivals. But Trajan never fully trusted Hadrian. He steadfastly refused to name him as his heir publicly".

"Last year when Trajan was ailing, Hadrian became desperate. He knew that the whims of a dying man cannot be controlled by anyone. He was used to bullying and intimidating and threatening to get his way but he could not do it with the emperor, it would have been counter-productive. So he resorted to stealth".

The atmosphere in the room had transformed. None of us knew this story, and the relevance to us was obvious. Lucius looked around, and this time he was confronted with eager looks and bright eyes. Our hostility was forgotten and as Lucius continued he began to react to the enthusiasm of his listeners, his voice becoming more animated.

"Trajan was foul in his final years. His fat, flatulent body had swelled to a revolting size. He was covered in boils that discharged constantly. He was incontinent, and as a result was rarely seen in public. Most of his time was spent under a mountain of blankets in an enormous bed that covered his indignity. He spent his time looking out over a narrow terrace from his villa, down the valley of the Tiber to Rome in the distance. The stench in that room was infamous. It is said that it was worse than the stench in the ports of Aegyptus".
He winked at us, and we grinned back.
"Because of his humiliating ill health his temper had become foul. Courtesans refused to visit his villa. The only physical satisfaction that he received was from reluctant slaves. For a man who had always prided himself on his prolific carnal activities, this had a devastating effect on his self regard".

"Hadrian had always been close to Dremona, his mother. Some say unnaturally close. They loved each other with a mutual obsession that made some jealous and others uncomfortable. She was a fine woman of great charm, but had one fatal flaw: she was as ambitious for her son as Hadrian was for himself. Hadrian hatched a simple plan to secure his succession. He sent his mother to persuade Trajan to name him as his successor. One day this beautiful, cultured, genteel woman came to him. Her dignity and reputation were exemplary. I really think that when she first went to him, she had no intention of doing more than just charming him. But she had not reckoned on Trajan's need to regain his feelings of self worth. Unfortunately for Dremona, this need manifested itself in an obsession to obtain her willing sexual submission. Dremona flattered him and flirted with him. She hinted that she found power to be a great aphrodisiac. In his loneliness Trajan came to look forward to her visits, and attempted to install her in a neighbouring villa. She refused, teasing him. He fell right into her

trap of honey. Dremona was sure that she would not have to go further to secure her son's status. In all probability Trajan was wise to what she was doing but was so tantalised by her that he did not care. But he wanted more than her innuendo and promise. One day when she went to see him he attempted to put his hand under her toga. She allowed him to fondle her heavy breasts, and even leaned forward to accept his tongue in her
mouth. But when he attempted to move his hand lower down her body she pulled away".

Greto let out an involuntary sigh, and everyone turned to look at him. He just looked back with an innocent expression on his face, and Numba couldn't resist.
"Poor Greto" he said. "I suppose that was the most excitement you've had from a woman in years!" We all laughed as Greto blushed. As Lucius resumed Rani was still giggling at the back of the room.

"Trajan was furious and humiliated. He lost his temper and shouted a tirade of abuse, banishing her from his presence. The old man's anger did not pass, and he knew exactly how to hurt her most. When the hot flush of humiliation had passed it was replaced by a determination to overcome her resistance. He summoned her once more and told her that her son would never amount to anything. Hadrian was to be disgraced and cast out of society. Dremona panicked. She tried to placate Trajan, but his anger ran deep. In desperation she agreed that if he would declare her son to be his successor then she would succumb to his desires. Before she would remove her toga, she made him write and seal the decree".

"When Dremona took the decree to Hadrian he was thrilled. When he was told about the circumstances in which it had been written he flew into a violent rage. The idea of his idolised mother being humiliated in such a way made him murderous. Within days, Trajan had been poisoned. His mother too died from poisoning. It has been suggested that Hadrian acted out of jealousy. I am not so sure. I think that his pride was damaged by his mother's action. I think that he could not bear for everybody to know what his mother had done on his behalf.

In some perverse way he felt that by killing her he was atoning for this humiliation and regaining his dignity. To most, though, it was the unaccountable action of a very dangerous man. I have known Hadrian for many years, since before he was even a senator and he is a viper. But underneath he is a coward. When he became emperor this year he did it largely through the intimidation of others".

Lucius leaned forward and took a long draught from the cup in front of him. As he did so there was silence. He had not finished and no one was going to interrupt him. When he resumed his voice was stern.

"This is the man who we have set out to fight. He is extremely intelligent. He is rigorous in weighing up risks versus benefits and his primary instinct is for self-aggrandisement and self-preservation. Understanding Hadrian, what motivates him and what he responds to is vital if one is to understand what conditions might persuade him to do as we desire. Hadrian understands force. He understands intimidation and bullying. He is governed by his ambition and his fear of humiliation. For that reason I have no doubt that he will be a great emperor. He is not a risk taker. He is a consolidator and an accumulator. But most of all he is a good judge of probability. So in order to be successful we must present him with odds that he does not like. We must offer him an option that allows him to retain his dignity and his kudos, but most importantly it must allow him to retain his position. He would risk everything to fight against something that does not guarantee him this. But he must also be certain that if he does not agree to our demands he will be humiliated and lose everything. If we present options in such a way, he will agree to anything".

Lucius paused. All eyes were fixed on him. We could not wait to hear how we could put ourselves in the position to bully the emperor. This was the sort of talk that we liked to hear, and the prospect of doing some soldiering seemed imminent. Lucius recognised the momentum, so he outlined his plan.
"I have come to the conclusion that we require the application of an irresistible force to Hadrian. The force must be visible to him, tangible. He must know it is there and know that it cannot be resisted.

He must be able to see it in front of his face and believe that it can destroy him. But at the same time it is vital that no one else knows that it is there. No one else must see it. If they do, then Hadrian's pride will force him into a standoff. He cannot allow himself to be seen to give in to force. His ego would not allow such a humiliation. And in many ways he would be right not to, for an emperor cannot show such weakness. Both Hadrian and I have seen before how the predators and scavengers gather before a weakened leader and pick at him until his power is undermined. So we must come at Hadrian with a force that is invisible to others. As well as being unseen by his colleagues, this force must be numerous. It must be sufficiently numerous that its power cannot be doubted and its personnel cannot just be made to disappear. The option of murder and cover up cannot be open to Hadrian, for if it is he will surely use it". Lucius paused and looked around him. "So the conclusion that I have come to is obvious".

*****

When Lucius had finished he was confronted by eight mouths hanging open. All of us were resourceful and experienced soldiers, but the audacity of what Lucius was suggesting amazed even us. Whilst the men and I wondered at the simplicity of what had been suggested, Marius was thinking through the details. Quickly he isolated the only part of the plan that hadn't been properly set out. But he was excited, for as he asked Lucius to explain it he had fire in his eyes. Lucius smiled appreciatively at the question. He was prepared for it.

"The answer lies in something that no soldier is ever told. It is known as 'the cult of the leader', and it is spoken of only in the highest political circles. The reason that we do not speak of it will become clear as I explain".
Lucius had long since relaxed and was enjoying himself.
"It was first officially recorded by Nero and he handed the experience down in the imperial inheritance. Early in his rule, within five years of becoming emperor, Nero fought a campaign against the powerful

Parthians with the objective of extending the empire into Armenia. The general who fought the Parthians was a man named Antonius Octavian. He was an impressive general and a superb soldier. Antonius was sent as commander of the IIIrd legion to conquer the distant land. They were isolated from all support and comforts. For several months he enjoyed many glorious successes harrying the Parthian patrols. But then, as he led his army out of the mountains of Armenia Minor near to Carana he stumbled across the whole Parthian army of over twenty five thousand men lined up in full battle order on a barren plain. His scouts had been captured by the Parthians, and their whole army was waiting for him. The IIIrd were outnumbered by five men to one and faced certain death. In contravention of all military manuals and conventional wisdom, Antonius immediately split his force. He ordered seven cohorts to turn and run, feigning panic and desertion. Then he waited for the great host of Parthians to advance. He waited there on the edge of the plain, with the mountains at his back and just two thousand men. He must have had nerves of iron".

Lucius had a note of genuine respect in his voice as he recounted the legend.

"Antonius formed his men in a v-shaped phalanx, and as they were attacked he ordered them to retreat steadily and slowly towards the valley from which they had come. Losses were kept to a minimum by the sharp teeth of the phalanx. The valley forced the enemy to fight on a narrow front, so they were unable to make their vast numerical superiority tell. They would probably never have entered the valley had they not believed that the seven cohorts, over four thousand of Antonius' six thousand, had deserted and fled".

"When they were well into the valley the seven cohorts entered it behind the Parthians. They had skirted round the hills to the north and formed up out of sight near the valley's mouth. Antonius was able to hold the Parthians at the front with his two thousand men while they were eaten up from the rear by the larger section of the legion. They panicked and fled. Antonius had snatched victory from the jaws of total annihilation".

Lucius' eyes were alive. We were hanging on every word.

"Over the following months, in that remote and wild outpost of the empire, the response of his soldiers was to elevate Antonius with such hero worship that in their eyes he attained the status almost of a god.
In Rome Antonius had a well earned reputation as a trustworthy, reasonable and measured man. He was universally popular and perceived as a man of great potential destined for the highest office. But the adulation of his men affected him. A model of Roman virtue became carried away with the myth of his own invincibility, and he began to believe that he was above the jurisdiction of the emperor. In that desolate place, his unquestioning and adoring subordinates became his subjects and he became a mini emperor. He began to refuse orders and act instead according to his whim. He negotiated with the Parthians for his own benefit. He sought to carve out a sovereign territory for himself and his men in that outpost. His men knew what he was doing and followed him regardless. Their loyalty was total".

"In the end Nero was so incensed that he sent a small team of assassins to Parthia. They did not find it difficult to murder Antonius. His personal security was remarkably lax, a result of his knowledge that there was not one of his own men who would lift a finger against him. The murder precipitated a crisis in the legion. One of the assassins was a senior senator from a distinguished family and had papers that appointed him as the new commander of the legion. But the legion would not accept him. They virtually deserted and Nero was forced to compromise with the Parthians, despite their weakened state. He had no choice but to return Armenia to them and withdraw to the eastern fringes of Cappadocia".

"And so it was that the theory of the cult of the leader was born. There have been many examples since of the same thing happening, albeit not so dramatically. No doubt it had happened before. A strong and able leader of men in a remote and dangerous outpost can take on the status of a quasi god. Ever since that incident in Parthia emperors have been on the look out for evidence of the phenomena repeating itself. And evidence has been found. Whenever it looks like it might be beginning to happen, the general is recalled to Rome under some spurious pretext and reassigned somewhere that enables a closer eye to be kept on him. But even so, it is difficult to keep such an eye on some of the remoter outposts".

Lucius paused.

"In the case of your remote outpost, I will take it upon myself to keep an eye on it".

Lucius looked around, making sure that he caught our eyes. There was the suspicion of smile on his lips as he finished.

"When you are ready, I will arrange for your legion to be recalled to Rome".

*****

We talked late into the night about the plan. We had literally hundreds of small, detailed questions to be answered. Lucius had brought our official postings with him. As he handed them over, it became too much for Rani. I don't think that any of the rest of us had stopped to think about how all of this would leave her feeling. We were too caught up in the excitement of our plans. But Marius had. As soon as Rani rose, Marius followed her out. We did not see him again that night because as soon as Lucius departed we went to the tavern. The release from being cooped up for so long and our excitement at Lucius' plan meant that it was not long before the wine made us incoherent.

*****

Marius grabbed Rani's arm as she reached the flight of stairs. When she turned round there were tears in her eyes.

"I won't go" he said simply.

"What?" Rani had scorn in her voice.

"I won't go" he replied.

"Don't be ridiculous" she spat.

Marius was perplexed. "I thought that you would . . ."

"What, Marius? I would what? I would want you to neglect your duty to yourself, to your men, to me and to God? I would want you to be a

pathetic coward turning his back on what was right? I would want to take you from your obligations for my own selfish reasons? You have a low opinion of me, Marius. I deserve better."
Marius did not know what to say, but her aggression angered him. He kept hold of her arm and almost dragged her to the end of the corridor. "It has taken me twenty years to find you, and I am not going to leave you now. Lucius does not need me. Neither of us asked for this. We can walk away now, and Lucius can find someone else to execute his plan. Why should it be me? Why should I leave you? I cannot be separated from you for so long, and I will not risk what we have found together. I will not go!"
Rani was still angry, and her voice was hard.
"You will go because you are the only person who can make Lucius' plan work, and you know it. We could never be happy together if we walked away now. I could never forgive myself for being the cause of such selfishness, and I could never love you if you allowed yourself to succumb to it. You know that, Marius. Part of the reason that I love you is that you cannot just stand by and watch this injustice. You cannot wash you hands of it when you can see that there is something that you can do. The man I love will lead brave men to see Lucius' plan through, for if he didn't he would not be the same man."
Marius was furious. He glared at her before almost shouting.
"Well maybe I am not the man you thought I was!"
He turned his back and put his hands on the low wall, looking out across the softly lit buildings of the Transtiberine. He remained there in silence, brooding.
They heard footsteps as Lucius and the rest of us left the building and descended the stairs.

It was some time before he felt Rani's soft touch around his waist. She rested her head on his back and stayed like that for a long time, until both of them had been soothed by the touch of each other. Then she spoke softly.
"I'm sorry, I should not have taken it out on you, Marius. I don't want you to go either. It's the injustice of it that gets to me, because you have to go. You have no choice, and we both know it. We must not take it out on each other, and we must not pretend to each other that

we can escape from it. You must go, and we must be strong. I will be able to come to you in time, but until that moment we must be strong".

Marius turned and the light caught the tears that streamed down his face. Without a word he embraced her. They stood there, alone in the darkness for a long time, clutching each other tight. Then, without a word, Marius picked her up and walked slowly back towards their rooms. Rani buried her head deep in his chest as he walked, and when he laid her down on their bed she drew him to her. That night they discovered a tenderness that neither had previously known.

*****

The following day, whilst the rest of us nursed our sore heads, Rani and Marius went to retrieve the manuscript from its hiding place out beyond the Tivoli gate. They returned subdued in the late afternoon and that evening it was strapped to Marius' torso as we left Rome and Rani behind. We travelled north to find the cohorts marching to relieve counterparts serving in a legion garrisoned in a frontier outpost known as Eburacum. Our orders said that we were to join them as the staff of Marius Sextus, who bore papers confirming his appointment. He was to be the Deputy Commander of the IXth Legion of the Western Army of the Empire of Rome, and we were proud to march with him.

21

Rome welcomed them by considerably lightening their pockets for the ferry ride across the Tiber and shamelessly overcharging them for a tiny room in the Transtiberine. Their ship had docked at the port of Ostia at dawn, and they hurried along the road to the city. Perridac wasted no time once they had dumped their bundles of clothes and supplies in their seamy little room. Sufficient daylight just remained, and all four of them felt that every hour was crucial if they were to catch Marius before he did something stupid. They set off for the centre of the city immediately to find the man who owed Tertullian his life.

Despite being from villages near to Ephesus, a great port in its own right and a city of considerable majesty, Perridac, Beziac and Radjic were impressed by Rome. Benjamin was overwhelmed. Brought up in Sidon, he had never been outside Ituraea. As he passed the glorious buildings on either side, he found himself wishing that Gideon could be with him to see it. He had been thinking about Gideon increasingly, and was unable to forgive himself for abandoning him in Creta. Despite Perridac and the other's assurance that he had done the right thing, he felt terrible. He prayed about it constantly, praying for the safety of Gideon and for forgiveness for what he had done. But now, having crossed the Tiber on the Augustinian bridge and passed the great Temple of Concord, everything was forgotten as he stood open-mouthed looking at the vast, teeming city ahead of him.

Beziac stood grinning at him but Benjamin did not see. He laughed and clapped him on the shoulder.
"When this is all over you must come to see us in Ephesus. That too is a great city, but when you come it will be to celebrate."
Benjamin had to work hard to tear his eyes away from the spectacle. As he did his face was sober.

"If I come it will be with Gideon. And if we do, it will be a great celebration indeed".

*****

They had no idea where to find the Via Flaminian, but according to Tertullian this was where they would find his contact's ancestral villa. It was some time before they found themselves in the forum, fighting against the crowd returning to their cramped homes. As they spilled out into the great space, a stall holder saw Benjamin's expression of awe as he looked at the huge buildings that lined the square.

"You, country boy. Want to buy a jar?" he called. He held out a beautiful piece of blown glass craftsmanship. Benjamin had never seen anything like it. Without thinking he walked over to take a closer look. As he approached, the trader withdrew the jar and hid it under his robe. When Benjamin asked to see it, the trader narrowed his eyes.
"It'll cost you, country boy" he said.
Benjamin was confused.
"I only want to look" he protested.
"Who do you think you are? A look is one dinarii, and you pay just like everyone else." The trader's tone was indignant.
Benajmin couldn't believe that it cost money just to look at merchandise, but then again this was Rome. He decided that since he was in the great city he had better abide by its customs, so he felt in his purse for change. He withdrew a dinarii and handed it to the trader.
The trader then produced the jar and roared with laughter. He showed the coin to a neighbouring stall holder.
"This halfwit paid me a dinarii just to look!"
Benjamin felt a hot rush of blood to his cheeks. He lowered his eyes, and with cruel laughter ringing in his ears he quickly turned to rejoin the others.

They were nowhere to be seen. He shoved through the seething crowd, desperately searching the massive sea of foreign faces. He began to feel afraid, for he knew that would not be able to find his way back through the maze of the Transtiberine to their rooms. All of the buildings there looked the same. He continued to wander around, increasingly aimless and desperate. People barged past and cursed him for getting in their way. He felt panic begin to take hold. Unaccountably he began to think of Gideon, abandoned by him on a small island to the mercy of people like this.

*****

Initially Benjamin had not associated the civilians wandering the streets with Roman soldiers. But as he was jostled and cursed and knocked to the ground he discovered the same virulent hatred for these men and women of Rome that he had felt for their soldiers since he was a small boy. He couldn't think straight. Hatred and frustration and panic built up in his head as he frantically looked about him. All he could see were faces that showed only indifference or irritation.

Suddenly he felt a hand on his shoulder. He jumped around, expecting a fight. Radjic had a concerned look in his eye. Benjamin once again felt a hot sting on his cheeks as he felt relief and embarrassment in equal measure.
"Are you alright, brother?" asked Radjic.
Benjamin took a deep breath and tried to regain his composure. After the disastrous episode in Creta he was desperate not to disgrace himself again.
"I'm fine. Sorry, I'm just not used to these crowds. I hate these evil Romans"
Radjic's eyes widened and he leaned close to Benjamin's ear.
"Never speak like that in public. We are going to be here for some time, and hatred will be one of the things that will give us away if we're not careful."
Radjic's tone was not unkind, but it was firm.
"And please try to stay with us".
Benjamin tensed at being spoken to as an inferior, but he said nothing.

*****

They found the house. It took them a while but they found it. When they knocked on the front door they were not even shown in. They handed Tertullian's letter to the doorkeeper and were told to wait outside by the side of the wide thoroughfare of the Via Flaminian. It was well past dark, long after they had first arrived, that the doorkeeper opened the door once more. Out came a small man who subtly gestured them to follow him. He moved remarkably quickly for one so small, and it was a little way before Perridac managed to catch up with him to ask him where they were going. The man was not in the mood for talking, but he did utter one sentence under his breath. "Back door, fall back, pretend you don't know me".
The little man walked into a narrow alleyway and pushed past a group of small children who were baiting a mangy looking dog. After a couple of minutes he reached a small doorway in a battered and rundown house. He took out a key and turned the lock, leading them through a derelict hallway and up to another door at the rear of the house. Again he had to unlock it, and they entered a small, windowless room. The door was locked behind them. The room was black as pitch and they heard some scrabbling about on the floor and the turning of another lock. Suddenly some light appeared from under the floor, startling them. The little man had opened a hidden door in the floor and was descending a wooden ladder that led down under the ground. The rest followed him, and as the last man Beziac closed the door behind him. As he did so he heard the lock click back into place. They were in a tunnel lit by dim oil lamps. They were led through the tunnel for quite some way until they came to a final door. When their guide unlocked and opened it, they were led into another passageway. They were shown into a room with a long table and few other furnishings and left without a word.

Several minutes later the door opened and a grizzled old patrician walked in. He was holding Tertullian's letter. Behind him came a striking looking girl. It was not just her luminescence and sparkling eyes that made the men sit up. She looked Iturean, or at least from somewhere at the Eastern end of the Mare Nostrum and the visitors were disorientated by it. The old senator made no effort to introduce her to them, but something told Perridac that he ought to know who she was

Their host got straight to the point. As he spoke it was clear that he was furious.
"Good day, gentlemen". His voice was flat and hard, and he spoke through gritted teeth.
"I apologise for the strange way that you have been admitted to my house, but these are dangerous times for certain people in Rome. From the note that you gave me, I would imagine that they are dangerous times for me" his tone was sarcastic and hostile.
Implicit in his words was a rebuke to the Christians for arriving at his house without warning. His manner made it overt, and it was not lost on Perridac.
"I apologise for coming unannounced. I had not realised that it would put you in danger, sir".
The old man could not contain his contempt. "Not put me in danger? I am the most senior man in the Senate of the Empire of Rome. As a result my every move is scrutinised by enemies and friends alike. Perhaps you think that four raggedly dressed eastern vagrants turning up at my door and handing a papyrus to my doorkeeper is a regular occurrence?"
Perridac was clearly embarrassed. "You have my sincerest apologies, sir. It was my fault. I am the leader of these men and I was not thinking."
"No you were not" came the terse reply.

Lucius Merutii Scripius was indeed angry. But the real cause of his fury was the quandary into which his ancient promise to Tertullian had put him. He could not keep his word to Tertullian without betraying his conscience, and his conscience was telling him that he must not give the Neronian confession to Origen's men. It told him that the plan he and Marius had embarked on was right and must be followed through. Yet his conscience was also telling him that he had an ancient debt to repay and an oath to keep. He was in an impossible position. This had been part of the reason for his delay in seeing the visitors. It had taken over one hour before the doorman had an opportunity to pass the note to Lucius, but the instant that he read it he had cancelled his evening engagement, pleading an illness, before agonising over what he should do. Eventually he had summoned Rani

There had been the most terrible argument. They argued about many things, but mostly they argued over whether Rani would attend the audience that Lucius would grant to these Christians. At first Lucius was violently opposed. He knew that her presence could reveal a link between Marius and himself. Lucius' instincts were to secrecy. But they were also to use events to his favour. During the course of their argument, it suddenly struck Lucius that to have Origen on his side could be perfect. If he could get Origen to realise that the confession would not be forthcoming unless the plan involved using it in the context of continued Roman government, then he might just be able to enrol him. This would serve a dual purpose, firstly of stalling the Christians and preventing them from doing anything that could jeopardise him, and secondly of involving the considerable abilities of Origen.

Lucius had reasoned that if Origen came up with a plan that was better than his own, they could simply adopt this new plan and recall Marius. As Lucius had argued with Rani, he changed his mind. Rani had been suspicious of such a sudden change of heart. When he told her his idea, Rani had been infuriated by the implication that Lucius was not totally committed to the plan that had sent Marius to Eburacum. They had not resolved the conflict before Lucius ordered the Christians to be admitted.

As a result of this, both Rani and Lucius were in a foul mood as they walked in to meet the Christians, and Lucius was taking it out on the people who were the cause of his agony. He rounded on Perridac and his men.

"What is it that you have come for, anyway?" he asked abruptly
Perridac didn't hesitate. He could see from the mood of this man that he must come straight to the point.
"Our request is simple. We request that you, Lucius Merutii Scripius honour your pledge to Tertullian of Sidon and do everything in your

power to help us to retrieve the document known as the Neronian Confession"

Lucius had known that it was coming, but was still shocked to hear it. He replied with a gambit that he knew was pointless.

"My pledge was to Tertullian personally. I have never met any of you before."

"Sir, I have a letter from Tertullian saying that you will be fulfilling your oath personally. He is too old to travel to Rome to make his request". Perridac had anticipated the objection.

Lucius leaned forward in his chair to answer.

PART III

BRITANNIA

22

The journey from Rome was hard. Marius drove us relentlessly, for he wanted to catch up with the cohorts as soon as he could. They had followed the Via Iulia, the metalled road that travels along the coast to the south of the region of Narbonensis through Nicaea. On reaching the great cities of southern Gallia, Arelate and Aix, they struck out to the north along the banks of the huge Rhodanus river.

We did not follow them. Instead, Marius decided to take the direct route. It was easy sailing up the coast of Italia to the port of Genua but from there we retraced the steps of the great Hannibal over the Appeninus Mons, the mountains that rise directly out of the Mare Nostrum to the south of Liguria. We procured horses at the military stores near the docks at Genua and immediately began to climb on the winding, unmetalled road. That first day we climbed to the top of the great pass of Giovus and spent a cold night in a cabin amongst the clouds. During the subsequent days we followed the winding road down through the mountains onto the flat plains of Liguria. The pace was hard and we were all out of condition after so much time sitting around in Aegyptus and Rome, but even so morale was exceptionally high. We were thrilled to be back on the road, to be heading somewhere with a clear purpose. We were delighted that we would be joining a legion and had a job to do with it, and we rejoiced in the prospect of some fighting. But most of all we revelled in the secret that we all shared, the secret of what we would accomplish in Eburacum and the effect that we would have when we returned to Rome.

We skirted round towards the west so as to avoid the great mountains of Helvetii, and went through a low pass in the Alpes Cottiae. At Lugudunum we joined the great road that connects Narbonensis with Ludgunensis and Belgica. We had virtually no rain, and it was only as we approached the lands of the Belgae in the north that the clouds thickened and descended, making the land seem grey and hard. The road was beautiful, passing through fertile valleys and rich hills. The villages were orderly and peaceful, the farms prosperous and full. This was an area that had embraced the pax romana and had benefited. The people were confident and plump, the infrastructure highly developed. It was a pleasant land, but to us it looked a boring one. We continued north, and were just two days short of the great city of Darocortorum when we came across a magnificent sight. As we reached the crest of a hill, laid out below us we saw the five cohorts that we sought, the soldiers from Umbria who were travelling to join the IXth legion of the army of the Western Empire of Rome in Eburacum. When we saw them we all had the feeling of euphoria that only soldiers know. We were returning to the place where we belonged.

*****

We had been trudging up a great hill for most of the afternoon. As usual, Artorius was alone at the front, a tall, purposeful presence setting the pace. He was followed by Tobias, Silus, Marius and myself. Numba brought up the rear with Greto. Since Aegyptus they had been increasingly close, the oldest and the youngest striking up a strong friendship. Numba would ask the advice of the older man, and constantly pester him to tell of past campaigns. Most of the time Greto was patient, but Numba could not resist playing tricks. One evening we heard an angry yell just after Greto had gone to bed. The rest of us quickly moved to see what had upset Greto – not a man to raise an alarm unnecessarily – only to find him nursing a nasty bite mark on his arm. Numba had caught a baby boar and wrapped it in Greto's sleeping blanket. It had surprised him as he prepared to sleep, and bitten him before he had a chance to break its neck. Although Greto was angry, the way he shouted at Numba was reminiscent of how a father might discipline his son. Despite Numba's jibes and ribbing, Greto and he were coming to value each other as the family that both had lost.

There had been the odd downhill stretch that afternoon, but they had been outnumbered by long uphill slogs. Many times we saw what we were sure must be the top only for it to be a false crest, undulating to another hill even higher than the last. It was not long before sunset when we finally reached the top of a bluff. Below us the road continued arrow straight for several miles, but we were not looking at it. About two miles ahead of us, on a great plain just to the west of the road was the encampment of the five cohorts. In all, there were just over three thousand men. Each cohort contained six centuries, each with about eighty men. There were one hundred and twenty horsemen, and an additional thousand auxiliaries. They had only just finished their days marching, for the camp was a hive of activity. The surveyors had laid out the camp, using flags to indicate where everyone would be billeted. Large tents were going up in the camps centre. This would be the praetorium and would house the commander and some of his senior staff. All the other parts of the camp were orientated around it. Each century was then given a space of thirty six paces length and ten paces width. These areas were easily discerned by following the flags laid out by the surveyors. As we surveyed the scene of rigorous order and discipline, I looked at the others. Marius had an expression of burning pride as he looked down at the men he would command. The rest had grins spread wide across their faces. Our packs felt light as we strode down the last two miles to the camp.

We were still well short of the camp gates when we were intercepted by a small group of auxiliaries. On account of our uniforms they were courteous and respectful. They wore the same woollen tunics as we did, made from two rectangular pieces of dark brown woollen cloth joined together at the shoulders leaving a hole for the neck. On top of this they wore a cloak draped around the shoulders and buttoned down the front. On their feet were caligas made from sturdy leather uppers sewn up at the back and stitched to a thick leather sole studded with iron hob nails. They wore no armour or helmets, and carried just a standard gladius attached to their belts. The swords were of plain design, the length of a man's leg to the knee and had a straight double edge. It was clear that these men expected no hostile engagements and they had no reason to. Even so, they were firm as they demanded of us who we were. Marius responded to their courtesy with stiff formality. He withdrew his letter of appointment and showed it to the

principales of the guard. Upon reading it, the principales' eyes widened. He looked at Marius and immediately stood to attention.
"You are welcome, sir. I will escort you to the legate immediately."

We walked in tight order into the camp. Without exception the men there were filthy, and all had thick beards. When we marched we did not shave and there were rarely bathing facilities, so our bodies took on the stink of the barbarians and our faces the beards of the uncivilised. But although these men did not look like Romans, their behaviour made it clear that they could be nothing else. On either side of the marked path along which we walked legionaries were going about the business of erecting their tents and striking their camp with practised efficiency. Their mood was good, for marching through this sort of country was relatively easy. The roads were in excellent repair, and the twenty five miles covered each day took about five hours. There was no need to build a defensive camp in this land, so the work at the end of the day was minimal. Their packs were heavy, as heavy as a boy of ten summers, but it was a familiar burden and one which lightened with experience.

Some of the legionaries erected leather tents that would sleep eight people, whilst others were sitting on bedrolls and shields preparing food. Over a fire they rested an iron grid on which they placed two pans. In the pans porridge and bacon were being prepared. Dry biscuits, cheese and fruit were laid out on the grass nearby. The shields, helmets, javelins and belts were all lined up outside the tents in perfect order. The soldiers were relaxed in their tunics and cloaks, most not even carrying their daggers with them. We strode through this familiar scene and we drank in the familiar smells of tired men and bland food. We rejoiced in the hammering and the chatter, the clank of metal pots and the baying of donkeys being unloaded and freed to graze. I heard Numba turn to Silus and ask if he had ever seen a more beautiful sight.

We continued through the orderly rows of tents in silence, and finally we reached the Praetorium.

Whilst Marius went inside with the auxiliary principales, the rest of us stood outside to wait.

*****

On entering the Praetorium the first thing that Marius noticed was that there was no ostentation, and none of the home comforts so beloved of most legates. It was not unknown for the legate of a legion to travel with over thirty female slaves, with cartloads of antique furniture and art and with vast herds of animals with which to furnish his table. Almost without exception these men proved to be poor generals, and the morale of their men was usually low. Victrix was the opposite. Just by looking at his quarters it was obvious that he was a soldier's soldier. There were none of the comforts of home save the one concession of a writing table. Other than that there was merely a field table, which could seat twenty on folding canvas chairs. This would be used for the council meetings that the legate held involving his six tribunes, his favoured centurians, his optio legatus legionis and any other officials that he should decide to include. Victrix himself was deep in conversation with a cleric, a man holding a large papyrus.

Victrix was a small man who exuded a warm energy. His eyes burned with an ironic sense of amusement at his life as a soldier. I suppose that we all had to cope somehow with our strange way of life as professional soldiers - the regular lack of women, the physical hardships, the long periods of boredom followed by intensive and petrifying brutality. Most managed by forming close friendships with the men of their century. Some became introverted and antisocial. Occasionally a man would lose his mind and would have to be left behind. Victrix responded to it with a relentless wry humour.

When Marius strode into the tent Victrix turned. He met and held Marius' glance with his own. It was as if he recognised something in Marius, because he immediately broke off his conversation with the cleric and walked over to him. Victrix did not bother with ceremony. He just walked over to Marius and grabbed his hand, shaking it. Marius was taken aback. This was most unusual, and particularly for one soldier to another. As he shook Marius' hand he looked hard at him. Then he smiled.

Marius saw Victrix's instinctive liking for him, and it told him a considerable amount. It said that Victrix had complete faith in his own ability as a leader and therefore was not in the slightest threatened by Marius. Without a word, Marius handed Victrix his letter of appointment.
Victrix read it quickly.
"You are welcome. I can see from your eyes that we will want you to stay".
He looked back at Marius' letter, reading it once more. When he had finished he looked up.
"Excellent! What a refreshing change to be given a soldier rather than a bureaucrat as one's second in command. Welcome, Marius Sextus. Welcome to what will form half of the ninth".
Marius smiled back. "Thank you, Victrix. It will be a refreshing change for me, to be led by a soldier ".
Victrix chuckled. "You and I are of one mind, Marius. I see that this order is written by Lucius Merutii Scripius. Do you know him?"
Marius was instantly on his guard. "I do" he replied somewhat formally.
"You are a well connected man. You are going to have to tell me how a man like you has connections like this. I would also like you to tell me of your career because I've heard your name, Marius, and it is good. But all this can wait. According to the date on this order, you have travelled here from Rome in impossibly quick time. I'm sure that you and your men are tired, and do not wish to make polite conversation to your legate right now, so I will not detain you. You will return later to dine with me?".
Marius replied that he would. Victrix then turned to the scribe who had been taking notes on the large papyrus. "This is Sergius. He is the tribune who looks after the inventory of the train". Marius stepped forward to shake Sergius' hand. Sergius took it warmly.
"You are welcome, sir. I will show you to your tent. How many men do you have?"
"Thank you, Sergius. Six men".

"If you will come with me, sir, I'll show you to your quarters".
Marius turned to Victrix who dismissed him, slightly embarrassed that such formality was required.

By the time the sun had set the men had already eaten, and had gone to have a look at the camp and meet some of their new comrades Marius and I went to dine with our new commander.

*****

With the exception of fresh meat, decent wine and freshly baked bread, Victrix's table served identical food to that which the majority of the other three thousand men would be eating that night. Around the table were sitting the four tribunes that Victrix was taking with him. Sergius, two tough looking primi ordines, Marius and myself. They were courteous and friendly and all were impressed by the speed with which we had come from Rome. Marius dismissed it as nothing, which impressed them even more. They were interested in Marius and wanted to know his story, but it was clear that he was reluctant to tell it. No man other than a fool enjoys telling others of his greatest moments and Marius tried hard to deflect the enquiries. At first he succeeded by asking about Victrix's history. Like Marius, Victrix would not speak of it but one of his primi ordines, Euphatin, had served with him for years. Amid the legate's protests Euphatin began to tell us of our commander.

"I was centurian of the XXXVIIIth century of the Ist Legion (Adiutrix) for twenty three years before I transferred here. I was offered citizenship and a plot of land out east after I had served my twenty five years, but I refused it so that I could continue to serve Victrix. He first earned a reputation as a tribune in the Ist Legion under Commodius, who is now serving as the Legate of the Imperial Guards in Rome. We were on campaign against Decebalus, then leader of the Dacians, over twenty years ago. It was in the east and Victrix was the tribune responsible for the baggage train and the supplies. The land was hard and had been frequently pillaged. The local people were so disheartened that they had not bothered to rebuild their farmsteads. Instead they scraped a miserable existence from the forests. But we ate like kings. Victrix started to earn his reputation on that campaign not for fighting but for food. The victuals of that campaign have gone down in history as the finest any roman army ever enjoyed, and Victrix was responsible. I was there and I have been on many campaigns since. In all my years of service I have never eaten better".

Fighting and food were the only two ways that reputations were made or destroyed in the legions. I could well believe that if the food was as good as Euphatin claimed then Victrix could have earned a reputation as a hero.
I was surprised to hear my own voice.
"Marius too fought a campaign in that area at about that time. He was in Moesia, fighting Pintreich. Was it the same campaign?"
Euphatin replied "If Marius served in the XIXth or the VIIth, then it was. The Ist and the VIIth moved on to cross the Danubus and fight Decebalus whilst the XIXth went south to fight Pintreich in Moesia".
Euphatin stopped to allow Marius to tell us who he was with.
"I was with the XIXth", he replied simply.
Suddenly Victrix started forward. His brow was furrowed and his thumb and forefinger held his temple.
"There was a junior soldier who made his name in Moesia. The XIXth was attacked at dawn by Pintreich and his forces. Their scouts were killed and they were taken by surprise from higher ground. A decurian, pretty much on his own initiative gathered a few men and went to hunt the barbarian leader. He surprised him in a forest and killed Pintreich himself. Another lesser chieftain whose name I forget was also killed. Unless I am very much mistaken the decurian's name was Marius something."
As he said the name he looked straight at Marius. Marius shrugged and muttered something about Marius being a common name, particularly for a soldier. I couldn't help myself.
"The name of the decurian was Marius Sextus and the name of the lesser chieftain was Rheistoln who was killed by a legionary named Greto, a man who is with us here".

I was worried that I might have antagonised these men by appearing to boast. Looking round the table, it was clear that my concerns were groundless. They were enjoying themselves.

Victrix went on to tell the story of Marius' killing of Pintreich. Marius had been looking embarrassed, but he allowed Victrix to finish. Then he quietly asked Euphatin to tell us of what happened to the Ist and the VIIth after the XIXth had left for Moesia. Euphatin looked at Marius appreciatively before launching into the story.

"Decabulus was clever. He would not be drawn into a fight with us, it was like fighting a shadow. He hid behind the mountains and behind the great Danubus river because he knew that it would be a struggle for us to cross the mountains, even in the summer. As far as he was concerned, that was the only way that we could ever get to him. He was sure that if we wanted to fight him we would have to cross those mountains. It suited him perfectly, as he could wait until the train was spread out over miles before picking off sections at his leisure. It had not occurred to him that we could cross the great Danubus. Because it was so wide and so fast flowing it had not occurred to us either. We were at a loss, and the general was considering simply building a series of forts at the foot of the mountains and withdrawing the majority of the forces. We would have contained Decabulus but would also have abandoned any hope of defeating him".

"That was before Victrix's intervention. He argued that when the spring floods had subsided we would be able to build a bridge. At the time, no one really believed him. The river was simply too strong and too wide. But rather than return in failure, the general challenged Victrix to build this bridge. The spring was spent building the barges that would be moored in the river as supports. The wooden roadway that would be suspended from barge to barge was prefabricated and built using the new method, devised by Victrix, of interlocking the struts in the construction rather than just binding them together. Within three weeks of starting, the bridge was ready. The two legions crossed it and marched right into the heart of Dacia. Decabulus was killed, as was the majority of his army. We lost just under six hundred

men in the battle". Euphatin stopped abruptly. He was not a talker and had only told this story because he wanted his master's deeds to be known. For a moment there was silence before Serbius punctuated it.
"Well, gentlemen, it appears that the rest of us have an impossible job of meeting the standards of our commanders. But I have no doubt that we will have fun trying. Allow me to raise a toast:
'Britannia'"
The company stood up and raised their wine glasses. "To Britannia!"
I glanced at Marius. His was the only face in the tent that lacked any merriment or humour.

*****

The following morning we woke at dawn and set off on the road to the north. The clouds were low in the sky, but occasionally they broke and the rays of sun slanted steeply towards the rolling hills.
We sat by the side of the road as we watched the head of the column leave. The auxiliary scouts had left earlier, whilst the rest of the force was still packing up the camp, so that they could scout the area ahead. After a lengthy gap the vanguard marched, just one cohort strong in our reduced sized force. Following them went the pioneers, who would repair the road where necessary and clear it of obstacles. After a fairly long wait the baggage train pulled out. Its eighteen large wagons were pulled by oxen and were flanked by the contingent of horsemen. It was the middle of the morning by the time that they had passed and it was our turn to march. Marius and Victrix were mounted, but the rest of us walked. Our men were given the honour of marching with them as part of an augmented bodyguard. Behind us came the tribunes and other senior officials at the head of the rest of the cohorts. Our relatively light loads made us feel guilty. They were half what the rest of the soldiers were carrying, for although we carried the same armour, weapons, clothing, bedrolls and cooking equipment, we did not carry any tools. The other legionaries carried heavy mattocks for digging ditches, turf cutters for building ramparts and wicker baskets for moving soil. All of these tools would become essential when we entered hostile lands, and they weighed heavy.

We used two long sticks to carry our equipment. The shorter was bound to the longer at right angles, forming a cross that was strapped to our backs from which our equipment was hung.

From that place the march was not a long one. It took two days to reach Darocortorum where we took on more supplies. It was then a further ten days due north until we reached a small fishing village that also served as a port for boats to Britannia. The land was densely wooded all the way, and the road cut in a straight line right through the forest. On the final night before we reached the port Victrix ordered every legionary to cut two long, sturdy wooden stakes. They would have to be carried in addition to the rest of our equipment, as they would serve as parts of the defensive wall whenever we camped or came under attack of any kind. In theory legions were supposed to carry them at all times on a march, and it had been a concession of Victrix to allow us to come so far without them. But they weighed heavy on the men, and in the safe lands that we had passed through they would have been a wasted load. It was the sort of gesture that went a long way with soldiers.
Despite the extra load, cutting the stakes released an excitement in the ranks. We were about to enter hostile territory.

Boats had been ordered and were waiting for us at the port. The day that we marched into the coastal village it began to rain. We were told that on a clear day the island province could be seen from the coast of Gallis, but that day it was shrouded in mist beneath the grey skies. It was with this ill omen that we boarded the boats and sailed for Britannia.

23

When Lucius replied his voice was steady and his eyes looked straight into Perridac's.
"I will not help you"
Perridac's face turned red. "You would break your sacred oath?"
Lucius did not flinch. "I would".

There was silence. It seemed that there was no more to be said. But Perridac was a wily man, and knew that the great man sitting opposite him would not break his word lightly. A guilty conscience always makes a man talk more than he would like to, so he sought to use it to try and make Lucius talk.
"Sir, we have travelled half way across the empire for this interview. We have lost a man on Creta in the course of getting here. You have a reputation as an honourable man, a man of your word. I believe that we are due some explanation of why you would break your oath. You still have your faith?"

The implication that no man who still retained their faith could break an oath to a brother would hit Lucius hard, and Perridac knew it.
Lucius knew what Perridac was trying to do, but there was respect in his voice as he answered.
"Sometimes I wish that I didn't still have my faith, Perridac. It would make so many things simpler. But I do, and I am acting as my faith dictates that I should."

Perridac had been unsure as to whether Lucius would even have heard of the Neronian confession. But now he was excited. It was not only obvious that Lucius knew about it, but judging by the seriousness with which Lucius was taking the matter it was almost as if he had the confession in his possession.

Perridac was a quick thinker. He knew that if there was some link between Lucius and Marius then the confession would almost certainly be in their possession.

"Where is Marius Sextus?"
At the mention of the name, Benjamin tensed. He had never met Marius, but he knew him to be the man who had murdered his brother. Perridac noted Lucius' discomfort at the question. He also noticed the look of intensity on the serving girls face and the colour that mention of Marius' name brought to her cheeks.
Lucius considered lying and denying all knowledge of Marius. But there was no point, the connection had been made. Despite his better judgement, he answered.

"Marius is awaiting instructions" replied Lucius.
"Is he trying to blackmail the emperor?" asked Perridac.
"No he is not. He realises now that if he had tried he would have failed."

Perridac felt that he had discovered all he needed to know from those questions. He asked one final question.
"Do you have the confession?"
"No" replied Lucius firmly and instantly.
"So what are your plans for it? Why will you not give it to us?"
Lucius flushed lightly as he replied. "I have not decided. I need to talk with Origen to hear his views. This manuscript could change the nature of the world as we know it. The question is whether it would be for good or for evil. I cannot allow the destruction of Rome. People would be thrust back into the darkness of anarchy and all the death that it brings. I cannot allow myself to be a part of making that happen. However the confession is used, it must be used within the context of the survival of Rome. I will not surrender the manuscript to Tertullian or to Origen unless I have heard what they intend to do with it and unless I agree that their plans will be for the good".

Perridac was satisfied. It was clear that there was no more to be gained. At least Lucius had been honest with them, and had given them a way forward.
Perridac got to his feet and stretched out his hand towards Lucius.
"Thank you for being honest, sir. I cannot say that we are pleased, but we will take what you have said to Tertullian and Origen, and you will no doubt hear more from them".

Benjamin had been listening to this exchange with increasing agitation. He could not understand Perridac's willingness to be stonewalled by Lucius. His mind was filled with the image of his brother David and Gideon. Their faces were drifting together in his memory, and he was beginning to find it difficult to distinguish the two. David had been killed by Marius, and Lucius was protecting him. This made Lucius more Roman than christian. He had more loyalty to a fellow roman than to a christian brother who had been murdered. His frustration boiled over.
"We are not going", he announced loudly as Lucius and Perridac shook hands.
Both of them turned to look at him in surprise.
"We are not going until we are told of the whereabouts of the manuscript".
He looked straight at Lucius as he continued. "You know where it is. Gideon will not be palmed off by your silken words".
Lucius' eyebrows were raised in a look of incomprehension. Benjamin had a desperate look about him. He needed a threat and he found one.
"If you don't tell us where we can find it we will expose you as a christian".
Lucius did not look at all worried. He simply looked at Perridac. "You would blackmail me?" He knew the answer before he asked the question.
"No, we won't. Benjamin, we're going". It was clear that Perridac was embarrassed by this crude intervention from Benjamin. Benjamin sullenly folded his arms and made it clear that he would not move. Perridac leaned forward to him and spoke gently.

"Come on, Benjamin. Blackmail is a sin and it will not get us anywhere. I understand how you must feel after what happened to Gideon and David. But we've all lost people we love and it is no good to let bitterness overtake us. I don't agree with the way that the senator has chosen to deal with this, but we cannot do anything else here. We must return to Sidon and report to Origen".

It was more the way that Perridac spoke than his words that made Benjamin crumble. He looked imploringly up at Perridac and then abruptly stood up and walked to the edge of the room. He would not shake hands with Lucius, or even look him in the eye.

As they left the house the same way that they had entered, Benjamin silently brooded over his humiliation.

Once they were back in their room in the Transtiberine, Perridac looked around.

"What did you make of that?" he asked no one in particular.

Benjamin looked chastened. He knew that he had made a fool of himself, and it almost made it worse that no one was acknowledging it.

Beziac shrugged his shoulders. "There isn't much to say, really" he said. "Lucius was quite clear".

Perridac settled himself down on the kilim on the floor. "Yes, quite clear. Did anyone notice the girl's reaction to the mention of Marius?"

The others just looked back at him blankly. Perridac continued.

"I think that I know who she is. Origen told us that Smenkhare's daughter had disappeared with Marius and his men. I would wager my shirt she is Rani of Assyut".

He paused to see realisation dawn on the faces of his men.

"I would also wager that Marius is still is in possession of the manuscript. He's the key to getting it. And the key to Marius, I suspect, is Rani".

Perridac's tone changed as he explained what he proposed to do.

"Two of us must remain in Rome to try to discover where he is. I think that the best way to find him is to keep a close watch on Rani. She will lead us to him eventually. The other two will travel back to Sidon to tell Origen what we have found. Lucius is up to something. I think that he has a plan, but he hinted strongly that the plan could be changed to include us if we think of a better one. That makes the trip back to Sidon an urgent one. I will go and Benjamin will come with me. You Beziac and Radjic will stay here and try to find Marius."

Benjamin knew that he was being taken back because Perridac did not trust him. He was seething with frustration and indignation, but he held his tongue.

Two days later a ship sailed from Ostia for Sidon. Perridac and Benjamin were on it.

24

Carrion birds gathered under the grey, heavy skies. They circled overhead a small, gutted village and some had already landed to start to peck at the corpses that smouldered amongst the ruins. It had been a poor settlement, just five or six tiny homes made of twigs and clay with rooves of thatch. Gwdloych had only vaguely enjoyed dismembering its head man. Unusually for him he hadn't even participated in the rape of the headman's two young daughters. It was their eyes that the carrion birds were now beginning to peck at. They always went for the eyes first.

None of Gwdloych's men noticed his distraction. They were sitting around the smouldering huts, waiting for pigs to roast on the embers of their dead owners homes. There had been more this time than Gwdloych could ever remember having for a raiding party. Tens of hundreds of men, perhaps as many as three thousand. Ever since he first struck at the Romans, men had started to materialise out of nowhere to come and join him. But since his first attacks on the columns that came for the people, this trickle had become a stream.

For three generations, since the Emperor Claudius first conquered Britannia, these lands had been used as a source of slaves. Slaving parties would march out of Eburacum into the hills and forests to the north and seek out strong young people to be taken to Londinium, and from there to the slave markets in provinces across the empire. They could never be household slaves as the Greeks or Phoenicians tended to be, but they had begun to gain a reputation as labourers. They were strong and fit, so were in great demand from commercial farmers. The slaving parties were composed of up to two hundred men. They moved fast and they were armed to their teeth. If they came under any sort of attack they refused to engage with their assailants unless they could not avoid it. They were not there to kill, but to harvest. But when they were engaged, they would be brutal. Until Gwdloych no one had been possessed of the courage to attack these columns properly. Most of the hill people had been reduced to cowering at their approach, hoping that they would not be singled out. Any assault had been restricted to desperate villagers, husbands and parents who vainly tried to save loved ones from being taken away. But they never could, and unless they were discouraged quickly they did not escape with their own lives.

Gwdloych was not particularly bothered by the idea of people being stolen, but he was irritated by these columns of swaggering foreigners marching through the lands of his people. So he had begun to fight back. He never touched a column unless he outnumbered them at least two to one. Even then he would not engage them unless he was able to plan the attack and come at them from a significantly superior position. He had done this three times now. The result on each occasion was the retrieval of the slaves and the killing of at least thirty roman soldiers. His losses had been heavy, usually about the same as those of the Romans, but he felt that it was worth it. The columns no longer came into his lands.

But Gwdloych had not anticipated how the people would react to his raids. The numbers that had come to him had taken him by surprise. What particularly surprised him had been the degree of fear that the slave takers had instilled in the people. When he started to attack the columns he had no idea of the numbers that were being taken or of the consequences that it could have for a family. Often the weak left behind were unable to fend for themselves, and ended up starving, or been killed in those bleak hills. But now they had a leader. Almost by accident Gwdloych found that he had become the champion of the Brigantes.

At first he wallowed in his role. His fame was spreading to many far-flung parts of the tribal lands. The Brigantes had been without a leader for several years, and Gwdloych knew that he would be endorsed as soon as he deigned to claim leadership. But he did not want to claim it until he had done something that was worthy of a chieftain, something that would make his acclamation special. Gwdloych needed a grand gesture, and he needed it not just to satisfy his own desire for glory but also to feed the increasing numbers that flocked to him. His land was not used to sustaining such numbers.

He was so engrossed, trying to decide whether his latest idea was too much, that he barely noticed the rape of the two young girls.

Gwdloych was caught in two minds. Originally he had restricted his raids to other tribes of Britons. He had heard much of the strength of the Romans, so had been wary of inspiring their wrath. But since he first decided to see if they were as invincible as he had been led to believe, he had come to enjoy baiting them. His first attack on a remote fort that guarded their long straight road had been successful. His men had loved him for having the audacity to try it, and he loved anything that brought him the adulation of his men. So he had continued the attacks on the forts, and had found that if he employed overwhelming force, the Romans bled and screamed and begged like everyone else. The attacks on the forts intensified, and it was then that he had begun his raids on the slave trains. His uncharacteristic indecision was caused by the idea to take one of their towns. He would kill everything in it and then send some of the death to the chief of the Romans, and the prospect excited him. But he could not decide which town he was to take. His first thought had been Eburacum because he knew that if he took Eburacum the bards would sing of him forever. But then, the bards would probably sing of him forever anyway.

Gwdloych had learned the lessons of the past well. He would only strike when the Romans were not expecting it, and leave as soon as he had done his work. His were hill people. They had no use for towns or roads or baths or villas. Their villages were remote and well spread, their strength their understanding of the land. They could go to ground and disappear, and the Romans could not fight something that they could not find. Gwdloych knew exactly what he was doing. And despite his desire to take Eburacum, he knew it was too risky. There were too many soldiers and they could move fast. Isurium, on the other hand presented a different prospect. Yes, it would be hard. No one had ever attempted such a raid since Boudicca. She had sacked

Camulodunum, Londinium and Verulamium. It was said that after Camulodunum the chief of the Romans had not even tried to defend Londinium and Verulamium. He had just abandoned the cities and instead lured Boudicca's people out to the plains of the Trinovantes, just below the Iceni's own lands. There he had inflicted his slaughter. No, these lessons had been well learned. Isurium would yield sufficient food to keep the Brigantes alive long enough for Gwdloych to give them an acclamation feast the like of which they had never seen before. It would give him the victory that would make his acclamation a celebration remembered forever. And after his acclamation he would be able to order the people back to their villages before they all starved.

As he thought he fondled the tiny heads that dangled from his ears. When he had come to his decision he stood up and surveyed the scene of devastation about him. Thousands looked at him, and he shouted loudly to ensure that he could be heard by them all.
"In three days we march from this place. We need all the men that we can find, for the victory we will win shall be great. From that victory we shall return to Dunn Sccyrebb where I shall be acclaimed as the chief of the Brigantes. Let any who would challenge me come there. So go, go and find men who want to be part of a famous victory".
With that, Gwdloych turned his back and marched south down the vale towards Dunn Sccyrebb.

*****

Three days later, shortly before noon he was back. The day was sunny as he marched up the vale. He had with him the three hundred men of fighting age from his and nearby villages. They had left Dunn Sccyrebb at dawn. All of them were covered in their battle dress of enormous furs. Bear fur and wolf hair cloaks were regarded as more prestigious, but leather hides from cattle were equally practical. All the men were filthy and had long, shaggy hair and thick beards. Most wore iron rings through their noses and various trinkets through their ears. Their weapons were mostly huge wooden clubs. Some men had long, two handed swords. A blow from them was lethal, but they could be unwieldy and cumbersome in the tight press of battle. From their belts dangled short daggers and on their backs were strapped small round shields made from cowhide which derived structural strength from the heavy oak staffs that crossed at their backs. The other piece of equipment that they carried was an enormous skin which contained a potent local mead. If there was to be a great victory, it could not be done with a sober head.

When Gwdloych and his men rounded the last contour of the vale they drew breath at the number of similarly armed and dressed warriors that were there to greet them. Most had been there for the last three days, simply remaining after Gwdloych's announcement. But many had gone to spread the word of the great victory and celebration that was planned. There were nearly five thousand men there that day. Gwdloych was not one for lingering, nor was he one for long speeches. He simply walked straight to the centre of the crowd and shouted.
"Any who want to see glory, come with me. Tomorrow will be a great day for us".

*****

They marched south. It took ten hours of marching to reach the hills surrounding the town of Isurium. By then it was well after dark, and the men were tired. They had marched due south for twenty miles since noon. Ahead of them they could see flames that lit the gatehouses of the town's wall. An amphitheatre sat deserted outside the walls, with an entrance close to one of the town's main gates. The barracks of the garrison were inside the walls. At most there would be five hundred in the garrison, so Gwdloych felt confident of the odds. After a brief conference, Gwdloych and his army walked into the deserted amphitheatre and started to drink. It was well into the early hours before they began to pass out.

An hour before dawn the word went round that Gwdloych was ready to make his move. There were only about one thousand men who were able to listen. They tried to creep quietly to the town walls, but fuzziness from drink and sleep meant that they were not as quiet as they could have been. They pressed themselves against the walls and skirted around until they came to the main gate. There they waited, arranging themselves on either side of the gate. At dawn the gate would be opened and the towns daily business would commence. As the gates opened they would storm in and take control of the gatehouse. But the plan relied on the men having sufficient discipline to remain under the town walls outside the gates for upwards of an hour undetected.

Discipline was appalling. Because there was no sign of any defence, the men soon became bored and began to talk to loudly. A few mead fuelled arguments began to break out. It was not long before the gate keepers heard the talk and threw down torches to see where the noise came from. They were greeted by the sight of over one thousand chattering barbarians.

The story of what happened next is still probably being sung by the bards in that part of Britannia. Gwdloych obtained a vast tree trunk from somewhere. Because he was so quick with the order the gates were rammed before they were reinforced and before the majority of the garrison were able to rouse themselves and raise the defences. It only took a few charges for the gates to buckle. By that time, the noise had not only summoned the rest of the barbarians but also woken most of the town. When Gwdloych's men entered, they were crazed. Fuelled by mead and bloodlust, five thousand barbarians staggered and stormed into the soft underbelly of a Roman town.

The theatre was on fire within minutes. Almost immediately it seemed that there was barely a house without its door smashed in. But the carnage was not as extensive as it could have been with better organisation. Gwdloych left no one to guard the gates of the town, so when the inhabitants realised what was happening and ran screaming into the streets, those that were not cut down by the great clubs and swords simply ran out of the town into the surrounding fields. Neither did anyone bother to destroy the garrison while it was rousing itself from sleep. Instead the vast horde of barbarians began the business of raping, killing, looting and drinking immediately they entered the town. Fires broke out everywhere. Big, smelly, drunk, hairy men carried large quantities of food, gold and wine out of the city gates to put in a great pile next to the amphitheatre. Severed limbs and bloody corpses littered the streets. Screams punctured the air and the sound of wailing became so pervasive that it went almost unnoticed. Eventually the garrison sallied from behind the gates of the fort, and when they did they marched straight to the basilica but found it in flames. People were running everywhere. The barbarians refused to engage the garrison, running instead from house to house to find more valuables to steal and girls to rape. As the garrison advanced through the town the barbarians retreated in their path.

Within forty five minutes of first entering the town most of the barbarians had left, carrying as much as they could. Their booty consisted of all manner of goods, as well as a significant proportion of the town's female population. They retreated some way from the town walls before Gwdloych managed to regroup them. He was exultant, the joy of spilt blood running through him. He let out a great roar of triumph. A sizeable number of barbarians had got carried away and ended up being captured. Gwdloych did not care, for anyone stupid enough to get caught deserved what came to him. And what came to them was to have their heads stuck on a pike strapped to the walls of the town. Triumphant, the horde retreated into the forest and slowly made their way back to Dunn Sccyrebb. With their heavy loads the journey took four days.

*****

The acclamation of Gwdloych was truly a feast to remember. Over eight thousand mostly women and children had gathered in that valley, camping around the village that Gwdloych had inherited from his father. The numbers swelled to nearly thirteen thousand when the men who had destroyed Isurium reached it. Many of their captives had died on the way. The brutality and sheer volumes of men who had indulged themselves in their bodies had killed large numbers of them. When the army marched into the valley and saw the crowds already there, they raised Gwdloych on their shoulders and roared their triumph. The women and children all pressed forward to meet the returning heroes. There was a great crush, and Gwdloych yelled to be set down. The moment that he his feet touched the ground he drew his sword. Immediately those surrounding stepped back. Slowly Gwdloych began to swing his sword round him. The crush became one to retreat from their leader. He swung around and around, making the circle about him ever greater. One woman was shoved back into the circle by an irate man who had grown tired of her constant pushing of him. Gwdloych's sword caught her on the hip, cutting it badly. She fell and was immediately dragged to the edge of the circle. Gwdloych continued to circle with his sword until he had created a space twenty metres across. Then he stopped, red in the face and puffing hard. He walked to the centre of the circle and said in a loud voice.

"I am Chief of the Brigantes. Is there any man here who would be chief?"

There was silence. Complete silence.

Gwdloych continued. "Is there any man here who would dispute my claim?"

Again there was silence.

Three men then came forward. One was a warrior and two were druids. Both druids were naked, their hair long and falling down their backs in ringlets. Some sort of grease or fat gave it a grey white tinge. Their bodies were covered in a greasy slime and their smell was so foul that it penetrated even the stench of the crowd surrounding them. They hopped and danced forward, jigging about in a state of high excitement. The taller of the druids held a squirming child of about four years. He shouted:

"This child's life says that Gwdloych is chief of the Brigantes"

A woman could be heard sobbing not far away. It was unclear whether it was the mother of the child or the woman who had been maimed by Gwdloych's sword. Other than that there was no other sound. The druid set the little boy down onto the ground where he stood looking perplexed. It was clear that he was searching the crowd for his mother. As he stood there looking around, the warrior brought down his sword on the top of the little boy's head, cleaving it in two.

Blood and brains spilled out. The smaller of the druids picked up the slimy brain in his hand. Part of it slipped out and spattered on the floor.

"This is a good omen", he said. "The brain has fallen in two. So it will be that Gwdloych's era will cause us to multiply". He paused as he looked about the crowd with a defiant, challenging look in his eye. At his feet the corpse of the dead child was twitching.

"I will serve him" he shouted.

On this proclamation the crowd around Gwdloych fell to their knees. Gwdloych tried to suppress a smile of triumph. When he had regained his composure he spoke.

"Tonight we will feast. And then I will tell you how we will drive the Romans from our land".

With that, Gwdloych, Chief of the tribe of the Brigantes of Briton grabbed a tall, thin Roman hostage of about fourteen years old, strode past his wife and dragged her into his low slung, stinking home.

25

We should have been glad to get to Londinium.
To its west, low green hills lay around the valley of a great river, and to the east the wide flood plain stretched out towards the mouth of the river. When Julius Caesar had originally visited Britannia he built a fort at the first place where the river could be forded west of its estuary. When he left the fort fell into disrepair, but a small community of local oyster fishermen had remained there. When Claudius returned to conquer Britannia properly, he, like Julius Caesar before him recognised the strategic importance of the place and set up his campaign headquarters by the ford. When the governor was appointed he had decided to build his capital here. It developed into a large provincial town, surrounded by a high wall and dominated by the enormous army barracks that sat outside. As we came over the wide rump of a low hill to the south east of the town we caught a glimpse of it through the afternoon sun.

The clouds were bulky and grey, but the sun frequently broke through. The weather had been like this ever since we landed on a desolate beach beneath imposing white cliffs. It was the kind of weather that brought heavy showers followed by sunshine, and it made marching inconvenient. Our journey was constantly slowed by the need to switch from the heavy skins that kept our kit dry to marching tunics that prevented us from overheating.

The march itself was mostly uneventful and dull. We were on the road for just five days before we saw the walls of Londinium in the distance. The only thing that was worthy of note on the march was the attitude of the local people that we saw. Serbius reported that they would not sell him food. There was nothing strange in this until he pointed out that it was not because there was any shortage of it. Even though their farms were primitive affairs worked with old tools that had long ago been replaced in most parts of the empire, the exceptional fertility of the land meant that it yielded an abundance of food almost despite the methods of the people who worked it. Our problem was that they refused to sell it to Romans, even Romans who were offering way above the market rate for it. Victrix would not allow us to requisition it, so morale was poor as we continued to survive on dried biscuits and porridge whilst passing through fields packed with ripening produce.

The local tribe, the Cantii, made their feelings towards us clear. To them we were hostile outlanders who had no right to be there. Passive resistance seemed to be their favoured tactic and it was effective. They were clearly savage, living in crude little mud huts and shouting abuse at us in their gutteral, ugly, throaty language. They had damaged sections of the road, and as we passed some of them would throw stones if they felt that they could get away with it. Shortly after we landed one of the legionaries was struck on the head and died. Usually we would bury the body by the side of the road and continue, but we were afraid of it being dug up so we carried it with us.

Strangest of all was the number of druids that turned out to curse us. Anyone who had served for any length of time in the legions of Rome was used to pagan barbarians and their strange priests. But in the land of the Cantii there were just so many of them. Legionaries were superstitious and hated to be cursed by these ranting madmen. At that time I myself was unsettled by them, and they had a bad effect on morale.

We had to make full defensive camp every time we stopped. This was usual practice in hostile territory, but it did mean that the evening ritual became protracted and tiring. All of this attrition wore the men down, so that by the time we spotted Londinium we were expecting to find some relief in it. But the ordinary little town on the edge of the bleak, flat flood plains of the estuary did not inspire relief. We did not know it at the time, but the south of that province was a good deal more hostpitable than the north.

Londinium was as underwhelming as Rome was overwhelming. It looked much like any other provincial Roman centre, except for the extent of the barracks which were considerably larger than would be normal for a town of Londinium's size, almost as big as the town itself. That sight was ominous, for it was a visible symbol of what we had already began to suspect. It suggested that we were in an untamed land. There was a hatred constantly simmering beneath the surface of the whole province. We had felt it ever since landing, and none of us liked what it implied. To march as a Roman there was to feel that at any time you could run into a savage horde driven by bitterness and loathing. We knew that we were well trained. All of us in that force were trained killers. Some were good at it, some not so good. Some had done a lot of it, some none at all. But even so, there was a dark mood among the men of our small army as we marched through this brooding, sullen land. It was unusual that so long after conquest the pax romana should still be rejected by the savages. Usually within a few years they would have seen the advantages that the Roman way could bring to their standard of living and would begin to aspire to citizenship. But these people seemed immune to all of that. They seemed to despise the progress that Rome brought to their land, wanting nothing but to destroy it and remove all evidence that it had ever happened.

*****

Our small army was welcomed enthusiastically by Caracalla, the governor of the province. He was a large, slowmoving and rather dull witted man of exceptionally high birth. He was delighted to have a diversion to take his mind off the boredom of life in Londinium. The mood of our army was slightly improved by two things. The first was the enormous amounts of food and drink that the XXth legion had in their stores. They had copious quantities of a delicious local drink brewed from hops called ayle. The XXth lived on it. The second was the number of spare barrack blocks that they had in that camp. It had originally been built to house two full legions. Because there was now only one legion stationed in Londinium it meant that there was plenty of room for us to stay. So our army was well looked after, and quickly settled in to eat, drink and exchange glorious stories with the men of the XXth. They were pretty downcast, the XXth, but were pleased to have news of the outside world and new soldiers to drink with.

I left Greto and the rest of our men tucking into the ayle and gorging themselves on chicken, pig and fresh fruits to return to Marius in the praetorium. As his assistant I was invited to the welcome banquet that Caracalla had insisted on holding for us. It was to be held in the governor's palace inside the town itself and Marius was quartered there. I left the camp and walked down the special walled avenue that led between the camp and the town. It had two heavily guarded gates at either end. This innovation began in Britannia and had caught on elsewhere. It meant that the soldiers could have immediate access to the town unimpared, and the townsfolk could escape to the barracks in the event of an emergency. When I reached the gate leading into the town it was open, so without breaking step I walked through and entered Londinium. The town was well spread out, with large open spaces all around. The fertility of this land was demonstrated by dense luscious gardens all around, and I marvelled at the work it must take to keep them under control. The homes were simple and sturdy, not grand like in Rome. All of the streets were metalled as one would expect, and they were quiet. There was none of the bustle and vivacity of a normal Roman town and there were hardly any hawkers. I remembered how in Rome I had thought that a town without hawkers would be a peaceful and welcome relief. But now, in this souless, empty town I began to miss them. They might be irritating but at least they were evidence that the place was alive. There was something spooky about the silence. Even the people in the streets seemed to by hurrying, so there was none of the familiar chatter. Instead, just silence punctuated by the occasional bark of a dog and bray of a donkey. Unintentionally I quickened my step toward the palace.

At first I barely noticed the shrines, but as I proceeded through the eerie streets I began to pay more attention. There were just so many of them. There were a large number of shrines to Vesta, goddess of the home, and to Lares and Penates, the guardians of the family. Saturn, god of farming was also unsurprisingly well represented. But what made me shudder were the number of shrines to Mars, the god of war and to Mithras, the sun god from the east. Mithras was a god who presided over death.

Rome had more than its fair share of shrines and temples, but what was different about Londinium was the fact that these tributes to the gods were so carefully tended. In Rome, almost no one paid any attention to the gods. We all knew that they were just an invention of legend, much as the allegorical story of Romulus and Remus. But here they were being taken deadly seriously. Many of the shrines had wax candles burning in them, and at their feet were considerable offerings of meat, fruit and cereals. As I walked through those streets I considered this new omen. I didn't like it at all, and looked forward to finding out more about this land from Caracalla and his men at dinner.

The palace was magnificent, a jewel amongst the mediocrity of that town. In Rome it would not have stood out as anything particularly special but here it was a great sight to behold, raised high above the level of the street and reached by a grand, fan shaped staircase of over thirty steps. I savoured the majesty of the place as I climbed to a colonaded façade dominated from above by a wonderful frieze. There were two huge carved doors of eucalyptus wood standing open and allowing a warm light to illuminate the staircase like a beacon in the wilderness. I strode up to the door and was greeted by a well dressed doorman. He led me through an enormous atrium that was entirely covered by an intricately gilded painting. It covered the walls and the ceiling, and was continued on the floor in the form of a stunning mosaic. On the walls were spectacular bronze oil lamps fashioned into the outlandish shapes of grotesque human heads, satyrs and parts of animals fused with parts of humans. Those sculptures somehow summed up the mood of Britannia.

*****

The banquet Caracalla laid on that night could only be described as sumptuous. When the doorman led me into the hall most of the guests were already there. It was an enormous room with columns supporting a balcony lined with lilies. In the hall were about twenty men and forty women. Victrix and Marius were seated either side of Caracalla, the three of them deep in conversation. I was amused to see that he was wearing a greek synthesis, making Victrix and Marius look like clumsy soldiers beside his elegance. I was led to a man of medium build, a large gut and small, deep set eyes and introduced formally as Tolus of Corsica. He replied formally that his name was Marcus Priorus of Rome, and then he smiled.

"You are welcome, Tolus of Corsica. You have come with the contingent to join the IXth in Eburacum?"

"I have", I replied.

"I've never had the pleasure of going there myself but I hear that it is one of the great joys that this world has to offer". At first I didn't pick up the sarcastic tone in his voice.

"And you, Marcus. You serve with the XXth?"

"I have that honour". He spat out the word 'honour' with such vitriol that I couldn't contain my look of surprise. He quickly moderated his tone. "I am sorry, Tolus. You have just arrived and I am already inflicting my disillusionment on to you. But this is supposed to be a happy occasion. We are welcoming some fellow Romans to help us in our quest to bring this place some measure of decent society. Tell me of your journey".

We ended up having a lengthy conversation notable only for its banality and Marcus' rather pained attempts to show an interest in inconsequential matters. He was obviously no good at small talk and was deliberately avoiding the subject of Britannia. From his initial comments it was fairly clear that this was because he would struggle to find anything positive to say about it. But I wanted to find out about this land, and it was clear that Marcus had plenty to say on the matter if only he would allow himself to say it.

"I noticed the shrines on my way here, Marcus. They are numerous and well maintained, and they show a great devotion to our gods of conflict".

He regarded me shrewdly. "You want me to tell you of Britannia?" he asked.

He was asking for permission to be honest with me. I looked him squarely back as I gave my reply.

At that point a great bell began to toll. The murmur of voices in the hall died down quickly and Caracalla stood up.

"If everyone would like to take their places, the banquet can begin" he said loudly.

Immediately the sound of music came from behind me. I turned to see an elderly man playing twin pipes. Next to him was a beautiful young girl with castanets, swaying gently to the rhythm. Slowly she slunk forward, swaying her hips and breasts provocatively. The pipe player followed her until they were both in the centre of the room. She ran her hands over her curvaceous form in such a way that no man watching could fail to be stirred. Marcus showed me to a couch by a low set marble table with fantastical winged creatures engraved into it. I reclined on the couch as beautifully robed serving girls came out with great platters of food and flagons of wine. The wine that we began with was yellow in colour and fairly strong, and I could taste the honey in it. The first course consisted of sweetbreads and stuffed figs and was followed by songbirds served in an asparagus sauce with quails eggs. It was the most delicious dish that I had ever tasted. While Marcus talked to me of Britannia I concentrated on my food and tried not to look too obviously at the nubile young serving girls.

"I have been here for nine years now and I have no prospect of getting out in the near future. My twenty five years service is not up for another six, and the chances are that I will be expected to serve them out here . . " he paused, wondering whether to continue.

"Whether I can survive for that long I do not know". He had decided. He took a long, deep draught of his wine. As he did so he noticed me regarding him.

"Don't worry, Tolus. Before long you will seek solace anywhere that you can get it in this country. I have never seen men who drink so much as the soldiers posted to Britannia. There is precious little else to do. One would have thought that with a province to build there would be plenty to occupy us, but there is no point. Even Caracalla would agree with me. We have tried. We have built aqueducts and roads, towns and temples, even plumbing systems and fountains. But whenever we do, the local savages do their best to destroy them. They are totally unable to build anything themselves other than the stinking little holes that they like to live in. But when it comes to destruction, there are none better".

Bitterly he drained his goblet once more, and as he did so he leaned over to refill mine.

"I have never known such hate, Tolus. They see everything that we do only as something that is Roman. They do not see it for what it is, progress, something that can make their lives better. I swear, they would rather give their children poisoned water from a bad stream than clean water from a roman pipe. You can't fight that. They will never again raise an army to challenge us in battle because they know the hopelessness of it. Instead they pick us off one by one. They harry us and wait until we are vulnerable. When they strike they are brutal. I don't mean brutal in the roman sense of the word. These people do not believe in a clean death. They believe in screaming death. They believe in exacting their hatred on our living bodies and then afterwards on our dead bodies. They do things that even Nero would not have had the sickness to think of. It is a war of attrition and the savages are winning it".

Once more Marcus paused to refill our goblets. His hand did not release the flagon as he drained his goblet. He refilled it once more before he reclined and continued.

"We prefer not to leave our barracks unless we are more than a couple of centuries strong. We have all but given up trying to build an infrastructure that can make this place truly Roman. You may have noticed that apart from the provincial staff there are barely any Romans in this town at all. The reason is that no sane person will come to live here. Even in the towns Romans disappear. Often they are never found. Sometimes their mutilated bodies, or parts of their bodies are found in the strangest places. So we have nothing to do. We cannot just go out and kill the locals, for we cannot wage war against an enemy that will not meet us. We cannot build, and we cannot even go on exercise without large numbers. So we sit around in our barracks, getting steadily more bored and more angry. The only way that we have to release the boredom and anger is to drink".

He took another long draught of his wine. Already he had drunk several goblets and our flagon had been replaced twice. Every time he replenished his own he replenished mine too, and I was beginning to become fuzzy headed.
"And that's not the worst of it. Things are bad down here, but I hear that things are worse up in Eburacum. Only a few days ago . . . ."
Marcus stopped himself. Through his alcoholic haze he decided that he had gone far enough. He would not disillusion me further by telling of recent events in Eburacum. I tried to press him, but he withdrew into a stubborn silence.

By now the party was in full swing. Almost all of the local soldiers were very drunk indeed. The sweet courses were being brought on, and I was feeling extremely full and considerably more drunk than I was accustomed to. The combination made me sleepy. Marius and Victrix stood out in the room, for they were the only two people who looked completely sober. They also looked perplexed and concerned. By contrast Caracalla was roaring drunk. There was a rather portly lady well into her middle years reciting Greek poetry, which I always find intolerably boring. Caracalla obviously agreed, for he was shouting at her to remove her toga. At first she tried to continue the recital, but he was insistent. She looked around the room confused, and then turned and ran out. Caracalla burst out into great guffaws of laughter. It was an undignified sight. As soon as he recovered from his mirth, he clapped his hands and a group of young girls came on and began to dance slowly to the music of several lyres. I watched for a few minutes in silence before I could no longer ignore the demands of my bladder.

As I stood I felt unsteady on my feet, and nearly toppled onto Marcus. He did not appear to notice, but I had to concentrate to remain in a straight line as I moved to the back of the room, where I relieved myself into a large bronze pissing pot. I decided to take a quick walk to clear my head, so I wandered along the arched walkway and passed though a wide arch that led to a pretty courtyard with a fountain in the middle and statues all around. I could so easily have been in Rome. The air had the chill edge of the north about it, and it felt good on my flushed skin. A quick walk round the courtyard would be perfect before returning to the banquet.

My head was already feeling clearer as I turned to walk up the far wall of the courtyard. Suddenly I heard a scuffling sound followed by a short whimper ahead of me. I thought it was a cat so paid little attention. But as I proceeded up the path towards the far corner of the courtyard I began to make out a shape in the gloom. The light from the oil lamps barely reached the recess, but I could tell that it was too big to be a cat. I continued to approach until I could see that it was a young girl of perhaps sixteen years and a fat Roman. The girl was a slave and her tunic had been ripped at the front, whilst the Roman had lifted his toga and looked as though he was about to rape the girl. I do not know what I would have done had I been sober, but in my impaired state I did not stop to think about where I was or the consequences of my actions. Instead, I asked the Roman to step forward. He told me, in no uncertain terms, to leave him alone. I should have gone but I stood my ground. He let his toga fall back and walked slowly out of the shadows. Almost before I knew what had happened he had punched me on the nose so hard that I saw stars. When my head cleared, I realised that I was sitting on my backside in the courtyard. Without a second glance the big roman turned back to the girl and resumed his attentions. I got up, and repeated my request for him to step forward. When he turned his eyes were burning with anger, and he reached under his toga and drew out a long dagger. I knew that I was drunk, but with the irrational confidence of the inebriated I believed that I could better him man despite being unarmed. He leapt at me. I jumped aside, trying to grab his arm, but I missed it. He circled to his right, and I to my left so that the girl was behind me. The roman lunged once more. This time I managed to grab his stabbing arm as I stepped out of the way. I twisted it hard and yanked it behind his back. The knife went clattering to the marble floor, and I flung the flat of my hand as hard as I could into his shoulder. I felt it dislocate from its socket and he gave a great yell as he fell to one knee. I grabbed the girl.
"Get us out of here now" I hissed.

She did not hesitate. She led me back to the corner of the courtyard and then through a small door to the right. We ran down a passageway and through another tiny door that led down some stairs towards some storerooms in the bowels of the building. Under an oil lamp she stopped and looked up at me.
"Thank you" she said.
Then, to my great surprise, she threw herself into my arms and began to sob.
I held her. I had drunk considerably more wine than I was accustomed to, and I held her for longer than I should have. She was young, but her breasts were perfectly formed. Because her tunic was ripped they were bare and I could feel them pressing through my toga. I stroked her hair. I stroked it to calm her but I found that the action, combined with the feeling of her tears on my shoulder, her breasts rising and falling and her breath on my chest was beginning to arouse me. I began to whisper softly to her that all would be right. I thought that if I asked her what her name was it might help her to stop crying.
"Olivia" she replied quietly. "And what is yours?"
"My name is Tolus" I replied. Had I been thinking I would never have given her my real name.
I think that she could tell that I was aroused. There was precious little clothing between us to disguise the fact.

We stood there for some time like that, holding each other. Eventually, for some reason I asked her of herself, and for an equally unaccountable reason she began to tell me. After a few minutes we heard the door open at the top of the stairs. Without a second thought she grabbed my hand and led me deeper into the cavernous cellars beneath the palace. She tried to push open a door but it was too heavy. I stepped in front of her and lent the weight of my shoulder to it. I really don't know what I thought that I was doing, but at the time it felt like the most natural action in the world. The door gave, and we stumbled into the darkness. She closed the door as I blundered into the black with my hands in front of me. My shin struck a hard object. I cursed as I fell headlong into a large piece of wood. My head struck it, and I hit the floor. I heard Olivia giggle as she felt forward. Her outstretched hands struck my left leg. Rather than withdraw, they rested there. I sat up with my back to the piece of wood and reached for her. In the pitch black, with her nestling in my arms and I asked her to continue her story.

Olivia had been born to a rich family in Greece. She had been educated by tutors and spoke Latin and Greek. Her town, in northern Achaia, had been conquered by Rome when she was still a girl. She had been taken by traders and sold in the forum in Rome to a politician, Caracalla's predecessor, two years before he was appointed to Britannia. When he had moved to Londinium he had taken his household with him, and when he had been recalled to Rome he had sold many of his household slaves to his successor. Thus Olivia had come to be owned by Caracalla. She hated his household. It was a place of drunkenness and misery. Because she was of fine birth and tender years she began to serve at some of Caracalla's feasts. Part of the duties of such a slave was to please the guests in any way that they desired. Apparently Caracalla never indulged in sexual behaviour in public himself, but he did like to watch. He had quickly become fond of Olivia and had decided to keep her back for himself, so she was forbidden to serve anyone other than Caracalla himself.

Olivia was not bitter as she recounted her story. Instead she had an air of weary resignation. She brightened as she described the first time that she was summoned for a private audience with Caracalla. She had been dreading the occasion, and it had not been long in coming after her release from service at the banquets. She was expecting to be set upon immediately. Instead, he sat her down and served her with wine himself before asking her to read Greek to him. As she did so he closed his eyes, and before long he was snoring. She was perplexed, and left him to return to her servants quarters. In the morning she was summoned. Caracalla was furious.
"Where did you go to last night?" he demanded
"I returned to my sleeping quarters after you had fallen asleep, sir" she replied
"Well in future you are not to leave until you are dismissed".
Ever since then she had been summoned to read to Caracalla at night. He had never tried to touch her but he did expect her to sleep in his

chambers and not to leave the following morning until after he had breakfasted. It seemed that he hated to sleep alone. Because of her "special duties" she was absolved any responsibility for any other chores in the household. Her lot, she said, had to be the easiest that any slave had to bear. Yet it was clear that this intelligent, well-educated girl was frustrated.

When she had finished her story she asked me of myself. I was still feeling the effects of the wine, and I was much franker with her than I would usually have been. I told her nothing of the secret element of our mission to Eburacum, but otherwise I was honest about my past as a soldier. As I spoke she began to caress me. She slipped her hand inside my toga and ran her hands through the hairs on my chest. I felt myself becoming aroused again. Her hand slid slowly down my chest to my abdomen. I hadn't had a woman for over a year. I was a young man in my prime and the proximity of this beautiful, firm young body and youthful, exploring mind was too much for me. I began to caress her head once more. My hands wandered down over the nape of her neck to her strong, smooth back. By now I had stopped talking altogether. We were just lying there, caressing each other's bodies. I ran my hands over the soft flesh at the top of her hips and round to her belly. It was flat and taut. My hands rose to the base of her small breasts. They stood pert from her chest and her nipples were hard. She let out a small moan as I took them in my hands. When she moaned it became too much for me. I put my hands about her hips, and she giggled as I rolled her over.

I do not know what time we woke. It was still black when I felt Olivia's tongue trace the outline of my lips. I opened my eyes but could see nothing. I took her tongue in my mouth and we made love once more.

It was an odd experience trying to stand up in that room. I put my toga back on and left Olivia there. She had asked whether she would see me again. My head told me that there was no way, but my heart told me that I had to. It was like I had spent years dying of thirst in the desert and had finally come across an oasis. Not just any oasis, but an

oasis with the sweetest tasting water and the most comfortable caravanserai in the world.
"I can see that you're different, Tolus. Make sure that you come back for me?" she said as I opened the door.
"I do not know if it is possible, but know that I want to and I will if I can" I replied feebly.

*****

When I got back to the barracks, the men were packing up. The light on the horizon told me that dawn would be coming at any second. To my relief, the banquet had degenerated to such a degree of drunken confusion by the time that I had left it that no one had missed me. Silus was the first to see me.
"What the hell happened to you?"
I was bewildered. "What do you mean?"
"Have you seen a looking glass this morning, Tolus?"
I felt my face. I had a large bruise just under my eyebrow and could feel dried blood. And my nose was swollen and extremely painful to the touch. The nose was the punch from the roman, and the eyebrow must have been from when I tripped and hit the piece of wood in the cellars.
"Oh, that" I tried to be nonchalant. "I got drunk and fell over".
Silus and the rest of the men thought that this was enormously funny. From my sheepish demeanour I think that they hoped that there might be an accompanying story of how I disgraced myself somehow at the governors banquet. They realised that they would not get it from me and so began to tell me of their night of revelry.
"We got absolutely routed in the drinking competition, and in more ways than one", said Numba cheerfully. "I've never seen a group of men who can drink like the XXth. We were pathetic by comparison. Most of us were vomiting and falling over whilst they were still just getting warmed up!"
I was not listening. My mind was with Olivia's firm body and soft words.

By noon we were on the road again. I didn't want to leave. I wanted to stay and work out a way to see Olivia again. Before we had left I had written to her. The letter had been formal in tone and brief. But Olivia would understand the implication and was sensible enough to destroy it as soon as she had read it.

"IF YOU EVER FIND YOURSELF IN NEED OF WORK, YOU WOULD BE WARMLY WELCOMED INTO THE SERVICE OF THE HOUSEHOLD OF MARIUS SEXTUS. HE CAN BE FOUND IN THE PRAETORIUM OF THE IXTH LEGION IN EBURACUM".

*****

On the journey out of Londinium I was anxious to talk to Marius, for I wanted to find out what had happened the previous night after I had left. But Marius spent the whole morning riding beside Victrix, the two of them deep in conversation. It was not until that night that I had the opportunity to talk to him.

"Finally I get the chance to talk to you" I said in his tent when everyone else had gone to bed.
"What is so urgent, Tolus?" he asked. He was tired and irritable, and I think just wanted to go to bed.
"I was just wondering what happened last night" I replied
"You were there, weren't you?" he said tetchily
"Tell me of Caracalla" I said.
"Must I? It's late and I really need to sleep".
I had not seen him in this sort of state since we were in Aegyptus. I made to go, but he summoned me back.
"Sorry, Tolus. It's just that this country is beginning to wear me already and we've only just got here. Some of the stories that Caracalla had to tell chilled the blood. But it is not surprising that they are failing so totally with these savages given their attitude to them. That lot in Londinium are good for nothing. They are a bunch of drunken layabouts and a disgrace to the uniform. We will be different. I swear it."
"What about Caracalla?" I asked again.

It was so important to our plan that Marius made a favourable impression, and I was nervous that he seemed to be avoiding the question.

"He is a lazy, pompous old fool. He loved having us as it gave him an excuse to get even more drunk than usual and gorge himself on even more food than he would usually allow himself. But he hates this province and cannot wait to be recalled to Rome. Victrix and I didn't talk tactics before the dinner, but just naturally fell into the role as each others greatest advocates. I told him what a great leader Victrix was, and Victrix duly obliged by telling him what an incredible service record I have. As far as Caracalla is concerned, we are the two bravest and most heroic Roman soldiers since Agricola and we will bring him fame and glory. What is more, we made our unreserved admiration and respect for our governor completely clear, and showed him that our obedience to our leaders is beyond question. Good, traditional soldiers both who follow orders and would never think to question them. We did a good job on him, Tolus."

He paused and the haunted look returned to his eye, the haunted look that I had first seen in the oasis between Alexandria and Misr.

"But worst of all, Tolus, I really like Victrix. He is a superb soldier and a fine man. We had such fun pulling the wool over Caracalla's eyes. We were enjoying it so much that we nearly went too far with our exaggerated respect and deference and our stories of each other's heroics. I got the giggles at one point and nearly gave the game away. He is a fine man, and I am seriously questioning whether I will be able to do that which I must".

I wanted to change the subject. "What did Caracalla say of Eburacum?"

Marius fixed me with his eyes as he told me what he had learned.

"Caracalla is terrified of this province. He believes that it is untameable. He told us that he will not travel further than Aquae Sulis in the west, and Deva and Lindum in the north. We shouldn't expect any visits from him in Eburacum. After dinner he took us up to the administrative rooms at the rear of the palace. There he showed us a crudely made wooden chest with an undecorated iron clasp. He turned his back and bid us to open it. When I opened it even I was shocked at what it contained. It contained an array of small human remains – eyes pulled from sockets, ears shorn from heads and index fingers severed from hands. And on each of the index fingers there were gold rings. Roman rings".

Marius paused as he waited for the implications of his words to sink in.

"I looked to Caracalla for an explanation. He sounded more like a child than a provincial governor as he told us of a local chieftain by the name of Gwdloych who has been causing trouble up near Eburacum. At first it was just the occasional raid on remote forts. Then it was the columns of slave gatherers. Apparently our harvest from the north of Britannia has all but dried up, and it has made Caracalla extremely unpopular with Rome. Then, a few weeks ago, Isurium was attacked. The savages got in and put the town to the sword. Then they burned it. They made off with as much as they could carry, including over four hundred women. The contents of the chest were some of the remains of those women. Many of the rings have been identified as coming from Isurium's families. He also sent a box full of severed heads, but Caracalla disposed of those".

I must have had a shocked look on my face, because Marius paused.

"I gets worse. There was a letter enclosed, written by one of Gwdloych's female hostages. Caracalla showed it to me, and although I cannot remember exactly what it said, it told of the things that were being done to them by the savages. This woman said that there were fewer than one hundred and fifty of the original hostages left. Those who died had died badly, from the abusive attentions of scores of men. She said that she had no desire to keep her own life and spent every waking moment hoping for it to end. She had been instructed to warn that until the foreign filth had left the lands that do not belong to them, then this sort of thing would continue to happen. She finished by saying that these were the words of Gwdloych, the king of the Brigantes".

Marius gritted his teeth.

"The man is obviously causing mayhem up there. Isurium was a major town. Apparently it has now been totally abandoned. No one will go back to live there. The garrison have returned to Eburacum and are mad for revenge. But Caracalla has no faith in Flavius Tiberius, the commander of the IXth. Apparently he is as afraid as Caracalla and virtually refuses to leave his walls. Things are bad here, Tolus. Things are very bad".

It took us three weeks to march to Eburacum. Three hard, frightening, miserable weeks.

26

Perridac and Benjamin landed in Sidon just after noon. It was so hot that the tar smeared between the boards of the boat was soft, and the two men's eyes could barely be seen beneath their squinting brows. Benjamin smelt the familiar stench of fish in the port, and to him it served as a welcome confirmation that he was, indeed, home. He was anxious to see if Gideon had returned, and was relieved that he was finally back to a place where he felt a degree of control. Benjamin's confidence had been badly rocked by his experience in Rome. Ever since leaving Lucius' house he had felt like a blunt instrument beside Perridac. It would be good to be back among people who respected him and loved him for who he was, and saw him as wanting for nothing.

Perridac was businesslike. He was keen to see Tertullian and Origen as soon as he could. During his theological debates with Tertullian he had come to respect him profoundly, not only as a religious thinker but also as a man. He was a living example to all the brethren, and Perridac felt sure that he would know what to do in the face of the vexing problem that they had brought with them from Rome.

They walked quickly through the town, probably too quickly. Having spent so long on the more temperate swells of the Mare Nostrum they were unused to the intense heat of the land. The ground seemed to bake, and the dust and rubble under foot was painfully hot to the touch. Despite the rasping dryness, both men were drenched in sweat as they left the town behind them and continued on to Tertullian's home on the edge of the desert. By the time that they were spotted by Ruth, both were dehydrated and filthy. She hurried out to greet them, a look of relief on her face.

"Thank God you have returned safely" she said.

"How is Tertullian?" replied Perridac immediately.

"Alive" Ruth said simply. The implication was clear.

She noticed Benjamin's downcast looks.

"You must be tired after your long voyage. Come and sit outside for a while. I will bring you food and drink whilst we wait for Origen to come".
Ruth turned to lead them towards the house.

Tertullian was lying on the cushions on his kilim under the large olive tree. He had a waxy pallor that made Perridac think of the dead. If it were possible, he was thinner than before. His skin was drawn across his face so taut that it looked ready to split, and the deep lines that had characterised Tertullian for so many years were now no more than light indentations. It was like looking at the mummified faces of the ancients. His legs were deep brown but the skin was excessively wrinkled and the flesh sagged lifelessly off the bones.
It really won't be long now, thought Perridac.

Ruth gestured for them to go and sit with him while she returned into the house. She soon returned bearing stuffed figs and deliciously cool water from a large jar in the shade of a cool room. Origen strode across the dustbowl behind her. He walked right up to Perridac and embraced him. Then he embraced Benjamin and greeted Tertullian with deference and tenderness.

Perridac saw this as a good sign. The two men had managed to continue to work together, obviously. But Origen was impatient. He had no time for small talk, and Tertullian too was keen to hear news. Just as Perridac was about to begin their story, Benjamin interrupted.
"Has Gideon returned?"
Origen looked at him with surprise. "Returned from where?"
Benjamin told him the story of the events on Creta. He was full of self recrimination as he told of Gideon's capture by the Romans and his subsequent abandonment of him. Despite his anxiety to hear of events in Rome, Origen had to work to be patient as he consoled Benjamin.
"You did the right thing in leaving him there, Benjamin. You could not have done anything for him, and the role you had to perform in Rome was much more important. There is a good chance that he will be released at some point and make his way back here. Do not hate yourself for what you did. You have no reason to".

He put a hand on Benjamin's shoulder before turning to Perridac.
"Come, brother, and tell us of Rome".
Without ceremony Perridac told their story.

Origen listened impassively with his massive frame hunched over, his head held in his hand with a thumb on his cheekbone and his fingers splayed across his forehead.
Perridac finished his story with Lucius' point blank refusal to help them. He looked up.

The fury in Origens eyes could have scorched the sun. Abruptly he stood and began pacing, muttering under his breath. His huge bulk seemed to quiver with agitation. To and fro he paced, like a wild animal that might pounce at any time. Perridac and Benjamin were too frightened to speak. They had never seen such fury in a man. Tertullian closed his eyes and gave the impression of being asleep, or dead. For some time Origen paced before he came to stand menacingly over the kilim under the olive tree. He stood rigid and coiled and when he spoke his voice was dangerous.
"So, the truth is revealed. We should not be surprised, I think. This senator has shown where his loyalties lie and they lie first to Rome".
His tone became sarcastic. "His belief in the Christus must be profound. He must be a brave and righteous man".
Suddenly he shouted. "Bastard! Bastard! Bastard!"
It was a great cry of frustration and it was shouted with all of Origen's might. His face was contorted, his mouth wide as his voice screamed out the words. A long stream of sticky drool escaped the side of his mouth and hung down below his chin. Perridac and Benjamin looked on in astonishment.

His anger was not diminished as he continued, but he did regain a modicum of self control. His tone was full of malice.
"I am going to Rome. I am going to get Nero's confession off these Roman scum if it is the last thing I do. I won't let these treacherous bastards get in the way".
The bile in Origen was spilling out.

"We are going to make the worms beg. We are going to pull the rug from right under their feet so that they fall on their arses in front of the whole world. We are going to drag them from their orgies and cut their genitals out from under them. The evil snakes deserve everything that's coming and I am the person to make sure that they get it".

His hands were clenched, and as he said the last few words he gave a great sweeping motion with his arms to indicate how he would smash through the resistance that they represented.

Origen's contorted features revealed how these events had revived the pain of his family's murder. The other men could see that Origen was close to falling into the abyss. The abyss where nothing but revenge could soothe his pain, where reason was no longer something that could reach him and where death, and death alone, would stop his rampage.

Tertullian was very ill but his mind was still sharp. He knew Origen better than anyone. He knew the demons that fought inside him and he knew that Origen understood the great sympathy and love that Tertullian had for him. He also knew how close Origen was to losing control, so he measured his words carefully.

"You will do no such thing, Origen. Remember the words of the Christus that Matthew quotes: 'But if ye forgive not men their trespasses, neither will your Father forgive your trespasses'. Revenge is not the way of the Lord, and you know it. Perhaps Lucius has a point. Perhaps he is doing what Jesu would have done. He is trying to preserve the law. Jesu was a great respecter of the law, Origen. Indeed it is he who is the law giver. Maybe Lucius is right that we should not just destroy the law. Maybe the ensuing anarchy would make it impossible for us to spread our message. Maybe we are better served by working within the Roman administration. We were taught that we must 'render to Caesar that which belongs to Caesar'. Be warned: If you ignore what the Christus has told us in this, He will not be with you. You will be doing it on your own for your own ends. Do not give yourself over to darkness, Origen. Do as He bid us and walk in the light".

Origen was sitting down with his head once more in his hand. When he looked up the fury had left him. In its place was a look of desolation. Tertullian's words had reached him. He stood up, and mumbled something about returning tomorrow to decide what to do. When he walked away he did so slowly, with his great shoulders hunched and his back bent forward. His feet shuffled along, barely clearing the small stones of the dustbowl. He looked like a very old man.

There was not much left to say. Benjamin and Perridac walked to Benjamin's family home, where they were greeted with great relief by his family. The household had already lost one son in this matter, and their joy at having the other return was great indeed.

*****

The following day was burning hot. Shortly after dawn, Perridac and Benjamin again walked down the dusty road through the edge of the desert to Tertullian's home.

When they saw the house in the distance, they could make out the distinctive form of Origen walking straight into the house without breaking step. Then they began to hear the sound of wailing. At first it was barely perceptible. It might have been wind whistling through branches had there been any trees. Soon it was evident that it was the wailing of several women. The two men quickened their pace. The wailing was coming from Tertullian's home, and it was terrible to hear. Perridac vainly hoped for some other explanation, but he knew what it meant. As they arrived at the house they did not even pause to knock on the door. They walked straight in to the main room of the house.

The room was cool and shady. Origen stood in the corner with tears streaming down his face. Before him, with their backs to him were five women surrounding Ruth, wailing loudly. In the centre of the cluster a sleeping cot had been brought out from one of the peripheral rooms and laid out on the floor. On it was the body of Tertullian. His skin had turned a curious waxy grey colour, and it looked even more drawn than it had the previous day. The body was covered by a white shroud, with only the face exposed. It was striking for its expression of tranquillity. The eyes were closed and the mouth was almost smiling. Both Benjamin and Perridac put their hands together and fell to their knees. Their entrance was unnoticed by the women, the noise of their arrival drowned by the grief.

Eventually Origen walked forward and touched Ruth's shoulder. She turned, her eyes red rimmed and filled with tears. He made to embrace her and she flinched. He looked into her eyes enquiringly and was met by a hard stare.
"You did this" she said.
"When did he die?" asked Origen levelly.
"Last night, in his sleep".
Ruth made to turn back to the body of her dead husband in dismissal. Origen stopped her.
"Truly, Ruth, I am sorry. I am sorry for what I have asked him to do and the strains that I have put on him. He was a great man, and he would want us to be friends".
Her despairing fists landed feebly on Origen's chest.
"You had no right" she sobbed.
He drew her to him and engulfed her in his enormous arms. Slowly she gathered herself and she pulled away from him. Her hard stare had softened as new tears welled in her eyes.
"You are right, Origen. I am sorry. He had to go some time, and God would not wait any longer. He is at peace now."
Origen embraced her once more, and she clung to him.

*****

Later the men met at the home of Benjamin's parents. It seemed strange to sit down without Tertullian, and with his body lying so near. But they did so because they had to resolve what to do and Origen wanted it resolved quickly. When they were all sitting down on the floor Origen spoke.

"I am going to Rome and Perridac is going to stay here to take over the leadership of the movement in my absence. Benjamin, I would dearly like you to come with me, but if you choose to stay here then I will not stand in your way. It will be dangerous for you, and I will not have your life on my conscience as I have David's. I can, though, offer you the prospect of revenge on the man who killed him".

Origen looked to Benjamin. Before he could reply, Perridac spoke.

"I cannot remain here to take over the leadership" he said simply.

"Why not?" shot back Origen.

"Because . . . " He was uncomfortable with what he had to say. He did not know Origen well, but he had seen enough of him to know that he had to say it. He shifted uneasily on his cushion and then looked up, straight at Origen.

"For God's sake, Origen, you have done exactly what Tertullian feared that you would and exactly what you know to be wrong. You have chosen the path of revenge over righteousness. I cannot remain here to take over the leadership because I do not believe that you should go to Rome. I would be endorsing your trip, something I cannot do. Tertullian spoke wisely, Origen. He knew you better than any. And he knew the demons that beset you. I do not know you so well, but I can see that you have the bile of hatred eating away at you. I can see that you are engaged in a constant struggle to contain it. By deciding to go to Rome you are giving in to it, and if you go you will not control it. Benjamin has the same fury".

Perridac's eyes were like iron as he continued.

"We have a responsibility to do what is right for our brethren in all of the empire. But you are not facing up to it. Instead you seem to prefer to do what your fury dictates. You would rather be led by your need for revenge rather than by your duty to do the right thing for the brethren. I will not stay here."

Once more Origen looked like he might explode. His voice took on its threatening, brooding quality.

"I am disappointed to hear it, Perridac. You leave me with no choice. I will go to Rome and I will have to find someone else to perform my role whilst I am gone".

Peridac looked at him incredulously.

"But there is no one who can do it" he spluttered. "You know that. We had this conversation with Tertullian before, when it was agreed that I would go to Rome".
He looked to Origen angrily but Origen just looked back with his eyebrows raised. There was the hint of a cynical smile on his lips.
Perridac looked away but his eyes were not focussing. He was thinking, making up his mind about something. He raised his gaze to the ceiling and sighed.
"I will go back, Origen. I will go back and put a plan to Lucius".
Origen's jaw was set. "No. I will go. This is the most important thing that has happened to our movement since the death of the Christus and there is no way that I can continue to sit on my hands in Sidon whilst other people fail to take the donkey by the balls. I will go".
Benjamin interjected. "And I will come with you. I have to meet this Marius. For the sake of my brother, I have to meet him".
Origen looked satisfied. He knew that he had backed Perridac into a corner.
"You know that we cannot survive without you, Perridac. You must stay and lead the movement from here. Things will fall apart without you".

Perridac got to his feet and walked out of the room. He could not think in there, with Origen's smug certainty. Origen would not listen to reason, Perridac was sure of that. Tertullian's death had slipped the anchor that had kept Origen in the light. He had fallen into the abyss, and seemed to be taking a perverse pleasure in letting Perridac know it. As he walked out of the house his head cleared, and he realised that he was cornered. Origen would go to Rome even if it meant leaving the movement to crumble in his absence. He was beyond caring. Perridac had no choice, and he knew it. He must do what was best for the brethren.

When he returned silence immediately descended on the company. Perridac was resigned, but he could not hide his anger as he looked directly at Origen.
"This is blackmail. You are forcing me to become involved in something that I know to be wrong, but you give me no choice".

There was a pained look on his face as he continued, and he spoke slowly.
"I will stay, Origen, but I want you to know that it is with grave misgivings and a heavy heart. You play too dirty. Never count on me as a friend, and know that when you return here there will be no place for you. For the good of our movement you will be cast out. You will be left in the abyss that you have cast yourself into".
He spoke the last sentence with gritted teeth and cold eyes. The effect was menacing as he got to his feet and stalked out of the house.
"Do your worst" shouted Origen defiantly after his retreating frame.

Origen looked at Benjamin and smiled a cynical smile. "We will find Marius. His girlfriend will lead us to him, and when we find him we will find the manuscript. When we find the manuscript we will bring Rome to her knees. Those bastards will suffer. I swear they will".

Within a few days the two of them had left for Rome.

27

The march to Eburacum was the most depressing thing that I have ever had to do. I have never seen a place with so much potential as that untamed land. It was so fertile that forests covered almost every inch of it. Food grew in prolific abundance wherever ground had been cleared by local tribesmen. Wild fruits grew at every turn, but how they managed it I do not know because the atmosphere was one of acidic hatred the like of which I have never encountered before or since. It seemed to permeate the landscape and cast an unsettling pallor over everything. The people were consumed with obsessive loathing for us. Even from afar we could see that they constantly spat in our direction. They stood on hills in gangs of up to one hundred waving farming tools at us. They pilfered our stores and sabotaged us at every opportunity. They were like shadows – we knew that they were there watching us but when we stretched out to grab them we found nothing. They just melted away and disappeared into the impenetrable forests. We lost fourteen men on that march, most of them in the first few days. Each time a man disappeared he would reappear within a day or two. Usually his head would be left on a stake driven into the grass on the side of the road ahead of us. Our scouts would remove it and not tell anyone save the commanders. Occasionally other body parts were found, most commonly genitalia, often dangling from the branches of a tree near to the road. On two occasions the scouts failed to see this and the main body was marching by before anyone spotted the gruesome sight. Soon orders were issued that no job was to be undertaken with less than twenty men. On cloudy days, the gloom of the woods was such that it never really got light.

Every night after the day's march was over, the men needed no encouragement to construct the camp. It was the standard camp that we had all been trained to dig in enemy territory, but it was an impressive sight. Two of the cohorts, over one thousand men deployed into battle line. The rest of the men cut down trees and cleared the undergrowth, with weapons always close to hand. They then dug a huge ditch, wider than the length of two men and deeper than the height of one. The ditch was two thirds of a mile long, and the soil from it was piled up on the near side of the trench to form a rampart. Flags were laid out by the surveyor to indicate the space allotted to each century. The two wooden stakes that every man had carried since before we crossed the sea to this grim land were driven deep into the rampart. With the ditches they formed an imposing defensive position. Within each century the manpower was divided up into specific tasks of cutting the turf, felling the trees, clearing the area, digging the ditches, shovelling the earth into wicker baskets and handing the soil up to those working on the ramparts. Unlike the early stages of our march in Britannia there was no reluctance to take on this task. On the contrary, the men were keen to finish it as soon as was possible. None of us felt safe until the baggage train was safely resting behind the ramparts. The whole camp could be finished within two hours of the arrival of the last part of the column. A heavy guard rota was set, ensuring that the camp was constantly patrolled whilst the rest of the men slept.

Victrix pushed the men as hard as he dared. He was in a hurry to get to Eburacum, for it felt like we could be attacked at any time in that place. Despite our scouts there was a general concern that we may have no warning of an attack in the heavy woodland that constantly surrounded us.

Each day we would pass a few villages. The land in their clearings was cultivated, but it seemed clear from the humble hovels that squatted in these miserable quagmires that the cultivation was for subsistence only. There was no great concept of trade among those people.

Other than these few primitive villages we saw nothing but trees and resentment. It was frustrating to feel so vulnerable, yet not be able to see a coherent threat. The fear showed itself amongst the men in the form of testiness and quick tempers. The officers had to work hard to remind them that we were all on the same side.

During the nights strange noises came from the forest. Constant howling, screaming and moaning unsettled the men. Occasionally crude shafts with iron tips would sail into the camp from the surrounding trees forcing the night patrols to keep low. Every day the vanguard and scouts reported dismembered animals lying in the road ahead of us. We were being watched and spells were being cast to prevent our progress. The general scepticism towards the power of our own gods did not prevent a deep-seated superstition emerging in our ranks.

Despite their orders to travel in large groups, our scouts were twice attacked by groups of savages who looked and behaved little better than wild animals. Although the parties returned to camp relatively unscathed, the men were severely shaken by the experience.
The only consolation was that the environment was perfect for the development of that which Lucius had spoken.

*****

It took us one week to reach Durobrivae, a small town with a large garrison that was responsible for keeping the road open, but we did not stay there. Among rumblings from the men we pushed on up that dark road, back into the close woods that held nothing but the promise of violence. A few days later we reached Lindum. The town was comparable in size to Londinium, and like Londinium had a vast barracks just outside the town walls. A large area of trees, stretching for more than five miles around the town had been cleared. They said that it was essential for keeping would-be attackers at bay. The open space was a relief as we marched into it. Suddenly we felt safer, being able to see with our own eyes that there was no great force that might try to obliterate us. That open land was cultivated according to Roman methods, and was well managed. The place was an oasis of normality, no different to any of the other northern domains that had accepted the pax romana. The sun was shining that day, and when we came to the vast expanse of clear land – several times larger than that around Durobrivae – all of our hearts lightened. Victrix allowed us to rest for two nights in Lindum. For Britannia it was relatively safe, and the men were relieved to have a day to nurse blistered feet and soothe sore shoulders. The weather was kind to us there, too. The sun shone without interruption for two whole days, and whilst the men just lay around trying to imagine that they were somewhere civilised, my mind was back in Londinium. I dreamed of Olivia.

*****

Things have changed since, and as I write the wild tribes from across the Danubus are once more threatening to overrun some of Rome's eastern provinces. But at that time the empire was peaceful. Most provinces had accepted the pax romana and were prospering as a result. Tiny garrisons were required, and the only fighting most of the men of the legions of Rome had seen was in the taverns on feast days and public holidays. Instead, they spent most of their time building roads and aqueducts and sewer systems and barracks. Most legionaries had a trade, whether it was stonemasonry, carpentry, foundry, engineering or one of a whole myriad of others. The result was that the fighting men of Rome had become unaccustomed to battle. Most of the men of the cohorts who had come with us from Italia had never been in truly hostile territory before. So this was a rude shock to them, and to their credit they took it well. It was a shock to Greto and me and the others, and we had seen more than our fair share of service in hostile lands. Those days spent sunning ourselves in Lindum made us remember what life was like in the civilised world, and we somehow forgot the horror of the nightmare into which we had marched. In the sunshine the men began to picture the potential that this province would have if it were civilised. It had all the requisite natural features and wealth to make it a beautiful and prosperous place. I don't know if it was my imagination, but I sensed a feeling of mission developing over those two days, a feeling that we had a job to do and a willingness to do it.

Any optimism that developed in Lindum was banished soon after we left. The weather turned. The skies became dark grey and the wind began to howl. Down on the road we were protected from most of the wind but we could hear it whistle through the tops of the trees, and the effect on our morale was devastating. It felt like a threat, a warning us to turn back and return whence we came. The low clouds raced past, occasionally spitting horizontal rain down at us. It was an ill omen and the men were not slow to seize on it. In the area around Lindum there had been a definite lightening of the harassment from the local savages. One day's march further north it resumed with renewed fury. A group of scouts was attacked in the woods and only fifteen returned. They had killed a good number of their attackers but they had been taken by surprise on the banks of a small stream and five had fallen. Worse, they had been unable to retrieve the bodies as they fled. The five bodies turned up the following day. Each had been mutilated. The legs and arms had been removed, leaving just the naked, bloody torsos. Their eyes had been gouged out and their genitals removed. Carrion birds, large black ones with a wide wingspan and hooked beak were busy ripping at the exposed flesh of what remained of their faces, and between where their legs had been. When the scouts reported this news, Marius caught my eye and I approached him. He was grim.

"Gwdloych is known by many names, each of which relate to how he murders his enemies. It is said that one of his favourite entertainments is to dismember his enemies whilst they are still alive. I hadn't realised that we were in his territory already. I was told that he only operated to the north of Eburacum."

Two days later we arrived in Eburacum.

*****

Our relief at arriving was exceeded by the IXth's relief at seeing us. The sun was shining bright as we approached the town. We came out of the dense forest that spread all the way from Lindum and as we did so the geography of the area was clear to see. Eburacum was magnificently situated for a frontier town. Two rivers met, and where they did they formed a v-shape. A hill rose between the two rivers, and the walls of the town surrounded the hill. The high stone walls were set back as little distance from the rivers as possible, and they were strong. Very strong. On the far side from us the walls could be seen stretching across the top of the v-shape, about two thirds of a mile long. There were three double gates, and a deep ditch before those walls. The result was a town which was impregnable on three sides, and close enough to it on the fourth. Even a Roman legion would have taken a significant time to break through those defences. It was a welcome sight. The barracks were inside the walls. There was no separate stockade for the soldiers, but the rows of long low garrison blocks made it clear that the north west part of the city was used as their quarters.

Our contingent marched proudly under the sunshine. We did not carry an eagle, for we were not a legion. But we did carry the elaborate insignia of over twenty five centuries. Victrix ordered them to be hoisted by each of their respective standard bearers, and he sent the cavalry on as the vanguard. We took on the closest shape to a ceremonial formation that Victrix dared. Our spears were carried high, having been removed from their straps on our packs. Just after we had crossed the western bridge, Greto, myself and the rest of our men went forward to attend Marius. He and Victrix had moved to the front of the column, ahead of the cavalry vanguard. The soldiers of the ninth were lining the city walls to watch our arrival. On seeing them, I got the feeling that something was not right about them.

When we got closer it was obvious. They were not wearing the traditional uniform of the legions. Instead they were wearing animal skins and leather hides, crude woollen cloaks dyed various colours and tatty tunics. Many of them had no shoes on. They looked more like a ragged bunch of savages than a legion of Rome. None of them were shaven. Nor were we, but that was only due to the concession on clean shaven faces that was granted to men on the march. In camp, the law concerning facial hair would be restored. Something had broken down in this wilderness fortress.

The main gate to the town swung open and an enormously fat man dressed in a grubby toga came out to meet us. Although it was not yet midday he was unsteady on his feet. He raised his arm and greeted us formally.

"I, Flavius Maximus Angelicus, Legate of the IXth legion of the Western Army of the Glorious Empire of Rome do greet you, Romans".
He was trying to sound majestic and intimidating. Instead he conveyed only whining self-importance and slight drunkenness.
Victrix could barely suppress a snort of derision at this old fashioned pomposity. He spurred his horse on and cantered up to Flavius. He pulled his horse up and spoke in a quiet voice.
"I am Victrix and I have orders from the emperor Hadrian".

*****

Once we were in the town the extent to which things had deteriorated became clear. The place was a mess. The dung covered streets had not been swept for weeks. Soldiers were everywhere, but mostly in taverns. There were also many civilian Romans. Eburacum had a large number of farms surrounding it and none had been attacked for years, but the citizens who farmed them had all moved into the town. There were many large, luxurious old villas in the surrounding countryside but since Gwdloych's destruction of Isurium all had been abandoned. The resulting overcrowding in Eburacum might have been tolerable had it not been for the appalling discipline of the ninth legion. There were none of the services that a normal roman town would expect, and virtually no evidence of any discipline being applied at all. That night as I settled into new rooms that I was to share with Greto, Silus, Artorius, Tobias and Numba in the barracks, we agreed that if there was ever an opportunity for Marius to succeed in what he had come here for, it was here and it was now. I have never known such terrible morale in a place and it was obvious where it came from. Flavius was a drunkard and a hedonist. Victrix and Marius did not even pretend to be civil to him after he had shown them round his villa. His neglect of his duty and his men was so obvious that they could not get rid of him fast enough.

It took two days for the departing cohorts of the ninth to pack up their things, say their farewells and be ready to go. In the meantime, Victrix had several long arguments with Flavius, who was planning to relieve the villa of all it's furnishings, personnel and arts. They were not his, for they belonged to the villa which in turn belonged to Rome. But he tried. He also tried to take most of the slaves with him. Victrix became impatient with the haggling and allowed him to take far more than he should have, including some of the beautiful young serving girls. But Victrix just wanted to see the back of the fat slug. On the third day Flavius left with five cohorts of men, muttering and moaning. They would return to Londinium and thence to Italia for their next posting.

Those three days were depressing for us new arrivals. Eburacum had been well built by Agricola. His men had done a fine job and built a town that was beautifully situated, superbly defended and solidly constructed. It was laid out in the traditional grid pattern, but the irregular shape forced on Agricola by the two rivers gave it a significant amount of personality and variation on the standard town design. But it was in a terrible state. In parts, the walls had begun to crumble. The town refuse had been thrown into the defensive ditch, half filling it in and smothering the whole town under the revolting stench of decay and rancidity. The streets were submerged in filth and most of the houses needed attention.

The night that Flavius left, Marius summoned me to the Legate's villa. Victrix had allowed Flavius to take his cook with him, so the food was much as it had been on the road. It did not seem to bother Victrix. Sitting round the table were nine men. Beside Victrix was his assistant Simone, a Greek with dark, handsome features and hazel brown, intelligent eyes which flashed with amusement often and revealed a mischievous nature. His advice was valued by Victrix, and rightly, for he was wise beyond his thirty or so years. I liked him. Then there was Marius and myself. At the opposite end of the table to Victrix sat Jaffa. He was fairly tall, and was distinguished by long ginger hair that rose in spindly curls above his head. They sprouted out in all directions, almost like an elaborate plumage. Beneath his hair were small, beady eyes and a flattened nose. He was a ruggedly handsome man but a quiet one, and he was the most senior tribune left among those of Flavius' men who remained. He had with him one other tribune, Riccus, a short portly man with clear blue eyes and a turned up nose, and Dunam, his most senior centurian. He was tall and would have been strikingly handsome had his face not been beset with angry red boils. Serbius, Victrix's tribune who managed the baggage train and Benton, Victrix's most senior centurian were also present.

Dinner began with Victrix giving a robust assessment of the abilities and personality of the departing Flavius. He was quite funny about it, describing Flavius as "the sort of Roman that the Greeks would like, and like to be". Jaffa, Riccus and Dunam laughed loudest at this criticism, but Victrix appeared not to notice.

Before long, conversation turned to how we were going to make the town presentable. Marius was advocating that we should set the legion to work immediately on restoring the fabric of the place. The defences needed work, the streets needed cleaning up, the sewers and drains needed unblocking, the defensive ditch needed clearing, the men needed new uniforms and shoes, everyone needed to shave and discipline needed to be completely reestablished. The list was intimidating.

As he spoke he, like Victrix, appeared to completely ignore the men of the ninth who were in the room. He spoke of their neglect freely, seemingly totally oblivious to their sensibilities. As he finished, he looked Jaffa straight in the eyes.
"Am I being fair, Jaffa, or have I been too harsh in my judgement of your 'achievements' in Eburacum?"
Jaffa looked back at Marius. His face was impassive and he gave a shrug.
"You are fair, sir. But do not be surprised. When you have been in this hell hole for a few weeks, you too will lose any desire to improve it. There is no point. We will abandon it soon enough, for this is a land which cannot be tamed. Even those bastards in Rome will come to that conclusion eventually. So what is the point of investing any effort

in making this place decent when we will be here for such a short time?"

I would have expected Marius to be angered by the man's impertinence, but if he was he didn't show it.

"You think me naïve, Jaffa, but you will come to know me".

Victrix was of a different opinion.

"If we were to do that, Marius, I think that it would be a constant battle with the men who have served here under Flavius. These men have clearly been poorly led . . ."

He broke off and turned to the three who had not come with him.

". . . I mean from the top. Corruption, laziness and weakness at the top corrodes the morale of men. Its effect permeates throughout an organisation and undermines its self respect. Before we do anything else, we must restore the self belief and pride of the men. If they have pride they will want to rebuild the town. If they think that there is a valid reason for doing so, they will be willing rather than resentful. If they don't, it could easily be divisive between the new arrivals and the veterans. Once such a division is created it is almost impossible to destroy. And if such a division is created it is my experience that everyone sinks to the lowest common denominator".

Jaffa coughed, a cough that came close to derision.

"If we can make all of our men believe in what they are doing, we might succeed. Without this it will be a constant fight against them. They will despise us for it and it will not be done well. I have never believed in forcing men to do anything that they do not believe in. We have a duty to show our men why they should do what we are asking of them".

Victrix paused. He looked around. Jaffa and his men were looking cynical, but Marius was paying close attention. Victrix resumed.

"Jaffa, is morale amongst the men who have been here good or bad?"

Jaffa raised an eyebrow in surprise at this question with such an obvious answer. When he answered, his tone was patronising and bitter.

"What do you think? We have been here for three years now. We have been led by a man who cared not a fig for us. Whenever we leave the safety of these walls we lose men. The columns that used to leave here to collect slaves were so decimated that we had to stop sending them. Our garrison at Isurium was powerless to stop the sacking of it's town and the abduction of one hundred and forty of it's women. Decent Romans will not come here to live. They know that it is a wild place. We are roman soldiers and we are running scared from a bunch of savages. No one wants us here and we do not want to be here ourselves. What do you think morale is like? We feel like the Christians in the coliseum, but without the comfort of an absurd belief. We believe in nothing. We no longer believe in ourselves and we no longer believe in Rome. Flavius saw to that".

He paused, realising that he was probably saying too much.

"No, 'sir'. . ." The venom with which Jaffa said the word 'sir' made me wince. ". . . morale amongst the men here is not good".

Victrix continued immediately.

"And can you think of anything that has been a particular blow to morale lately?"

I could see where this was going. Victrix knew the answer to this question just as surely as he had known the answer to his first. Jaffa looked slightly puzzled. I think that he thought that he was talking to an idiot.

"The loss of Isurium, of course", he replied.

Victrix's eyes were shining.

"So, morale is poor. Before we do anything else we are going to restore morale. And the way that we are going to restore it is to reoccupy Isurium. We are going to teach the savages that they cannot just sack a Roman town without paying for it. And believe me, they are going to pay for it."

*****

Five cohorts, half the legion, would march out of Eburacum in two days time. The five cohorts were to be composed of both the veterans of this place and the new arrivals. We were going to find the villages of the savages that lay within a ten mile radius of Isurium, and then we were going to torch every one of them. We would lay waste to the whole area, and we would kill any savage that we found.

"They need to be taught that our revenge is terrible. We will spare no one. We will make sure that they do not attack Romans again by reclaiming Isurium from their destruction. We will show them that they cannot chase us away, that it is not worth resisting us. For our wrath is terrible. This is the lesson that Boudicca learned. This is the lesson that is still heeded in the south. This is the lesson that the north must learn".

I agreed, but when I looked over to Marius he seemed to have an uncomfortable look about him.

*****

Two days later we set off. Greto and the rest of my men stayed in Eburacum as they were not part of the force that had been chosen to come. All were frustrated to miss out on our first prospect of some real fighting. Artorius, Silus and Tobias accepted my promise that there would be plenty to come, but it took some strong words from Greto to pacify Numba. Two and a half thousand men marched north at dawn and continued through the forests for most of the day. In the middle of the afternoon Jaffa informed Victrix that we were at the tenth mile marker from Isurium. Victrix ordered us to make camp right there. We slept by the side of the road behind our stockade and listened to the howls and screams from the forest, but this time we were not afraid. We were on the offensive and it felt good. Well before dawn the following day we were ready to move out.

Victrix ordered the force to separate into centuries. He believed that a century was a sufficiently strong force to defend itself if attacked, and strong enough to lay waste to a village. No one was going to argue with the latter belief, but Marius challenged him over the former. It was Victrix's belief that there would be no organised resistance to us. Gwdloych's camp was way to the north and we all thought that most of his men would be up there with him. There had not been nearly enough time for Gwdloych to receive word of our leaving Eburacum the previous morning, let alone time to gather men. He ordered that two hours before sunset we must all be inside the gates of Isurium where we would camp until the town's defences had been rebuilt. Jaffa added his objections to those of Marius, counselling him against splitting up the force to such an extent. He tried to warn of the dangers of smaller bands of savages under local commanders often in the woods. But Victrix would not listen. Marius tried once more but Victrix was impatient. As dawn broke the centuries dispersed and the killing began.

*****

By the late afternoon I was in Isurium. Gwdloych's destruction all those weeks before had been considerable, but it had not been total. Nevertheless, the town was deserted. Its only residents were Roman corpses lying in the streets, a few wild animals and the heads of the captured barbarians that had been hewn from their bodies, placed on stakes and strapped to the town walls. A family of wolves fled as soon as we marched through the gates. The corspes were mostly just bones, all their flesh eaten, first by the birds and wolves and then by insects and maggots. Other than the bones all that remained was the odd patch of dried out skin hanging against them, with wispy hair blowing in the wind. Maggots still crawled over some of the remains. About one third of the buildings had been burned. The rest stood abandoned, but the town's defences were just about intact. The wall still stood, as did the barracks. We did not clear the corpses when we entered. We just sat down in the barracks and waited for the rest of the centuries to return.

Of the twenty five centuries that went out that day, Victrix had fully expected twenty five to be within the walls of Isurium by nightfall. Only twenty three returned.

Of the two that had not, one was led by Dunam and was part of the force that had been in Eburacum for years. The other was one of the centuries that had travelled up with us from Gallia. Of those that had returned all were unscathed. Or relatively unscathed. Three had lost men to iron tipped spears thrown from the woods and one to a desperate farmer defending his home. But such losses were very occasional and were to be expected. The total losses of the twenty three centuries that returned that evening were just eight men, and four of those had been from one century. When the story of those four was recounted, no one mourned them much. One of the four had been raping a woman and the other three had been looking on, so distracted that they had not noticed her brothers come into the hut behind them. Their centurian agreed that they deserved their deaths for such carelessness. But two entire centuries had not returned at all. Whilst we waited for them to return, we collated the information from each of the centurians about their day of destruction. Fourteen villages had been found and each one destroyed. Not one person survived from any of them and the estimated number of enemy dead was nearly four hundred and fifty. None of us doubted our right to behave in that manner. It was normal for us then.

We were concerned about the two centuries that had not returned by the appointed hour, but not unduly so. But by the time that darkness fell and our force was well established in the ruined town and its defences made adequate for the night, we were becoming seriously worried. We ate largely in silence. As most of the men were finishing their evening rations a sentry ran up to Victrix.
"Men have just entered the gates, sir" he reported breathlessly.
"How many?" replied Victrix instantly. He could not hide the concern in his voice, and he frowned when he heard the reply.

Victrix was on his feet striding out of the barracks. Marius and I were right behind him. He walked quickly down the devastated main street of Isurium. As we got nearer to the main gate, burned out shells replaced the stone facades nearer to the barracks and bodies still lay where they had fallen in the streets all those weeks before. At the end of the main street was a bedraggled group of men. They were led by Dunam. This tall, handsome man looked exhausted and shocked. He walked forward and stood before Victrix.
"Where are the rest of your men?" asked Victrix.
"They are fallen" replied a breathless Dunam. He barely concealed the anger in his voice.
"What happened?" asked Victrix. His thoughts were unreadable.

"We were taken by surprise on a narrow path through the forest. They came at us from all sides. I do not know how many of them there were, but there were more of them than of us. We tried to fight, but it was hopeless. We were surrounded. We fought our way back down the path and fled. Many of our men fell, we could not return to seek survivors. The men panicked, we continued to run, and after a few minutes we came to a wide valley with no trees".

Dunam was barely able to control his distress. He had a wild, haunted look in his eye as he continued.

"We were being followed and after a few minutes running down the valley we began to come across legionaries lying in the grass. Every one of them had had his head cut off from his body. Mostly their heads were just lying beside their necks. In some cases they had been placed on the midriff of the soldiers. We ran on. But then we saw a large group of savages. They were heading north with about forty legionaries under heavy guard. We could not attack them. We were weakened and there were too many of them, at least two hundred, and we did not know whether we were still being followed by the other group. So we turned to the east and carried on running. Soon we were back into the forests, but we were lost. We headed south to seek out the road. It took us several hours to find it and when we did we came straight here".

"How many men have you returned with?" asked Victrix softly.

"Sixty eight" replied Dunam.

"How many corpses did would you say were lying on the grass?" Victrix's face was expressionless.

"Up to fifty or sixty", he replied bitterly.

It was obvious that the fear and distress of the day had got to Dunam. He had been getting increasingly agitated as he recounted his ordeal, and as he did so the anger rose in him. Suddenly he lowered his voice and began to speak in an acid tone right at Victrix.

"This is all your fault, you arrogant bastard. You would not be told that this place is evil. You would not believe us when we told you of the danger that oozes from the very earth of this hole. You just saw us as useless layabouts who needed a bit of glory. You have no idea,

Victrix. The sooner you get that into your thick skull the better. We would be better off without you. It was madness to separate us into centuries. It made us vulnerable. They were good men, and they did not deserve what happened to them. It should have been you who was killed".

By the time he finished his voice had risen to a shout that was clearly audible to his men. But Dunam's tirade had exhausted itself and it looked like it had exhausted him. He said nothing further. He just stared defiantly at Victrix. All of those within earshot knew that he would have to die. Such talk could never be tolerated from a subordinate, and particularly not from a centurian in front of so many of his men.

Victrix's face remained impassive. He turned to Marius and spoke in a level voice.
"Marius Sextus, you will place this man under arrest and you will personally bring him to my quarters in one hours' time". He turned to Serbius.
"Have these men quartered and see that they are well fed".
He turned away. He knew, as we all did, that his expedition had been a disaster. We had lost the best part of one and a half centuries. But worse still was that the enemy, whoever it was, had got almost half of one of our centuries as prisoners. And we knew what they did to their captives. The effect on morale would be terrible. It would reinforce the fears of all the men who had been there for so long, and would only serve to increase the dread of us newcomers. Whilst everyone else returned to the barracks silently, I helped Marius with Dunam. He made no effort to resist as we led him away.

When I rejoined the men it was clear that no one wanted to talk, so it wasn't long before everyone retreated to their barracks and tried to sleep. It was a long time coming.

*****

Shortly after dawn a breathless Serbius burst into the quarters that I was sharing with Jaffa and some of his men. He looked distressed and did not stop for breath as he spluttered.
"You'd better come with me, Tolus". Without waiting for a response he turned and strode out. I had to hurry to keep up as he strode to the commanders quarters. He walked straight through the door without knocking and into the antechamber.

The floor was sticky with blood. One of the walls had a thick red smear on it, and at the base of the smear lay Dunam. His eyes were open and his legs tucked up unnaturally behind his back. His mouth was open and he had an expression of surprise frozen on his face.
To his right lay Victrix. He too had his eyes open and his tongue was hanging out to the left of his mouth. He was lying on his side and the front of his tunic was caked with the deep red, almost black of long dried blood. On the other side of the room lay Marius. His tunic was bloodstained. As we entered he moved his head fractionally.
"Thank the gods you're here", he whispered.

*****

Marius had a deep cut to his side which impeded his ability to move, but it was just a flesh wound and it would heal cleanly. He told us that when he had led Dunam into Victrix's rooms, Dunam had one intention, and that was to kill Victrix. Everyone had seen how incensed he had been at what had happened to his century and where he placed the blame. Most people secretly agreed with him. On entering Victrix's quarters he had not hesitated. He simply walked straight up to him and buried his sword in his belly. Victrix had been so surprised that he had not had time to respond. Dunam then turned on Marius. Having had more warning Marius managed to draw his sword to defend himself. But Dunam was quick and he had known what he wanted to do. He lunged at Marius, piercing his side. Marius staggered backwards and as he did so he had hit the rear wall of the room. He pretended that he was so badly wounded that he could not move. As Dunam advanced forward to finish him of Marius suddenly sprang forward and stabbed him in the guts. Due to his forward rush of weight and his injury, he had overbalanced forward and pushed Dunam right back until he hit the wall on the far side of the room. Dunam sank down the wall and died bleeding on the floor.

When I saw him I ran across to bind his wounds, shouting at Serbius to get the medics. Despite his injury it didn't take Marius long to take command. His first order immediately established a degree of popularity for him. For he ordered us to form up and return to Eburacum. He had to be helped onto a horse, and have his wound tightly bound to keep it closed. But he made it back.

We were a sorry sight when we marched back into Eburacum the following day. The men were distressed and silent. They had lost their legate to a deserting centurian. They had lost the best part of a century and a half to the savages, including up to fifty men alive. And they had as their new acting legate a man of whom they knew little, except that he had a bad wound in his side.

Worst of all was what they didn't know.

28

A messenger rode through the Ostia Gate, his horse almost ready to drop. He had cantered without a break since his boat landed at Ostia, nearly thirty miles from Rome, and made it in well under half a day. He was tired, for his voyage from Londinium had been rough. But with the wind howling from the north it had been fast. As he approached the gates to the eternal city he slowed his horse to a walk and dismounted. Only patricians were permitted to ride within the city walls. He hurried up the Ostian Way until it met up with the Appian Way that came up from Puteoli, in the depression between the Aventine hill and the Caelian Hill. The road then curved round to the west, and as it did so the intimidating grandeur of Rome was revealed. He headed straight for the villa of Decimus Marcellus, the whereabouts of which, like every military messenger, he knew well. It was a little out of town, across the Tiber on the slopes of the Vatican Hill. He crossed the river at the only bridge on the north side of the city, the bridge that had been originally constructed by Nero to allow easy access to his great amphitheatre on the west bank. Once he was over the river he was able to mount his horse once more, and he made speedy progress to the villa of the general.

Decimus received the messenger without much delay. It was rare for him to hear from Caracalla, and that was a good thing. He knew that the governor would not trouble him unless he had to. Decimus had never met him, but knew all about him. He knew him to be competent if lackadaisical, a man once considered able who, like so many others, had been corrupted by drink and sloth. He had been irritated to hear from Commodius that the previously reliable stream of new slaves from the north of Britannia had all but dried up. But it had irritated him only mildly, and on the whole Decimus was pleased with Caracalla. There had been no catastrophes, the place had been quiet, and it had paid most of its taxes promptly. Most importantly, though, since his conversation with Commodius and their decision to appoint

Victrix, Decimus had not really had to think about the province. As far as he was concerned this meant that Caracalla was doing a good job. The man was an old hand and he knew the rules. The first is that you do not speak unless you are spoken to. You do not trouble your superiors unless you have a real problem that requires their involvement to solve. The second is that you do not have that kind of problem. The only time that Decimus wished to hear from the provinces was once a year when they made their tax returns and their annual report. So when he broke the seal of the message from Caracalla, he was slightly concerned as to what this untimely intrusion could be. The message was simple.

"CARACALLA, GOVERNOR OF BRITANNIA, A PROVINCE OF THE WESTERN EMPIRE OF ROME GREETS YOU, DECIMUS MARCELLUS, SUPREME COMMANDER OF THE COMBINED ARMIES OF THE EMPIRE OF ROME. I ASK YOU TO APPOINT FOR US A LEGATE FOR THE IXTH LEGION (EBURACUM). THE PREVIOUS LEGATE, VICTRIX, WAS KILLED BY A DESERTING CENTURIAN. VICTRIX'S DEPUTY, MARIUS SEXTUS, KILLED THE CENTURIAN BEFORE HE WAS ABLE TO INFLICT ANY MORE CASUALTIES. MARIUS SEXTUS IS CURRENTLY ACTING LEGATE, AND MY RECOMMENDATION IS THAT HE BE ALLOWED TO CONTINUE. I HAVE MET HIM AND CONSIDER HIM TO BE OF THE HIGHEST CALIBRE AND UTTERLY LOYAL. I WILL AWAIT YOUR APPOINTMENT WITH INTEREST, SIR. I REMAIN YOUR HUMBLE SERVANT
CARACALLA"

Something in the back of Decimus' mind jarred. Briefly he tried to isolate the feeling, but when he could not he dwelt no further on the matter. As was his way when he had something to do he summoned his secretary, who entered the room immediately.
Decimus handed him the papyrus. "Have this taken to Lucius, and ask him to include it on the agenda from tomorrow's meeting".
The secretary nodded and was dismissed. Decimus thought no more about it.

*****

Benjamin did not know how he did it, but he found the rooms in the Transtiberine that Radjic and Beziac had kept on after he and Perridac left. The crossing from Sidon had been slow and tedious. Their boat put in at Cyprus, Rhodos, Creta, Sicilia and even Sardinia before docking at Ostia. Origen nearly went mad with impatience, and as a result his mood had been foul all the way. Most of his time had been spent pacing the deck like a caged animal, almost as if he believed that by doing so the boat might reach Rome more quickly. Being surplus to Origen's requirements meant that Benjamin got horribly bored with his own company.

When they landed at Ostia, Origen had been so impatient that he had not wanted to wait for the boat to be unloaded before heading up the Tiber to Rome. Instead he paid the premium rate for the uncomfortable stagecoach that bumped and jumped it's way across the stones of the main road into the city. So it was with considerable relief that Benjamin led Origen up the staircase of the vast tenement in the Transtiberine. It was with greater relief that they found Radjic and Beziac there, both of them looking well.

Sitting on the kilim in the cramped room, Origen brushed aside Radjic's questions about his voyage. Both he and Beziac were surprised at how long it had taken Origen to return.

"It was dreadful. We stopped at every port in the Mare Nostrum, but we are here now. What have you found?"

Radjic's answer was brief.

"In order to make it easier for us to watch Lucius' house we have set up a stall across from the front entrance and we sell fruit. At first we were resented by the local stallholders, but because our business has been poor they have reluctantly accepted us. Every day for the last three months one or both of us has manned that stall. If Rani or Lucius go out anywhere, one of us follows. There have been no occasions when Lucius and Rani have gone anywhere together, and only two when Rani and Lucius have been out of the house at the same time. When this happened we packed up the stall and each of us followed one of them. From what we have seen, Lucius is going about his normal business. Most days he attends the senate, and he frequently visits the villas of his colleagues. During the evening he is usually at home, although he does sometimes visit the theatre or the villas of his friends. He even once went to the coliseum on a Sunday when they were killing Christians".

At this, Origen's face reddened, but he did not say anything.

"We are sure that he has not met with Marius".

Origen looked thoughtful. "And what of Rani?" he asked.

Beziac leaned forward and answered. His answer was even briefer.

"She rarely leaves the house. When she has it has been to visit the forum. She has brought a few clothes, but not much else. Most of the time she just wonders around the market, looking at the performers in the street and browsing through the stalls. She has been to the baths a few times, and obviously we couldn't follow her in there. But there has been no sign of Marius at all. Nor has there been any sign of the men that he had with him".

Origen's look of thoughtfulness gave way to puzzlement. He stayed like that for some time whilst the others sat waiting. Eventually he spoke.

"I will go to see Lucius. I will speak to him myself and see if I have any more luck than you did. But first I will spend a few days on your stall with you. I want to see for myself how 'normal' things are".

*****

It was not until late that night that Lucius returned home. Despite his exhaustion he had the candles lit in his study and ordered a slave to request Rani to join him.

It was not long before there was a soft knock on the door. Rani knew what Lucius had been doing, and she was glad that he wanted to see her. But when she entered and saw the old senator she was concerned. Lucius looked worn. He smiled wanly as she entered and sat opposite him.

"How did you fare?" she prompted softly.

Lucius frowned. "I don't really know. I am too old for this politicking. I am known for the openness of my dealings in the Senate. I have never made secrets out of my motives, and it is years since I did this".

Weariness had overcome him, a consequence of the risks that he had been forced to take that day.
"I think that I have got the support we need. I only hope that in doing so I have not made us vulnerable".
Lucius retired to bed soon after, but despite his fatigue, sleep was a long time in coming.

*****

The following day the Council for the Administration of the Combined Armies of the Empire of Rome met. As he padded up the stone steps leading to the council chamber of the Senate House, he felt the unfamiliar tautness of apprehension grip him. The chamber was not large but it was grand. It had high gilded ceilings of considerable beauty, and inset into the walls were small alcoves which each housed a marble bust of a previous emperor. The Chairman's place at the head of the oval table was free, but all of the other places were filled.
Decimus Marcellus was the most powerful man present. As the commander of the armed forces he carried ultimate responsibility. He was also in a foul mood. The word on the grapevine was that his position was unstable. Hadrian, it seemed, had continued to see the young Greek tutor of his friend's son, and Decimus' charms were continuing to prove less attractive to him. Decimus, it was said, was becoming increasingly desperate in his efforts to win back the favour of his lover and patron.
Lucius nodded to the men seated at the magnificent eucalyptus table and took his usual place at its head. He had been the chairman of this Council for over seven years.

As well as Decimus and Lucius, there were four further senators present. There were also five members of the Plebs, whose interest derives from the fact that so many of their men folk serve in the army. They are tolerated by the patricians because built into the eleven man council is a natural majority for them.

The council itself does not have any jurisdiction over the political decisions concerning the armed forces. It does not decide where war is waged, what campaigns are fought, who is to be conquered, what tactics or strategy are to be used or even how many legions should be sent to a particular province. All of these things are decided by the emperor in whatever way he sees fit. Nor does the council have any jurisdiction over operational practices, which is done through a council on which primarily soldiers sit. The Council for the Administration of the Armed Forces is there to establish the pay and conditions of the army, to allocate funds and to administer the movements of personnel. This includes bodies of men and individuals, and so one of their duties is to appoint legates and generals.

As he opened the meeting, Lucius had the unfamiliar experience of having to make a conscious effort to keep his voice level.
"Good morning, gentlemen".
Lucius looked around the table, trying to sense whether there was anything different in the atmosphere of the meeting today. Everything seemed to be as he would expect, and he began to move through the agenda. The meeting opened well. Most of the first items on the agenda were easily dealt with, mainly due to the rigorous preparation that Lucius had put into them. It was not long before they came to the heading "Appointment of new Legate to IXth (Eburacum)":

Lucius offered a silent prayer, settled himself, and began to explain the background. He passed Caracalla's message around the table and put his suggestion to the Council.
"It seems that this Marius Sextus is now the de facto incumbent. Does anyone have any alternatives?"
There was silence. This was a good sign, as it meant that there was no one present who had come to sponsor their own candidate. One of the plebs offhandedly asked a question.
"What is the man like?"
The secretary shuffled some papers. The secretary had no vote in the meeting, but was a senior soldier from the Imperial Guard whose job was to be fully briefed on all of the issues discussed by the council. He looked up.
"I have made enquiries of various sources. The man is essentially a pleb. He was born in Rome and is the first son of a centurion who

served in the XIVth. His mother died in childbirth with her second child. His father was killed in action when Marius was ten. Whilst his father was on campaign he lived with his cousin, and after his father's death he continued to do so until he joined up aged sixteen. He rose through the ranks, serving in Dacia, Moesia and Pannonia. He distinguished himself in Moesia and rose to the position of centurion in the XIIth".

The secretary continued his concise biography and abruptly brought it up to date.

"Four months ago he returned to Rome and was almost immediately appointed as deputy Legate to the IXth. The command of that legion was in transition, and his appointment was approved by this council two months ago, at the same meeting that Victrix was appointed Legate. His record is exemplary, his reputation fearsome and his abilities rated very highly".

He shuffled the paper to one side and folded his arms.

"I remember this man. He made a report to me. I liked him" said Decimus mildly, barely interested.

It was obvious that none of the plebs was going to object. They were always trying to get more plebs appointed to senior roles in the military, their major complaint against the army being that it was run by patricians who did not care for their men. Lucius held his breath. He could not believe his good fortune in Decimus voicing his vague recollection of Marius. By doing so in favourable terms, he was likely to pre-empt any objection from the senators. The appointment of such a low born to such a high position was extremely unusual. The senators would usually not stand for it. There was a moment of silence before Brutus, an elderly, pompous senator of impeccable birth and questionable intelligence spoke. As he did so Lucius felt his heart sink.

"I don't feel comfortable with such a man being given a job as Legate. None of us know him, and he's not one of us. Surely there must be a more appropriate person of decent birth?"

The plebs stiffened in their seats. This was the sort of comment that was guaranteed to rile them. Decimus was also irritated. He had just said that he had met the man and liked him, and Brutus was treating his opinion as though it were irrelevant. When he spoke he allowed himself to be scathing, as he knew that in doing so he would have the support of over half of the room. Besides, it never did any harm to ingratiate oneself with the plebs.

"Perhaps Brutus has developed a hearing defect. I said that I knew him, and I said that I like him. Lucius knows him too, don't you Lucius?"

Lucius gave a start. He had hoped that he would not need to reveal any association with Marius. But in the face of such a direct assertion he had little choice.

"I do, and I like him also" he said simply.

"Good, then it is decided. A show of hands. Who is for Marius Sextus as legate of the IXth?" said Decimus.

Ten hands went up. Everyone looked at Brutus, and finally he allowed his hand to rise too.

"Excellent, it's unanimous" said Decimus. Lucius quickly moved on to the next item on the agenda.

An hour later the meeting was finished, and Lucius was still tense. He had no desire to talk to any of the Council, so he busied himself putting papers back in order and gathering his notes as they left.

On the great staircase of the Senate House, the huge wide marble steps that sweep down from the tall doorways into the magnificent forum of Augustus, Brutus and Decimus were standing talking.

"Strange, that business about the ninth" he said. "To be honest, I'd have protested more if Lucius hadn't touched on it yesterday when he visited me to talk about my wife's birthday celebrations. I mean, the man's a pleb. It would never have happened in the old days, I can tell you. We always used to make sure that a decent fellow with a good upbringing got the job. We certainly wouldn't have let some jumped up little rank and filer, some urchin from the streets to take over a legion. To be honest .."

Decimus interrupted him. He had only been half listening to Brutus, and even that was more attention than he was accustomed to devoting to such bores. But some of Brutus' words had penetrated his reverie.

"Say that again, Brutus".

Brutus looked at him as if he were a little mad. When he repeated what he had been saying he did so much more slowly.

"I said, Decimus, that when Lucius was advising me on venues for my wife's birthday party he did mention that the acting legate of the ninth seemed just the chap to get the supply of slaves going again from the north of Britannia. Frankly I never knew that he had an interest in slaving, but I suppose that it's a solid way to ... "

He looked up at Decimus, only to see his retreating back.

"Rude little upstart", muttered Brutus. "He'll get his comeuppance now that Hadrian's found a prettier little boy".

Vatican Hill

Decimus charged back into his villa. All the way back he had been thinking about what Brutus had told him. The more he thought, the less he liked it. Lucius was definitely up to something. Originally the appointment of Marius to Eburacum had seemed a good idea. A neat way to dispose of a man who had been involved in something that they would prefer no one to know anything about. It would have made an ambitious man very happy whilst getting him right out of the way. But it had definitely been Lucius' idea. And now he was lobbying the Council to get the man promoted to legate. This was an entirely different matter. A legate in a place such as Eburacum had a significant amount of responsibility, and power.

Decimus had caught up with a couple of the other senators who had been at the meeting, and found that Lucius had visited them the previous day too, each ostensibly for different reasons. In the course of the visits he asked each of them to support the candidature of Marius as legate of the ninth. As he strode home, Decimus' mind turned to his only meeting with the new legate of the IXth. With a conscious effort he reconstructed those events several months ago.

The more that he thought, the more Decimus' thoughts ran wild. Suddenly all manner of impossible dangers seemed to threaten. Hadrian had found a new favourite. And hadn't Brutus ignored his opinion at the meeting? He even began to wonder whether he was a dead man.

By the time he reached his villa Decimus was seething with frustration, but he had made his decision. As he crossed his threshold, he shouted loudly.

"Send for Nihilo. Right now".

*****

Just over an hour later Nihilo walked in. As usual he was composed. There was no evidence of the hurry that he must have been in to get from town to Decimus' villa so quickly.

Nihilo was a scaly little man. His eyes were small, beady and utterly cold. To many they were chilling. Although he was small there was a sinewy strength in his body, with no suggestion of any spare flesh. His skin was thick, dark and rough, and it stretched across his features in a way that gave him the appearance of a snake. Nihilo was an unpleasant little man and Decimus knew it. But he also knew that Nihilo was about the best at his job in Rome. Nihilo was a spook.

Decimus wasted no time.

"That bastard Lucius is up to something. It involves the newly appointed legate of the ninth legion, a Marius Sextus. I want to know Lucius' every move. I want to know every single coming and going from his house. I want to know details of all his correspondence, what his servants are gossiping about, what is new and what has been happening that could be described as unusual. I want to know everything and I want to know it now. Go."

Nihilo did not say a word. He just gave a reptilian smile, bowed and walked out.

*****

From behind their stall, Origen and Radjic observed Lucius returning to his house as the sun went down. As he entered, Beziac approached the stall and resumed his place.

"Where did he go?" asked Origen.

"Only to Senate House" replied Beziac. "He is often going there. It's where he works".
Origen looked sour. He had only been watching for a day and a half and already he was bored and frustrated.
"Tomorrow I'm going to pay him a visit".

The following morning Origen, Benjamin, Beziac and Radjic had only just got to their stall, and were still unpacking their wares when a young soldier led a donkey to the front of Lucius' house. The donkey was laden with two large bundles. As soon as it arrived, Rani hurried out of the house. She did not notice the stallholder who crouched down behind his crates as she greeted her escort. Origen had recognised Rani and was sure that if she were to see him she would recognise him, from their meeting in Assyut all those months ago. She was dressed simply but not as a slave, and over her tunic she wore a travelling cloak. She walked with the young soldier and the donkey towards the centre of the city. Origen grabbed Benjamin and turned to Beziac.
"Benjamin and I will follow. Keep your watch. Keep it even if we do not return for some time".
With that, he and Benjamin were gone.

*****

From his vantage point on the first floor of a house directly opposite Lucius' main entrance, Nihilo watched. He had not paid any special attention to the stallholders before, but the behaviour of the big, bearlike one had caught his attention when the pretty young girl had walked out of the house. Were he a suspicious man he would have thought that they, too, were watching Lucius' house. Nihilo was paid to be suspicious.

*****

Origen followed Rani and the young soldier through the centre of the city and out under the Palatine hill to the Ostia road. They passed through the Ostia gate without stopping and continued all day. Origen and Benjamin had not been prepared for a long walk so carried no water or food with them. It was past sunset when they walked into Ostia, tired and thirsty.

Although some vessels sailed up the Tiber and docked at the wharves underneath the Aventine hill, most docked at this port, at the mouth of the great river. This was what earned Ostia her the synonym, 'the gateway to the empire'. Clearly Rani and her soldier were planning a long journey.

Rani and the soldier went straight to the docks. Origen and Benjamin kept their distance as the soldier spoke to many captains. After about an hour of searching he found a ship that the two of them boarded, unhitching their bundles from the donkey and taking them aboard. They left the donkey tethered to the quay. Origen and Benjamin waited for a while in case they re-emerged. After about half an hour, Benjamin went off to get food and discover the destination of the ship. When he returned he looked surprised.
"The boat sails for Londinium on the morning tide" he said.
"Then we will be on it", replied Origen.

29

They were dark days after the death of Victrix. Marius, the new legate of the IXth legion, holed himself up in his residence and would not receive anyone. He despatched messengers to Rome and Londinium and he issued orders for the town to be cleared up and restored. He also sent scouts to bring back detailed information about the whereabouts of Gwdloych's forces and his headquarters. But then he shut himself away. It was three days before I was granted admittance, and they were bitter-sweet days for me. I knew why Marius would not see me. But I passed the time by thinking of Olivia. It seemed that the further that I got from her, the more I dwelled on those hours that we had spent together. I could spend hours picturing her soft hair and firm body, and remembering her quick wit and her courage.

When I was finally admitted to see Marius, I was not surprised to find him consumed by self-loathing. But I was surprised at the extent to which the horror of what he had done was beginning to break him. He railed against Lucius, and even me. He lay in bed, despairing over what he had become. I urged him to tell me about it, but he just looked back at me with scorn. Eventually he sighed heavily.
"You couldn't understand because you weren't there, Tolus"
"Then make me understand. Tell me what happened" I was annoyed by his attitude and it showed.
He did not respond. He just lay there, looking blankly into space. I sat silently. Presently tears began to seep from the corners of his eyes. I leaned forward and put a hand on his shoulder.
"Tell me, Marius. Tell me, for it may be easier to bear if you do", I said gently.
"I cannot" he whispered.
"Tell me" I replied simply.
So he did.

"When I walked in with Dunam, Victrix looked up and motioned us to sit down. Before either of them knew what was happening my sword was in Dunam's belly. The last thing that he did was look at me with complete surprise. He had no time to react. I carried on pushing, until the sword was in to the hilt. It went straight through him. I shoved him up against the wall, and then let go. He fell down the wall, leaving that terrible trail of blood. Victrix was on his feet, looking on in horror
'What the hell was that?' he asked, furious.
I did not want to kill Victrix. I believed that I could enrol him into what we were doing. So I showed him the confession. I had brought it with me, under my cloak. He didn't want to read it and I had to practically force him. When he had finished, he looked up at me and said two words that I will never forget. He said, 'So what?' I knew then that I would have to kill him, but I continued to try to persuade him. I told him of our plan. I told him of Lucius' involvement. I told him everything. He knew then that one of us was a dead man. But still he tried to talk me out of it, Tolus. He talked of loyalty to Rome. He talked of the duty of a soldier. He spoke the words that I have refused to allow myself to think, Tolus. And he reasoned well. He told me that I had no place doing this. He told me that I was going to put a whole legion into impossible danger. He told me that I would have their lives on my conscience. He was right, damn it. He then offered to forget about the whole thing. He said that if I were to burn the confession then and there, he would pretend that nothing had ever happened. He liked me, Tolus, he really did. But I refused. I thought that I knew what we were doing. I thought I knew why and I thought that it was right. But I don't know any more. I wish I'd just agreed to do as he asked. But I refused".

We always knew that Marius would have to murder Victrix. We had discussed it with Lucius. At first I could not understand his desolation. We had killed Alaric and Cassius in Aegyptus when they refused to join us and we believed then that what we were doing was right. But as he spoke I came to see it as he did. He had not only killed a man who he had come to like and respect, and who trusted him implicitly, but he had also murdered Dunam, a centurion he had no quarrel with.

"Tell me what followed, Marius" I prompted.

Marius almost cowered in his chair and looked at me, almost beseeching me to allow him not to. I gave him a nod of encouragement, and he continued softly.

"It was strange what happened next. We both knew what had to be done and we formally drew our swords. Victrix was no coward. He could have fled the room and called for me to be arrested, but he didn't. He drew his sword and touched his blade to the drying blood of Dunam that covered mine. Then we fought, and he was good. It was he who inflicted this wound in my side. When he saw me injured he thought that I was hurt more seriously than I was. He thought that I would be incapacitated. He lowered his guard and I was able to take him by surprise. And then I lay down and thought up my story".

Marius looked bitterly out of the window.

"I cannot go on with this, Tolus. I am going back to Rome. I will give the confession to Lucius and tell him that I am not his man".

He became worked up as he continued.

"I curse that day that we found it and I curse the day that we opened it".

Marius was on his feet, standing by the window and fiddling with the tassels on the curtains.

"I will be damned for what I have done. Leave me, Tolus. I curse you, too."

He would not listen to me or look at me, so I left him.

*****

It took another week for him to come out of that room. It took him even more time to return to anything like vigour, and during that time I think that he came almost to hate me. Every time we were alone together I spoke to him of why we were doing it. I reminded him of the great injustices that the Christians suffered at the hands of the Romans, of all the murdered innocents that our leaders were responsible for and of all the souls that were endangered by the lies first spread by Nero. And I reminded him of Rani.

It took time, but it worked. Had it not been for Rani and her family, I don't think that it could have. He would have given up and returned to Rome. But gradually Marius became convinced all over again. He read and reread the confession, and I think that the great lie set out so clearly put the death of Victrix, Dunam and the others into perspective.

As he became more convinced he became a better leader. His soldiers had not seen their new leader for two weeks. As far as they were concerned he had been badly wounded in his heroic attempt to save the life of their legate. Because of this they did the tasks that were asked of them. They cleaned the streets and mended the town walls. They cleared the defensive ditch and helped to repair some of the rotten infrastructure of Eburacum. Marius' wound had, in fact, healed quickly and was not deep. When he was feeling mentally strong enough to begin his task, he ordered the whole legion to assemble in the parade ground.

He wore his full dress uniform that day, and cut an imposing figure standing on the platform that had been specially erected for the occasion. He was flanked by a standard bearer who proudly bore the Eagle of the Ninth. The centuries were lined up ahead of him in tight order, all in full uniform. On Marius' orders all six thousand men were clean-shaven. Decent uniforms had been made for most, although many still did not have shoes. The cobblers had been working constantly for two weeks, but they could not make the shoes quickly enough. Marius' voice was deep and rich as he began to address his men.
"Men of the Ninth! My name is Marius Sextus and I am your acting Legate. Ave!"
Six thousand voices shouted back as one. "Ave!"
"This is a hard land. Neither those who have served here for years, nor those who have recently arrived require me to tell you that. I have already sustained an injury, and that is not a common occurrence!" There were a few laughs in the crowd. The irony of what he said was not lost on them.

"I want to start by commending you on the work that you have done over the last two weeks. Eburacum is beginning to look Roman again. It is right that we should start with the town, but we must not finish with the town. We must continue with the province. And to make the province Roman we must subjugate any rivals to our power. Our rival is the leader of the Brigantes. We must subjugate Gwdloych".

Marius paused, and as he did so he looked around. He was in no hurry, and he had the undivided attention of all six thousand men present. They liked his tone but they were sceptical.

"There will be a parade in four days time. On the merits of that parade, forty centuries will be selected to march the following day. We will march to the headquarters of Gwdloych and destroy it. Do not be the sad bastards left behind, who will hear of a great victory second hand. Be sure that you are the glorious ones who win the victory".

Marius's voice had risen to a crescendo as he finished. He paused for a moment, stock still on that platform. The eyes of every man were fixed on him. He knew how to hold a crowd, Marius. He always had. He slowly opened his mouth, and shouted with all his might.

"Victory".

The host seemed to waver for the briefest of moments before six thousand right hands were raised as six thousand voices shouted the word back.

*****

Frantic activity followed. Kit was repaired, weapons sharpened and tools polished. Shoes were begged, borrowed and stolen from anywhere they could be found. The standard of each century was polished so hard that they reflected the sun undimmed. The motivation took me by surprise. I had been expecting the men to be almost reluctant to go on this campaign, particularly after the disaster at Isurium. But it was quite the opposite. There was almost a desperation not to be left behind. I was puzzled, so I did what I always did when I wanted to know what was going on in the heads of the rank and file. I asked Greto.

"Oh, don't be surprised, Tolus. The men adore him already. The story of what Marius did in Moesia when he killed Pintreich has been told thousands of times since he was injured. His bravery has been proved by being the only survivor of Dunam's madness, and half of the legion feel that they know him personally since he spent so much time on the journey up here from Londinium getting to know them. They believe in him. They already feel better about themselves now someone is taking an interest in them. They are no longer ashamed of this town, mainly because Marius has ordered them to make it a decent place, and they trust his talk of famous victories to come. You know that he has a way with people, Tolus, and his magic is working here. I just hope that he knows what he is doing by taking on this local chief. If he fails now, all will be lost. But if he succeeds . . ."

*****

I have to confess that I was caught up in the mood of excitement that accompanied the build up to that parade. Which is why I felt such acute disappointment when Marius called me in two days before to tell me that he had decided that I would stay behind to help guard the town. I tried to argue, but it was futile. Marius had made up his mind, and there was a certainty about him that precluded any dissent. He was completely transformed from the weeping shell of a man that he had been just two weeks before. Replacing it was the personification of confidence, and it was infectious. He spent those four days touring round the town, encouraging and joking with the men as they worked to restore it. A new atmosphere developed. We were going to war, and we were going to win.

I spent the day before the parade commanding a working party clearing a section of the ditch outside the city walls. It was a foul job, shovelling away the accumulated waste of months. The stench was such that we all wore masks of linen, and the mulch was heavy. Nevertheless the men did not need any coercion to make them work. All day we toiled under the imposing city walls, with fields stretching out to the north and with our backs to the pale sun. By sunset we had cleared our section so I dismissed the men and returned to the barracks to find Greto and the rest.

The barracks were a hive of activity. In the long, low blocks soldiers sat on their bunks with their equipment laid out beside them. They worked with intense concentration, ensuring that all of their kit was glistening, well stitched, robust and properly greased. I listened to the cheerful chat and nodded to those that I recognised as I walked through. When I saw my men, they were doing much the same as the others.

"Tell Marius that if we don't get selected, then we leave to find Rani and tell her what he's really like". Numba grinned. He had the certainty of a man who knew that he would be selected.

I looked to the others. Silus and Tobias were looking at their kit, avoiding my eye. Greto busied himself polishing the buckles on his sword belt, and Artorius just stood around looking awkward.

"What's going on?" I asked.

The response to my question was the absurd spectacle of grown men squirming, looking anywhere except in my direction. I began to lose my temper, but just as I was about to shout, Artorius' face broke into a grin.

"We had word from Marius. He says that we will be seconded to his staff for the campaign to Dunn Sccyrebb".

They were almost ashamed of their luck, and clearly felt bad for me being left behind. But they all looked so proud. I was pleased for them, but my pleasure was soured by jealousy. I wanted to fight.

*****

The parade was magnificent. The whole legion marched past the podium. Marius stood rigid in the centre, surrounded by his tribunes. Sergius stood to his right and Jaffa looked proud on his left. Marius was clever about who he chose. Those centuries that he chose to stay behind were the worst turned out. But it was relative, and the standards were generally very high, even by the standards of Rome. But some had to stay behind, and Marius was painstaking in the trouble he took to ensure that they still felt valued. He used me as an example, speaking of my value in a fight and saying that he was leaving me behind because of the importance of protecting Eburacum. And then, the following day, he marched out of Eburacum at the head of four thousand beautifully turned out legionaries. Greto and the others walked tall by his side.

It was a spectacular sight. They took no baggage train with them. Every man carried all the food that he would require and they only took five days supplies. But other than that they travelled as lightly as possible. I felt a great envy as I watched them march that morning.

*****

They marched north for the whole day, covering over thirty miles. Marius selected a large plateau to camp on and the night passed uneventfully. At dawn the following day they resumed the march and covered a further twenty five miles. Progress was slower on that second day due to the terrain. The low, rolling hills gave way to larger, more imposing valleys and peaks. Again they built a full defensive camp on high ground. They were just five miles from Gwdloych's headquarters, a large and grim village that is no more but was known then as Dunn Sccyrebb.

Two things distinguished that march from Eburacum. The first was the use of the cavalry. The legion had one hundred and twenty horse. Usually these would travel with the main body of the soldiers, guarding the flanks. But Marius split them into two groups. The first he assigned to travel ahead of the vanguard, to scout the paths through the thick woods a mile or two in advance of the vanguard. Their job was to cut down anyone who retreated down those paths in the face of our on-coming army, to prevent word of the legions presence from reaching Gwdloych. Experience and discussions with veterans of the ninth had told us that our enemy would not stay to fight if they had word of the approach of such a force. They would melt away into the woods and the hills, so Marius was keen to catch them by surprise. The other sixty cavalry were assigned to roam the woods and the hills searching for war parties that might engage us, and report back. Fortunately they heard of none and they saw none.
The second thing was the marching order. Instead of marching in a long line, drawn out for miles behind each other, Marius ordered that

as much as possible the men should march abreast of one another, in a horizontal line. This was difficult in the forests, but in the wide valleys it meant that they were constantly in battle order, ready if they were attacked. In the event they weren't, but it gave the men great confidence to know that they could defend themselves adequately at a seconds notice.

On that march every village found was razed, and every inhabitant killed.

The scouts who had found Dunn Sccyrebb drew a map of the terrain surrounding the village. It was set on the edge of a wide valley, with a high pass to the west. To the north and the south the valley meandered through the hills. To the east was a great hill with sides so steep that it could not be readily negotiated, neither up nor down.

The cavalry had been successful in their task. None had been lost, and they had cut down over one hundred savages as they ran in the face of our army. At dawn that third morning, our scouts reported that there was no sign of the enemy being aware of the legions presence. Three and a half thousand fighting men were camped in the valley around Dunn Sccyrebb. Every day a few left, but it had only been a trickle. All those that departed to the south were killed silently.

The morning of the third day Marius revealed his plan. Fifteen of his forty centuries were to march up the valley from the south. He reckoned that one and a half thousand men would be a sufficiently strong force to make the barbarians turn and flee. They would have two options. They could either scramble up the pass to the west or they could continue up the valley to the north. Marius believed that their instincts would be to go for the hills. They would head west, rather than up the northern valley. So of his remaining thirty centuries he sent fifteen to the west under the command of Jaffa, to skirt round behind the hills and approach the pass from the far side. Under the command of Serbius he sent ten centuries to skirt round to the north, to cut off the northern escape. It took most of the day for the three sections of the army to get into position. Marius remained behind to command the section that would reveal themselves from the south. It was mid afternoon before Marius received word that the other two contingents were in position.

He did not waste any time. Immediately he gave the order for his section to march forward. They were in full battle order, spread out in century groups across the valley floor. The valley curved round to the northwest and the village of Dunn Sccyrebb became visible. More importantly, they could see the rough camp of the horde that stayed on the valley floor to the east of the main village. As soon as they saw the approaching force they scrambled about for their weapons. Shaggy haired warriors, covered in filth ran to grab their cloaks and their great two handed swords.

30

Nihilo recounted to Decimus what he had seen outside Lucius' house. There were two things that particularly interested his master. The first was the mysterious departure of the striking Eastern woman with the soldier. But of far more interest was the revelation that Nihilo was not the only person watching Lucius. It confirmed that he had been right to suspect something, and it only served to increase his frustration.

Decimus was furious that two of those other watchers had disappeared to follow the woman and that none of them had returned. He felt that he was being excluded from something. He did nothing for one day, leaving Nihilo to watch the house in the hope that the young girl and the soldier would return. Nothing happened. When Nihilo reported to him on the second day Decimus made his decision, although he knew that it was a risky one. There was a good chance that the watchers were in the employment of Hadrian. If that was the case, then Decimus knew he was about to put himself in extreme danger. But if they were not, he could use whatever he found to win back his lover. It was a gamble, and Decimus felt he had little choice.
"Bring one of them in, Nihilo. We'll see what he has to say. Leave the other, but have him followed".

*****

From his vantage point above their stall, Nihilo watched as a man wandered up to it. The man looked at the sad looking fruit laid out and picked up an apple. He put his other hand into his toga and withdrew his purse. From his purse he produced a small coin and a small fragment of papyrus. He handed both to the man on the stall, and then quickly disappeared into the crowds walking down the Via Flaminian..

Beziac was so taken aback by the piece of papyrus that he reacted slowly. By the time he did the man was gone. He turned and beckoned to Radjic, and then he unfolded the papyrus. As he read it, Radjic looked over his shoulder.

"IF YOU SEEK A MAN NAMED MARIUS SEXTUS THEN YOU WILL WANT TO SPEAK TO ME. OPPOSITE THE MAIN DOOR TO THE RESIDENCE OF LUCIUS MERUTII SCRIPIUS IS A DOOR WITH A SMALL SHRINE TO MITHRAS BY IT. ENTER THAT DOOR AND ASCEND THE STAIRCASE OPPOSITE TO THE FIRST FLOOR"

The note was unsigned. Beziac turned to Radjic with a raised eyebrow.
"I will go" said Radjic. "If I do not emerge within ten minutes, come in after me".

Radjic turned and walked the few paces to the door mentioned in the note. From the outside it looked like a normal residence. He pushed the door and it opened inwards. He stepped inside and as he did so the door was closed behind him and he felt a splitting pain in his head.

A cart drew up by the door. It was led by a donkey and was surrounded by eight soldiers. Nihilo walked out of the front door and joined the driver of the cart. Two of the soldiers entered the house, and came out carrying a large pile of linen, which they hoisted onto the cart. The procession then moved off in the direction of the Vatican Hill. Beziac looked on with increasing unease. Something wasn't right. When he entered the house he found it empty.

*****

It was mid afternoon when Nihilo reached Decimus' house. He took the cart round to the back entrance and unloaded the bundle of linen. Nihilo summoned one of the guards to help him, and between them they took the bundle inside. Decimus was too busy to join Nihilo, but ordered him to make a start.

The bundle lay on the floor of a basement room. The room was well proportioned and beautifully crafted. The sandstone walls had no gaps in their joins, and the stone flagged floor was perfectly smooth. If one looked closely at it one could make out a mild discolouration. Despite enthusiastic and repeated scrubbing, it had not been possible to completely erase the dark stains. There was no furniture in that room other than a large, heavy chair. It was made of wood, and each leg was inset into a deep hole cut into the stone flagging. On the front legs were straps, and there were more half way up the back of the chair, on the reverse side. There were two men in that room. Nihilo was there, and with him was a heavily scarred Numidian slave. The slave could not talk because he did not have a tongue. Nihilo had removed it as a precaution. This man would not be able to communicate anything that he heard because neither could he write, but he could hear and he could obey orders.

Nihilo drew his knife and cut the linen bag open. Inside, Radjic was conscious and naked. His hands and feet were tightly bound and an old rag had been stuck so far down his throat that he had gagged. When he saw Nihilo's face and the knife held close to his chin his eyes widened in terror. The slave and Nihilo manhandled him onto the chair roughly. Nihilo held the knife to his throat as the slave cut the bindings on his feet and strapped each of his legs to the front legs of the chair. They were sufficiently far apart to result in Radjic's legs being well spread, his genitals exposed. The slave then cut the bindings on his hands and pulled the wrists back, twisting them up so that they slid into the bindings high up on the back of the chair. This caused Radjics shoulders to be pressed far forward, inducing a dull, aching pain. He would soon learn that this dull pain did not really deserve to be called such.

Nihilo set to work. Radjic was surprised, for as he did so he did not speak a word. He did not ask any questions, nor did he seek to explain what was going on. He just set to work on Radjic's body with his knife. The lack of an explanation was what terrified Radjic more than what Nihilo was doing. He made small incisions on the edge of each of Radjic's shoulder blades. The pain was bad, but what was worse was the feeling of the blood seeping down his back. With precision and care he made more nicks on the top of Radjic's shoulders, and he was just starting on the top of Radjic's thighs when the door opened and Decimus walked in.

Decimus did not say a word. He simply nodded at Nihilo to continue. In front of his eyes, Nihilo made a long, shallow incision on each of Radjic's thighs. He inserted short stubs of a hard wood at intervals into each of the incisions to keep the wounds open. Because they were not deep, the incisions only opened about one centimetre, and because they had been made into muscle they did not bleed too profusely. The slave then walked forward from behind Radjic and handed Nihilo a large ceramic jar. Nihilo placed his hand inside, and when he brought it out he had a fistful of squirming white maggots. Carefully he dropped them along each of the open wounds on Radjic's legs. Radjic tried to scream as he felt them wriggling in his leg, burrowing slowly into the wound.

The process of breaking him down had begun. Radjic was being eaten alive.

It was two or three minutes before Radjic stopped straining and fighting his bindings. He could not scream due to the rag half way down his throat. He took long, deep breaths through his nose, and his face was puce. As soon as calmed down Nihilo began to speak. He did so in low, nasal tones. He had a slight lisp, and the effect of his matter-of-fact manner was terrifying.

"You are probably going to die. If you tell us all we want to know quickly enough we might allow you to live. But if you leave it too long, your body will be too weak. If you get to this stage, we will kill you quickly as soon as you have told us what we want to know. If you do not, you will die slowly. My personal record is eleven days. The man in question was brave, and he was down to less than half of his original body weight when he cracked. When we strapped his head down and forced his eyelids open, we found that the maggots enjoyed the taste of his eyeballs. That did it for him, and within a minute of

beginning to speak there were no maggots in his body. An hour later we rewarded him for his co-operation. When I cut his head off I think that he was grateful. But the choice is yours"
He paused to gesture at Decimus.
"Now my colleague has some questions for you".

Decimus stepped forward. Radjic had turned his head to one side and his eyes were shut tight. Decimus put out his hand to remove the rag that was stuffed in Radjic's mouth. As he removed the gag, Radjic's head jolted forward and he tried to take a bite out of Decimus' hand. But Decimus was too quick.
"What is your name?" asked Decimus.
There was silence.
"Why are you watching Lucius?" he continued.
More silence.
"What do you know of Marius Sextus?"
Nothing.
Decimus turned and strode out. As he closed the door he spoke over his shoulder
"Summon me when he is ready".
Nihilo stepped forward and replaced the gag in Radjic's mouth.

Radjic lasted three hours. It was extraordinary how quickly the maggots worked. Nihilo was careful to replace the maggots at intervals of half an hour. This ensured that they were never sated, that they continued to eat away at the flesh and muscle of his leg. Each time he removed the maggots, he left Radjic's legs clear for several minutes. The relief from the sensation of the squirming creatures working through his living flesh was incredible. As soon as they were removed, blood began to ooze slowly from the wound. Already after two hours each wound was three centimetres wide, and much of the flesh under the skin eaten away. The sixth time that the maggots were about to be replaced, Radjic began to moan frantically. Nihilo removed the gag and Radjic spoke.
"I will answer your questions" he said.
Nihilo ordered the slave to replace the gag and the maggots, and left the room.

Radjic urinated where he sat.

Ten minutes later Decimus entered the room. The maggots were removed, as was the gag.
Radjic immediately turned his head to one side and vomited on the floor. It left a trail down his chin. He vomited from the sheer agony coming from his thighs, but also with disgust at the sensation of being eaten alive. It was an acute pain but within it he could feel the movement of the maggots in his legs, working his muscle into a digestible pulp and chewing at his nerve endings. The others in the room ignored his vomit and the puddle of urine on the floor.
"What is your name?" asked Decimus once more.
"I am Radjic of Lydia".
The words were delivered in a monotone and were edged with pain. The pain was intensely physical, but there was more to it than that. Radjic's voice was empty. It was the voice of a man who knew that he had been tested and found wanting, a man who had examined his soul and failed to find the courage that he had hoped that he possessed. No man can tell in advance how he will bear such trials, and thankfully most never have to find out.
"Why are you in Rome?"
There was a pause. Nihilo moved forward to replace the gag, and Decimus looked as though he were going to leave. Radjic couldn't bear it.
"We are searching for the Neronian Confession" blurted out Radjic.
Decimus could not hide the look of surprise that came over his face.
"Who has it?" he immediately asked.
"We don't know, but we believe that it is Marius Sextus" replied Radjic.
"How do you know that it exists?" asked Decimus. He could not hide his excitement.
"Because Marius found it in Alexandria and brought it to Rome. He was going to use it to blackmail the emperor. But Lucius talked him out of it. Lucius and Marius have a plan of how they will use it, but I don't know what it is."
Decimus' eyes were bright. "And why are you searching for the confession?"

"Because of its value to us" replied Radjic.
"And who is 'us'?"
Radjic was looking down at the spongy pulp of his thighs.
"Origen's men. Followers of the Christus. The Christians" he murmured.

Decimus leaned back and his eyes moved from Radjic to the heavy stone ceiling. He stood there for some time in silence. Nihilo knew not to speak. Decimus was thinking, and he hated to be interrupted.
"How do you know all this?" he asked eventually. "How do you know what transpired between Marius and Lucius?"
"Because we went to see Lucius" replied Radjic.
"Why?"
"Because of his oath to Tertullian".
Decimus was beginning to get confused.
"Who is Tertullian?" asked Decimus
"His is the former leader of our movement" replied Radjic.
Decimus became aware of a vague realisation coming over him. He needed time to think in order to understand what it was. There was a link that would make this all fit into place, but he couldn't work it out. He decided to press on in the hope that Radjic would tell him.
"And why did Lucius give an oath to Tertullian?" he asked.
"Because Tertullian saved him from capture at a secret meeting in Rome many years ago".
Decimus felt a shock of adrenaline as the realisation came together in his mind.
"Lucius is a Christian?" he burst out.
"Yes" replied Radjic.
"Keep him alive." he said simply as he stalked out of the room.

Decimus was excited, and as he thought more about it, he began to feel elated. His first instinct was not to tell Hadrian, but he rejected it. It did not take him long to realise that there was no way that he could use this situation to oust Hadrian and take over. But nevertheless, the significance of this discovery for him personally could be huge. Hadrian would be grateful to him for uncovering such a dangerous plot. So grateful that he would be sure to reinstate him as his favourite, and maybe even consider naming him as his successor.

*****

Within the hour, Decimus was awaiting a private audience with the emperor at his palace.

When Decimus first told Hadrian of his discovery, the emperor would not believe him. But as Decimus continued, the implications of his words began to sink in. Hadrian's face became progressively whiter. At first it was shock, but it quickly gave way to rage. It only when Decimus told him the news that he had received just that morning that Hadrian began to believe what he was being told. For that morning Decimus had received a short message from Britannia that told of a great victory won by Marius Sextus in the north of the province of Britannia, a victory over the king of the local tribe that was called Brigantes, over a man named Gwdloych.

Hadrian was in a white rage. He walked out of the grand reception room, across the striking mosaic on the floor and into the peristyle. Decimus followed. Hadrian was muttering under his breath, cursing. When Decimus caught up with him, he put an arm round Hadrian's shoulders. Hadrian shrugged him off violently and continued pacing. Suddenly he let out a great howl. There were two slaves working on the gardens in the quadrangle in the middle of the peristyle, and Hadrian screamed at them.
They looked terrified and ran away towards the servant's quarters. Decimus then walked up to Hadrian and put a hand on each of his cheeks. He did so firmly, but not without tenderness.
"Talk to me, Hadrian. Tell me what you want to do."
Hadrian sat down on a bench beside a fountain. The water spouted out from the mouth of the Goddess Venus. She had a face of sublime beauty and her full lips surrounded a mouth that was open in a smile. Venus, Goddess of Love. How ironic, thought Decimus as he sat there with his arm around Hadrian's shoulders.

"I don't know, Decimus. I don't know" His voice was whining, almost like a petulant child. Decimus wondered whether his lover was about to burst into tears.

Decimus was exasperated. "Let's look at this sensibly. What do we know?"

Hadrian looked back blankly.

Decimus continued. "We know that Marius found the confession. He came to Rome with the objective of blackmailing you, but before he could Lucius got hold of him and got the truth out of him. Lucius is a Christian, and he wants to use the confession for his own ends. He arranges for Marius to go to Eburacum".

Decimus paused and looked directly at Hadrian, ensuring that the emperor was taking his words in.

"We know about the cult of the leader. We know what happened with Antonius Octavian?"

Hadrian nodded.

"What if Marius were to establish this kind of loyalty from the Ninth? I would bet that the death of Victrix is no coincidence. He is leading a legion in one of the foulest lands that has ever been discovered. And he has started to win great victories. He has the Neronian confession with him, and he could well have begun to enlist the support of some of his senior officials. The ninth is due to return to Rome in three years time. It is not beyond the bounds of possibility that by that time Marius would have achieved the power that Antonius Octavian held over his men. Particularly if he continues to have successes like the one that he has just had. We could be facing a legion of full strength, loyal to them and not to you being stationed at the gates of Rome. If you were given an ultimatum whilst facing that sort of threat, what would you do, Hadrian?"

Once again Hadrian went white.

"Impossible" he shouted.

"Not impossible. That is the whole point. No legion has ever marched on Rome. Our defences are pathetic, because we know that there is no enemy in the known world who could come within a hundred miles of us. But we rely on the loyalty of our men and we rely on the loyalty of our commanders. If both were to be lost to us, it is not impossible."

For the rest of the afternoon, Decimus and Hadrian talked. It was long after the sun had set before they agreed what they would do, and Hadrian was delighted with the plan. He wrote the necessary orders in haste. Then he felt for Decimus' hand and grasped it. Without a word he stood up and led Decimus towards his private chambers.

31

Marius' men marched forward slowly, careful to keep their order. After about five minutes of scrabbling about, the savages began to flee. Marius was relieved, because the only vulnerability in his plan had been if they decided to attack the contingent that they could see. Even then, Marius was confident that he could hold them, despite being outnumbered two to one, until the others could run down from their hiding places. But rather than attack the forces they could see, they turned and ran. Marius' men continued to walk forward slowly. The savages were trapped, and there was no need to risk breaking up the line by hurrying. The savages ran in both directions. Most ran for the hills, east up towards the pass. But a sizeable number ran north up the valley. There was no order to their retreat. They made no effort to stay together in any sort of cohesive group. Instead, they straggled everywhere.

Those who were there with Marius' southern force told me that the most magnificent sight that they had ever seen was the move of the two other contingents after that. The fifteen centuries guarding the western flank moved forward. Suddenly, a vast line of fifteen hundred men was visible at the pass. It stretched right across it, and from below it looked magnificent. The straggling savages stopped in their tracks and looked to the north. But the northern contingent had stepped forward too. Although there were just a thousand of them, it looked like the same number as on the pass. The savages started to run in all directions. On all three sides our legion closed in. Some of them got through the gaps as it advanced, perhaps as many as a thousand. But they were ignored. There were plenty who would not get away. Still the savages had no order. Still they did not form up to make any sort of concerted attempt to break through. It made the work of killing them easy for our men. They just continued to advance, as desperate, panicked barbarians threw themselves at our shield wall. Their druids were in a frenzy. They tore about and cursed us in great screaming rants. Our men ignored them, treating them as they did the rest. None of them had a chance, not like that. The business of killing went on for two hours. The field ran red with blood and the carcasses of enemy dead impeded the slaughter. It was like a machine, the efficiency of it. The savages could do nothing. Their huge, two handed swords were powerless to break through the legions lines. Disciplined men just took the cutting, horizontal blows on their shield wall and stabbed their short stabbing swords from between their shields. Most attackers were killed immediately. The three forces continued to close in, stepping over great mounds of dead. Jaffa's men, coming down from the pass, were first to reach the village. Their wall would split to enable it to go round a hut or obstacle, and would then reform on the other side. Some legionaries would break off to search the huts and kill anything inside. By the time the butchering was finished, the sun had gone down behind the pass to the west. And a butchering it was. Over three thousand lay dead. Most were men of prime fighting age. The few hundred inhabitants of the village had also been killed, most of them women and children. There was no sign of the hostages that Gwdloych had taken, either from his raid on Isurium or Victrix's disastrous attempt to retake the town.

That night the entire force moved back to high ground. It was well after dark before the defensive camp had been completed. Despite the physical strains of the day, most of the men could not sleep for a while. They were too exhilarated by their days killing.

At dawn the following morning Marius ordered them to return to the village. Some of the savages had not been killed. All of those still lying injured on the field were despatched, and all of their weapons were retrieved. There were no enemies still wanting to fight.

*****

The legion was preparing to move out when a breathless scout ran up to Marius. His face was white and vomit stained his tunic. He had found the hostages. Marius ordered him to lead him there, and the scout began to shake. He led Marius to the east. The hill was steep, so steep that the only tracks on it were those of wild goats. It was a treacherous path and it traversed the hill right to the top. It was a long, hard climb. The peak of the hill had large black carrion birds circling above it. And it was there that the remains of the hostages were found. On the summit was a large, deep pit. The smell was not too powerful, because most of the flesh had been removed by scavengers. Instead there were piles of bones in the pit. But this was not what caught the attention. What did was the grotesque horror that surrounded it. It was like a forest. There were over one hundred stakes driven into the ground. And on those stakes were the heads of over one hundred Romans. And attached to those heads by the skin of the necks were the complete skins of the victims. They hung down limply, blowing in the wind and giving the nauseating impression that they were dancing. They were yellowing and stained with black patches of dried blood. Body hair was matted on them. The flesh from the inside had been largely pecked away by the birds, and the result was punctured, ragged skins resembling old, frayed papyrus. None of the faces had eyes left. Most of them were rotting, the skin beginning to flake off the bones of the skulls. The sheer number of them, and the way that they had all been arranged, each of them facing east as if in some horrendous reconstruction of the audience at a play, or a group of people watching the sun rise, made it a sight that would affect all who saw it. Marius was a hard man, but he immediately leaned over and threw up. He did not stay long. Instead he hurried down the hill, and as he did I heard him mutter one of the names by which Gwdloych was known. The name was "Sangueskayne", and it meant "hide of blood".

Marius ordered one hundred men up to bury the skins with their bones in the pit. This took two hours, so by the time the legion was ready to leave it was almost midday. Marius wasted no time. He ordered the march south to begin immediately. The discovery of the dead hostages and the manner of their death had removed all the pleasure that Marius' great victory had brought him. His hatred of this land returned, and he wanted to get back to Eburacum as soon as was possible. The other thing that slightly soured the victory for Marius, if not for our men at that time, was that Gwdloych had escaped. A small group of barbarians had been observed running, with a roman woman in their midst, right at the beginning of the battle. Marius was sure that it was Gwdloych.

He drove them hard on the way back. He drove them hard and the men did not mind. For they were still revelling in their victory, and most had not seen the gruesome sight on the top of the eastern hill. It was the late afternoon of the fourth day that our sentries announced their return. The gates of Eburacum swung open to welcome the bulk of the ninth legion back. They had lost four men in the brief campaign, and in the eyes of his men Marius was well on his way to achieving the status of a god.

*****

Over the days and weeks that followed, Marius had been staggered by the degree of adulation that he received from his men. He was treated with something approaching reverence. The men began to take on tasks that they had not been asked to do, tasks to improve the town. It was not long before the place was spotless, the very model of a clean and efficient garrison town. And Marius was not slow to catch on to what it meant. He had not shared Lucius' confidence of his ability to engender the cult of the leader. He had been concerned that it would not be possible. But here, he was watching it develop before his own eyes. Fear had drained morale and those who had served in Eburacum for years had lost their confidence. It was they who deified Marius more than any. They had been used to no leadership at all. Suddenly they rediscovered their confidence and with it they conquered their fear of the land. Their faith in the incontrovertible power of Rome was restored, and in their eyes they owed all of this to one man. They owed it to Marius Sextus.

The men who had travelled with Marius from Gallis felt possessive. They saw Marius as their leader, the man that they had brought with them from across the sea. As a consequence, a sort of competitiveness built up between the two groups of men. It was friendly and good humoured, but both wanted to show that their devotion to Marius was greater. This phenomenon only served to increase the degree to which Marius was revered by his men.

*****

In the middle of all of this, Marius summoned me. As I entered his quarters and he barked rather than spoke.
"Why did you knowingly put my life in danger?" he spat. His face was thunderous.
I had no idea what he was talking about.
"What?"
Marius repeated the question deliberately, as if to a halfwit.
I racked my brain for what could have made him so angry. I genuinely could not think what it could be.
"Marius, really, I don't know . . ."
"How dare you lie to me!" he shouted back.
He glared at me and I just looked back. I was beginning to get angry myself, but before I could reply, Marius made his accusation.
"Why have you been giving slaves my name and saying that I would welcome them?"
Realisation dawned, but before I had a chance to answer, Marius was off again.
"Why have you been encouraging them to flee their masters?" His face darkened.
I began to stammer an explanation, but Marius was shouting again.
"I should have you arrested for trying to lure a slave away from her master. And not just any slave, but a slave of the governor of the province no less! What were you thinking of?"
By this time I was not able to answer, because my mind was racing. Olivia must have been caught escaping, a crime that she would pay for with her life. Until that moment I had no idea what a strong grip this young girl gained over me. The thought of her execution was more than I could bear. I looked back at Marius as he was in mid sentence.
When he saw my eyes he stopped. To my surprise, he turned on his heels, stalked over to the corner of the room and opened the door. As he turned, I had not thought of the fact that Marius would have to find

a scapegoat. All I could think of was the fact that Olivia was dead. I closed my eyes and sat down on the floor with my head in my hands.

I heard the door close, and footsteps approach me. Suddenly there were hands running through my hair. I looked up at Olivia standing over me. She looked nervous, but the moment her eyes met mine they lightened and she threw her arms around my neck.
I looked into her gorgeous eyes and felt my stomach turn somersaults.

I was speechless. Marius was in the corner and he was smiling widely as he spoke.
"You're a sly one, aren't you? Olivia, it seems, ran away from Caracalla. If he finds her, she will die".
He looked at Olivia. "I should really return you, you know."
She looked back defiantly, and I saw her strength. He wouldn't stand a chance, but neither of us knew that at the time. Fortunately he did not try, for even though he could be harsh I knew that he would not be when I was involved.
"I suppose that we should just make sure that our governor never sees her again" he resumed grinning. He was enjoying himself, and winked at me. I could have killed him for putting me through that. He turned to Olivia and feigned officiousness.
"You will serve on my household staff and you will be assigned private quarters".
He raised an eyebrow. "I am sure that Tolus might be spared from his duties, occasionally".

*****

Olivia had found a group of travelling iron traders travelling north. They had taken her on as a cook. They knew that she was not a Briton, but she spoke their language and was willing, so they had not asked too many questions about how she came to be on the road. They had been a tough bunch, and they needed to be. It was a perilous occupation in that wild land to be a trader of any kind, and particularly a trader who travelled with something as valuable as iron.

As a result, the caravan in which they travelled was heavily armed and often moved under cover of night.

She had come because it was her only hope of happiness. She saw that fleeting encounter in the cavernous cellars of the palace of the governor in Londinium as her best chance.

The rest of my time in Eburacum was one of incredible discovery. This spirited Greek girl was only sixteen, but she had seen much of the worst that this world has within it and it had made her old beyond her years. I spent every night with her. While I idolised her, she loved me back. She had never received much love, at least not for many years. At first it was difficult for her, as she learned more about me and discovered that she did not like all that she found. I was not the ideal that she had built up in her head on the dangerous road from Londinium, but in time we found great happiness together. We spent the nights discovering each other's bodies. I had never had a regular woman, and what we both lacked in experience we made up for in enthusiasm. And we talked for hours. She had a perceptive and mischievous mind and she taught me many things. Her exuberance and vivacity made her a favourite in Marius' household, too. Our happiness was so obvious that people wanted to spend time with us. We became frustrated at not being able to spend enough time together, but we managed. They were good days.

*****

Marius continued to behave in a way that only served to increase the reverence that the Ninth had for him. He became a totemic figure, a great symbol of what could be achieved in this desolate land. The men were happy as they continued to work on the town. Regular patrols began to roam the surrounding area, even venturing into the forests. Marius ordered more tree clearing, increasing the open lands around Eburacum for miles. This increased our feeling of security, and the farmers moved back into their villas and houses outside the town. Olivia took to going for long walks outside the city, and it made me worry. But she was insistent, saying that she had not come all this way to be cooped up like she had been in Londinium. Her wilfulness was the source of some conflict between us, but we both knew that it was one of the reasons why I loved her so much.

Normality began to return to the town. Occasionally the patrols would see evidence of groups of fighting men. The camps of the savages were easy to find, and they were even easier to track. Whenever such evidence was discovered, Marius would send a party to find and destroy them. He often led these parties himself, and was clever in ensuring that the first places on these parties went to those who had been forced to remain behind in Eburacum when Dunn Sccyrebb was destroyed. In this way everyone had a share of the glory.

All the while, Marius was subtly working on his officers. He introduced the subject of religion at his dinners with his tribunes. He talked briefly of his posting in Ituraea and of his encounters with the leaders of the movement of the Christus, but he always did so in a way that implied that there was much left unsaid. He gave the impression that he had a lot to tell, but was unable to until he trusted them totally. Cleverly he began to sow the seed that the version of the events of Judea that everyone knew to be true might, in fact, be questionable. He inferred that he might have discovered information about Rome's motives for discrediting such a movement. He hinted at the threat that such a movement might pose to the authority of Rome, and gave the impression that he had gained an alternative understanding of how the power of Rome worked. He did all of this slowly and he did it subtly. There was much time then for conversation, and most subjects were exhausted. Because of his standing, Marius' hints were taken seriously. A feeling developed that he had some sort of knowledge that was dangerous, and that his loyalty to Rome was preventing him from sharing it with them. His senior commanders became intrigued, and Marius encouraged them by giving the impression of being in a dilemma. He played the part of someone whose honour prevented him from being disloyal, yet was outraged by what he had discovered. The tribunes' interest led them to actively encourage Marius to reveal things of which he was reluctant to speak. At first he would not give anything away, so the men tried to show their own loyalty, their own trustworthiness. In response, Marius revealed more of his secret knowledge, little by little. It was masterful.

After a few weeks, I think that if he had shown them the manuscript most would have fallen in with him instantly. But he didn't. He wanted to make sure that the conditions were perfect, that he would not fail. He believed that he could only achieve such certainty once he had won them more glory.

It was not long before his chance came. And it came from the unlikely source of the emperor himself. For, seven weeks after his glorious defeat of Gwdloych's forces at Dunn Sccyrebb, Marius received a messenger from Londinium. The messenger carried a scroll from the Emperor Hadrian himself.

32

Origen had not enjoyed the voyage. He had been forced to stay in the squalid cabin for virtually the whole crossing, whilst most of the other passengers spent their days on the deck. Benjamin had no such constraints. Because Rani had never seen him before he was able to move freely, and there was a benefit to this. Benjamin had used the opportunity to learn that the young soldier accompanying Rani was an imperial messenger and that he carried a message for the governor of Londinium.

Separately Origen, Benjamin and Rani were unimpressed with Londinium. Origen had been quick to catch the mood of the land, as the hatred and resentment reminded him of home. He procured new clothing for himself and Benjamin. They travelled bare foot, and wore crude jerkins made from skins secured with belts of gut. The early progress had been painful as their feet had been slow to harden, but they felt safer without their roman tunics. They dressed like savages and Origen reasoned that they would be treated to some degree as savages. They were not harassed. Instead, the local tribesmen ran away when they saw Origen and Benjamin. At first they could not understand why.

Rani did not stay in Londinium for long. When the imperial messenger delivered his message to the governor he was immediately sent back to Rome. The governor then ordered a detachment of ten horsemen to take the message north. Rani went with them. Under grey skies Origen and Benjamin stood by the towns gates watching Rani leave on horseback with the messengers. They followed the only road leading north, a road known as the Via Erminus. Origen and Benjamin were not in any hurry as they procured two horses for themselves. There would be ample time to catch up, as the Via Erminus did not have any major junctions for many miles.

They got talking to a Roman farmer as they purchased two of his horses. Origen was pleased to be able to engage in conversation, since he had talked to almost no one other than Benjamin since leaving Rome. What they learned from the farmer confused them even more. For he told them about the glorious victory that had been won by a man named Marius Sextus in the far north of the country, north of the most northerly garrison town, a place known as Eburacum.

By the time that they rode out of Londinium, Origen and Benjamin were sure that they knew where Rani, and therefore themselves, were going. But no matter how much they discussed it, they could not work out why. There was no possible explanation. Despite Perridac's conviction to the contrary, Origen began to believe that Lucius did have the manuscript after all. He began to feel that this whole trip up to the wild northern lands was a complete waste of time. And as he did so he became irritable once more.

Over the next few days, as they passed the gruesome evidence of rituals and spells cast at the sides of the road, Origen became quiet. He seemed to resent Benjamin's attempts to pass the time with small talk. Each night they made a crude camp in the woods, at least a few hundred metres from the side of the road. Benjamin had bought a small tent made of stitched hides soon after they had arrived in the lands of the Cantii, and they had provisioned themselves with dried biscuits and porridge oats in Londinium. They found a fair amount of wild fruits growing in the forest, and these supplemented their diet sufficiently to make their meals palatable. The trees were beginning to turn in the land, gold, russets and reds taking over the green of their leaves. The days were becoming shorter, and there was a cold bite to the air at night. Each night they would camp as the sun set, and would be asleep shortly after it became dark. Each day they woke with the dawn. At first, neither of them had any idea how much danger they were in, camping near those wild roads at night, but Origen's obsession with secrecy meant that they did not camp right on the side of the road. If they had, they would probably never have survived beyond the first night.

On the fourth evening they discovered the danger. As the sun set they saw a vague trail leading off from the cleared area by the side of the road. They turned off the road, dismounted and walked the horses across the grass that bordered it and entered the woods. The path was sunk down, and had high banks on either side. The trees grew from those banks so thickly that they covered the path completely, giving it the feeling of a tunnel. They continued along the dark path, and before long came to a small clearing. Dappled light filtered down amongst the trees, but it was murky and would be dark before long. Benjamin was making a fire, and Origen removed his fur cloak to reveal his bronzed, heavy boned, vast hairy chest. He was trying to erect the tent when there was a rustling at the edge of the clearing. Both of the horses started and looked up, sniffing the air. Origen immediately grabbed his sword and the short hunting spear that was secured on the larger of their two horses. With luck it might be a wild animal, a boar or a fawn. Origen stood poised with the spear when suddenly several men stepped out onto the edge of the clearing. It was the first time that Origen had seen the savages close up. They were filthy. Long, dank hair was matted down the sides of their faces. They wore wolfskins and bear furs. Most had necklaces hanging round their necks, thin cords from which grey bones hung. Some wore iron rings through their ear lobes and their nostrils. All had thick greasy beards and sunken eyes, and few had any teeth. Their faces were painted with some sort of black substance, probably charcoal. And they were all armed with clubs. Great, wooden clubs. One of them, a small man with a wrinkled face carried a vast broadsword, a weapon that dwarfed him and looked like it would take all his strength just to lift. There were about eight of them, and gawked with open mouthed wonder at the two strangers. Benjamin stood straight, watching out of the corner of his eye as Origen examined the savages. Origen thought quickly. It would be impossible for them both to get to the horses and flee before they were set upon. They could not win in a straight fight. Despite their superior weaponry and his confidence in their fighting skills, there were too many of them. The savages were looking at both Benjamin and Origen closely. There was a wonder in their eyes, a look that suggested that they had never seen anything like Origen and Benjamin before. Origen racked his brain to think what could prompt this. They were dressed as savages, so it could not be their clothes. He could not believe that it was the horses, for he knew that the savages had learned how to tame horses themselves. It was their skin. They were looking particularly intently at Origen's torso. It had to be their dark skin. All of these savages were a pasty white. Benjamin and himself were the dark, swarthy, leathery brown of the middle east. The savages had never seen brown people before, and particularly not brown people dressed like themselves. The look of open mouthed wonder began to give way to fear. Origen realised that he had to act quickly. Without warning he began to howl. He howled and he began a crazed dance. He hopped around and waved his arms frantically. Benjamin looked on in bewilderment, and Origen motioned for him to follow suit. Without knowing why, Benjamin too began to howl and wave his arms. The look of fear and wonder turned to terror on the faces of the onlooking savages. Suddenly, and with remarkable speed the old one with the sword turned and ran. He crashed through the undergrowth, followed by his fellows. The sound of their retreat quickly gave way to silence. Origen stood half naked, looking at Benjamin. Suddenly he began to convulse with laughter.

"We are ghosts, Benjamin. These simpletons think that we are some sort of ghosts, or gods. They have never seen people with skin like ours before. We have our protection in this land, Benjamin. We are untouchable. We are ghosts!"

Once more he roared with laughter. Suddenly it dawned on Benjamin. He, too laughed. Mostly he laughed with relief.

*****

Ever since she arrived in this dark, cold province, Rani had been feeling increasingly excited. Every step that her horse took was a step nearer to Marius and to her that was all that mattered. The road was hard, particularly as her pregnancy was becoming so full. Her belly had swollen considerably, and it gave her some degree of discomfort. She found that she needed to urinate much more regularly than she usually would, and her hunger was often almost uncontrollable. Yet she was happy. The sickness that had dogged her early days in Lucius' house had gone, and she felt radiantly healthy. They had been on the road for two and a half weeks, and she was assured that it would not be many more days before they reached Eburacum. Her heart lifted with every step.

The driving rain had made their progress slow that day, and Rani was finding it increasingly hard with the baby kicking within her tummy. As usual they left the road shortly before sunset, pitched camp and ate a simple meal. Like so often since she had been heavy with child her sleep was disturbed by the call of her bladder. She rose and padded bare foot out of the clearing a short way into the trees. Everyone else in the camp was asleep, but she was always careful not to expose herself when there was a possibility of the messengers seeing her, even in the dead of night. The wind had died but the rain still fell, and it dripped softly in the wood. The cloud cover meant that there was virtually no light to see, but Rani felt her way rather than go to the trouble of lighting a torch.

She was about to squat with her back to a tree when she heard a twig snap behind her, from the direction of the camp. She assumed that it must be one of the messengers, but was not concerned as there was no way that she could be seen in the dark.

She began to undo the belt that bound her tunic, and as she did so a great hand covered her mouth. She tried to bite it, hard, but her teeth could not get a purchase. The hand that held her mouth jerked her head back, leaving her off balance. Hard hands grabbed her wrists and pulled them behind her back, where they were tied together. She tried to scream but the only sound from under the rough hand was a muffled moan.

She could feel hot breath on her neck from behind, but could not see her assailant. Silently she was led further into the woods, shaking with terror. She had been told the grim stories about what barbarians did to outsiders. She had listened with horror as their sickening brutality had been described, and now she was going to find out for herself. She could smell the powerful odour of unwashed bodies and feel the skins that her assailants wore.

She stumbled across the branches and bracken that lined the narrow forest path, but she did not struggle. It would have been pointless, such was the strength of the grip in which she was held. They continued like that for many minutes before the hand was removed from her mouth. She did not scream, because they were too far into the woods for her voice to carry to the camp. Instead she continued walking, biting her lip to prevent herself from weeping. She had been so close. Two days away, the messengers had told her that day. Two days from Marius. Rani was realistic enough to know that a lone woman taken in this land would not survive, and she fought the despair that threatened to overwhelm her. Two days away.

They walked for most of the night. Shortly before dawn they entered a clearing, and she heard horses give a nicker of alarm. They had reached her abductors' camp. With the first light of dawn she saw them, and when she did she shuddered in horror.

33

Lucius' grizzled head hung down to one side. Despite the shady cool of the room, it was covered in beads of sweat. He had been abducted in the Via Flaminian some days previously. Lucius had no idea how many days it was, but it felt like a lifetime. When he had become conscious again after being knocked out on his own doorstep, he found himself in a dimly lit room with beautifully crafted sandstone walls. There were only two furnishings in that room. One was the ominous looking chair in which he was strapped with his wrists behind his back and his legs to each leg of the chair. The second was a bloody, half rotted human carcass lying on the floor. The corpse had been cleaned, and the wounds dressed with some sort of liquid that had stopped it from smelling too strongly. It was ravaged, particularly the face. The eyes had been eaten out by something. He did not know what, then. It was not long before he discovered the answer, and by the time he did he was incapable of coherent thought. Parts of the eye remained, so it was obvious that they had not been cut out. He had felt chilled then. When Hadrian walked in accompanied by Decimus' notorious inquisitor Nihilo, Lucius had vaguely wondered why Decimus was not with them. He had also known that he was a dead man.

He would have killed himself back then. He knew instantly that somehow he had been found out. He would have killed himself but he had been tied to that cursed chair and could not inflict any injury on himself. But he did not have long to wait before the injuries began to be inflicted. Hadrian had begun personally, and he had been crude. His fists had been his weapons of choice, and as he set about his work Nihilo had appeared bored. Lucius lost consciousness fairly soon after Hadrian had begun to vent his anger. But it was not until Nihilo began his work that the real pain set in. The sweat that he could feel collecting across his head now had nothing to do with heat. For the past two days, Nihilo had been slowly drilling holes in his body and inserting maggots. He had started with his legs and had moved on to his feet and his genitals. Lucius thought that it had been the previous day that he had been castrated, but he couldn't be sure. Structured thought was virtually impossible in the midst of the keening pain. But Lucius felt that it would not be long now. Had he been capable of proper thought he would have known it, and he was dimly aware of his spirit lightening at the prospect. The more his physical strength left his body, the more his spirit rejoiced. He did not have long before he would meet the Father. He did not have long before his body would surrender and release him to eternal peace. And his strength was failing. He could no longer lift his head in reaction to the pain. He could sense that even Nihilo was about ready to admit defeat and end it. And as these thoughts whirled around his mind, fragmented in the acute agony that shot through all the parts of his body there were four words that repeated themselves in his head like a mantra. He had shouted, screamed, whispered, imagined, willed, prayed, dreamed, chanted, pleaded and wept those four words constantly ever since he had been brought to this place. "I will not talk. I will not talk".

Four hours later the naked, mutilated body of the most respected patrician of the senate of Rome gave up on life. It was never buried, but instead flung out of a chariot to the side of the road ten miles north of Rome. The mutilation to his face was such that the corpse would never be identified.

34

A group of ten horsemen had ridden into Eburacum, and brought with them an official scroll from the Council for the Administration of the Combined Armies of the Empire of Rome. It was two days ago, and it should have been the cause for a private celebration. But instead Marius fell into a dark morass of hopelessness. The scroll was Marius' official appointment document confirming that he had been elected as Legate to the Ninth Legion in Eburacum. Lucius had fulfilled his promise and the plan was working. But what cast Marius into black despair had been the other news that they brought. They told of the disappearance of the slave girl that they had been accompanying. She had vanished from their camp three nights previously, and they found no trace of her. Marius, like the messengers, concluded the obvious. She had been taken by the savages. There was no hope.

Until the messengers arrived, Marius had been satisfied with his progress. His legion adored him, and he found that he liked their adoration. But more than that, for the first time he had an utter conviction that what he was doing was right. He had seen how Lucius' plan could work. The past few weeks had banished all his doubts that he could succeed in that for which he had been sent.

He had been meticulous in his efforts to ensure that he got to know each of his centurions personally. His tribunes were already converts to the cult of Marius, and they spread the word liberally. There was a buzz about the place then. Within a few weeks, everyone knew that Marius had discovered some kind of momentous secret in his past campaigns, some great piece of knowledge that could teach them much about their overlords in Rome. They were intrigued. Marius tantalised them, he hinted and he inferred, but he was never overt. The result of this was an almost obsessive desire from his men to find out. The other result was credibility. Marius' reluctance to share this information spoke to them of loyalty, of professionalism and of honour. It was a masterly tactic, for when the time came for him to reveal his secret he was assured of their total trust, and of total sympathy for whatever position he might take. But the time was still not right. Marius was patient, and he knew that for his men to take the leap that he required them to take, he must be even more revered than he currently was. He needed another great victory.

But now Marius was again in pieces. He seemed listless, uninvolved, disinterested. He would not leave his chambers. He resented my presence, probably I think because he could see how happy I was. I had Olivia, and the past few weeks had seen the two of us flower as one. We wallowed in the pleasure of each other, and I stayed every night in her quarters. We explored each other's bodies with an obsessive joy, and when we had exhausted them we explored each other's minds. When the news came of Rani's disappearance, my happiness contrasted uncomfortably with Marius' desolation. For two days I was virtually banished from his company. But on the third, a damp, grey day when the drizzle never stopped, his grief was interrupted.

*****

Summer began to leave us over the previous two weeks, and it was replaced by an unsettled, stormy sky. The leaves were turning on the trees that lined the hills around Eburacum. The nights were closing in, shortening the daylight by more and more each day. We had heard much of the northern winters, and we braced ourselves for our first. Wood for the fires was piled high in the barracks and the under floor heating was stoked up for the first time. I had finally been granted admittance to Marius' apartment in the Praetorium, and was talking of nothing and of everything in my attempts to elicit some response when we received word that a messenger had arrived. Marius would not react to the news, so I ordered the messenger to be sent up.

The man carried nothing with him at all. His sword had been removed from him as he entered the Praetorium and there was no sign of any message. As he walked through the door to the private apartment I had the shock of foreboding. I think that Marius did too, for he no longer lounged absently but sat ramrod straight in his chair. The messenger was dressed as a savage, wearing a great wolfskin cloak over a tunic made of hide, held by a belt of gut. But he was clearly not a savage. His skin was of the east. He came from a distant land, a land that we both associated with the cause of our stay in Eburacum. A land we associated with Rani.

The man stopped in front of us and looked a little awkward, saying nothing. There was a flicker of interest in Marius' eyes. He looked straight at him and bid him speak.
The man looked around him and began in a nervous voice.
"My name is Benjamin. I have come from Ituraea with a man who you know, with Origen of Sidon".
I could feel butterflies fluttering about in my stomach. I glanced at Marius. His teeth were gritted and there was a slight colour to his cheek. I think that at that time he dared to hope. But he did not respond. Benjamin was gaining in confidence. He continued brusquely.
"We have with us something that you desire, and you have something that we desire. We propose a trade. Rani of Assyut for the Confession of Nero".
Benjamin issued his proposal with a certainty that belied his earlier nervousness. As soon as I heard it I felt my stomach fall away. I looked across at Marius, and apart from his gritted teeth I could not discern a reaction.
Marius spoke, and when he did his voice was almost gentle. His relief must have been huge. His heart was surely singing with the knowledge that Rani was alive and well. His reaction was a measure of his coolness under the most terrible of pressure, because his reply was the last thing in the world I was expecting to hear.
"And if we refuse?"
"Then Rani and the child within her will die", replied Benjamin.
Marius recoiled visibly, whether from the threat or the revelation about the child I do not know. His fingers had coiled to form fists and his knuckles were white.

"When and where?" His voice was flat.
"Come to the front gates of Isurium tomorrow at sunset. Bring the confession".
"You will bring Rani?" asked Marius through gritted teeth.
"We will".

*****

When she had first seen her abductors, Rani saw what it could mean for Marius, and she had been horrified. But her second instinct was relief. She was with a civilised man. She was with a Christian brother. She was not going to have to undergo the unspeakable atrocities of which she had heard.

Her questions came out in a tumble of words.

"How . . . what are you . . . why . . when . . . . what on earth are you doing here?"

"I have followed you here, Rani". Origen's voice was weary. "I have been to Aegyptus, I have been to Rome and now I am in this godforsaken wilderness, and all because Marius Sextus stole something that does not belong to him. I have come to retrieve that which is rightfully mine".

Rani stuck out her bottom lip. She did not like Origen's attitude.

"It was never yours, Origen. You have a claim, certainly, but no better claim than Marius".

The petulance of her answer revealed that she did not totally believe what she said.

"That manuscript was left in the safe keeping of your family, Rani. They had no right to give it to a Roman who is not even a follower of the Christus!"

Rani's attitude had in turn annoyed Origen.

"We did not know that he was a Roman when we told him where to find it, remember?" Rani was rising to Origen's provocation.

"But when you did know that he was a Roman soldier you still helped him to keep it from us, did you not?"

The thought of this beautiful young christian girl betraying her movement for the love a murdering Roman was almost too much for him.

"I did, and I did so because you cannot be trusted, Origen. You will not do what is right. You will do what your hatred dictates!" Rani was really angry now. She was angry because she recognised that in his way Origen was right.

Origen was disgusted by Rani's behaviour. But he was also aware that her anger might lead her to say things that she would later regret. He knew enough of this girl to know that she would probably rather die than betray the man she loved. But he also knew that she was fiery enough to lose her self discipline in an argument, fiery enough to volunteer information that she might otherwise die to conceal. Origen deliberately riled her.

"And what of the Romans, Rani. Can they be trusted? This man who seduced you, this Roman. He is not acting for the benefit of the brethren. He is acting for the benefit of Rome!" His tone was deliberately scornful.

"You know nothing, Origen. Marius is acting for the good of everyone. He is doing this to save souls and to prevent the injustices that are daily perpetrated against our people. He is an honourable man who is more of a Christian than many who would call themselves such. He is a good man!"

"If he was a good man he would give the manuscript to me!" Origen was fairly sure from her earlier answers that she had all but confirmed that Marius still had the manuscript. But he wanted to be sure. Her answer confirmed it for him.

"He would not. He will never give it to you. He will not allow you to use it to try to inflict damage on the empire. He knows you, Origen".

So, it was becoming clear. Marius still had the manuscript. Marius and Rani had a plan for its use, and it must surely involve Lucius. They were actively planning something, but Origen could not fathom why it involved Eburacum. He could not think of a subtle way to put the question.

"Why Eburacum?" he asked.

Rani calmed down. By changing the tack of the conversation so suddenly, by asking such a level question after such an emotional exchange she had the horrible feeling that Origen had been manipulating her, playing her for a fool. She had lost her temper. She had fallen right into his trap, and had said more than she would ever have done under straight questioning. Immediately she clammed up. She folded her arms and shut her mouth. Origen could not resist one more vengeful dig at her.

"You did it for love, Rani. You were seduced by a Roman who was cynical in his exploitation of your desperation. Without you he could never have succeeded, so he pretended that he loved you to get you on side. You have been shown up, Rani. You have been taken for a fool. Wait until you get to Eburacum. Do you think that he will be pleased to see you? Of course he won't. He is the legate of a Roman Legion. He will have tens of female slaves to attend to his every sordid desire. Go home, Rani. Go home and forget that you ever met him".

Rani just stood there, alone in the darkness, staring back at Origen defiant and silent. Origen moved forward and tied her wrists and ankles together. He then carried her into a tent and made sure that she was well covered with blankets. Then he went to sleep.

The following day, the three of them moved deeper into the woods. They were fairly sure that the Romans would not look for her. If they did, it would be for no more than a day. They had an imperial message to deliver to Eburacum, and they could not afford to spend time searching for a slave who was probably lying dead somewhere in the huge forests that surrounded the wild road. Rani refused to open her mouth all day, and both of them recognised that she was not the kind of person who would talk if she had chosen not to. Neither of them had the stomach for torture, and particularly not of a woman so self evidently with child.

Origen did not really believe what he had said about Marius. He had seen the look on the Roman's face back in Aegyptus, and it was not the look of a cynical man exploiting a naïve young girl. It was the look of man completely smitten, the look of a man who was in love. Marius would surrender it. If he loved her like Origen suspected he did, then he would surrender. If he didn't, then Origen would probably die. But without any prospect of obtaining the manuscript Origen could not think of any particular reason to live. As he coldly considered his own death, he did not even think of Benjamin or the family who had already lost their other son in the pursuit of the manuscript. He was not sufficiently concerned to even give it a thought.

*****

The following day Marius and I left Eburacum on horseback alone. We were dressed in the clothes of the savages with great furs covering our tunics, and the horses were equipped only with coarse woollen blankets rather than leather saddles. It was the only way for small groups to travel with relative safety in those lands. We rode hard to Isurium and got there an hour before sunset. The town was still abandoned. The heads of the savages strapped to the walls around the gate were now little more than skulls with bits of weathered, dried skin hanging off them. It was a dark place. When we got there we found Benjamin waiting for us at the gates.
"Have you brought the confession" he called to us as we approached.
"I want to see Rani" Marius shouted back.
Benjamin looked a little uncertain, but before he had time to respond the great mass of Origen stepped out from behind the gates. His huge forearm was around Rani's neck. She was more beautiful than I remembered her, but more striking than that was her new shape. She was heavy with child. Her belly was massively expanded, protruding heavily from beneath her filthy robes. Immediately he saw her, Marius shouted to Origen.
"You will not get the confession until I have had a chance to speak to her. Alone. You can take my horse and my weapons and even Tolus if you want, but I must be allowed to talk to her".
His tone was such that Origen did not argue. Marius did not even wait for a response, but dismounted and withdrew his sword. Holding it by the blade he walked slowly forward. Twenty paces from the gates he thrust it deep into the turf and tied his horse to the hilt. He withdrew his dagger, threw it into the ground and walked forwards. Behind him I also dismounted and copied his actions, disarming myself and tethering the horse to the hilt of my sword. Origen was careful. He ordered Benjamin to gather the two horses and the weapons. Once

Benjamin had led them behind him and retrieved Marius' sword, he spoke.

"If you try to escape, I will catch you. I have horses and you do not. If you do, Benjamin and I will kill Rani first. Even if we do not survive Rani will die, of that I can assure you."

I believed him. We would not try anything. I stood there watching Marius walk forward slowly, deliberately. As he approached, Origen withdrew his forearm from Rani's neck and she walked forward. They fell into each other's arms. They stood like that for a long time, holding each other tight. Then they withdrew into the town. We watched as they stepped over the bones that littered the main street.

It was strange standing there in the silence outside the abandoned town, eyeing Benjamin and Origen. After a few minutes, I decided to speak. I did so not because I wanted to talk to them but because I thought that I might distract Origen and enable Marius to spend more time with Rani. I asked them how they came to be here and how they had discovered where we were. They told me freely. I think that they were relieved by the opportunity to tell their story, to distract themselves from the tension of the moment. They did so without relish, without joy and without boastfulness. It was not something that they were proud of. They had derived no pleasure from their pursuit of the manuscript. They did it with the grim determination of people who know that they have no alternative. And I got no sense of them believing that they were on the brink of success. They had been misled and disappointed on so many occasions that to them this was just another episode in a long and miserable tale. They were in a wild land further from their home than any other province in the empire and they were not enjoying it. I don't think that either of them were bad men. Both had a love of righteousness and justice. Neither could match Marius for his obsession with truth, but they were not bad men. God forgive me, for as I listened to their story I liked them. I could see why they felt that we had stolen the confession, but they did not know our motives then, and I was not going to tell them.

It was a long time before Rani and Marius re-emerged. When they did so, it was clear that both had been crying. Marius' eyes were rimmed red, and he made no effort to hide it. Reluctantly he returned Rani to Origen. He had no choice for had he tried anything at least one of us would have died, and we believed Origen that it would have been Rani. Origen returned our horses to us and we retrieved our weapons. Marius mounted his horse and I followed suit, perplexed. Until he spoke I had no idea what Marius' was planning to do.

"I do not have the confession with me. I came here today to be sure that you could be trusted. I thought that it might be an ambush. But now I know that you are sincere in your offer. I will return tomorrow at the same time, and when I do I will bring the confession".

Without waiting for a response, Marius turned his horse and rode off.

*****

He was grim faced and silent as we rode away and I knew him well enough to leave him. We rode hard, and it was over an hour before he broke the silence. The horses were breathing heavily, and Marius allowed them to slow to a walk. When they did the first thing that he did was curse, extensively. When he had finished, he looked towards me.

"She won't let me hand over the confession, Tolus. I would willingly give it to those bastards in exchange for her life. But she won't let me. She says her life is irrelevant in comparison to our sacred mission. She believes that it must be valued more highly than both her own life and our love for one another".

He looked to the sky, his face screwed up in frustration. I thought that he might scream. Gradually his face relaxed and he continued.

"I would abandon our mission to be with her, but she won't hear of it. She said that if I give Origen the confession in exchange for her life, she will never speak to me again. She even threatened to kill herself if I tried. And I believe her".

I was sure that there must be a way out of this.

"Why don't we call their bluff? Just tell them that we are not going to give them the confession and they can do what they like with Rani? I spoke to them, Marius. They are good people. They are men of conviction, not men of spite. I do not believe that they would kill her. They do not have it in them."

I thought myself a good judge of people, and it seemed reasonable from what I had just learned from them. I would never have said it had I known what I know now. Marius flared.

"You fool! You have no idea about these people. Rani does. She knows that they will kill her. She knows of Origen, of his hatred and of his past. He hates Roman's more than we hate these savages. I am telling you, Tolus, they would not hesitate. They are ruthless, and they have come here from the other end of the empire. They will get what they have come for or they will die".

I was stung by Marius' vitriol. But I was not willing to give up.

"Why don't we hand over the confession as they have asked, retrieve Rani and follow them. We can ambush them and retrieve the confession. How difficult can it be? There are only two of them."

Marius was scathing once more.

"Don't you think we have thought of that? There are two problems with it. Origen is good. He knows that if we were to hand over the confession we would try something like that. He would know and he would take precautions. Rani forced me to think like Origen will. When I did, I realised that it would not be too difficult. These woods are easy to lose yourself in. Yes, they are full of savages, but they are superstitious and stupid. Rani told me that all the savages they have met in the woods have fled, petrified. Even bands of warriors have run from them. Origen has found a way that he can disappear in this land. He uses his dark skin to make them think he is some kind of phantom. We cannot follow him into the woods. He would get away.

The second problem is Rani. She says that to do that would be to act in bad faith. She says that it would be dishonest, and she will not have it".

I couldn't help myself. Before I realised what I was doing, I scoffed.

Marius saw, and was sympathetic. "I know, Tolus, it's ridiculous. These people have abducted her and are bargaining with her life. They have used the existence of my unborn child as a bargaining chip. Yet she maintains that to do a deal with them and then hunt them down would be contrary to her beliefs, and she will not let it happen. We had a terrible argument about it but she would not be moved".

There was only one more thing that I could think of, but I was afraid to suggest it because in many ways it was the most dangerous of all.

35

Origen was furious. He manhandled Rani roughly across the fields that surrounded Isurium, fields that were already looking tatty from the neglect of the past couple of months. The late summer had been damp, and the wilderness was beginning to spread into the previously well-tended fields.

Their progress to Isurium from where they had abducted Rani had been mostly uneventful. On two occasions they had been accosted by savages in the woods, and on both Origen and Benjamin revealed their torsos and put on the ridiculous performance of being some sort of pagan ghosts. However it was interpreted it was effective. Origen had found the skull of a cow, a great heavy thing with two large horns and carried it with him. When the savages appeared he grabbed the skull and used it as a prop. The effect had been quite funny and both times the savages fled in terror. Fighting men had fled at the sight of two dark brown lunatics dancing in the woods. Despite the danger and the circumstances there had been empathy between the two Christians and their captive. Rani had been expecting to detest Origen and Benjamin. She had been taken against her will and was being bartered as they exploited a good man's love for her. But she could not dislike them. She deliberately tried to form a relationship with them, reasoning that by doing so she would be making it more difficult for them to harm her. She found Benjamin to be sweet, brave and rather stupid. Origen bullied him mercilessly, and she found his weary acceptance endearing. And she could not hate Origen either, despite his exploitative behaviour towards Benjamin,. He was so unhappy. Never before had she seen such contradiction in a person. He was the embodiment of the conflict within all of the brethren and it made him a walking paradox. On one hand he was all that is heroic and righteous about the movement, uncompromising and absolute in his beliefs. Yet he allowed bitterness to conquer his judgement, and had given in to the darkness of his hatred. Despite her predicament Rani could not help but sympathise with him for the experiences that had led to his torment.

Mostly the road had been deserted. No one travelled along it unless they had to, and then only when armed to their teeth. Twice they had seen groups approaching, and both times Origen led them into the woods until they passed. One had been a fairly large force of Roman soldiers, the other a tough looking group of traders. On several more occasions they caught a glimpse of people on the road who disappeared into the woods as soon as they saw them approach. Sometimes they felt eyes watching them from the forest, and Rani could not work out if it was her imagination or if they were really there.

*****

Rani's arm was badly bruised by the time they reached their camp. It was completely dark when they entered the woods. The camp was set in a clearing, not far into the forest beyond the cleared land of the disused farms around the town. It consisted, as it always did, of their tent and their two horses tethered to a tree. Leaves littered the ground as the first of the trees shed their summer glory. Entering the clearing by the light of a torch that Benjamin had lit in the fields, Rani felt a searing pain in her abdomen. She let out a cry of alarm, and Origen and Benjamin gave a start. Benjamin ran to her, supporting her as she staggered. Beneath her tunic, her waters had broken. Benjamin did not know what to do, for he had never been present at the birth of a child. But Origen had helped to deliver his own. He wasted no time as he laid his own cloak down on the ground and helped Rani on to it. For a few minutes nothing happened. Rani tried to get up, but Origen immediately moved over to her side and pushed her back down.
"Your baby is coming" he said softly. "You must lie here until it has come".
He left her, and went to the horses to retrieve their spare tunics, the Roman tunics that they hadn't worn since Londinium. He sent Benjamin off to the stream to wash them whilst he moved over to Rani and took hold of her hand.

It was six agonising, noisy hours later that Origen delivered the daughter of Rani and Marius. She was covered in blood but had a healthy scream. He cut her cord with his dagger before wiping her down with the damp tunic and wrapping her in an old piece of linen. Then he handed her to Rani and told her to feed the wrinkled red face of the new born. Rani was exhausted, but she put her baby to her breast, and as she did so she blessed Origen for his experience and his gentleness. In those hours she had seen what tenderness he was capable of.

None of them had much sleep that night. It was not until the early hours that the baby was born, and both mother and daughter kept the two Christians awake for most of the rest of the night. After sunrise, Origen and Benjamin tried to sleep through the morning.

*****

Tobias and Silus were stationed either side of the main gates, high up on the wooden platform at the top of the inside of the town walls. They were hidden from view by the balustrade built onto the edge of the platform to prevent hapless soldiers from falling to the open space below. Their role would be to close the gates if it became necessary to block Origen and Benjamin's escape. Inside the gates was a small forum twenty paces across before the main street began. The houses at the end of the street nearest the gates were mainly just burned out shells. Greto was to hide in the first house on the left, and Numba in the house opposite. Artorius was hidden outside the town, his job to cut off any attempted escape if the Christians were to get outside the walls. Just inside the gates, Marius and Tolus would wait in the open space, with the theatre to one side and the baths to the other.

Once everyone was in position they sat down and tried to pass the time by sleeping. Marius could not relax and became increasingly agitated as the day progressed. As the sun sank towards the forests on the horizon he was extremely edgy. I was too. I did not like that ghostly, abandoned town. The heads strapped to the wall seemed like a warning, and the bones in the streets did not auger well. But I kept my misgivings to myself.

By mid afternoon, Marius and I moved outside the town walls and sat down by our horses to wait. An hour before sunset Origen, Benjamin and Rani approached from the west. They came slowly, their horses plodding. Benjamin and Rani shared a horse, and Rani appeared to be carrying something. As they got closer we saw what she held in her arms. Marius began to move forward but I caught his elbow and he turned round. His eyes were blazing, but I gave a slight shake of my head, for our plan relied on getting them inside the walls. Marius got the message, and we both returned through the gates into the town. We stood on the open space inside the gates and it was not long before the two horses of the Christians entered.

Marius immediately walked up to Rani and took hold of her hand. He looked into her eyes with wonder, and then down at the baby.
"A daughter, Marius" said Rani.
He looked so happy and proud, a man united with his family for the first time. It was as if he had completely forgotten the circumstances under which they met. Origen sympathetically interrupted the familial scene.
"You will forgive me for intruding, but we have come for the confession. You have it?"
Marius took several steps back to ensure that he was out of grabbing range of both of the Christians. He then put his hand inside his tunic and brought out a large leather wallet. From the wallet he pulled out the sixty year old confession of Emperor Nero. Origen's expression was as intense as I have ever seen anyone. I had not understood how much this piece of papyrus meant to him until I saw his face then. I suppose that in many ways Marius was holding open the doorway to his life's work.
Rani took the opportunity to slide off her horse. For just a few seconds, Origen neglected to control the situation. She was standing by the side of the horse, holding her baby and looking like she might just walk over to Marius. But Origen quickly regained control. He

reached forward and grabbed her by the hair. Just ten paces separated us from them. Origen broke the silence.

"You will walk to me and hand over the confession. Once I have it in my hands I will release Rani. Do you understand?"

Marius did not reply. He simply replaced the confession in its wallet and handed it to me. He gestured with his head that I should approach Origen. My heart was beating so loud that I feared that everyone would hear it. Our plan was simple. We would conduct the handover, and the minute that Rani was safe the doors to the town would close. Then we would go after Origen and Benjamin.

Marius had been completely insistent that Rani was not to be endangered. Her safety was to be our only priority until we had her. Only then would we turn our attentions to her abductors and the confession. So I walked forward with the clear intention of handing the confession to Origen. Those ten paces felt like further, and time seemed to be suspended as I walked. Even now I can see myself there, walking across that open space towards Origen. As I reached him I watched my arm rise and stretch out toward the great hulking figure sitting on his horse, the wallet outstretched. Origen's hand was outstretched to receive it, and as he gripped the wallet I let go. He pulled the wallet to him but did not release the hair of Rani. He held the wallet in his teeth to free his remaining hand. It delved into the wallet and pulled out the confession. He glanced down at it, his eyes intoxicated by the realisation of his quest. It was the manuscript of Nero. It was obvious at a glance. The seals and the signatures, the stamps and the artistry were all unmistakably imperial. Slowly and carefully he replaced it in its wallet and looked up. His eyes were moist as he loosened his grip on Rani's hair and she began to walk away.

What happened next happened so quickly that I was left completely bewildered. I never thought that bewilderment would cost me my life, but there it very nearly did. I don't know why and I don't know how, but from where Tobias sat high up on the platform in the walls a wooden strut fell. I watched it fall through the air behind Origen, and there was an agonising second when I knew that it was going to make a loud sound when it hit the ground. There had been complete silence whilst the handover was conducted. But suddenly the silence was broken by a sharp rap as the strut clattered into the stone flagging below. Origen grabbed forward for Rani's hair once more and jerked her back. As he did so he spun round. I wasn't sure if he would catch the glimpse of Tobias' foot as it withdrew from the hole in the balustrade but he did. He saw the foot, but more importantly he saw what it represented. He saw the ambush that was awaiting him, and he did not hesitate. Before I could react he moved his left shoulder backwards, stretched out his arm to the rear of his horse and grabbed the hilt of his sword. In one motion he drew the sword and brought it down in a great arc over his horses back and down onto Rani's skull. He did not strike her straight on but at an angle. His sword sliced through her head and lodged six inches in. Brains and blood spattered out and landed on Origen, his horse, Rani's baby and me. It was the resulting bewilderment that nearly killed me, for Origen pulled back on his sword and the corpse of Rani collapsed. The baby was still in her arms and began to scream. Origen swiped his great sword backwards at me with incredible speed, and I ducked as I saw the blade coming for my face. I was only just in time. Benjamin's horse was panicking and he was struggling to bring it under control. The gates to the town were closing and Greto and Numba were running out from their hiding places. Origen wheeled his horse round and charged for the gates. He was quick but he was not quick enough. He could not get to them before they shut. Marius was kneeling by Rani's body, looking down with total incomprehension, almost a quizzical look. He was moving slowly, a sense of unreality about his movements. When the gates closed Origen wheeled his horse around and charged at me. By now I had recovered some degree of composure, and God forgive me but I even began to feel the thrill of battle. Rani was lying dead just a few metres away and I was feeling exultant. When Origen's horse was close I jumped to the side and as I did so I thrust my spear as hard as I could between its two front legs. I was lucky, for the horse faltered and collapsed onto its knees. Origen rolled off and began to advance towards me. He was an intimidating sight, his eyes blazing with fury and his face contorted with hatred. I stood my ground. I was vaguely aware of Benjamin. He was fighting with Numba hand-to-hand, the two men going at each other in a frenzy.

As I braced myself for Origen's onslaught he stopped five paces in front of me. He was looking at something over my shoulder. I was not going to turn to look. It was an old trick. But I felt a hand on my shoulder and looked round to see Marius. His eyes were flat and blank, his face expressionless. With a barely perceptible flicker of his eyes he motioned for me to stand back. I did not want to. I wanted to kill this great monster. I had the craving of battle running through my veins and I wanted to satiate it. I wanted the man's head. But I stood back. I honestly think that if I hadn't Marius' would have killed me then.

When I did so I was able to look around at Benjamin. Numba lay on the ground in a large puddle of blood. He had been sliced in the neck and the life was draining out of him. Greto was fighting him now, tears running down his cheeks.

Origen advanced towards Marius and brought down his great sword hard. It was a two handed sword, but Origen only needed one, such were the size of his fists and the strength in his arms and shoulders. Marius stepped aside, parrying the blow with his short stabbing sword. Our weapons were not really designed for one on one combat in open spaces. They were designed for the tight press of battle, for working in confined areas. Nevertheless, Marius was good. They exchanged blows, mostly Origen raining down mighty swings onto Marius' sword. Marius was retreating in the face of the onslaught, trying to contain Origen's attack. He knew that it could not go on forever. No man can generate blows of that vigour for long. I was so intent watching the fight that I hardly noticed as I was joined first by Tobias and then Silus. Silus had picked up the baby, and it was nestling quietly against his shoulder.

Marius' tactics were clear. He was waiting for Origen to exhaust himself, but it was a dangerous gamble. Origen was good, and on several occasions Marius had to be incredibly quick to withstand the onslaught. There are not many men alive who could have done so. I for one doubted that I could have. But Marius continued to retreat until he had his back to the first burned out house at the top of the main street. Origen was breathing heavily, and despite the cold air was sweating profusely. He had nicked Marius' shoulder and the leather there was torn. Blood slowly seeped through but Marius appeared not to notice. He had two or three opportunities to lunge when Origen had over extended himself, but he didn't. It was almost as if he was deliberately stringing the fight out. Suddenly, after Origen had given one more lateral swipe with his sword Marius sprang forward. It took us spectators by surprise, and we were twenty paces away. Origen was equally surprised. Instead of aiming for the large and obvious target of Origen's torso, Marius instead gave a flick of his wrist and sent his blade skimming through the air and crashing into Origen's sword hand. The blow pierced the skin and shattered the small, fragile bones on the top of the hand. Origen dropped his sword. He had no choice, his hand was destroyed. Instead he stood up to his full height and he looked at Marius. He must have known since the minute he buried his sword in Rani that he was going to die that day. But as he stood up and faced Marius he was not afraid. There was a defiant look in his eye. We were all expecting Marius to finish him quickly. The natural thing to do would be to thrust his sword deep into the chest of his victim. But he didn't. Instead he toyed with that brave man. Origen did not move or flinch as Marius set about him with his sharp blade. He hacked down at his arm, across his chest and then at his legs. Origen fell to the ground, and the minute his head hit the cobble Marius sank his sword with all of his might into the centre of Origen's face. I have never seen a blow of such hatred and fury. The sword completely destroyed his nose and eye sockets. Blood gushed up and quickly receded. When Marius withdrew his sword and looked up it was as if he was waking from a dream. We watched with fascinated horror as he turned away from the enormous carcass lying on the ground and walked up to Tobias. Before any of us knew what was happening his sword was deep in Tobias' chest. Tobias had a look of shock on his face as he fell to the ground. He was dead before his body hit the floor.

I turned to see Greto on his knees hacking at Benjamin's corpse. He was covered in the blood of the dead Christian. It ran in rivulets down his face and his forearms, yet still he chopped at the pulp that was left of Numba's killer. Quickly I moved to him, and put a hand on his shoulder. He turned to me, an expression of madness on his face. His sword fell to the ground and he stretched his hand out towards where Numba lay. I had to manhandle him away.

Without a word, Marius walked over to Rani's corpse. The abandoned town was completely silent as he fell to his knees and buried his head on her soft, white neck. Her lifeless eyes stared straight up to the heavens, unseeing. Marius rocked silently, the sinews of his neck straining, his mouth wide open and his eyes tight shut in a silent scream. Ravens circled overhead as Marius' knuckles whitened under the intensity of his grip on Rani's cloak.

I led Greto towards Silus and took the baby from him. As I took the child she began to whimper but I ignored the noise. Quietly I ordered Silus to take Greto and find Artorius, and then bury the dead outside the town walls. I helped them to remove the corpses and left them to dig the graves.

In the forum, Marius still rocked on his knees as he looked down at Rani's butchered head. I closed the gates to leave Marius to his desolation.

*****

Night had closed in by the time Marius silently walked through those gates. I had retrieved the wallet with the confession from the saddlebag on Origen's dying horse, but he did not even notice it as he mounted and rode off. Holding the baby in one arm, I gestured for the men to follow. We kept our distance. Without a backwards glance Marius guided his horse down the road that led to Eburacum.

No one said a word on that journey. Marius wept silently. I could tell because I could see the tears glistening on his cheeks in the moonlight. He made no effort to brush them away, letting them stream down his face as he stared straight ahead.

*****

The following days were terrible. Greto was heartbroken and silent. He had loved Numba as though he was his own son, and he retreated into his shell.
Silus and Artorius, too, were sullen. I think that it was the cold way that Marius had killed Tobias without any warning that disgusted them. I shared their disquiet.

We had arrived back in Eburacum before dawn. Fortunately the guards were awake and had opened the city gates as soon as they identified us. Wordlessly Marius stalked up to his chambers with the now screaming baby. I was planning to stay there, to make sure that Marius was all right. But as he got to his door he turned to me. His eyes were completely blank, and he spoke in a voice devoid of life.
"The child will die without food. Find a woman who still has milk in her breast". With that he shut the door in my face.

It took most of the following morning to find a woman who was willing to nurse Marius' daughter. At first she was reluctant, but she relented when I told her that the baby's mother had been cut down by a savage. I hurried the baby to her, for it was a day since she had fed and she was screaming almost incessantly. When I left, I paid the woman handsomely and promised that someone would visit regularly to check on the baby's progress. Olivia held my eye when I asked her to look in on the baby every day. She would have preferred to nurse the child herself, but she had no milk in her breast.

When I returned to the praetorium I was met by Riccus the tribune. He had a concerned look on his face.

"There is an imperial messenger who says that he has urgent orders for the legate. But the legate will not see him. The messenger arrived yesterday morning and has been waiting for him to return."

I did not like my chances of persuading Marius to see him, so instead I asked Riccus to bring the messenger to me. When he came we walked together to Marius' apartments. The doorman tried to turn us away. He was afraid, and said that he had orders that no one was to be admitted. I had to reassure him that no harm would come to him before I led the messenger through the door and into the large reception room of the praetorium.

Marius was standing by the window. As we entered he turned and I caught a glimpse of the stricken look on his face before he tried to compose himself.

I introduced the messenger. "This man brings orders. We must hear them" I said.

"I said that I was not to be disturbed" replied Marius in a weary monotone.

An awkward silence followed. I turned to the messenger and requested that he leave the message on the low table and leave us. He did so. As soon as he had left the room I walked over to the scroll and broke the seal. I read it aloud and as I did I felt relief. Relief that we would see action, that we would have an opportunity to distract Marius.

"I AM HADRIAN, EMPEROR OF ROME AND I GREET MY LEGATE MARIUS SEXTUS OF THE IXTH LEGION (EBURACUM). I AM DISPLEASED THAT THE INSURGENT GWDLOYCH LIVES. I ORDER HIM TO SEND THE HEAD OF THE INSURGENT TO ME FORTHWITH. I AM HADRIAN, EMPEROR OF ROME".

The message contained all of the necessary seals and verification to make it a binding order. As I finished I looked up at Marius. His eyes had narrowed, and some sort of life had returned to them. He sat for some minutes before he stood up. When he did so it was with a new staccato energy.

"So be it", he said. "Gwdloych will be butchered and his tribe will be silenced forever".

There was a brutality in his tone, a bloodlust that was uncharacteristic and ugly. Suddenly he was a tense bundle of energy. He ordered me to summon all of his tribunes and named five centurions that he wanted with him immediately. But he was not himself and I did not like it.

Marius was going to try to exorcise his grief through death, and I obeyed him.

*****

Within half an hour there was a war council. Eleven officials were present as well as myself. Marius wasted no time. His first words were to thank everyone for coming. He was still playing the part of the great leader. Then he read the Emperor's order. Everyone in the room was greatly impressed that it had come directly from the emperor, and offended at the suggestion that Hadrian was displeased with Marius. They took it as a personal affront, so when Marius told them what he required of them they rushed to obey his orders. Scouts were sent out to locate Gwdloych. The entire legion less one century was to be ready to move out three hours after dawn the following day. The one century he named, a fine group of men, were to stay behind to garrison the town. One hundred men were not enough to guard it properly, but Marius knew that there would not be an attack. There would not be an attack because in a few days there would be no one left in the lands around Eburacum capable of mounting one.

*****

At dawn the following morning there was a frost on the ground, but soon afterwards the clouds rolled in and it began to drizzle lightly. But the weather did not dampen the mood that day. The legion formed up in marching order outside the town walls and it was a spectacular sight. The vanguard was over two miles up the road as the rest of the legion marched out of the town gates behind them to take up their positions in the column. Like the previous campaign, we travelled light with the most meagre of baggage trains. The mood among the legion contrasted sharply with the lethargy that had set in amongst my men. They were buoyant, for they had absolute faith in Marius as a general and were looking forward to another great victory. They were beautifully equipped, as they had begun to take pride in their uniforms once more. Despite the grey day all the buckles, weapons and standards glistened. The column that stretched along the road towards the thick forests of the north was twice as large as that which had marched on Gwdloych previously. With the beautifully tended farmland on either side, we could not help but feel proud to be Roman.

The eagle was raised, and we marched north to win a famous victory. But Marius marched to vent his grief and feed his hatred. He marched to immerse himself in blood.

36

The Via Wattlus had taken them through Verulamium, Durocobrivae, Magiovintum, Venonae, Mancunium and Coccium, and they had picked up men from each of those garrisons. By the time that they arrived in Bremetennacum the XXth was augmented to over seven and a half thousand men.

The messengers had done their work. The IInd (Augusta) arrived from Isca Silurim a week after XXth, a week used to send messengers to Gwdloych and conduct intensive training exercises with the XXth. Decimus was pleased.

Each day a few hundred men drifted in from garrisons as far afield as Camulodunum and Lindum. They were immediately assigned to a cohort and ordered to join the training. There was the purposeful air of preparation for a major campaign, and morale was good. This was what they liked in the ranks – the promise of glory.

As soon as the IInd arrived, on a dry, overcast day Decimus ordered a full parade in the fields surrounding Bremetennacum. Decimus stood on the strong walls of the pathetic little garrison town and looked out at the farmland beyond. Except that the farmland could not be seen. He felt the surge of power that only a general of a great army feels when he holds the lives of thousands of soldiers in his hands. He stood on the walls with the legates of his two legions. He had divided the soldiers from the town garrisons between them, augmenting their strength beyond those of normal legions. The legates were in awe of him, and this was how he liked it. Their legions paraded by. Their men marched rigidly in rank, with standard bearers carrying gleaming banners high, horsemen riding the flanks and centurions marching at the head of their centuries. There were well over twelve thousand men, and they were magnificent.

*****

They marched from Bremetennacum for over a week, through rolling forested hills that seemed like they might go on forever. Progress had been easy on the road but after three days they veered to the north, away from the road and into the beautiful moorland west of Isurium. They walked across the soggy ground, through the mud and the drizzle. On the eighth afternoon the scouts reported that they were no more than half a day's march from Gwdloych.

Decimus ordered the legions to make camp and left with his senior tribunes, including Bonnicus, the legate of the XXth. He also took two hundred of his three hundred horsemen. He wanted a show of force, and he wanted the security. With horses they would be able to escape at the first sign of trouble. Decimus did not trust Gwdloych.

He was welcomed warmly. Gwdloych had moved his camp to a stretch of open moorland on the edge of a forest. He could disappear into that forest at a moment's notice if necessary. The stores were full after the summer harvest, and for the time being Gwdloych had plenty of food. But the encampment was a miserable affair. Great shelters had been erected to enable the fighting men to sleep out of the rain, but there was no other protection from the elements. Decimus could not help but feel a shiver of distaste and fear as he entered the camp.

Gwdloych himself strode out of the grim camp to meet him. He must have had over two thousand fighting men there, and almost as many women and children. His men were all heavily bearded and pierced, great furs and skins covering them, and great weapons at their belts. Many were tattooed on their cheeks. They slowly advanced to inspect the horsemen that Decimus had brought with him. They were intrigued by their weapons and uniforms, and by their bridles and saddles. They themselves had no such equipment for horses. The prowling advance of these inquisitive savages unsettled the men, but it unsettled the horses more. They began to stamp their feet and snort, wide-eyed. Decimus knew that the savages must keep their distance or else some of the horses might panic and bolt.

As Gwdloych strode out he shouted something loudly in his unintelligible language, all clicks and grunts. Decimus looked back dumbly wondering what he was supposed to do, when he heard a high-pitched voice break the awkward silence, speaking perfect Latin. "King Gwdloych of the Brigantes welcomes the Roman king and thanks him for his gift of gold" it said.

Decimus scanned the crowd for the woman who spoke Latin. When he spotted her he realised why he had not seen her sooner. She walked directly behind Gwdloych, taking cover behind his back. She was a barbarian, filthy and, no doubt, stinking. Lank hair hung down over her cheeks, and the ragged skins she wore looked like they had been rolled in dung.

Decimus was curious, so rather than answer Gwdloych formally he spoke to the woman.

"How is it that a barbarian speaks the tongue of the Romans?" he asked.

"I am no barbarian, Decimus Marcellus. I am a citizen, from Isurium"

Decimus suppressed his anger at her, anger at her failure to keep her standards, at her evident willingness to stoop to the level of these savages. When he spoke his voice was measured and warm, and he addressed his words to Gwdloych, who was already beginning to look impatient with proceedings.

"Decimus Marcellus thanks the King of the Brigantes for his kind welcome and requests the honour of a conference".

The Roman woman spoke to Gwdloych in low tones. He barked something to her and turned around. Decimus reddened at this insult, but the words of the translator pacified him.

"Gwdloych agrees and invites you to dine with him. Do not interpret his manner as insulting. Their manners are different from ours".

Decimus curled his nose in contempt.

"Ask the king to order his men to keep their distance from my horsemen. The horses may panic, and it will frighten both my men and his. It will be peaceful that way".

The woman nodded and spoke rapidly to Gwdloych. He barked an order towards his men and they fell back instantly.

Dinner was an extraordinary affair. It was raining, so the only place that it could be eaten was under the low shelters that the barbarian army used for sleeping. Gwdloych sat in the centre with Decimus on one side and his interpreter on the other. Surrounding them were Decimus' senior officials and Gwdloych's biggest and most frightening warriors. The contrast was striking. Whilst Decimus' entourage had impeccable manners and impeccably clean tunics, packed separately from their marching gear, Gwdloych's men were, without exception, filthy. Whilst Decimus' men were chosen for the quality of their birth and their brains, Gwdloych's had obviously been chosen for their size. The barbarian Roman was the only interpreter, and as a result conversation was impossible for all but Gwdloych and Decimus. But the barbarians had been ordered to be hospitable and to behave towards their guests. This did not stop them from piling the roasted meat and the corn porridge into their mouths as if they might otherwise starve. The Roman soldiers ate more slowly, but they enjoyed the food. They enjoyed the drink more, and as the two groups got more and more drunk they became friendly, patting each other on the back. The barbarians elicited strange grunting noises in their direction.

The evening deteriorated as the men became increasingly drunk. By the time that the feast was over several fights had broken out between the Roman soldiers and their barbarian hosts. Several Romans and barbarians died. Things looked like they might get out of control, so Decimus stood up and ordered his men back to their horses. He left quickly, confident that Gwdloych understood what was required of him. To ensure that there could be no misunderstandings, Decimus left two of his tribunes behind, to guide Gwdloych to do as he did as he had promised.

Decimus rejoined his army, and early the following morning they began to move deeper into the highlands that lay to the north of the moor.

37

The hills were shrouded in cloud, the mist often descending so low that it brushed the tops of the trees in the thick forests. After two days the forests gave way. We marched into a majestic, uninhabitable land. The hills were so vast, the valleys so deep and the passes so high that they dwarfed even our great body of men. The land was not fertile enough to sustain crops or even trees, and the few tribesmen that did live in those wild hills scratched a pitiful existence grazing their livestock on the coarse grasses. We saw virtually no one on that march, and little evidence of human habitation. The hovels that we did pass had been abandoned recently, no doubt because of our approach. Marius ordered that all animals were to be captured or killed. The men were to eat as well as possible, and he had no scruples about taking from the land. All attempts to appease the locals had been abandoned.

Many of our scouts did not return. It was an ominous sign, but Marius seemed oblivious. They had been travelling in groups of ten, and of the six groups sent out only two returned. The two groups who did return had discovered where Gwdloych's forces were gathered. To our surprise, they reported that he had a sizeable army with him. We had imagined that the tribe would have dispersed to their pitiful homes for the winter. When Marius heard that they had not he gave a grunt of satisfaction, for to him it was good news. It meant that our victory would be all the more crushing.

After the first day we had left the road and negotiated our way through the hills using the long valleys. We had traversed two high passes already. The ground was soggy under foot, and by the time that a few hundred men had passed over it the grass was worn away leaving a quagmire for the rest of the legion to trudge through. Not one man had dry feet and no one was warm enough. We donned our animal skins and wore them constantly to keep out the biting cold. On the afternoon of the third day the snow began to fall, and when it did it was almost a relief. The cutting wind lessened, and the peaceful silence of the beautiful white flakes drifting down on to us cast a dreamy pall over the whole legion. Our feet were cold and our legs spattered in mud, but this was war. This was what we had trained for and what we knew we could not be matched in. We were happy.

On the third night we camped on the floor of a wide valley that opened out to a plain to the north. The men were in high spirits but they were tired, for we had marched hard. Because we were still a day and a half march from Gwdloych's camp no engagement orders had been issued. We expected to be briefed the following night.

The next day it was still snowing lightly, but the coarse grass was only partially covered. By the middle of the morning our force was spread out over about half a mile, unusually compact for a travelling legion. Marius believed that we were at our most vulnerable when spread out, and as a result he rode up and down the column reprimanding centurions who allowed their centuries to be the cause of a gap larger than was absolutely necessary between themselves and the men in front. He assigned the one hundred and twenty horse to ride up and down the column, ensuring that it was as tightly bunched as possible.

The snow began to fall harder. Men stuck out their tongues to feel the flakes tickle them. Already their faces bore the stubble of four days and soon they would be bearded once more. Half of the legion had never seen snow before, and were full of wonder at the gentle grace with which it floated down from the sky and settled on the ground. For a while the conditions in which we walked became easier. The ground had frozen the previous night, so the thick mud was replaced by a crisp frost topped with icy, hard packed snow. I still remember the stinging, followed by numbness as my toes gradually froze. But our march kept the rest of our bodies warm, and every time we stopped the men would down their packs and frantically rub their toes to try to restore some life to them.

The day was silent and windless. The clouds were low, the peaks of the hills invisible. I didn't feel any disquiet about the march. I just felt a peace and calm sense of wonder at the whiteness that was engulfing us. I knew that there was bloodshed to come, but in some ways I welcomed the prospect. I believed that by destroying Gwdloych, Marius would vent his grief and we would become free to continue with that for which we were in this godforsaken land.
As the snow drifted down I enjoyed the silence.

*****

All morning we had been following a deep valley as it rose ahead of us to a low pass. A stream ran down from the pass, and we marched on both sides of it. The sides of the valley were steep. To the south they were impassable, and to the north they could only be climbed with great difficulty.

My reverie was interrupted at around noon, when a wide-eyed scout appeared from the foggy hill to the south and rode towards Marius. Without waiting for a tribune to escort him, he barged through the surrounding officials to where Marius was walking his horse beside Jaffa's. The commotion created by tribunes trying to prevent his progress made me look up. As one of them attempted to hold him back Marius told him to approach. The scout was breathless and excited as he recounted his news.
"The IInd (Augusta) is ahead of us, sir. I saw the eagle myself. It is at full strength, lined up in battle order".
I will never forget the look on Marius' face at that moment, because it was then that he saw our fate. At first he was silent. There was a colour on his cheeks, but otherwise he did not react. Everyone was looking on, incredulous. Most thought that the scout had gone mad, that the pressure had got to him and he had lost his mind. But not Marius. He knew that somehow we had been betrayed. That was the first time that I saw what Marius had become over the last few days. His mind was filled with the vision of Origen's sword burying itself in Rani's head, and it was his reaction to this that sealed our fate. He could have gone to Decimus then, he knew he could. Had he done so I

think there was a chance that we would have been spared. But he had lost his humanity. His face hardened and he made his decision. Hatred and bloodlust, despair and desolation led him to turn his back on what he knew to be true. He knew that he was beaten but he chose to ignore it.

Immediately he issued orders for the legion to draw up in full defensive battle order facing west, up the hill toward the pass. As he did so Riccus came forward and grabbed his arm. Marius turned on him, furious at being interrupted at such a crucial moment. But Riccus did not flinch. Instead he leaned forward and whispered.
"A scout from the rear has reported that another eagle had been seen several miles behind us. It is the eagle of the XXth, and they are at full strength".
Marius did not even look surprised. His face was set as he issued more orders.

He called me forward and reached under his jerkin to pull out the leather wallet.
"They have come for me, Tolus. Take it. Take my daughter to her grandparents and leave the confession with them. Do it for me. You are the best friend a man can have". He looked at me with such intensity that I could not refuse him. I could not refuse him for the sake of the child and for Rani.
"I will do as you ask" I replied formally.
I knew then that I would never see Marius Sextus again. He did not need to give voice to his gratitude. His eyes glistened as he transformed his tone. My friend was replaced by my master.
"You will take the front, and you will hold off the IInd with two cohorts. Hold them for as long as you can, and when your line is broken order a retreat. If you can find your way over the hills, rejoin us". With that he turned to issue orders to the other eight cohorts, the four thousand men who would congregate at the southern side of the valley.

I obeyed, but I was surprised by my reluctance as I did so.

*****

My two cohorts were to dig in a full defensive position to the west, facing up the valley towards the pass. The rest of the legion turned around and retreated down the valley. Their aim was to break through the XXth and reach the place where we had camped the previous night. They would regroup there, at the place where this valley met another heading south and a plain to the north. There would be an escape route from there. As Marius issued these orders the tribunes looked on agog. They were still trying to comprehend the fact that there were three full strength legions in this wilderness. Marius was way ahead of them, but then he knew what they would never know. Marius' swift series of orders, rattled off at bewildering pace in a voice that left no room for questions confused them even more. He was assuming that these legions were hostile to us. They did not understand why, and it is a measure of their regard for Marius that they did not question. Instead they rushed to obey. Within fifteen minutes one thousand men under my command were retreating down the valley to a point where it narrowed. We began building a defensive rampart in the thickening snow. I knew that we could only hold the IInd

for a limited amount of time and I knew that when we were over-run there would be no hope for us. We would be slaughtered. Marius was sacrificing us. Yet we were essential to him, for if the main body of the legion was attacked from the front and the rear simultaneously there would be no hope. We would be eaten up. As we built the rampart, the rest of the legion trudged through the deepening snow behind us, moving eastwards as quickly as possible. Our men worked frantically, and after half an hour we began to see shadows through the snow. They loomed darkly through the delicate white flakes. The only sound was the grate of frantic shovelling and shouts of officers encouraging men in their tasks. It was an hour before we could make out individual shapes ahead of us, and by that time the rampart was strong. I ordered the men to take up their defensive positions and swap their tools for weapons. It would not be long now.

*****

Marius retreated, and it was a long time before he saw the outline of the pursuing legion ahead of him. Instantly he ordered battle lines to be drawn. It took no more than a few minutes for the men to be poised, for they had been well trained, and Marius immediately ordered a charge. No one could believe the order. A legate was ordering his men to charge another Roman legion. The officers knew Marius to be a great man and a fine general. They believed in him and most of all they trusted him, so they did not question that he knew what he was doing. None of them understood why two legions surrounded them. It was an impossible scenario that contradicted all logic. Many in the ranks did not know that they would be charging at Romans. They had not been able to see the uniforms and the standards of their foe. All they could see through the falling snow was a dark, amorphous mass of an army. By the time they were charging and they did start to see the standards, it was too late. The joy of battle had overtaken them, and the momentum meant that they were committed. They fell on the XXth with the full ferocity of Rome's finest soldiers, completely surprising them. The IXth had not been expected to react like this.

Initially Marius made good progress. He kept his forces as compact as possible and had them hugging the base of the southern hillside. Boniccus' men had been strung out on the road in a linear column, so initial resistance was sparse as Marius tried to break through their flank. But they quickly organised, and Marius found that his men were having to fight laterally, from south to north, as they sought to work their way east.

*****

When the IInd came out of the snow they were in full battle line. They would have been able to see the dark outline of our hastily constructed rampart, so they knew that they were attacking a strong defensive position. With just two cohorts we would never have been able to hold the valley at a wider point and as it was we were spread too thinly, our line no thicker than one deep across the width of the valley. Decimus was clever. He attacked the full length of our line, believing that Marius had committed his whole legion to it, unaware that the XXth was to his rear. As a result, when Decimus attacked there was no real urgency about it. He wanted to engage us and wait for the XXth to eat us up from behind. When they arrived, the attack would intensify. But standing in that line it did not feel like anything less than the full fury of battle. Silus, Greto and Artorius stood with the rank and file as I rode across the back of the line encouraging the men. They stood shoulder to shoulder, their long spears ready to take the first onslaught and their swords stuck in the ground behind them, ready to be grabbed at a second's notice. There was a strange silence as they stood there, bracing themselves for an onslaught the like of which they had never had to resist in battle. All had fought other roman soldiers in training. They were aware of what made an attack devastating. They had simulated these attacks on the training fields in great exercises, with wooden swords and tipped spears. But this was for real, and it was terrible.

The IInd came at us. Their measured ferocity made me realise why it was that we were so terrible in battle. It was horrendous. I was used to seeing crazed, drunken savages in a chaotic, magnificent, disorderly rushing charge. They would come at us flailing and could be picked off as individuals. When the IInd came, they came as one and they remained as one. Slowly they marched forward. All that could be seen was a straight and unblemished line of shields with spears protruding from narrow slits between them. The second rank held their shields above their heads. Their line had no flanks. Instead, the shield wall extended right across the valley.

I ordered my men to stand firm behind the rampart. They crouched behind their shields and waited. We waited and we watched the wall approach. When it reached the ditch ahead of the rampart it stopped. The two lines were no more than ten paces apart. To get to us they would have to climb up the steep rampart bristling with our stakes.
"Stand firm" I called to our men. It was essential that we held our line and did not allow our excitement and nerves to prompt a suicidal

attempt to fall on the attackers. Both forces stayed like that for some moments.

"Stand firm" I repeated down the line. It was strange, unlike anything I had ever experienced in battle before. Neither side wanted to advance, because to do so would risk breaking the impenetrable defences of the shield wall and allow first blood to the enemy.

"Stand firm" I continued to shout. There was not a flicker of movement from my line, and I was glad. I knew that if we were patient we would force them into coming to us, making a direct attack on our defensive position. I also knew that we were not in a hurry. The longer we held the IInd, the greater Marius' chances of breaking through the XXth. The stand off lasted some time before the IInd began to advance. They did so slowly, and I think the only reason that they advanced at all was the press of men from behind. I reminded myself that this was as unique an experience for our attackers as it was for us. There was nothing in the training manuals about how to defeat a Roman legion. We were trained to fight against the armies that we met in the provinces, and those armies were barbarian.

When the clash came it was savage. The front ranks of the IInd advanced up the rampart and as it did so it broke up. They began their advance from just ten paces away, but within a couple of steps they had been forced to begin climbing the slippery bank. Some men lost their footing, others dropped their shields to use their hands to keep them upright. The line broke and for the first time we looked into the faces of our attackers. Their beards were longer than ours, but other than that it was like we were looking at ourselves. They were armed with the same weapons, dressed in the same kind of clothes, even bore standards fashioned in the same style.

"Spears" I shouted repeatedly, riding down the line. From our superior position, our men began to thrust their spears at the bodies that struggled up the hill. I saw the iron tips thrust into men's faces. I saw razor sharp points pierce jerkins before men fell. Some of the spears broke as their owners tried desperately to free them from the torsos in which they had been impaled. But mostly they were retrieved. As the attackers battled up the bank, red stains began to seep into the white of the slush to join the smears of mud that already mingled with the snow. Our line was holding well. I was most concerned about a loss of discipline at some point in the line, about a rush of exhilaration that could cause parts of the line to rush down into the ditch to drive home the slaughter. We would be lost if that happened. As soon as the line was breached it would be close to the end, for we would be attacked from all sides.

But the line held. For most of an hour the line held. Once the spears were lost, the men drew their short stabbing swords and huddled behind their shields. The bank was becoming increasingly treacherous, with blood, slush and mud all combining to make it almost insurmountable, despite the fact that it was no more than the height of a man from the base of the ditch. Still the men of the IInd came, and still they fell. The corpses were beginning to pile high in the ditch, several hundred at least, with many more on the slopes of the bank. The IInd used their fallen as footholds on that slippery bank, and when the bodies on the bank were sufficiently scattered to enable a relatively secure foothold right across the breadth of the valley the fight became much more even. We still had the advantage of the stakes, which hampered any concerted attack. But the fighting became hand to hand and there was no more role for a strategic commander. I would have one more duty to perform as commander that day, and that would be to order the retreat. But I would not order it until we could not hold the enemy for a moment longer.

The two lines met at the top of the rampart, and it was their shields that clashed. A great shoving contest ensued as soldiers swiped below their shields, trying to catch the legs of their opponents. Occasionally a shield would fall, its bearer struck from below or from a spear flung from in front. When a shield fell, opponents would thrust their swords forward through the exposed part of the wall and into the soft flesh within. The battle continued like this for an hour, and casualties on both sides were low. It was almost impossible to kill anyone through those shields but it was exhausting, and it was us who would get exhausted first. We were so few.

*****

Marius was making progress, for the XXth had been slow to react. They had been so surprised to be attacked, and by such a huge number, that at first they took defensive positions. This suited Marius perfectly. He did not want to engage them, he simply wanted to pass them. As soon as Boniccus realised what was going on, he had ordered his legion to fall on Marius. He tried to get as many men as possible down the valley to cut off any escape, but he had been too late. With his back pinned to the steep southern wall of the valley, Marius fought like a crab. He had spread his soldiers out on a front facing laterally across the valley. He ordered a v-shaped formation to make incisions eastwards along the southern wall of the valley. The rest of his men he ordered to move east as quickly as possible whilst guarding their rear. In this way the legion fought a glancing battle and held off the enemy whilst it outflanked them. It took two hours, but eventually Marius got behind the XXth. In doing so he had lost nearly one thousand men, and inflicted at least equivalent losses on the XXth. It was a strange battle, but Marius made it. And when he broke through to the rear of the XXth, he ordered a full retreat to the point where we had camped the previous night.

*****

I should not have fought with my men. Having been entrusted with the Confession of Nero and the stewardship of Marius' young daughter, I should have stayed out of the way. But I was not thinking of those things.

I found Greto, Silus and Artorius in our line, and it was there that I chose to fight. For a whole hour we shoved and jostled, and we became exhausted. There was no encouragement, just grunting and heavy breathing punctuated by the occasional scream. The moans of the first attackers who had fallen on the bank could still be heard, but other than that it was not a noisy battle, not like the battles that we were used to. At intervals we would support each other's shields whilst the other took a wide swing at the legs of our enemy. I felt my sword bury itself in soft flesh before it was stopped by hard bone, and I heard the scream as a shield in front of us fell. Greto and Silus pounced into the gap and there were more screams. They had claimed at least a couple of the enemy, but as soon as they fell their places were taken and the enemy shields would close up once more.

After an hour, suddenly, our line broke.

38

Some of our men had become exhausted, their shield arms no longer able to support the weight of their own shields and the weight of their attackers. Their arms dropped and they were forced to try to penetrate the oncoming shield wall. They fell, and our line was breached. The men of the IInd flooded through, and we were engulfed. Immediately I fell back to order the retreat. I could not find my horse in the chaos, but I screamed the order repeatedly in all directions. It was taken up by other men, but by then it was too late. We were overrun. All around small pockets of men were engaged in hand to hand fighting. The snow was falling even more heavily, and the white softness on the ground was littered with corpses. I turned from shouting and glimpsed a sword swinging from my left towards my temple. I ducked, and swivelled in the slush. The legionary was off balance and from my crouching position I lunged at his exposed left side. My sword penetrated his jerkin, his ribs and buried myself in his lung. Blood appeared on his lips and trickled out of his mouth before he hit the ground. I did not stop to watch, but swung around to see Greto defending himself. I ran over to him and swung at the neck of the man lunging at him. Blood spurted up and I grabbed Greto. He had a nasty wound to his side, and I half dragged him backwards. About twenty paces back we found Silus and Artorius engaged in hand to hand fighting. Both of them saw us retreat south, to the steep hill at the base of the valley. It looked virtually impossible to climb, but we tried. Greto was struggling with his injury and we did not have anywhere else to go.

We would never have made it up that southern hill had it not been for the depth of the snow and the hobnails on the underside of our sandals. We traversed the mountain towards the clouds and Artorius, Silus and five others from the IXth followed. The nine of us climbed into the clouds to lose ourselves. It was hard, particularly as we had to take it in turns to help Greto. He did not complain, but it was clear from the creases in his already wrinkled face that he was in severe pain. From our vantage point we made out the carnage below. Most of our two cohorts lay dead. The occasional man or small group ran eastwards down the valley, but each time they were pursued. There was no chance for them, for even if they managed to outrun their pursuers they would only come into contact with the XXth.

We continued up the hill and as we did I felt under my jerkin. The leather wallet nestling close to my skin felt like a heavy weight then. I looked at the wide valley stained with the blood of over two thousand men and I cursed it. But I kept it.

The light began to fade. We continued up until we could climb no more. We were well into the cloud, and the snow was lighter there. Visibility was terrible, and all of the men were bewildered, exhausted and frightened, me included. Once we were at the top we sought somewhere to sleep. There was barely any light when Artorius gave a shout. We followed the sound rather than the vague shadow we thought might be him. He was standing in a craggy overhang, sheltered from the snow and the increasingly strong wind. Silus lit a fire while those with rations shared them out. Greto's face was pale in the light of the fire, and he looked bad. No one spoke. I think that we were all too horrified at what had happened. It was beyond comprehension. That night was lonely and sleepless.

*****

Marius regrouped at the previous night's camp. The ramparts were still there, and the XXth had made no effort to pursue the three thousand men of the IXth who had broken through them. It was a fine place to camp, and most of the work had already been completed. To the north the landscape opened out into rolling hills and plains that marked an end to the dark hills. To the south was a narrow, steep valley and to the west was the valley that we had just come from. The light was fading, and Marius ordered the legion to camp in the same positions as the previous night.

To everyone's surprise the night passed uneventfully. When dawn broke it revealed clear skies and a wan sun shining down on a beautiful blanket of fresh snow. There was no sign of the other legions. It was almost as if the whole thing had been a terrible dream. Except that the legion was down to nearly half of its original strength. Marius ordered the legion to mobilise to march deeper into the hills. He knew that it was the best chance for such a significantly inferior force. There was nothing like steep hills and rough land to make a legion fragment. So Marius ordered his force south through the small, narrow valley bordered by the high mountains. His scouts reported that the IInd was slowly making its way down the valley, following the route that Marius had taken yesterday. The XXth had skirted round to the north and was camped on the edge of the plains there. This news unsettled Marius, for it gave him the impression that Decimus had anticipated his move. But Marius had seen their force. He knew that there were no more legions in Britannia. He was having everything that Decimus could muster thrown at him, and so he continued up that valley, marching through until sunset at exceptional pace. By then the men were exhausted, yet despite the snow and the sludge and the uneven terrain they made good time. At sundown Marius ordered camp to be struck.

*****

The snow was waist high when we woke on the top of that mountain. In contrast to the previous day, the skies were clear and the air crisp. I sent Silus and the other five legionaries out on a scouting expedition to see if they could get a view of where we were in relation to Marius and the two hostile legions. They took on the task with relief. I think that they just wanted something to do, and they wanted to make sense of what had happened to us. I stayed behind with Artorius and Greto. We had bound Greto's wound, a nasty incision just below his ribs, and he seemed stronger for some sleep. . Whilst the others were gone we ate our meagre breakfast rations.
"What's happened?" asked Greto softly. He was not strong, and talking seemed to take a big effort.

I looked at him and shrugged my shoulders. I did not really want to think about it.

There was an awkward silence as Greto's question hung in the air. None of us wanted to speak, for fear of what we might say.

*****

I would not allow a fire to be lit, for I did not want to give our position away to anyone. We sat in that crag and we waited for the scouting party to return. We waited for hours and we talked of our failure. It was mid morning before Greto finally said that he was not going to wait any more. I think that the pain was returning and he wanted something to take his mind off it.

We struggled out from under the crag through the thick snow, and soon we saw the scene laid out below us. In the far distance, to the south, we could see a bunched column marching down a high sided valley. We instantly knew that it was Marius, for forming up to the east, at the place that we had camped the night before last were two legions, clearly discernible, and they were moving out. They were going to follow Marius down the narrow valley. That day we kept to the hilltops and we travelled south. We had a vague idea that we would rejoin the Ninth and try to make Marius see sense, make him see that he could still surrender and save the lives of his remaining soldiers.

The only other people that we saw that day were corpses. We did not have to walk far to find our scouting party. Silus and the five soldiers lay dead less than a mile from where we had all slept. They had run into a patrol. With them were nine other corpses. Their blood had melted the snow around them, and some grass was exposed.

We travelled the whole day on those hill tops. Despite the constant climbing and descending across the ridges, peaks and troughs, and despite having to take turns in supporting Greto we managed to keep up with the IXth below us. As much as possible we kept to the eastern side of the hill to avoid being seen from the valley below.

As we moved south, the hills became smaller and a few trees began to appear. The undergrowth, almost completely absent in the high hills, became thicker affording us much better cover. At sundown we watched as the IXth made their camp in an unconventional semi circular shape, with the rear of the semi circle against the steep hill behind them. We too made our camp on the side of a hill in the snow. Sleep came more easily that second night as we surrendered to our exhaustion.

Shortly before dawn we were woken.

*****

Marius had been woken by his scouts. Within ten minutes the camp of the IXth was under attack from the south. At first Marius could not understand how it could be. He had kept a close watch on both the IInd and the XXth. He knew for a fact that both had camped to the north of him, in the steep sided valley. He knew that there was no way that they could have skirted round him during the night. There was just no way around.

It was the blood chilling howls that accompanied the attack that gave it away. Barbarians. Gwdloych. The surprise was such that it was not long before the marauding barbarians were in the camp. But Marius was quick. The legions coming from the north had been seen and he knew that they would soon be upon him. But he also knew that unless he could eject Gwdloych from the camp all would be lost. He ordered the whole of his force to drive back the barbarians. They lined up quickly behind their shields and formed a wall, advancing deliberately and taking great care to keep their shape. The barbarians were shoved backwards. Few casualties were inflicted as the advancing Ninth sought simply to drive them out rather than kill them. As soon as the barbarians had been pushed back over the rampart, the order was given for the legion to man the whole length of the semi circular defence. Quickly it was a solid shield wall and it only just formed up in time, for shortly afterwards the IInd and the XXth attacked.

*****

The IXth were glorious that day. They were glorious and they were lost from the start.

At first we could see nothing, for the clouds had returned and it was snowing lightly. Until the sun rose we could do nothing but listen to the sounds that had woken us. But as the dawn came we began to see carnage. As we watched from our vantage point on the hill we crept down, using the undergrowth for cover. The battle proceeded much like ours had the previous day. It was the second time that I watched Roman forces fight each other, and the pattern was distinctive. It developed into a shoving competition on the ramparts. The only exception was on the southern side, where the undisciplined forces of Gwdloych repeatedly threw themselves at the wall of shields and died as they exposed their torsos to bring down their heavy weapons. But the Ninth could not hold on indefinitely. There were too many attackers, too many fresh men to replace those exhausted at the front line.

By the middle of the morning the line broke much as ours had the previous day. And when it did, there was slaughter. Marius' men fought for their lives. The hand to hand combat was terrible, with Roman swords being driven into Roman flesh. Eyes were gouged, limbs severed, necks half hewn and genitals shorn. The carcasses of the dead lay thick on the ground, and the screams were chilling.

In the midst of the chaos, Marius spotted Decimus. He rallied some men and led a phalanx forward. Despite their predicament, there was a belief and energy to that charge that revealed just how far Marius had gone in winning the hearts of his men. Surely they must have realised that they were beaten, but they fought like men inspired. They cut deep into the line of the XXth, leaving many dead in their wake. Marius was at the apex of that phalanx, leading by vicious example. His sword smashed through the guard of many men, and such was his fury that the ranks began to yield to his charge.

I was watching Marius rampage forward when suddenly he shuddered. Blood spurted from his mouth and he staggered. Then he fell out of my view, speared by the unseen thrust of a man lying on the ground. The blade was deep in his lung.

News spreads quickly on a battlefield, and like a wind sweeping through the IXth they laid down their weapons. Their attackers stopped their work. The IXth was defeated and they knew it. There was no doubt. They had surrendered and it was over.

Instinctively everyone moved back from the fallen leader as Decimus approached him. As the ground around him cleared, I could see my commander once more. His lips were moving as the life seeped out of him, but to this day I do not know what he said. Then his eyes stared unseeing toward the sky.

Decimus turned and shouted an order for all the men of the Ninth to retreat back behind their rampart, and for all the men of the IInd and the XXth to leave the camp. An uncomfortable silence fell whilst hostile legionaries walked past each other.

*****

Decimus whispered orders to his tribunes, and they turned to ride around the valley, passing them on to the centurions. There seemed to be an uncertainty about them when they heard the orders in that white valley. No sound other than the moans and screams of the dying could be heard.

Suddenly Decimus stood high in his stirrups and shouted the order to attack. The legions hesitated. For a moment I thought that they would not obey. Uncomprehendingly the men of the Ninth looked on as their countrymen advanced once more. Belatedly they grabbed for their weapons, but most had left them on the field. Horror, hopelessness and sheer bewilderment had taken the fight from them. It was a repulsive sight. Even now, thirty years on I cannot bring myself to describe what I saw happen to those men. There must have been over one thousand men of the Ninth left when the butchery began. Artorius leaned over and vomited in the bush that hid us. Unarmed men were cut down where they stood. They raised no resistance, but just looked around disbelievingly as their comrades were slaughtered.

I felt nauseous too. I saw Riccus led away and taken to Decimus. As he was held Decimus cut his throat, oblivious to the blood that showered him. Every single man of the Ninth was killed that day, to the very last man. The snow was scarred with streams of blood and the corpses piled high. Gwdloych's barbarians stood by, grinning. Their druids danced and howled and gloated. Then, when the grim work was complete Decimus walked forward in the midst of that horror. His voice rang out clear in the cold air.

"Today is the darkest day in the history of Rome. This is what happens to those who would deny the divinity of the emperor. This is what happens to traitors. Let it be a lesson to you. Marius Sextus was the legate of the IXth legion, and he sought to undermine the empire. The men under his command became rotten because of his corrupt leadership. What you have done today must never be repeated. But what you have done you have done for Rome. Never forget that. Today you have saved Rome".

There was complete silence. Decimus' men looked at him with something close to hatred as he resumed.

"Roman soldiers must never again be put in the position where they must kill their own. The only way that this can be prevented is for men to obey the legitimate power of the emperor. You will never speak of this. Rome will be ever ashamed of what happened here today, and you must never tell of it. But know that it has happened on the orders of the Emperor for the greater glory of the empire. It has happened to prevent an unimaginable terror from being unleashed from this desolate land. It has happened that your children and your grandchildren can grow up in peace and safety under the protective wing of the empire".

With that Decimus dismounted his horse. He nodded in the direction of Gwdloych, who was listening without comprehension some distance away. Gwdloych strode forward and knelt. When he did so he reached for the hand of Decimus. He brought it to his lips and he kissed it as he had been instructed. Then he stood, turned, and returned to his men. They quickly disappeared southwards from whence they came.

The legion buried the bodies. They dug deep graves, and they stripped the bodies of everything before flinging the bloody corpses into them. It took the whole day to bury the legion in that hard ground. They made no effort to bury the savages. That night Artorius and I moved off silently into the hills. We carried Greto, for he was no longer able to walk.

Epilogue

The heat is more oppressive than ever, but Snofru has been kind over the months that I have been writing. She has encouraged me when I have weakened and comforted me when I have wept. I never believed when I started that it could be this hard, that the demons could be so potent. But perhaps peace will come now that I have finished.

Olivia is gone and I am alone. Alone but for our children, and the orphan who now might know who she is.

Greto died before we even got to Eburacum and we buried him where he fell. I entered the town disguised as a soldier of the XXth legion, and remained there with Olivia for a while. No one ever suspected me of having been with the Ninth. It took Olivia months of patience before I was able to talk of what had happened. When I finally did it helped a little, just as these months of pain have. It was while we were in Eburacum that I heard that the governor, Caracalla, had died in mysterious circumstances and had been replaced by a relation of Hadrian's.

It was not until the spring before Olivia felt that Marius' daughter was strong enough to leave. We named her Rani, after her mother, and loved her as our own. The winter was agony, for I had come to hate that place. But we couldn't leave for fear that little Rani would die on the road. It took us several years to get to Aegyptus. We did not have much money and had to travel most of the way over land. We stopped frequently, for me to work and for Olivia to be delivered of another of our children. I worked mostly as a labourer, and we had no cause to hurry.

Whilst on the road I heard some news that intrigued me, from a traveller who had visited Britannia some months before. A tall man with dark skin had settled in an area of the south west of the province, inhabited by a people known as the Durotriges. There he had established himself as some sort of chieftain, and developed a reputation as a great leader of men. His hatred of the Romans became legendary, and he enjoyed much success as a scourge of the occupying forces, winning many victories against them and becoming a great hero for the independent minded people of that province. The traveller's description of the man was familiar, and when I heard the name by which he was known I was sure that it was the same man that I had last seen when we had buried Greto together. The legendary chieftain went by a name of the Britons, and that name was Urtor.

Most people never knew why Hadrian became obsessed with Britannia, and they believed what they were told about why he built a great wall from the west coast of the province to the east, to the north of a town known as Eburacum. They believed that he did it to keep the untameable savages of the north out of the province. But I know the truth. I know that he built that wall as part of his deal with Gwdloych. I also know that it suited him to do so, for he wanted to keep the truth out. He built that wall to hide his shame, to ensure that word of what happened could never slip back into the empire to pollute his name. He built it to keep Rome in.

Smenkhkare had died by the time that we finally arrived here in Assyut. But Horemheb lived, and she welcomed us all as though we were her own. I had been worried that she would blame me for the loss of her daughter, but I had no cause.

I have still not decided about the manuscript. There have been so many times that I have wanted to burn it. When they were alive Olivia, Perridac and Horemheb urged me to destroy it but I refused, because the persecution of us Christians continues. If anything it gets worse. But we grow stronger every day, due in no little measure to the strong foundations laid for us by Perridac in the decades of his leadership. Rani is a strong christian woman, and I am proud of her. Once she has read this she can decide what to do with it. It is her right.

God was good to us, and Olivia and I were happy. He soothed my pain and He gave my wife patience. Little Rani and our own children were the source of much joy, and we delighted in each other. But I never really recovered from what I saw that day in the wild lands of the north of Britannia. It has cast a shadow over my life. Until now I have not spoken of it to anyone, but now that Olivia is dead I feel that I have nothing left to live for. I know that I should leave it in God's hands but I sometimes feel that he is punishing me by forcing me to live when all the others are dead. Our children are all good Aegyptusis and work hard, but they no longer need me.

No one who was there ever spoke of the events that happened in the wild lands north of Eburacum. I am not surprised. No one has any desire to raise those ghosts, to relive the horror and the shame of what was done. Part of me still thinks that I am foolish for doing so. But if I am to have any kind of life now I must exorcise the demons that have plagued me since I began to write.

If I am honest with myself, the demons never left me after that cold day thirty years ago when the IXth Legion of the Western Empire of Rome was massacred. They have lived in me and been given power by what I know.

I only ever believed in one man enough to murder my own men. In truth, the men of the Ninth Legion were massacred by that man's desire for revenge. They were massacred by the bloodlust of Marius Sextus.

Postscript

Mediolanum, Gallia Transpadana, Northern Italia. 313AD

Emperor Constantine I finished issuing the declaration to the assembled dignataries. It was more an imperial edict than a declaration and to future generations it would come to be called the Edict of Milan. It declared that the empire was legalising the religion of Christianity. The emperor was no longer divine.

After the ceremony, the emperor walked straight through an antichamber set up with couches, food, wine, concubines and several advisors, all waiting for him. One of his advisors jumped up off the couch and spoke to him in a manner that emperors are not accustomed to being spoken to. His voice was full of vitriol as he spoke.
"What you have done today will bring about the end of civilisation as we know it".
Without breaking step the emperor replied mildly.
"If you had seen what I have seen, you would have had no alternative but to do as I have done".
The emperor continued walking through his private rooms, and when he got to the innermost chamber he withdrew an ancient manuscript from his tunic. He pulled out the scroll that had arrived with it. It was written by a man in a village called Assyut in the province of Aegyptus and it read:

"READ THIS DOCUMENT. READ IT AND ACT ON IT, FOR ONLY BY DOING SO WILL YOU BE SAVED. THIS IS TRUSTED TO YOU BECAUSE THE TIME HAS COME FOR IT TO BE USED FOR GOOD OR FOR ILL. GOOD CAN ONLY COME THROUGH YOU, AND YOU HAVE BEEN JUDGED WORTHY. THE HOLY ROMAN EMPIRE WILL BE GREATER THAN THE PAGAN ROMAN EMPIRE EVER WAS".

The emperor smiled to himself, dangled the ancient manuscript into the flames of a candle and watched as it burnt to ashes. Once the last

ashes floated to the floor Emperor Constantine I dropped to his
and began to pray.